THE RED ROOSTER

BY MICHAEL WALLACE

PROLOGUE

June 2, 1940

A{MONG THE THRONGS FLEEING THE} port at Dunkirk was a young woman from Spain, seventeen years old, who wanted to return to the front lines. She had passage across the Channel, papers paid for with a man's life and a small fortune in twenty franc notes, and a cousin waiting in London. She kicked off her shoes, gathered her dress and prepared to jump overboard.

The captain of the overburdened boat grabbed her arm with a bandaged hand. His eyes were wild. "Stupid girl, you'll die, you'll never make it."

Gabriela barely heard him, could only think about her father and it made her angry and afraid.

You lied. You said you were coming back and you never meant it.

Instead, he'd left her on this shot-up listing fishing boat, lashed to the side of the British gunboat and crowded with children, embassy staff, and soldiers. He meant to face the Germans without her.

"What's wrong with you, aren't you listening?" the captain said. "Fine, die for all I care, I won't stay a minute longer."

Gabriela braced herself and jumped.

The water was cold. She went under and into silence. Gone

were the shouting, cursing soldiers, the rumble of artillery and the high-pitched whine of brawling fighter planes, the British destroyers hurling shells across the water and into the city.

She came up in a wreckage of splintered oars, broken barrels, shoes, army jackets, papers, flailing people with or without life jackets. The water tasted bitter, oily. An explosion, a spout of water. Anti-aircraft fire sliced the sky against two screaming dive-bombers. She paddled toward the beach, and the hundreds of British and French soldiers wading into the water.

A soldier pulled her onto the beach, asking questions in English, what sounded like a variation of what the fishing boat captain had been screaming.

"No, I'm going back, I need to find my father. Let go!"

More English, two soldiers now, trying to calm her, take her back into the water and toward the ramshackle flotilla evacuating the beaches. Gabriela struggled and kicked and finally they let her go. She ran barefoot across the sand, back toward town. Burning half-tracks littered the beach, together with overturned trucks, an aircraft fuselage, rifles tossed in piles by fleeing soldiers. The ground shuddered, threw her down. She picked herself up.

Her father had lied, he'd stuck his head in the noose to save her. He'd sacrificed himself, and for what? Did he think she'd take it?

CHAPTER ONE

T HE ITALIAN WAGGLED HIS FINGER in Gabriela's face. "Eleven francs. No more."

She extended the jade brooch until she held it under his nose. "Please, look closer." Gabriela fought to keep from sounding desperate, a difficult task two years into her nightmare. "The dragonfly wings are so delicate, and look at the detail. How about thirteen, it's just two more francs."

He shook his head without looking down. "Eleven."

"There are other stalls, you know."

Sure, and you've tried them all, haven't you?

A hundred other stalls, and ten thousand people in worn shoes and threadbare socks, empty stomachs, some with hungry children, all trying to offload their last, precious possessions.

Gabriela owed her landlords thirty, had sold almost everything she owned, and was down to selling half her ration cards so she could buy food with the other half. What good would eleven francs do? Thirteen, for that matter?

"Eleven. Take it or not."

She pulled back her hand. "My father gave this brooch to my mother. She's dead. I can't possibly sell it for eleven francs."

"Listen girl, nobody cares." The voice belonged to a woman

MICHAEL WALLACE

queued behind her, holding silk scarves. Behind her, a man with a pair of silver candlesticks who looked suspiciously like a Jew. In the *marché aux puces,* nobody much bothered with that.

She'd seen all types in the flea markets of Paris. Hadn't she been here a hundred times to sell her father's things? His boots, belts, greatcoat, books of Spanish poetry, leather journals, his watch, even paintings of mother; all brought a few precious centimes or francs. Two weeks ago she'd sold the trunk itself, brought from Spain.

She kept a few meager possessions, her favorite of which was his meerschaum pipe, amber from years of smoking. It still held the aroma of tobacco and she couldn't smell it without imagining him in his chair. When she came in and saw him smoking, she could almost see the cloud of thoughts rising above his head with the pipe smoke. He would urge her to sit down, pull out a small wooden box of imported Belgian chocolates, and then pontificate: rubber plantations in Ceylon, the proper ratio of shellfish to sausage in a mixed paella, or the development of the steam engine. It didn't matter the subject, he was so energetic that she would sit and listen, eating chocolates while he gesticulated with his pipe and his latest book.

Selling the pipe would be like selling those memories.

The stall owner's scowl hardened. "Eleven. Either make a deal or get the hell out of my line. I'm busy."

"All right, then, eleven." She made to hand over the brooch to the stall owner, already fumbling in his pocket for the bills, when a young woman took her wrist.

"Eleven francs, are you crazy?" the woman asked.

The speaker was close to Gabriela's own age. She had a fresh, carefree air and looked glamorous in her green dress with dainty straps over the shoulders. Nylons, a whiff of perfume, red lipstick, long eyelashes.

"That's all I can get," Gabriela said. "I've tried, God

help me."

"Don't let this man rob you. I'll pay you twenty, how about that?" The other girl opened her purse. She pulled out some mixed bills that included reichsmarks and francs. "Twenty. Do we have a deal?"

"Hey, what are you doing?" the Italian demanded. "That's mine, I bought it already." He shoved his money at Gabriela and grabbed for the brooch.

She jerked it back. "This woman says twenty. Will you give me more?"

"Dammit, we had an agreement." He turned his anger to the young woman. "You, who do you think you are?"

The young woman laughed and gave a brushing off motion. She took Gabriela's arm and led her a few paces from the crowd. Her heels clicked smartly on the pavement.

Gabriela worried the stall owner would pursue them, but he was already haggling with the owner of the scarves, while the queue of sellers patiently waited their turn. Meanwhile the crowd swirled around them. Children, begging. Young, shiftless men. An old war veteran in his cloak, toothless and smelling of whiskey and sour sweat.

"I can't believe he thought you'd take eleven. May as well steal it. Your brooch is worth at least twice what I offered, you know that."

"Maybe before the war."

The young woman held out the money. "If you want to ask around for more, I understand. Otherwise, I'm delighted to pay twenty. It's a beautiful brooch."

"No, no, I'll take it."

Gabriela took the twenty francs and handed over the brooch before the girl could change her mind. She tucked the money into her bra, glanced around to make sure she hadn't attracted the attention of pickpockets. Her gaze caught the uniformed Germans who idled in the shade at the edge of the street. The Eiffel Tower lifted behind them, topped by a swastika flag that flapped back and forth in a lazy salute. One man smoked a cigarette, while the other polished his rifle butt with a handkerchief.

She was always searching for one German in particular, the man who knew about Papá. These two were just ordinary soldiers.

"It's beautiful," the girl said. "I feel so guilty. I should have paid you more."

"Thank you anyway, you were generous," Gabriela said, using the formal address in French.

"Oh, don't give me that *vous* nonsense. It's so formal and stuffy, and I'm not that old. How old are you?"

"Almost twenty."

Am I? My god, has it been two years already?

"See, I knew it. We're the same age. My name is Christine."

"I'm Gabriela. Gaby, I mean."

"Well, Gaby, I took advantage of you, I admit it." She held up the brooch, admired it, then slipped it into her purse. Gabriela felt a pang of loss. Her mother's brooch, and now it was gone. At least she'd sold it for more than she'd dreamed just a few minutes earlier.

"Are you from Paris?" Christine asked.

"No," she admitted.

"I'm so glad. I'm tired of these snobby Parisiennes. Oh! I'm ready to faint I'm so hungry. You must be too, arguing with that horrible Italian. Can I buy you a sausage? I know a man who sells them out of a cart." She gave Gabriela a confidential smile. "No ration coupons required."

Gabriela would have declined out of polite habit, not to mention the punishing urge to go back to her cramped, dingy flat she shared with her landlords and curl into a ball, but her stomach growled so loudly at the mention of sausage that she thought it must have been audible over the shouting touts, the haggling, the crying children. "Yes, please. That would be very nice of you."

The sausage, when tracked down from the illegal vendor, was obscenely expensive compared to pre-war prices, and just as obscenely good. It had been weeks since Gabriela had tasted meat and that had been a scrap of chicken, so dry it was almost desiccated. This was thick and juicy. She took a bite and rich fat, hot and delicious, slid down her chin. Christine laughed and helped her clean it up with her handkerchief.

"I'm sorry," Gabriela said around mouthfuls. Her fingers were burning on the wax paper, her tongue burning too, but she didn't care. "I haven't had lunch. In fact, I haven't had a proper meal for about three weeks."

A thin girl of four or five stared at them eating. She clutched her mother's dress. The mother tried to sell bunches of daisies to passersby.

Christine took her elbow and led her away. "I know what that's like. Times are tough."

"Times are tough?" Gabriela put a smile into her voice. "Isn't that like observing there are Germans in Paris? Or saying a lot of Catholics hang around Notre Dame?"

Christine laughed. "Well, I hope the money comes in handy. Hey, are you waiting for someone?"

"What? Oh, no. Not really." Gabriela realized she had been scanning the crowd again. Looking for the Gestapo agent who could help her find her father.

"Who do you live with? Your parents? Husband?"

Gabriela shook her head. "I don't have anyone. I'm fighting it out by myself."

"But where do you live?" Christine asked.

"With my landlords in the 14th Arrondissement. Not so

nice, but it keeps me warm."

"You may not believe it, but I know what that's like. I have to work to keep fed."

"Oh, you have a job?" Gabriela found herself reappraising Christine. Not a rich girl then. But what kind of job paid well enough to buy black market sausages for strangers?

"I grew up near Marseille. Came up with my sister a couple of years ago, but her husband went east on a work crew — POW, you know — and she got permission to join him in Germany. My mother wants me back in Provence. Probably to get married, but she won't admit it. I don't want to go, so I got a job in a restaurant called Le Coq Rouge, in the 4th. You know the place?"

"No, I don't think so."

"Good food, nice people. You should stop by some time. Maybe you could, I don't know, get a job."

Work in a restaurant sounded perfect. Something to feed herself while she continued her search for Papá. Gabriela had already scoured the city for work, of course, but never managed to find anything, and wondered how Christine had managed.

"What do you do, wait tables?" Gabriela asked.

"Not exactly. I'm more of an entertainer."

"And that's what you do at the restaurant? Entertain Germans?"

"In a manner of speaking," Christine said.

"But how, exactly? Is it singing or something?"

"No, not exactly. Companionship, more like. They're a long way from home and you know, the *boches* aren't monsters. Most of them, I mean. They get lonely like anyone else."

"Ah, I see."

Her new-found friend must have caught something in her tone. "No, it's not like that. You know how it is when you get a boyfriend? Maybe you like him because he's cute and you think you want to marry him, but that's not always what it's like, is it? Sometimes you're just bored and you think it would be fun to walk along the canal holding hands and stopping under the bridges to kiss. Or maybe he's kind of dull, but he's rich and he buys you nice things. It's kind of like that."

"So they buy you nice things?"

"Sometimes," Christine said. "And sometimes it's just good food and wine and the chance to feel pretty again, like a woman, a real woman. You understand, it's not like those *en carte* girls, who work for money. It's not like a job."

"I don't know."

She did know, actually. It sounded disgusting.

"Try to be open minded," Christine said.

"But if it's not a job, why does the restaurant let you in?"

"Pretty girls attract business, and besides, Monsieur Leblanc puts us to work and doesn't have to pay us. It's better than it sounds. Besides, one doesn't have to work as a hostess. Sometimes girls help in the kitchen while they figure out what they want to do."

"Kitchen work doesn't sound so bad."

"You know, he's looking for another dishwasher. I could introduce you."

Gabriela was suspicious enough of the whole arrangement that she started to say no, but then thought about the Germans who made up the restaurant's clientele. Could it be a new place to search?

The truth was, she'd run out of places to look. Over the last two years, she'd worn holes in her shoes walking back and forth to the German embassy where she'd queue in the drizzling rain only to be turned away. She'd written stacks of letters to Vichy officials, to work-camp officers, to Todt representatives. To anyone and everyone who might have news of her father. No word of him or the man who'd arrested him.

And food. The restaurant would mean a break from the ever-present gnawing, that feeling of being eaten alive from the inside.

"Hey, come over here," Christine said. "I want to show you something."

The something turned out to be the art Christine had discovered in an outdoor shop, tucked behind an armoire that smelled like mothballs. The paintings should have been hanging in some gallery, rather than stuffed into a dented metal footlocker. By the time they finished admiring the art, Gabriela had decided to take Christine's advice and stop by Le Coq Rouge, to see if this Monsieur Leblanc needed help.

"That's great," Christine said. "It'll be so much better than surrendering your treasures to thieves in the flea markets. You'll see."

"But in the kitchen, you understand."

"The what?"

"Working in the kitchen," Gabriela repeated. She spoke as firmly as possible. "I'll wash dishes, but I'm not going to be a hostess."

"Oh, that. No one will ever make you. I promise.

CHAPTER TWO

A ND YET IT WAS ONLY a few months before Gabriela stood before Christine, wearing her only dress, her last sliver of lipstick and a borrowed dab of perfume.

"Don't I look like the sexiest prostitute in Paris?" Gabriela asked.

Christine grabbed her arm. "The colonel? Did you listen to anything I taught you?" Gabriela felt like she was watching the scene from a distance. She couldn't possibly be leaving the comforting warmth and anonymity of the kitchen to seduce the Gestapo officer. Surely that was someone else. But then why was she dressed up like this?

"Gaby, are you listening?"

"Have you heard about the nuns buying bread?" Gabriela asked. "A German tried to jump the queue and they attacked him with their rosaries."

Christine blinked. "That sounds like the start of a joke."

"The *boche* lost two teeth. Fourteen nuns arrested. And what about the paper this morning? They caught an English spy in the 3rd Arrondissement. Turns out he was a Jew. Or so the Gestapo is claiming."

"I heard."

"The girl who did his laundry turned him in, and know why?" Gabriela asked.

Christine shrugged. "Because he was a Jew?"

"The laundress didn't care if he was a Jew or English or a spy. But his French was terrible and he wouldn't take any correction. That's how she knew he was no good."

Behind them, the clank of dishes, the smell of caramelizing onions, the cook complaining to Leblanc about the impossibility of working under these conditions: the dish needed butter, the carrots were limp, this chicken was tough and stringy. Where the hell was the garlic?

"Gaby, what are you doing?" Christine asked.

"I'm going to seduce that man. I already told you that."

"Listen to me. There are two other Germans at the table. Better looking, richer, safer. Why does it have to be the Gestapo bastard?"

"You choose your clients, I'll choose mine."

"Gaby, for god's sake, it's your first. Play it safe."

"Just trust me, I'll be fine."

"*Mais, non.* You'll be dead." Christine shook her head. "What are you thinking?"

What was Gabriela thinking? She wasn't, not tonight. She'd had two and a half years of thinking. When she'd pulled the stitches from the secret hem in her coat to remove the bills she'd hidden inside, when she'd sold her grandmother's gold locket and her father's silver cigarette case. When she'd taken the job working in the kitchen and resisted Monsieur Leblanc's pressure to work the Germans instead. She'd thought for the last few months as she'd scrutinized every German to step into the restaurant.

Even in the last twenty-four hours, since she'd told Monsieur Leblanc that she was ready, she'd had plenty of time to think things over. Even after Christine shook her head and tried to talk her out of it, then reluctantly sat her down and shared tips, explained the nuances. It had all seemed surreal but the time had now come and she couldn't second-guess, not even a little, or she'd never be able to go through with this.

"Look at you," Christine said, "your hands are trembling. You're so scared you're going to drop the trays."

"I'm not scared, I'm hungry. I haven't eaten yet." She caught Christine's skeptical look. "It's true, a crust of *pain noir* with a cup of watery coffee for breakfast and nothing since. What do you think I'm doing here, I'm sick of fighting the other dishwashers over the garbage. I'm tired of struggling." The part about the crust of bread and bad coffee was one hundred percent true, the rest a lie. She may be down to her last five francs, but she had no intention of selling her body for money.

"Now please, let me go." She steadied the tray of drinks. The men at the table couldn't see her tremble.

"Please, Gaby. Just look." Christine parted the doors a crack.

Gabriela glanced into the lounge. Three Germans at the table. Colonel Hoekman stood out from the other two. He was pale-skinned, a strong-looking man with a weak chin and too-narrow eyes. He was watching the negro band with barely-concealed disgust. The other two men at the table sat as far from the colonel as possible.

"Gestapo agents need comfort, too," Gabriela said.

Monsieur Leblanc approached from further back in the kitchen, where he'd been arguing with the cook. "What's this? Oh, come on girls, gossip on your own time. We've got thirsty customers. Gaby, you said you knew what you were doing. Either get out there and prove it or change out of that dress and go back to washing dishes." He stepped into the lounge and snapped his fingers for her to follow.

Gabriela followed. Christine gave one final pleading glance, but said nothing more.

Christine may have recruited her to the restaurant, but

she really was as nice as she'd seemed that first day in the flea markets, if a little dreamy. When she was not out serving and seducing Germans, she sat in the back smoking Gauloises and fawning over the drawings of Monsieur Leblanc's son, Roger. And gushing about the pretty trinkets given to her by German lovers.

Monsieur Leblanc swept up to the table with the three Germans and gestured for Gabriela to follow. "Come, come, whiskeys for our fine guests. On the house!"

The whiskey was on the house in the same way that the Germans were in Paris as guests.

The Germans may not pay directly, but one way or another Leblanc would find a way to extract a few more reichsmarks from their wallets to cover the drinks.

Leblanc stepped to one side and flashed that wide smile again. "Our new girl. Very pretty, no?" He ran his finger along the lace at the plunging neckline of her dress.

The first thing Christine had done after Gabriela told her she was ready to move out of the kitchen was drag her back to the *marché aux puces* and buy her a red dress and a pair of shoes. It had seemed an extravagance, but Christine insisted she could pay her back when she worked her charms as a hostess. It was Gabriela's first time in the flea market as a buyer.

Gabriela fed the Germans her most seductive smile. She bent for effect when she put the drinks onto the table to give them a view down her dress. As expected, their eyes dipped to her freckled breasts.

The restaurant was slow tonight, with only a few *miliciens* — French paramilitary — and a larger table of German officers on the opposite side, who had waved away any company and feasted on a leg of lamb and loaves of *boules de pain blanc*, the kind of white bread the average Parisian hadn't seen in years. Nearby, a fat Austrian businessman sat having wine and

Camembert with his regular hostess.

The restaurant décor was faded elegance. Dark oak paneling. A thick, woven carpet on the floor, now showing its age, paint that hadn't been freshened since 1940 and the debacle. Always the debacle. One never used the words *surrender* or *capitulation*. It was as if the Germans were an act of God, like a volcano that had erupted in their midst, killing and burning. One didn't fight these things, one simply adapted. And what could you do anyway when they cut your rations or when they arrested your neighbor without explanation? Just shrug, drink your watered-down coffee and be thankful it wasn't worse.

She put a drink in front of each of the men. "Your dinner will be out shortly. Meanwhile, may I interest you in some whiskey?"

"You've outdone yourself this time," the first man said to Leblanc in lightly-accented French. "Free drinks with a pretty girl, how can we say no?"

He was a handsome Wehrmacht officer in a crisp uniform. The man to his right was just as good-looking, with blond hair and strong Aryan features. Unlike the other two, he wore a business suit instead of a uniform. The third man, the Gestapo officer, sat stiffly, his hat on the table in front of him. A silver eagle decorated his hat, straight-winged, gripping a wreath and swastika in its talons. Below the eagle, a silver skull. The man's gray uniform was finely pressed, his boots polished. It was late in the night, but nothing was out of place in his uniform or hair.

Gabriela served the drinks while Leblanc produced a brass lighter to light the candles.

The Gestapo officer held the glass to the light of the candle at their table, said something in German to the other two.

"You do not like the whiskey, *Monsieur?* It is genuine Scotch." Gabriela gave him a sly smile. "Isn't that naughty of us?"

"Very impressive," he said with a heavy accent.

"Only the best for my clients," Leblanc said. His smile looked forced. He would be worrying about this new customer. Did he look offended at the presence of the illegally imported Scotch?

A fourth glass sat on the tray. Unlike the other three, it held a strong, unpleasant French whiskey, made in an illegal still somewhere in the Dordogne. You could have bought a barrel of the stuff for what Leblanc would pay for a single glass of the Scotch given the Germans.

She handed the empty tray to Leblanc and slid into the seat next to the Gestapo officer with the fourth glass in hand. "May I join you *messieurs*?"

"But of course," the regular army major said in lightly accented French. He said something in German to the Gestapo officer, who nodded.

She took a sip, tried not to make a face. She imagined that a Russian soldier on the Eastern Front, hiding behind a barrier of dead, frozen horses with a rifle in his hand and suffering a gangrenous wound in the thigh, might find this drink a suitable companion for a chill winter night. She'd have preferred a nice Chablis.

"I'd better see to the kitchen," Leblanc said. "Gaby, anything for you?"

"I'm not hungry," she lied, "so maybe just a bit of bread." It was the agreement with Leblanc. She could work, but no salary and no freebies from the kitchen.

The alcohol slid straight through her empty stomach and to her head. "Did Monsieur Leblanc tell you about the new one-armed dishwasher?" she asked. "He can balance a stack of plates on his hook."

The major grinned. "Really?"

These three weren't friends; she could sense the discomfort the major and the businessman felt for the Gestapo agent. Was it business or circumstance that brought these men together? It didn't matter, she needed to warm things up if she didn't want them to leave the restaurant separately and alone.

"Also useful for hooking bits of food out of the garbage when he thinks nobody's looking. He's good with the hook, maybe too good. Claims he can unhook a girl's brassiere, but I've declined his offer." She winked at the Gestapo officer.

The major laughed, the businessman chuckled, but the Gestapo officer frowned and shook his head with a confused expression. The major repeated the joke in German and this elicited a smile. The story was obviously embellished, but the men didn't seem to mind. The next was a story about a cat that ended in the pot of their rivals across the street.

"Can you imagine, serving cats? *Ouai*, and an English cat, too. The former ambassador left it behind when he fled Paris in his nightgown. Please, if you're going to put cat meat on the menu, at least make them French cats. Everyone knows English food is *merde*."

Another laugh from the major, more translation for his SS counterpart.

"My name is Gaby, and you are, *messieurs*?"

The regular army officer introduced himself as Major Ostermann, and the businessman called himself Helmut von Cratz. The businessman was watching her, but she couldn't read him as easily as the Wehrmacht officer. The major's hungry look was obvious enough.

"*Et vous, Monsieur, le sérioux?*" she asked the Gestapo officer.

His French was good enough for that. "I am called Colonel Hoekman."

Colonel Hoekman. To hear it from his own mouth thrilled her. She'd spent more than two years not knowing, remembering that cruel face. Yesterday, Leblanc spoke it for the first time, and now she had confirmation: Hoekman. The bastard. She wanted to grab a steak knife and ram it through his throat.

"Ah, a colonel." She gave a teasing smile to the other men. "I'm afraid a girl must cast her net for the biggest fish." She put a hand playfully on Hoekman's knee. He glanced down and then met her gaze, but didn't pull away.

"Bah," Major Ostermann said. "Your so-called biggest fish is going to swim back to Berlin day after tomorrow, next week at the latest. You won't get a meal out of him."

We'll see about that.

"What this place is?" Hoekman asked in his imperfect French. "Like One-Two-Two club? The Egyptienne?"

"What? No, this is a fine restaurant."

"Then who are all the girls?"

"Well, Elyse is from Belgium, Christine is from Provence. Those two are *Parisiennes*."

"But are they...I mean, do they...?" He frowned, as if searching for the words. "Work, sexually?"

Major Ostermann blinked and there was a long, uncomfortable silence. "Please, just enjoy the Scotch," he said at last. "We don't want to insult our hosts."

Hoekman snapped something in German and Ostermann shrugged and stared down at his drink.

Like Gabriela, the other hostesses weren't exactly restaurant employees, but neither was this a brothel or a *maison close* like the Egyptienne. Leblanc and Le Coq Rouge offered opportunity, nothing more. Opportunity to meet someone who would buy you a few pretty things, move you out of your louse-infested rat hole. Opportunity to tear up your ration coupons and eat real bread, drink real coffee, a real glass of wine. Eat meat.

But you'd better sell yourself or you'd be fighting the dishwasher's hook for the tastiest garbage.

Ostermann and von Cratz picked up their conversation,

this time in German. Colonel Hoekman watched them without comment.

The lights flickered and then died. The jazz music continued in the dark without interruption and Leblanc materialized with more candles. He had them on the tables and lit within moments. Sconces on the walls. The light was dim, but passable. A few minutes later, the electricity came back on and the *patron* swept up the candles with the same practiced hand.

Leblanc brought a bottle of wine and a basket of bread. A few minutes later, the venison and potatoes. She took a pitifully small slice of bread, spread as much butter as she dared and nibbled at the corner as if participating in the meal out of politeness. Her mouth watered and her stomach gave an excited rumble. A moment later, she forced herself to put down the bread, unfinished.

She tried not to stare at the venison.

Colonel Hoekman ate deliberately, almost daintily, while the other two attacked their food with a good deal of cutting and chewing and clanking of silverware and dishes. Gabriela kept up a meaningless chatter. Her hand kept returning to Hoekman's knee. He'd come here for something other than food or hostesses. She could see it in the way he studied people as they came and went. What that was she couldn't guess. Something unpleasant, no doubt. Looking for the opportunity to arrest some poor, innocent bastard for the crime of voicing the wrong opinion about the war or for telling the wrong kind of joke.

But gradually, Hoekman's glances fell more and more on her neck and bust line and less toward the door. By dessert, she would make her offer. Word it cleverly enough and he'd think he'd seduced her, rather than the other way around. The conversation between the other two Germans switched back to French.

"Have you seen Roger Leblanc's drawings?" Major Ostermann asked. He had downed several drinks and loosened up considerably.

"Roger Leblanc?" Colonel Hoekman asked.

"The owner's son. He's quite talented."

"Ah, yes, the...how you say?" He said something in German.

"Deviant? Well, yes, I suppose he might be homosexual," Ostermann said with a frown. "They all are, aren't they? We wouldn't have a museum in Europe if you cleared out all the homosexuals."

Gabriela had no idea if Roger was or wasn't, but she didn't like the sneer in Hoekman's voice. The Germans were strange about these things. You might very well take a man like Hoekman for a homosexual himself. Big and strong looking, but with a pursed-lipped, almost pious look around his mouth and a perpetually arched eyebrow.

Her father had once told her that the priests and bishops who were most anxious about rooting out and denouncing sodomites were invariably acting out of self-loathing for their own, similar inclinations. She wondered if you could say the same thing about fascists. She hoped not, in Hoekman's case.

"He's not homosexual, just a sensitive artistic type," she said.

Colonel Hoekman snorted. "Another word for deviant, *ja*? This is why I do not like art. All deviants."

"But the drawings are quite good," Ostermann said. "You should see them, Colonel. Isn't that right, Helmut?"

Helmut von Cratz shrugged. "They're not bad, I suppose. For an amateur."

"Oh, come on. Where's the boy, I'll show you."

"There is no need," Colonel Hoekman said.

This was no good. A distraction, at best. But there was something else, like a warning. A bad feeling. A struggle between these three men coming to the surface, perhaps. She didn't need it.

"Oh, I agree with the colonel," Gabriela said. "There's no point. The boy's all right, but it's amateur stuff, really. Besides, it doesn't seem Roger's around. I think he went out."

But now that he'd staked a position, the major seemed determined to defend it. "How about Leblanc, where the devil did he get to?"

"Never mind," von Cratz said. "Didn't you hear what he said? The colonel's not interested."

Major Ostermann frowned and picked up his wine glass. It might have died there, but just then Monsieur Leblanc stepped out of the kitchen. Ostermann gestured impatiently.

Leblanc hurried over with hands clasped. "*Oui, monsieur?*"

"Where's your son? We want to see some of his drawings."

Leblanc licked his lips and glanced from one man to the other. Gabriela gave him a tiny shake of the head. She couldn't tell if he caught the warning.

"Well, you see I was about to send him out. We need mushrooms, and—"

"Oh, never mind mushrooms," Ostermann said. "Let's see these drawings. Come on, Hoekman is a real art connoisseur. I told him we had a budding *artiste* on our hands. This is the real stuff. Where's the boy? Bring him out. I insist."

"Yes, of course."

Gabriela brushed her hand against Hoekman's knee, tried to say something witty, but he was preoccupied now. He stared hard at Roger Leblanc as the boy came out with his father. Roger carried a battered leather portfolio under one arm. A cigarette dangled at his lips.

Roger had the untidy look of a zazou: long hair slicked into a duck tail in the back, too much color and cloth on his clothing in defiance of wartime rations, narrow tie. When she saw him in the street he always wore dark glasses and carried an umbrella over his arm, *a la* Neville Chamberlain, never open no matter the weather. The look had the odd effect of making him look much older than seventeen, and at the same time like a child playing dress-up.

Hoekman snapped his fingers. "Let's see them, come on."

"Easy, easy," Major Ostermann said. "This boy is an artist, let him show the drawings his own way."

Roger opened his portfolio and held out the first drawing with a look of practiced indifference. A woman feeding bread crumbs to pigeons. The old woman's face drew Gabriela's attention. Quiet desperation. And her hands, held out as if imploring the pigeons to eat, not offering.

The Germans leaned forward and studied the drawing. Gabriela returned her hand to Colonel Hoekman's knee. He glanced at her neckline and there was something smoldering in his look. Very good.

Christine and Virginie came out of the kitchen. Christine caught her eye with an imploring look, but Gabriela looked away.

Roger flipped to the next drawing. A man kneading bread. It was good, too. His hands, especially. Roger flipped to the next. It was only partially finished, but it caught her eye at once.

He'd drawn an elegantly dressed couple, strolling arm-in-arm through what looked like the *Jardin de Tuileries,* with other couples only hinted at with a line or two. The only other completed detail was the face of a child, playing with a line or two of what would become a dog. A look of innocent delight on his face. That look made her heart ache.

"I remember that," Gabriela said. "When people used to walk like that."

Hoekman snorted and said something in German. She understood without needing a translation. *What, people in Paris don't take walks anymore?*

Christine looked over Roger's shoulder. "Ah, that's good."

Her face looked younger at that angle. It was the expression she wore when Gabriela and Christine wandered the flea markets. Christine liked to look at the art. Once, they found what appeared to be a genuine Corot. Who had been desperate enough to sell such a beautiful thing to filthy, uncaring men?

Roger was no Camille Corot, god no. But there was a spark of native genius in those drawings. Roger flipped to the next. Too soon; Gabriela wasn't done studying the child's face.

"Enough." Hoekman waved his hand. "It is deviant art."

"Oh, come on. It's good, admit it," Ostermann said.

"It is deviant." The colonel turned to the third man, asked a question in German.

Von Cratz shrugged. "Don't ask me. I don't know anything about art. Or deviants for that matter."

"Go on, then," Monsieur Leblanc told his son. He sounded relieved. "You're done here, and I need those mushrooms."

Roger slipped the drawings into his portfolio. "Yeah, what kind of mushrooms?" He leaned over and insolently tapped the ash from his cigarette into the ashtray at the Germans' table.

"One hundred grams of *pieds de mouton*."

"Oh, is that all?" Roger asked sarcastically. "You sure you don't want some white truffles? I hear you can get them in Vichy, if you're friends with Marshall Petain and willing to sell the family jewels."

Leblanc darted a look at the Germans. Hoekman had produced a notebook and was jotting something. He didn't seem to have heard. Or maybe he had and he was now writing it down.

"Don't be smart with me. Look, if Pierre doesn't have them, get something. Use your judgment. Not the *girolles*. The last ones were terrible. Now make it quick, the sub-prefect will be here with his wife in twenty minutes, and you know what he always orders."

Roger stood for a long second, then shuffled off. Leblanc gave his apologies and disappeared into the back room. The three men started arguing in German — probably about whether all zazous were sodomites, or just most of them — until Gabriela said, "Oh, leave that alone. He's just a pretentious boy. Besides, everyone knows where to find the best art in France."

"Where is that, *mademoiselle*?" Major Ostermann asked.

"Why, Berlin, of course."

At last she coaxed a smile from Colonel Hoekman. He put his hand beneath the tablecloth and rested it on her knee. Gabriela gave him a raised eyebrow, put her hand over his as if she were going to push it away in shock, but then slid his hand higher, onto her thigh. She giggled.

And suppressed a shudder. Horror, hatred, anticipation. What would her father say, whoring herself to fascists? No, she knew what he'd say.

Hija, you never abandon someone you love.

Papá had shown her just how far to go. When he was in hiding and they arrested Mother, he'd made a bargain to turn himself over in order to free her. After six months in jail, and many tearful letters from family members, he was freed. But he didn't stop there. Papá voluntarily crossed back into Nationalist territory to search for a brother and an aunt in Sevilla. And then, tried to bribe Gaby's way out of France while he prepared to face the Gestapo.

And now it was Gabriela's turn. She wouldn't abandon him. Nearly two and a half years, it didn't matter. It wouldn't matter if it had been twenty.

She waited a few minutes until the other two Germans were chatting about something, then leaned over and whispered in Hoekman's ear. "This place is so boring. Want to get out of here?"

"What?"

"Let's go somewhere else, maybe your place."

"Go where? I don't understand."

His poor French was infuriating. She spoke slowly, as simply and directly as she could. "Can we go to your house?"

"What? Ah, oh, I understand." He glanced at the door, then back at Gabriela. His hand was clammy on her thigh. And, she swore, growing clammier. It made her whole leg feel slimy, as if someone had emptied a jar of live escargots on her thigh and they were now oozing toward her crotch. "Yes, we go. We go now."

Hoekman rose to his feet, gave a curt dismissal to the other two men, put on his hat with the eagle, the swastika, and the silver skull. He snapped his fingers at Gabriela as if she were a dog. She rose obediently to her feet.

Major Ostermann took a sip of wine and turned to the businessman with a wry smile as Hoekman and Gabriela made to go. "I told you, Helmut. French girls go crazy for a man in uniform. Throw on a few ribbons and bits of silver and they go quite wet between the legs."

She had to do this.

Gabriela smiled at the two men still sitting. *"Au revoir, messieurs.* Thank you for the delightful conversation."

She took Hoekman's arm and started toward the cloakroom.

But the front door burst open before they'd taken three steps. A young man in a gray uniform with the same lightning-like SS marks on his collar as the colonel strode up to Hoekman and snapped a salute. "Heil Hitler!" A stream of excited German gushed from his mouth.

Hoekman jerked free from Gabriela's grasp, turned to Ostermann and von Cratz and said something in a triumphant voice.

All at once, the conversation in the restaurant died and

attention turned to their table. A note faltered on the trumpeter's lips with a sound like a strangled goose. Monsieur Leblanc poked his head from the kitchen with a frown. Hoekman shot him a look and he froze in place.

Two more men jostled through the door. They dragged a young man between them who protested in rapid-fire French, mixed with a handful of German words. "Papá! I am innocent."

It was Roger Leblanc.

CHAPTER THREE

G ABRIELA PICKED OUT A SINGLE word from the otherwise unintelligible babble of German passing between Colonel Hoekman and his young aide.

"*Maquis.*"

Colonel Hoekman asked a sharp question. The young officer addressing him sounded eager. Again, that word: *maquis.*

The word meant undergrowth, the kind of brush you could cut out and would grow back the next spring. After the debacle, it had been used to describe the young men hiding from the Germans in the hills. Bandits, really. The *milice* — French paramilitary — had been created to hunt down and either arrest or kill the *maquis.* Only now the undergrowth had spread to Paris. A murdered German officer, a car bomb targeting a Vichy official, a truckload of stolen mortar shells. And that was just the past week in the 4th Arrondissment.

The table of *milice* looked just as surprised as everyone else as Colonel Hoekman barked orders to the men who'd dragged in Roger. One snapped his heels and broke for the entrance at a run. Hoekman took his gloves from his pocket and twisted them between his hands as he rocked back and forth on the balls of his feet. It was quiet enough to hear his boot leather creak.

Gabriela returned to her seat at the table, terrified. "What did Roger do?" she whispered to Major Ostermann.

Ostermann shook his head, expression stern. Helmut, the German businessman, looked at the bit of meat on the end of his fork for a long moment and then set it down uneaten. Leblanc burst out of the kitchen.

He rubbed his hands together. "A problem, *Monsieur*?" he asked Hoekman. When Hoekman didn't answer, Leblanc turned to Ostermann with a tone like a whimpering dog. "Your friend, can you ask him if there's a problem? My son is a good boy, I'm sure that whatever—"

"Quiet, man," Ostermann snapped. "This is Gestapo business." Ostermann put his hand on Gabriela's arm. "Don't you worry. You're in no danger, my love."

"Roger, what is this about?" his father asked. "What did you do?"

"I didn't do anything. I'm innocent, I swear."

Roger rose to his feet, tried to pull free. He crashed into the other table of German officers. They snarled at him and one man shoved him away. Roger fell toward the raised dais where the band still poised with instruments in hand and the three musicians shrank back as if he were poisonous.

Roger's eyes bulged and he looked from side to side, as if trying to spot an escape. He briefly met Gabriela's gaze with a pleading expression. The Gestapo officers got control of him again and threw him down. One man held him down with a boot on his back.

The young officer returned holding a bag. Hoekman grabbed it. He looked inside, then down at the young man who cringed at his feet. He tossed the bag to the ground. It spilled its contents onto the floor.

Major Ostermann rose to his feet and made to retrieve the bag. "What is this? Contraband?" he asked in French, with shrug. "It is just mushrooms."

Hoekman turned with a hard look and said something

in German.

"*Ja, Polizeiführer.*" Ostermann sat down hastily.

Hoekman said something else to Ostermann, who turned to Leblanc, "This is your son?"

"You know he's my son. You were just looking at his drawings."

"I'm translating for the colonel, you fool. Answer the question."

"In that case, yes, of course. But he's not guilty of any crimes. The mushrooms are just—"

"This is not mushrooms!" Hoekman snarled in his heavily accented French. He said something again in German.

"This is not about mushrooms," Ostermann translated. "Your son is a bandit. He works for the *maquis.*" A pause, more German from the colonel and Ostermann continued. "We caught him stealing petrol from the staff car."

"No, not Roger. He is a good boy."

"We caught him with the siphon in his mouth. He reeks of it."

Gabriela could smell it now, even from where she sat. It was splashed all over Roger's coat, as if they'd come upon him just as he was about to suck the petrol up the hose and then let it drain into a can. Perhaps they'd surprised him and he'd spilled it all over himself.

Colonel Hoekman had been waiting and watching. It explained why he'd appeared at Le Coq Rouge just a few days earlier. He was on the lookout for something in the *quartier*, and had found it. But a *maquis?* Probably Roger was just a petty thief. Leblanc might have even known what his son was up to, although surely he'd have never authorized theft from the staff car of a Gestapo officer.

"And now," Ostermann continued with Hoekman's translation. He licked his lips. "You will tell us about your cohorts before we kill you."

The two younger officers dragged Roger to his feet. To Gabriela's surprise, the young man seemed to regain his composure. He stood, pale, but very still. Not groveling.

The Wehrmacht officers from the other table had left their places and gathered around, either to help or out of curiosity. The French *milice*, too, rose to their feet, menacing in their black shirts.

"Tell us now," Ostermann translated.

Gabriela sat frozen. She had seen this show before. She knew how it ended. She knew the casual brutality that Hoekman could employ. And she could see Leblanc, his arms trembling. A vein pulsed at his temple. He was ready to do something terrible to protect his son. She could read that expression. He would say something, do something rash. Father and son would be hauled away to a dark, dripping, poorly lit place.

She shook off her fear. "Major, the *patron* will make it good. I'm sure of it. The boy could be punished here. Someone can fetch the police. Monsieur Leblanc will pay the damages. Tell the colonel, please."

"Yes, yes, of course," Leblanc said. "Anything to put the situation right. Major Ostermann, please, I beg you."

"Quiet," Ostermann said. "It is too late for the boy, there is nothing to be done."

To her surprise, the German businessman spoke up. Helmut von Cratz cleared his throat and said something softly in German. He reached for his pocket and pulled out a wad of bills. Reichsmarks. He peeled off several bills, which he attempted to hand over to the Colonel.

Hoekman looked at the money with a disgusted expression."*Nein.*"

An argument ensued between the two men. Helmut didn't back down as quickly as Ostermann. Colonel Hoekman grew more and more angry. At last, Helmut put the money away and looked down again at his empty plate.

"I didn't steal anything," Roger said. He sounded so sincere, so outraged, that Gabriela forgot for a moment that he was actually covered in petrol.

"You stole it," Ostermann translated, "and you are a faggot."

"I am what? I am *not!*"

It wasn't just the Germans who thought so. More than once she'd heard Leblanc telling his son how pretty Christine was, or saying, "That Virginie has nice legs, no?" Pleading with him to show interest in a woman. But the boy seemed to care only for his art and for slouching around with his zazous friends, not all of whom were homosexuals, but surely some were. And stealing petrol from the *boches*, apparently.

Gabriela remembered Roger's half-finished drawing. The couple, arm-in-arm, gazing adoringly at each other. The look of innocence on the boy's face as he played with the dog. The world passed them by and they didn't notice it.

Roger would never draw again. Petty theft was one thing, but if the Gestapo carried off a Jew or a homosexual or a communist, he'd never be seen again.

She rose to her feet without thinking about it. Before anyone could stop her, she was at Roger's side. She threw her arms around his neck. "Please don't take him. I was afraid to say anything, but we're going to get married, and I'm having his baby."

"No, my love," Roger said. He gazed at her with such a look of adoration that for a second she forgot he was acting. It was such a brilliant act, in fact, that it only reaffirmed his guilt in her eyes. "I'll be okay. It's just a misunderstanding, you'll see."

"You see," Leblanc said. "He is not a homosexual. They can hardly keep their hands off each other."

Colonel Hoekman spoke again, and Ostermann translated.

MICHAEL WALLACE

"Take the faggot away."

Monsieur Leblanc tore free of the German holding his arm. The grip, Gabriela saw, was a feeble one. Surely they'd have known the man was a threat.

He charged at the colonel with a bellow of rage and frustration.

Never once had she seen the *patron* lose his temper. Yesterday, the flour delivery cart couldn't get to the restaurant because a German soldier couldn't be bothered to snuff out his cigarette and move his truck, which blocked the alley. The baker had fumed, but Leblanc merely sighed and urged patience. He must have sighed endlessly over the last few years. You didn't serve Germans for very long without learning that practiced sigh.

The calm demeanor was gone now and he looked ready to tear off the colonel's head with his bare hands. Whatever privations France had suffered, Leblanc had been well-fed at his restaurant. He was a big man, getting older, but there was obvious strength in his chest, shoulders, and arms.

Colonel Hoekman rested lightly on the balls of his feet. Gabriela noticed, then, that he held his Mauser pistol in hand. The two soldiers who'd dragged Roger inside held submachine guns, gripped at the ready, but they did not appear particularly alarmed at Leblanc's charge. Merely alert.

The colonel had deliberately given his orders through Ostermann, had them translated into French so Leblanc could hear. To provoke.

Hoekman lifted his pistol as Leblanc reached him. He smashed the butt across Leblanc's forehead and the man went down with a groan. He tried to get up, but Major Ostermann rose again and held him down with a booted foot. The other Germans surrounded them.

Colonel Hoekman removed a cigarette case from the breast

pocket of his uniform and tapped out a filtered cigarette. He lit it and gave a satisfied puff. He watched the men drag Roger through the door. Leblanc gave up and sank back to the carpet with a groan, Ostermann's boot still resting on his back.

Hoekman grabbed Gabriela's arm. "You. Come with me."

She had a little knife in her purse. There might be a few seconds yet, as he got her to the car. She was a woman and they wouldn't think she was a threat. She'd never find her father, but she could take her revenge. One moment to finish it all; that's all she needed. And then whatever they did to her wouldn't matter.

Ostermann said something in German to the officer. Another brief argument, but this time the SS colonel backed down. He released Gabriela's arm with a violent jerk, then turned and strode for the door. In a moment, the SS officer and his men had all left the restaurant.

Christine and Virginie came from the kitchen and helped Monsieur Leblanc to his feet. They guided him to the back, whispering soothing words. Blood trickled from a gash in his forehead. He clutched his temples and moaned. The musicians started up again. The others returned to their tables.

"Come, sit down," Ostermann urged Gabriela. He took her arm and returned her to her seat. "Here, eat something, drink something. I can tell you're hungry. Leblanc is in the kitchen, he is preoccupied." He dished some of his venison onto her plate. "The colonel is gone. I took care of him, I told him you had nothing to do with this. You can relax."

She couldn't help herself. She was so hungry that she forgot everything for a moment as she ate the food offered. The venison was good, god was it good. And the gravy. Had she ever tasted anything so rich?

Ostermann smiled. "You see, I can be generous."

"But Roger...my boyfriend."

"Oh, please, he's not your boyfriend. He is a faggot. The colonel was right about that much. I don't know why you were protecting him. Loyalty for Leblanc perhaps. Never mind, it is over now. Nothing more to be done."

"He may be a homosexual," Helmut spoke up, "but it's not hopeless, not yet. Neither the boy nor his father helped matters any with that outburst, but something might still be done."

"Come on, Helmut," Ostermann said. "Don't give the girl hopes. She's already naïve enough. The boy is *maquis* and he is a faggot. And now the Gestapo has him. It is hopeless." He didn't sound particularly upset about it. Ostermann turned to Gabriela. "What this little French flower needs is a friend, don't you, my love?"

She wasn't French, she wasn't a flower, and she wasn't naïve.

She'd had no plans beyond tonight. Seduce Hoekman, find out where they kept her father. And if that failed? If they'd killed him? Then at least she could take her revenge, steal whatever she could from Hoekman's flat, and flee the city. Head for the River Cher and get to the south side somehow, into the formerly unoccupied territory. The *boches* had broken their promises—didn't they always?—and occupied Vichy all the way to the sea, but it was different to the south. Even now the Germans were thin in the Dordogne, she'd heard. But she'd have to evade the *milice* and the other Vichy authorities. It would be a desperate chance.

Gabriela faced desperation of a different kind now. Major Ostermann offered her an escape. The thought of going home with him made her stomach churn.

"The girl is shaken up, I think," Helmut said. "How about we give her a few francs and send her home for the night? Maybe tomorrow, when she feels better, we'll come back."

Ostermann shook his head. "She'd be safer with company."

"Safer from what?" she asked.

"Colonel Hoekman, of course. I just put him off for the moment, but I guess you don't speak German, so you wouldn't have heard what I said."

"So he'll be back?" There still might be a chance.

"Not here, no. If you see him again, it will only be when the Gestapo kicks down your door in the middle of the night."

She glanced at Helmut, but there was nothing on his expression to tell whether or not Ostermann was telling the truth. She thought he was bluffing about the Gestapo part, although she had never passed a German in the street without dreading a voice at her back shouting, "You! Halt!" The thought of the Gestapo coming in the night filled her with a secret terror.

But never seeing Hoekman again was almost worse. She had staked her last few resources on getting close to him. And if that was gone, what?

A sense of tightening panic gripped her. She had nothing left, no food, no money, nothing to sell. Even the clothes on her back came from money she'd borrowed from Christine.

"And you must be lonely," the major continued. "My apartment is very warm. I can draw up hot bath water. I had some pastries sent in this morning, but I couldn't eat them. How does that sound, Gabriela? What a pretty name, it almost sounds Spanish or Italian." After a moment of silence, he asked again, "How does that sound?"

Weighed against what? Going back to the bedbug-infested room she rented from the Demaraises? The old couple could not afford to heat their own flat, let alone the tiny, drafty converted hallway where there was barely enough room to stand up or lay down her mattress. If she stood and left the Germans' table, she'd be shivering in bed tonight with nothing but an aching in her belly. Listening to the rats behind the floorboards, inches from her head, always gnawing, fighting, fucking.

A hot bath, a warm bed. Pastries. Maybe a few francs in the

morning and a hot cup of real coffee. It sounded like heaven.

All she had to do was whore herself to a German officer. And pretend she liked it.

Another group of Germans entered, talking loudly and smoking. No sign of Leblanc, but Christine swept into the room, said something in German that made the men laugh, and led them to a table. Just moments earlier the restaurant had been a scene of terror and violence, but life went on. Christine glanced her way and the two women shared a look of understanding.

Gabriela turned back to Ostermann and gave her best charming smile. She hoped it hid her despair and self-loathing. She put a hand on his knee. "A hot bath sounds wonderful. I don't suppose you have any perfumed soap."

Ostermann beamed. "I can get some. You will smell lovely."

CHAPTER FOUR

GABRIELA THOUGHT IT WOULD BE harder to prostitute herself to a German.

She'd never, in fact, seriously considered it. Had only approached Monsieur Leblanc so that she could get close to Colonel Hoekman. And yes, she'd have slept with Hoekman, but for something far greater than money. And yet here she was, leaving the restaurant on Major Ostermann's arm and she felt more relief than anything.

Christine stopped Gabriela at the front door of Le Coq Rouge as she put on her coat. "Be careful," she whispered as they embraced.

"Of course."

She slipped something into the pocket of Gabriela's coat. Gabriela put her hand in the pocket and felt a slip of paper as Ostermann led her out. A note? She wished she could take it out and read it.

Gabriela had certainly misjudged Christine that day in the flea markets. First in one direction, then the other. Not so glamorous after all, just a prostitute. Gabriela would never fall so low.

And now she was leaving the restaurant in the company of a German for the first time. She fingered the note in her pocket and wondered what Christine had to say. Final advice? A warning? Something about the arrest of Roger Leblanc?

An old man was in the alley when she left the restaurant on Major Ostermann's arm, rummaging through the rubbish. The old man wore a battered blue military coat of the kind they wore in the *Guerre de Quatorze* and gloves without fingers. His face was filthy and he smelled worse than the garbage through which he pawed. But when the major stepped out with the young French woman on his arm, he stood proud and erect. He said nothing, did nothing to the German, but looked at Gabriela with an expression of such disgust and loathing that she shrank back.

What am I supposed to do? she wanted to plead to the old veteran. *For god's sake, tell me!*

Ostermann glanced at the old man, but the man's sneer was gone. A blank mask took its place. He turned back to the garbage.

Ostermann snapped his fingers at a young soldier, who left at a run and returned a moment later with a black car. A chill breeze flapped the flags above the headlights, which held the same straight-winged eagles above swastikas as his hat.

"A Horch Cabriolet," Ostermann said with a touch of pride. "There is some advantage to being in charge of requisitions, after all."

"Is that a good car?"

He looked at her with a frown. "A luxury car before the war." Then, when she didn't respond, he added, "The same car Rommel drives."

"Ah, of course. It's very handsome, Major."

This seemed to appeal to his vanity. He smiled effusively, but waved his hand. "Please, none of that major business here. My name is Alfonse."

"Okay, Alfonse."

He opened the door for her and she got in. He entered from

the other side. They sped off. Gabriela gave a glance through the rear window to see the old man still watching. It was too dark to see his expression.

Ostermann bragged as they left the 8th Arrondissment. It was the only way to describe his method of conversation. His boots were of Italian leather, he could get American cigarettes. He had a large flat, heated and with hot running water. He ate only the finest cuts of meat. Even Russian caviar was not unknown to his plate.

"And our boys on the Eastern Front have had a hell of a time of it lately, so you can imagine how hard caviar is to find these days." He seemed to catch himself. "Don't repeat that. The war is going very well."

"Of course I won't," she said in a shocked voice. "I never pass along any confidence."

"That's good. Anyway, I'm sure any setbacks will be reversed come spring. The Russians put up a fierce resistance in the winter, but they are rubbish once the tanks get rolling. War these days is a thinking man's battle and they're no good at strategy."

"I wouldn't know about that."

"Not to mention that they're more scared of their own commissars than German bullets. They throw down their weapons and surrender at the first opportunity." He lit a cigarette. "Or so I've heard."

For his sake it was a good thing she wasn't with the *maquis*. He was a babbler; it wouldn't be hard to pry out military secrets with a few questions and a bit of flattery.

She found herself hating him. His casual acceptance of Roger Leblanc's arrest and the accusation of homosexuality. The way he left food on the plate in the restaurant, while proud men had been reduced to rummaging through the garbage. The way his driver sped around traffic and nearly ran down a man trying to cross the street.

"Goddamn Jew, violating curfew," Ostermann said as the man leaped out of the way and they sped past without slowing. He said something in German to the driver, who chuckled.

The whole city had been under curfew since last February, but the Germans, in one of their periodic attempts to show largesse, had lifted the curfew, except for Jews.

But nothing about the man's appearance had given an indication as to whether or not the man was a Jew, so far as she could see. And never mind that the so-called *Ville-Lumière*—City of Light—was a dark, dreary place at night, what with electrical rationing and the forced blackouts. They'd been almost upon the man before the Horch's headlights caught his startled expression. If it was anyone's fault, surely it was the fault of the driver, not the pedestrian.

"I had the most delicious lamb with mint sauce yesterday," Ostermann said. "I know you French love to talk about food. You want to hear what my cook's secret is?"

She was so hungry she could almost faint. A few bites of venison had done nothing more than stoke her appetite. She didn't want to hear about lamb with mint sauce unless it were on the end of her fork. "Yes, of course. How was it prepared?"

Her mind went to another place as he gave the details, but the only participation he required was a nod and a smile and a light touch on his arm.

The driver stopped the car in front of a block of apartments, not far from the Luxemburg Gardens. "Ah, here we are."

"Oh, how nice. I've always loved these flats, Alfonse."

"First thing, hot bath. Then those pastries. They're delicious, you'll see."

"And after we eat the pastries?" she asked in a teasing tone.

He grinned back. "Then we have dessert."

ᛋᛋ

"Put your clothes on," a man said in a disgusted tone.

Gabriela sat up, half-awake, startled. Her head pounded and it took a moment to remember where she was, last night's debauchery. Ah, the food, those glorious pastries. Had they ever been so good before? She had never fully appreciated them.

Her eyes focused and she saw Helmut von Cratz standing at the doorway of the bedroom. He didn't look at her and she glanced down to see that she was naked, with sheets and blankets tossed around. She hadn't needed clothes or blankets to stay warm last night. Apart from their physical efforts, Alfonse (she'd stopped thinking of him as Major Ostermann sometime during the night) must have wasted a week's worth of coal heating the apartment.

Gabriela pulled a sheet around herself. She felt her face light up with shame. "How did you get in here?"

"The maid let me in."

Indeed, the maid was in the salon, cleaning. She passed by with a broom and a dustpan and did not look inside.

The events of last night came rushing back.

Gabriela had formed a plan: maintain a cold distance. She had to sleep with the German, but she could disengage her mind. She would let her body respond, but it would be an act, and she'd be detached, watching everything. It was the only way to keep her dignity. Just like the *maquis* were willing to be tortured for France, she would let Alfonse have his way with her sexually, so as to stay alive, to give herself a chance to find Colonel Hoekman again.

The French army would have been proud at how fast she surrendered to the German.

She had eaten two pastries, drank three glasses of wine. Felt light-headed.

Alfonse, when he wanted to, could be seductive. He flattered her, coddled her. Made promises and suggestive remarks.

When she seemed reticent, he buttered her with charm.

Gabriela had lived in isolation for two years, since she last saw her father. Four years since her first, tentative boyfriend in Barcelona. She didn't realize how much she craved attention and human touch.

There was no cold distance. There was no disengagement. When the time came, she shivered under Alfonse's touch, felt her body respond in every way. It was a lie to blame the wine.

He took her there on the couch, gently, like a lover. And then later, in the bedroom, harder, faster, more urgently. There might have been one more time, but she'd had too much wine by then and couldn't remember the details. But she had been willing, she knew that much.

"Where is Major Ostermann?" Helmut asked from the doorway.

She gripped the sheet more tightly. "How would I know?"

"Yes, I know. You're just the prostitute who spent the night. But my friend talks too much."

"I'm not a prostitute."

Helmut stepped into the room, made his way to the night stand. He picked up the folded German marks, sitting on a plate next to one of last night's half-eaten pastries, and tossed them to her. "Your pay. For services rendered."

She looked down at the money. It was quite a lot. In fact, if she was figuring the conversion right, it was only about five francs short of what she owed Christine for the dress and shoes.

"With that kind of money, you must have pulled a double shift. How many times did you give yourself to him?"

Oh, god. She was a whore. A filthy whore to the *boches*. What would her father have said? *I didn't leave Spain so you could whore yourself to fascists.*

No, he would have never judged her. Papá would have told her to do what it took to survive. But that didn't mean she hadn't shamed him.

"Go buy yourself a good meal," the German said. "You're too skinny. Too many bones, too few curves. It's not attractive."

"I'm skinny because the goddamned *boches* are stealing all our food." The words came out before she could reconsider. "You, you're personally responsible. I know what your business is. You steal the riches of France. That's your job."

"I pay money for everything I buy," he said.

"At the price you set. You buy up everything for nothing and you ship it off to Germany. Do you have a wife and children there? I bet they don't go hungry at night. Well here, in France, there are hungry children sleeping in the streets because of your job."

"Where did you hear that? The so-called Free French from London? Don't believe everything you hear from the BBC. It's propaganda."

"I don't have to listen to the radio to see what's right in front of my eyes. To see the little crusts on my plate while the German trucks rumble off from the bakeries every morning, loaded with bread for your soldiers."

Helmut pointed to the half-eaten pastry. "Wonder what the suffering children of France would say if they could see that. There goes a true patriot, stuffing herself with pastries and German sausage. She must truly love France."

This stopped her.

"What do you want?" she said at last. "Just to see me naked? Are you waiting until I get dressed so you can sit and gawk?"

"Yes, I know. One usually pays for that privilege."

"Are you just cruel by nature? Can't you see, I'm doing what it takes to survive, that's all."

And this seemed to stop *him*. "Yes, I guess you are."

"What is it you want?" Gabriela asked. "Please, just tell me and then leave me alone."

"I need to find Major Ostermann. I have business to discuss and it is rather urgent. The sooner you tell me what you know, the sooner I'll leave."

"I'm afraid I really don't know."

Helmut clenched his jaw. "God, this is annoying. He knew I was coming. I told him three times."

He turned, scanned the room, fixed on the major's desk in the corner. He flipped through a stack of papers on the desk. It was a familiar gesture, yet she caught him glancing back to see if she was watching. As if considering whether to break into the desk itself and if it would get back to the major if he did.

"Are you sure he'd want you to do that?" she asked.

"Mind your own business." He let out an exaggerated sigh. "Looks like my trip is wasted. Good day." To her relief, he turned to go.

Someone cleared her throat. It was the maid, standing in the hallway. "Excuse me, *Monsieur*," she said in a tentative voice. "The major left a note."

"Well, why didn't you say so in the first place?"

"I wasn't sure who...I—"

"Never mind, hand it over." He took the envelope, opened it and read with a frown. "Ah, I see now." He tossed the note to the bed. "It's for you. You must have been impressive."

Gabriela unfolded the paper.

You were wonderful last night. Please, stay in the apartment. Help yourself to whatever food you find in the flat. The maid will bring you anything else you may require. I shall be back after dark. I hope to see you then.
A.

"Congratulations," Helmut said, "you've secured full-time employment."

CHAPTER FIVE

"I AM AN AMERICAN SPY. I know when the Americans plan to invade France and how. I can either betray the Fatherland if I choose, or I can sell this information to the German High Command."

Helmut von Cratz talked out loud to himself as he drove down the motorway and into the Loire Valley. There was nobody else in the car to hear. A light snow fell from the sky and the bald tires slipped as they tried to grip the turns. Goddamned rubber shortage.

He came around a corner to see a farmer in the middle of the road, leading a donkey that pulled a cart. Helmut punched the brakes. The tires locked and he started to slide. The man must have heard him coming, because he was trying to pull the donkey onto the shoulder. He looked up, and a shared moment of terror seemed to pass between the two men.

Helmut caught control and slid around the cart, prepared to fly off the road and slam into the trees. There was a sickening moment when he could feel the future: car crumpled, head slammed into the windscreen, the steering wheel crushing his sternum. But the bumper caught the edge of the cart, spun both the car and the cart around, and he came to a stop.

He was sweating, his heart pounded. He looked out the window. The donkey jerked and tossed. The wood rail at the back of the cart had splintered from the impact. The farmer sat on his backside in the road, but appeared unhurt. He rose shakily to his feet, grabbed the reins and tried to calm his animal.

Helmut rolled down the window. "That was close."

The farmer looked terrified, as much to be talking to a German—probably the first he'd ever met, this being so far into the countryside—as over the near-fatal collision. "So sorry, *monsieur.*" His French was so thick that Helmut could barely understand. "So very, very sorry. Please, I have a family. Do not report me, I beg you."

He answered in German, recklessly. "I possess the Soviet battle plans for the spring of 1943. I can deliver the full blueprints of the new British super weapon."

The farmer gave a confused shake of the head. "*Monsieur? Je n'ai pas compris.*"

He switched to French. "I said never mind, it was my fault. I was driving too fast for the conditions of the road. If you're all right, we can both forget this ever happened."

"I am fine, *monsieur.* Thank you, you are very kind. Thank you."

Helmut rolled up the window and continued into the snow. Lies. What he needed were some even more outrageous lies. The more fantastical, the better.

"I once slept with my own mother. Josef Stalin is my godfather. Once, when I was little, I tortured a dog. I dropped it in the well and watched it try to climb out until it drowned. Did I tell you I love Jew girls? My secret desire is to father a half-Jew bastard and pass him off as fully Aryan. I will teach him to hate Jews and then, when he's an adult, I will tell him the truth and watch him suffer."

As he invented lies, he modulated his voice, to make it sound as convincing as possible. He would repeat a phrase with the emphasis on different words. This time sound self-hating, this time boastful, this time as if he were confessing under torture.

It was like practicing for a play. When the time came to step on stage, you would be ready. You would not feel stage fright and you would deliver your lines in such a convincing way that you'd forget, for a moment, that you were acting.

He had recovered his composure by the time he reached the next road block, some twenty kilometers south of his near accident. He handed over his papers. The soldier thumbed through without comment, then said, "You are from Bavaria?"

"Ja."

"My mother was from Mittenwald. Have you ever been?"

"Of course. My wife and I have visited many times. I love the pink church. Very charming."

The nature of the question was not important. The important thing was for the inspector to ask a question, watch to see how the questioned individual responded. Did he look away, talk too fast? Was there something in his accent that sounded suspicious? Maybe he sounded Austrian or even had a hint of a French accent that no length of time in Germany could erase. Did he sweat? Glance over his shoulder at a bag in the back seat?

Helmut knew all of this and he knew, too, how to defeat such simple interrogation techniques. In theory, at least.

The soldiers were all older than Helmut; not a one looked younger than forty. The young men were on the Eastern Front, getting killed by Russians and eating boot leather, if rumors about the ferocious battle at Stalingrad had any truth to them. Another year of this war and they might as well set up recruiting offices in the retirement homes.

The man thumbing through his papers was the oldest of the bunch. Most likely, his mother from Mittenwald was born before Bavaria had been absorbed into greater Germany. But if he was old, he didn't look soft. Helmut suffered no illusions as to what would happen if the man discovered the true nature of his business.

"Have a good day, Herr von Cratz. I hope your business in Tours is profitable for you and for the Reich. Heil Hitler."

In France, the Wehrmacht still used the traditional military salute, for the most part, and the old soldier's zealousness caught him off guard. In his mind, he heard his wife's irreverent joke. *Heal Hitler? Is he sick?*

He'd heard this same joke once while he and Alfonse were listening illicitly to the BBC one night, but it didn't carry the same weight since 'heil' and 'heal' didn't sound exactly the same in English. Nevertheless, the major had roared with laughter as if he'd never heard the joke before.

Helmut returned the salute. "Heil Hitler."

There would be another, more serious checkpoint outside Tours. Helmut continued toward it.

He was troubled by the girl in Alfonse's apartment. Gabriela. Was she a danger?

There was a hint of Spanish in her accent, although Alfonse seemed blind to it. Half a million Spaniards in France when the war started — mostly Republicans and Communists. Likely, she was one of the refugees, but he wasn't sure. It had occurred to him that the whole scene in the restaurant with Leblanc's son could have been a farce.

First Colonel Hoekman comes, arrests Leblanc's son on some pretense. The restaurant hostess mounts a spirited defense. Hoekman lets her off with a warning. She goes home with Major Alfonse Ostermann. Who now trusts her. She is pretty, Alfonse is weak and talks too much. And what does she report back to the Gestapo?

Helmut shook his head. No, that was just paranoia. She was a prostitute.

"I am feeding information to the *maquis*. They are planning to bomb the Gare du Nord tomorrow night when the munitions arrive." He licked his lips. "I would kill the Fuhrer if I could. He is a blight upon the German nation."

He paused after saying this last part. Considered.

Not all of his lies were one hundred percent false.

⚡⚡

Helmut was stopped at the bridge over the Cher near Chenonceau. To the south, the Vichy regime. Germans had recently occupied the south, but they were concentrated on the coast opposite the Americans in Algeria. Someday, everyone knew, the Germans and the Americans would lock in mortal combat, but for now the two armies glared at each other across the Mediterranean like a pair of big, mean dogs before a dogfight, wanting to go after each other's throats, unable to do so.

How would the Americans fight? They'd done well in North Africa, but they'd started with a huge advantage. The groundwork had been laid by their British cousins and the Vichy French had gone into full boot-licking mode as soon as the Yanks showed up with their tanks and guns. And the Germans were handicapped by that inconvenient barrier to logistics known as the Mediterranean Sea. Rommel couldn't keep his army supplied.

When Helmut and Alfonse were alone, the major opined often and strenuously that the Yanks had no stomach for fighting Germans on European soil. Americans preferred to let Russians die on their behalf and would keep supplying Stalin with tanks and jeeps and planes and the petrol to run them until the Russians started to win. And then the Americans and the Germans and the British would sit down over a hock and seltzer and work things out like civilized people.

"Roosevelt, that's a Dutch name, isn't it?" Alfonse told him once. "And that's just how a Dutchman would think, isn't it?

The Dutch are cunning bastards, but they're just Germans at heart, aren't they? This Roosevelt wants to weaken us, but he sure as hell doesn't want to see Russians in Berlin and Paris. God, no. When it comes right down to it, the Americans will be on our side. The Brits, too. You'll see."

Alfonse could be a smart man in many ways. On other occasions, he was the biggest idiot in the Reich. Seeing as the Reich was full of idiots these days, that was quite an accomplishment.

As for the prostrate nation that had once been known as France, the center of the country was still largely ruled by the French. One wave of his papers and any French police would send Helmut on his way. This German crossing was the difficult part.

When he reached the bridge, an SS captain ordered him from the car and took his papers. Helmut kept his briefcase tucked under his arm. A soldier walked around the car with a mirror on a pole, inspecting the undercarriage. If something looked wrong down there, they'd soon have the car in pieces. He was counting on the contents of the briefcase to distract them from a more thorough search.

A man with a German shepherd on a leash followed the riverbank. The dog's breath steamed as it paused to sniff at something in a clump of grass. A light mist rose from the river. There were several stone cottages along the riverbank and they'd been turned into some sort of barracks, guarded by sand bags and machine gun nests.

"Come with me, Herr von Cratz," the captain said. The man led him into the nearest stone cottage, which had been converted into a guard post. A corporal with a submachine gun gave a Hitler salute as they entered.

As Helmut expected, the money in his briefcase attracted interest. The captain took out the money and set it to one side, then ran his fingers along the interior as if looking for hidden compartments. Helmut felt his heart rate accelerate slightly. If they paid similar attention to his car, he would be in trouble. Perhaps outside they would be, perhaps at any moment a corporal would come in and whisper something in the captain's ear. Tell him what they'd found.

"Twenty-five thousand marks is a lot of money, Herr von Cratz."

"Yes, it is."

"Why not carry francs, if you are planning to cross into the Vichy zone?"

"I arrived in Paris last night from Munich," Helmut said. "Francs are rather hard to find in the Reich. And the reichsmark carries somewhat more weight these days than useless French paper."

The SS captain shut the case holding the stacks of 20 mark notes. He did not yet hand it back or order von Cratz to return to the vehicle. "And you travel alone, and by car. This is a dangerous part of the country for a lone German carrying a large sum of money. What a risk to take."

"If the *maquis* target my car, I'll have other things to worry about than losing a few marks."

"Still, why not take the train and ride with other Germans?"

"I have my reasons."

"Which are?"

"Are my papers not in order?"

The SS officer thumbed through them a second time. "Yes, they appear to be. But you did not answer the question."

"You may call headquarters if you must. But I can't divulge the nature of my trip. Surely you understand."

The captain seemed to consider this. He seemed a bright young man, alert, but Helmut didn't sense any malice. So many of these SS officers had to lord it over you, remind you that at any time they could drag you away somewhere and nobody would ever hear from you again. Maybe if more SS were like this young man. the world wouldn't be in its current state of absolute *scheisse*.

Which begged the question of why the captain was in the SS and not in the regular army. Why join up if you didn't harbor a sadistic streak, if you didn't enjoy power and its many uses? If you hadn't been the kind of boy who liked to skewer frogs and light a cat's tail on fire? Bully the little Jewish boy and all of that. Why bother?

The captain handed him the briefcase and then the papers. "Very well, Herr von Cratz. You are free to go." The man followed him back to the car, which sat undisturbed, to Helmut's great relief.

As Helmut climbed behind the wheel, the captain raised his arm. "Heil Hitler." This was an SS officer, so of course Helmut was expecting it this time.

"Heil Hitler," he repeated.

Heal Hitler? I'm not a doctor.

Moments later he was on the south side of the river.

He had no illusions that the arm of the Reich could not find him in so-called Free France. But at the very least, the local authorities would be deferential. They would take one look at the signatures and stamps on his papers and step meekly aside.

⚡⚡

Ten kilometers south of the border he found the Molyneux farm. It was late morning.

He parked at the top of the lane, so as not to get stuck in the mud, then headed to the trunk. It took a minute to pry open the secret compartment. From there, he opened the crate and took out a wad of ration coupons from on top of the main cargo. Moments later he was walking down the lane toward the farm house.

The house was a run-down version of what he clearly remembered. The gate hinges had broken and not been repaired. The stone wall still marked the boundary of the property in its solid, eternal fashion, but the barn on the other side was faded and the doors missing. Five years ago, there had been animals everywhere: chickens, cows, goats, pigs, draft horses. Now, a single, scrawny dog barked angrily, confronted him as he stepped out of the car and then slunk off with a whimper when he sharply told it to back off.

Two women were lifting a basket onto the porch, filled with coal scraps. They set down the basket and stared. Coals dust blackened their hands and smeared their faces. He'd passed the rail yard a few kilometers back, and they must have walked all this way, carrying the basket of gleanings.

"Marie-Élise," he said.

The younger woman stared. Her breath puffed into the cold air and her breast heaved from the effort. A light, chill rain fell from the sky and dripped off the end of her hair. She was an older, thinner version of what he held in memory. But still achingly beautiful. Her green eyes were hard, like stone, but a tremble at her lip betrayed her.

She recovered quickly. "Ah, a German. Sorry, we have nothing left to steal. Not even our wheelbarrow, as you can see."

He looked at the house with the broken shutters and a cracked window, unpainted, weedy and thought about how meticulously neat the Molyneaux patriarch had kept it before. "What happened here? Where is your father?"

"Gone to Germany to work."

"Your brother?"

"Him too."

"But he's just a boy," Helmut said, surprised.

"He was fifteen when they offered him the chance to volunteer." A note of irony as she said this last word. "They promised to send him home with a good wage when his term is up. I have doubts. You know how Germans always break their promises."

"Let me help with that basket."

"Don't bother, we can manage."

"Is there something I can do?"

"Why did you come, Helmut?"

"I brought you something."

"I don't want it."

The woman's mother turned. "Marie-Élise."

"I don't want it, mother. I don't want anything this snake has to offer."

"But we're desperate. We have nothing. We—"

"Go inside, mother. Go inside now and don't come out until he's gone. And when I come in, never mention this visit or this man's name again." Marie-Élise didn't take her eyes from Helmut's as she said this. The gaze was so intense he had to look away.

Madame Molyneaux nodded, then turned inside without another word.

"I'm sorry," he said when they were alone.

"It has been four years. Four years without a word."

"The war," he said. The words sounded even more feeble as he spoke them than they had in his head. "You know how difficult it became."

"You promised. You knew there would be fighting and you said you'd find a way to get me. I thought you must have been taken into the army and then what? Killed? You don't know how much I suffered just wondering what had happened to you."

"So why are you so angry? Why aren't you happy I'm alive?"

"Because I found you. I looked, and I asked, and I paid money—money we didn't have—and I found you. And I figured out why you never wrote or came like you promised. You got married."

"I had no choice."

"*Conneries!* You had a choice."

"It was the war. I was going to lose my business, everything. I couldn't marry a French girl. I needed help, contacts. Loise was the daughter of a man who could — "

"My god, I don't want to hear her name," she interrupted with a grimace. "Listen to you, you make it sound like you're some Jew, who needed to flee the country in the middle of the night. You're a man of privilege, no doubt you and your family have prospered greatly by the war. I can tell just by looking at you and your car too. So you got married, you probably have children. Well good for you, but after everything that happened between us, everything you promised to me, everything that's happened to me since then? Excuse me for not wishing you well."

"I understand," he said. He hadn't expected hugs and kisses and tears of joy, but he'd hoped for understanding and forgiveness. This vitriol hurt and it hurt more to think about what she must have suffered in the past few years. Look how thin she was, the pain etched on her face.

"You don't understand. There's no way you could understand. Not yet. Maybe some day, when the war comes to your own country, maybe then."

"I brought you something."

"You said that already. And I said I don't want it."

He reached into the pocket of his greatcoat for the ration cards, which he tried to hand to her.

"What is this *merde?*" she asked.

"You're not blind, look."

"Yes, ration cards, so what?"

"Look, this isn't just rotting potatoes. Look at these

cards, you can get milk, grain, even pork and sugar. Cooking oil! I brought enough cards for four people to live well for six months."

Ration cards were more valuable than money, at least for a French girl like Marie-Élise and her mother. And these were T-cards, for manual laborers, which gave extras to compensate for the heavier work load.

She shook her head as she stared at the cards, wide-eyed. "No. Don't do this, no."

"There are only two of you, it could last a year. Maybe longer, maybe the war will be over then. But you'll have to be careful. This much food could attract attention."

"I don't want your help, why won't you listen to me?" Her voice was anguished.

He stepped forward with the cards, but Marie-Élise snatched them up and threw them to the ground. She came down off the porch as if to stamp them down in the mud and he seized her wrists to stop her. She beat her fists against his chest and cried.

That day, he could only think of that day. The day they had walked hand-in-hand along the banks of the Cher. The chateaux were still open then, and they had visited Chenonceau and the gardens of Diane de Poitiers. It was a brilliant, sunny day and the flowers were in bloom in the garden. They'd perched on the stone wall overlooking the river and kissed like naughty teenagers. A pair of old French widows in black had clucked their tongues as they walked past.

A *policier* eventually tapped Helmut on the shoulder. "This is not Paris, *monsieur*. We behave properly in the Loire, *n'est-ce pas?*" Marie-Élise blushed and they shared a guilty laugh after the *policier* straightened his hat and continued on his way. That night they made love in the hay loft above the horses. He was certain Monsieur Molyneaux knew what the young lovers were about, but Helmut had not disguised his intention to marry Marie-Élise in a proper Catholic ceremony. Those were the days when many people still thought the war would be averted.

"I'm so sorry," he said as she wept. "It was the war. The war."

She looked up at him. "Go away, Helmut. Do not come back."

They stared at each other for a long moment, then he nodded and turned to go. He did not look back until he got to the car. As he did, he saw Marie-Élise on her hands and knees, collecting ration cards from the mud and wiping them clean on her dress. Her shoulders shuddered.

CHAPTER SIX

C OLONEL HANS HOEKMAN PICKED UP the gold coin in a
pair of forceps. He'd removed the top of the lamp, and
now held the coin in the direct flame.

"Does anyone know what the melting point of gold is?"
he asked.

One of the young lieutenants answered. "A little over one
thousand degrees centigrade."

"That high? I never would have guessed, are you sure?"

"*Ja, Polizeiführer.* I'm sure. One thousand sixteen degrees,
to be exact."

"Now if you had given me the exact number to begin with,
I never would have doubted you. You were afraid to say it,
because you didn't want to appear to be showing off. It sounded
officious, an affectation. Can you be more precise, still?"

"One thousand sixteen point one-eight degrees, *Polizeiführer.*"

"Excellent." Hoekman considered. "But that is interesting.
You think of gold, it is so soft. You would expect it to melt like
chocolate or butter. And look at that, it is not even turning red.
How would you even know it was getting hot? Apart from the
fact that I'm holding it in direct flame, of course."

He smiled at his own joke. None of the other three people
in the room seemed amused. The two lieutenants watched
intently; they were wondering what he was doing. Perhaps

hoping he would let them get involved, maybe scheming to get ahead. How best to please him, how to crush him in turn when the time came. There was always scheming.

The third — the boy — didn't speak German, but no doubt the conversation and the coin in the lamp flame had focused his attention. He must have noticed Hoekman's tone of voice.

Why was it that a calm, measured tone and perfect control — like a snake, never blinking, never agitated — inspired more fear than ranting, pacing, loss of temper, threats?

Hoekman was taking French classes, two hours a day, plus study when he had the chance. His French was coming along at a rapid clip and even the old man giving him lessons seemed genuinely impressed. Nevertheless, it was not yet strong enough to complete the interrogation.

"You will translate for me, now," he told the younger of his two aides. "Bring him here."

They dragged the third young man — Roger Leblanc — out of the chair and brought him across the room to where Hoekman turned the coin over in the flame to evenly distribute the heat. "Your French coins are very beautiful. I especially like the detail on this rooster. Where did you get this one?"

The lieutenant translated.

The boy was sweating, shaking so badly that he would have collapsed to the floor if the two lieutenants weren't holding him upright. He muttered something.

"What did he say?"

"He doesn't remember."

"You had a gold coin in your pocket. What a strange thing to find on a seventeen-year-old boy in Paris these days. And you do not remember where it came from? Even more strange." Hoekman removed the coin from the fire and brought it near the boy's cheek.

"*Non, mais no, s'il vous plait, non.*"

"Look at you. A faggot, it is disgusting. And look at your clothes, your hair. A Clark Gable mustache, hair untidy. You have been watching too many American movies, it is not healthy." He waited, while the lieutenant caught up translating. "You are a zazou, aren't you? A disgusting little group of faggots. Very soon we will clean the entire city of this scum."

He brought the coin closer. The fuzz on the boy's cheek curled and smoked. A whiff of burning hair.

"I found it!" he blurted.

"You found it? I think you are lying."

A frightened burst of French. "I swear, my god, please, you must believe me. I just found it, that's all. Please, for god's sake, please. You have to believe me."

Hoekman pulled the coin back a few inches as the lieutenant translated this. "You found it. Where?"

"I was in the major's car, looking for cigarettes. I suppose it had fallen out of someone's pocket. I didn't think it would be missed."

"The major? Major Ostermann, you mean."

"Yes."

Now this was interesting. Colonel Hoekman didn't trust Alfonse Ostermann. There was something underhanded about the man. At the least, he was a corrupt element within the Wehrmacht requisitioning department. But this business with the coin cast new suspicions on the major, assuming the boy was telling the truth.

Hoekman took the forceps and put the coin back into the fire. How long would gold hold its heat? He would have to ask the lieutenant later.

Could this have anything to do with the American spy they were trying to catch in Provence? There was something there about gold roosters, too. They'd raided a house near Marseille reputed to hold the spy. No American, but one of the items recovered was a small box filled with a few dozen gold rooster coins. It might just be a coincidence; there were a lot of these old coins in vaults and banks across the country. Even more had found their way to Germany, and not always by official routes.

In fact, one of Hoekman's earliest successes as a Gestapo investigator had been catching a Wehrmacht captain who had robbed a bank vault during the invasion of France, smuggled its contents back to Germany in sacks of feed. A number of French roosters and British sovereigns and even American eagles had turned up mysteriously in and around Stuttgart. The captain's house, when raided, had been filled with real coffee, chocolate, lemons, oranges, and other extremely expensive black market items. His wife had been wearing nylon stockings, like a cabaret girl.

After Hoekman had finished arresting and interrogating the captain and his co-conspirators, he'd received a curt telegram through official channels, ordering him to report to a castle in the Silesian highlands, near the old frontier with Poland.

This had been March 1941, before the war with the Russians on the Eastern Front, when Germany and the Soviet Union were, to all intents and purposes, allies. Suspicious, semi-hostile allies, of course, like two packs of wolves came together to bring down a wounded animal — Poland, in this case — and now circled each other warily with blood from the last battle still dripping from their jaws. Still, Hoekman had assumed war with the Soviets would be unthinkable so long as Britain remained unbroken and jeering on the other side of the English Channel.

But as he drove into Silesia, Hoekman couldn't help but notice the trains, the military convoys, the massive movement of material. And endless lines of men, thousands and thousands of them, all moving east, in excess even of what he'd see along the former border with Poland two years earlier. Hoekman had recognized at once the signs of a pending war.

So all the talk of peace and friendship with the Bolsheviks was a lie. And why not? Germany was surrounded by enemies. Germans had their superior organization and their brains, and if they needed to add a measure of cunning, so be it. He just hoped his counterparts in Department E were up to the challenge of rooting out and destroying the NKVD spies that no doubt infested Poland and would be watching and reporting to Moscow.

The guards didn't lead Hoekman into the castle, as he'd expected, but onto a path into the wooded part of the estate. The sound of an animal came from the underbrush, grunting, primitive sounds. A wild boar, from the sound of it. Hoekman found himself wishing the guards hadn't relieved him of his Mauser.

"Heil Hitler," a voice said.

Hoekman turned, snapped off a reflexive Hitler salute of his own, and then found himself staring at the Reichsführer-SS, himself. Heinrich Himmler. The man had come from a side path and somehow approached without Hoekman hearing. He was out of uniform, in a pair of trousers with a matching khaki shirt. A hunting rifle lay draped over one arm.

"You must be Lieutenant Hoekman, the one who uncovered the gold smuggling."

"Yes, Reichsführer."

"Come, walk with me. We can talk."

Himmler handed the rifle to his aide, then polished his round glasses on his shirt. He dismissed his aide and the two guards who'd brought Hoekman, then ordered him to report about the discovery of the gold coins. They continued to walk as Hoekman did so.

The Reichsführer interrupted several times in his Bavarian-accented German to ask pointed questions. Himmler looked thoughtful as he finished his recounting. "Hoekman, that's a Dutch name, isn't it?"

"My paternal grandfather was Dutch, yes." He kept his voice neutral, neither apologetic nor defiant. "I am not in any way Dutch. I grew up in Munich and had never been outside of Germany before the war started."

"And yet one could hardly claim that Hans Hoekman is a provincial man," Himmler said. "I understand that you expended considerable effort learning Polish during the few months you were stationed in Warsaw. Why would you do that?"

"It is useful to know the language of the enemy. People tell you things in their own language."

"A disgusting, unsophisticated language these Slavs speak, isn't it."

"No, Reichsführer, I didn't find it so."

Himmler's eyebrows rose. "You didn't? Well—" It was clear he was not used to being contradicted and didn't quite know how to respond.

"The more Polish I learned, the more I liked it. Indeed, I found it surprising that such a degraded, inferior people could speak such a beautiful, sophisticated language. I can only surmise that the Poles were, at one time, a superior race to what they currently present. They have mixed excessively with Jews, Cossacks, and Mongols."

"Ah, yes, of course. That only makes sense." He chuckled. "I misunderstood you for a moment."

"I apologize, Reichsführer, I should have been more clear."

"Tell me. As a boy, did you ever suffer abuse from other children about your Dutch family?"

"No. I kept to myself and the other boys were mostly wise enough to leave me alone. When they didn't, I made sure they learned their mistake."

"And you joined the SS when?" Himmler asked.

"I joined the brown shirts in 1930, when I was eighteen. I started working in investigations in 1936. I report to Department D."

D1, to be specific. Opponents of the regime in the occupied territories. He was not particularly interested in D2 business, except where he came across Jews and homosexuals and other deviants through the normal course of operations.

"Interesting. You have the file?"

Hoekman handed it over. Himmler thumbed through the pictures, the typed memos as they continued to walk. Hoekman was intimately aware of the contents of that file, having dictated most of the memos himself. He walked a pace back, feeling rather stiff.

Hoekman had felt vaguely disappointed by this encounter and it took him this moment of silence to realize why. He'd expected Himmler to be some superhuman in intellect and charisma, but of course he wasn't. Instead, he gave the impression of a Prussian Junker out for a walk on his estate.

Himmler stopped at the sheet that cataloged the exact quantities of gold and black market goods confiscated and sent to Berlin. "That is quite a sum of gold. Were you at all tempted? It might have been easy to take some of it, but still claim the glory of discovery."

"Money holds no particular temptation, Reichsführer. My goal is to serve the Fatherland."

"Some might question your patriotism, that it's a front to hide your Dutch ancestry. To prove that you are more German than the Germans."

"I am aware of that interpretation, Reichsführer. I reject it."

"An excellent answer. Perhaps a little too excellent, in fact. Everything about you is a little too perfect. Perhaps it is an affectation."

Himmler gave a half-smile and Hoekman could see a grudging respect. Also, a touch of caution. Hoekman had often seen such caution before — how to deal with such a strong-willed, unbending man as Hans Hoekman? — but it still surprised him to see it in a man as powerful as the Reichsführer. If that caution turned to fear, Hoekman's life would be in great danger. He was aware of that.

"You look very German," Himmler continued, and his tone made it clear that this was a high compliment. "Your actions, of course, were correct in every way. Even down to the extreme measures taken with this Wehrmacht captain." Himmler passed him a photo of the captain in his uniform. The young man looked arrogant, untouchable in the photo. He had worn a very different expression by the time Hoekman had finished with him. "Of course your captain looked very Aryan, too, but we have done some digging into his background and discovered a Polish grandmother. Sometimes it just takes a drop of impurity to contaminate the whole."

"Polish. I did not know that," Hoekman answered truthfully. Was this a dig at his own family background?

An animal exploded onto the path. It was a magnificent stag, with an enormous rack that looked almost too heavy to carry. The two men drew up short, Himmler letting out a startled gasp at his side. For a long moment, the two men and the stag stared at each other and then the animal was bounding into the meadow on the opposite side of the path.

"And to think," Himmler said in a rueful tone after it had disappeared into the woods beyond the meadow, "I'd unloaded my gun."

"It is probably for the best," Hoekman said. "You might have killed it and that would have been a loss, I think. Those antlers look better on a live animal than hanging on your wall."

The Reichsführer turned and fixed him with a frown that

turned first to a smile, and then to a chuckle. "You know what, I think you might be right. Well said, Lieutenant, well said."

⚡⚡

Six days later, Hoekman received a promotion. The papers were signed 'H. Himmler.'

Within ten months he had risen to the rank of Reichskriminaldirektor — a Gestapo colonel.

It was curious that he had come upon another case relating to gold coins. The government would be very interested; even the smallest amounts of confiscated gold would be sent directly to Berlin. Apart from the satisfaction to be gained by rooting out another conspiracy against the Reich, it was not lost on Hoekman that another big find might propel him to new heights in the SS hierarchy.

But this gold rooster now pinched between the forceps, heating in the lamp flame, was it the only one? Nothing more than someone paying Ostermann gold for black market goods? Or was there some sinister connection with the events in Marseille and the small cache he'd discovered? He was intrigued by the possibilities.

"Now," he said to Roger Leblanc. "Is there anything else you would like to tell me before we continue?"

"I told you everything I know."

"Maybe you have, maybe you haven't. We shall find out. Lieutenant, drop his pants. Underwear, too."

"Me, *Polizeiführer*?" the clever one asked, his tone reluctant.

"Yes, you," he snapped. "He is not going to sodomize you, look at him, he is helpless."

One man held the boy by the neck while the other stripped him naked from the waist down. They both looked revolted.

Hoekman felt a very different emotion than his two lieutenants. Hoekman hated this deviant because the state told him to hate deviants. If his superiors told him that French brie posed a threat to the Fatherland, he'd have arrested guilty dairy farmers, women queuing in front of cheese shops, and anyone whose breath stank in a certain way. Now obviously sodomites were a threat to the Reich in a way cheese that was unnaturally soft and smelly at room temperature could never be, but there was no need to get hysterical about it.

"Good, now hold him still."

"For god's sake, what are you going to do to me?" Roger asked.

"You are a faggot. There are punishments appropriate for such cases."

"It's a lie. I didn't...I never would..."

"Lieutenant, bend him over." The boy's backside thrust into the air, hairy, disgusting.

The colonel removed the coin from the flame. Heat shimmered from the surface of the gold coin. He stepped up to the boy.

Roger twisted his head to look over his shoulder. His eyes bulged. He started to scream.

CHAPTER SEVEN

HELMUT VON CRATZ WAS A rich man, but the first time he'd ever carried a bag stuffed with money was the first time he'd visited Gemeiner in eastern Prussia, in a castle not far from the old Polish border. That was last spring, when the Americans had just entered the war, the eastern campaign had stalled, and smarter people began to realize just what the future held in store. He hadn't fully understood his role in the conspiracy, or what, exactly, he was doing carrying so much cash.

The money bags had held mostly reichsmarks, but there were also several thousand French franks. Business profits, reduced to cash. Helmut thought about his father when he carried the bags through the portcullis, ushered in by Gemeiner's old butler.

When Helmut was still just a boy and realized that his father was a wealthy businessman, he'd naively asked to see all the money.

"What, you think I just keep bags of money lying around?" his father had asked with a laugh.

"You don't? Where do you keep all the money, then?"

"I don't keep it anywhere. I don't actually have very much cash."

Helmut was disappointed. "But I thought you were rich."

"You think that way because you're just a boy and you don't have any money. You're thinking like a poor person. Poor people have no assets except what they've got in their flat and have no money except what's in their pocket or tucked under the mattress."

"But if you don't have any money, then how come everyone says you're rich?"

"I have money, or I can get it, at least, with some effort. But that's not how rich people work. It's a different way of thinking altogether that makes you rich in the first place."

That had proven remarkably true when Helmut actually needed to raise money. It had taken a good month just to convert ten percent of his wealth to the cash he carried into Gemeiner's castle.

Gemeiner waved off his butler and led Helmut down a hall lined with suits of armor and into a huge library. It smelled of old wood and dusty books. The coat of arms of an old Prussian family hung over the fireplace, with the motto—near as Helmut could make out with his school Latin—Hammer of the Slavs.

Gemeiner poured cognac and indicated they take a seat in the wing-back chairs. "Thank you for coming. How much did you raise?"

Helmut told him.

"Hmm, well that's a start. It will convince our contact that we're serious about buying his hoard."

"And what is this hoard, Herr von Haller?"

The man looked pained. "No, never that name. Always Gemeiner."

Gemeiner was an old word that had become slang for a naïve, stupid country peasant. Gemeiner was from an old Junker family—those self-styled hammers of the Slavs—of a similar aristocratic background as Helmut von Cratz, and it was unclear why he'd chosen the pseudonym. Irony, perhaps.

Gemeiner fished out a key and opened a drawer in his desk. He handed Helmut a small wooden box, very heavy. Inside were fifty or sixty gold coins.

"French roosters? Where did they come from?"

"Unclear. Pillaged from France, no doubt. We carried off the bank reserves of the French state when we won the war, but it would appear that certain freelancers took advantage of the confusion for their own personal enrichment."

"In my estimation," Helmut said, "there's no greater contraband than gold."

Gemeiner's pale, curved lips lifted into the hint of a smile. "And why do you say that?"

"Official directives, for one. All gold must flow to the center. There must be no secret caches of gold. The only thing the National Socialists are more interested in discovering than secret caches of gold are secret caches of Jews. And that's largely because you often find the latter in possession of the former."

"Yes, I know that, but I'm not a sophisticated businessman like yourself. I don't understand the obsession with gold any more than I understand the obsession with Jews. With all the gold they've already looted, I would think the reichsmark would have sufficient reserves to back it."

"But the regime needs to spend the gold because the international currency market is dead," Helmut said. "We set rates with the French and so on, but outside of that, it's almost impossible to import anything not produced in the Greater Reich, because nobody but the Italians will take our money. Even the Swiss balk. So the government needs every scrap of gold it can get its hands on. It's the only convertible currency we've got left. It flows out of the country and never returns.

"In short," Helmut continued, "it's a one-way conversion from reichsmarks into gold. Outside of this room I can't even imagine how you'd liquidate a cache of gold roosters. Not under present circumstances."

"And strangely, this is exactly what makes them so valuable," Gemeiner said. "Short of American War Bonds, I can't think of anything that would suit our purpose so well. So valuable and yet so illiquid."

Helmut had no idea why that requirement was so necessary. He expected that Gemeiner would now tell him, but instead the man asked, "Tell me, how much cash can you raise without bankrupting your business or otherwise drawing attention to yourself?"

"I'll raise every pfennig of my share, if you give me time."

"It's a lot of money, even for men like you and me. Eight months, is that enough?"

"Yes, it's enough. War is good for business."

As was fascism. Together war and fascism drove up demand, eliminated rivals, created monopolies, and scared away competitors. A few more years and he'd be richer than his father had ever dreamed. Or would have been except that he had volunteered to invest his profits in illiquid gold coins.

"Take these coins back to France, turn them over to St. Claire," Gemeiner said. "Tell him we've made contact with the American."

"And then what?"

"Then you'll be an industrious little businessman. Get rich."

He had done so.

⚡⚡

"We will reduce your rent," Madame Demarais. "Twenty francs. And you can help with the wash to pay the rest."

"I don't have twenty francs," Gabriela said. "I couldn't pay you ten."

She regretted paying Christine back so quickly with the money Alfonse had left her. It was the first thing she'd done after sitting down to a glorious breakfast of eggs and sausage and real, fresh bread with butter. And real coffee. A pair of the *Parisiennes* had been standing near the door, gossiping, and had smirked when she entered the restaurant to look for Christine. Gabriela could almost read their thoughts.

Not so pure and innocent now, are you cherie?

None of that from Christine. She even feigned disinterest in the money. "Oh, you don't have to give it back yet. Go buy yourself a few nice things."

There had been a time, nearly a year earlier, when she'd borrowed money from a greasy man who lived in the flat over the Demarais, so that she could bribe a secretary of the sub-prefect, who had hinted to Gabriela that he could find her father. He couldn't. In fact, the secretary eventually stopped looking. After she'd stopped asking about her father and merely tried to recover the money, he pretended he'd never seen Gabriela before, claimed to be outraged by her suggestion that he could possibly be bribed, and threatened to turn her over to the authorities.

The bigger problem turned out to be that greasy man upstairs. He wanted his money back. Or perhaps, he'd suggested darkly, she could work off her debt cleaning his flat and providing other "services." Gabriela rushed to the flea markets and sold her father's gold watch for a fraction of its value. And paid off the bastard.

No, she didn't like debts. Christine was nothing like the man upstairs, but Gabriela wanted it paid off, all of it. She'd get the last five francs as soon as possible, but in the meanwhile, please, take it all.

Only now, at the apartment, she wondered. Would it have been so bad to hold back a few francs? Christine would have understood, and now she wouldn't be standing in front of the Demarais with her hands empty and feeling this horrid guilt at seeing their desperation.

Monsieur Demarais was wringing his hands, pacing back and forth in the tiny front room of their flat. At one time, they had been reluctant landlords. She had begged them for a room off the back, a storage closet, even a warm space in front of the stove.

Madame Demarais pulled at a strand of gray hair with fingers that protruded from fingerless gloves. There was no coal at the moment to heat the flat. "Perhaps you have something you could sell. That watch, what about it?"

"I sold it almost a year ago. My mother's ring seven weeks ago. The last of my father's books two weeks ago. That was the eight francs I gave you. I have nothing left."

Gabriela held all of her remaining possessions in a single carpet bag, which she clutched in front of her. A few threadbare clothes, some socks, a pair of shoes. And the last few remembrances of her father. The first was a photo with Papá and her brother Pablo, standing on Las Ramblas in Barcelona. The second was a smooth green stone her father had used as a paperweight. She couldn't remember her father attaching any special importance to the stone, and yet it was one of the possessions he'd brought from Spain, while abandoning a thousand other, nicer things. A man at the *marché aux puces* had offered twenty centimes, a price that was more than an insult, it was pointless. She wouldn't part with it for so little.

And then, finally, his pipe. It might have brought a few coins, but she couldn't do it.

"What about that dress you wore last night?" Madame Demarais asked. "That has some value. Maybe fifteen, maybe even twenty."

"I can't sell that. I borrowed the money for the dress to...to get a job."

"A job?" Monsieur Demarais looked up. "With the *boches*?"

"Yes, with the *boches*. What else is there for a girl without husband or family?"

"True, true. No doubt the job would be clerical work or something similar," he said.

"Yes, something similar."

"You're a good girl, I'm sure you will work hard and do well."

Marshall Petain was always going on about how to renew France through *travail, famille, patrie*. Work, family, homeland. It was the only way to restore the honor of France, make it whole again. As avidly as they listened to de Gaulle's BBC broadcasts from London every night at 9:00, the Demarais still worshiped the Marshall and kept up the fiction that both they and their lodger were respectable folk, suffering a rough patch.

Monsieur Demarais returned to his pacing. He muttered under his breath. Reached absently for his breast pocket and groped for a minute before seeming to notice that he had no more cigarettes.

"And there's nothing you could sell?" his wife asked.

"Leave the girl alone," Monsieur Demarais said in a weary voice. "She has nothing. Look at the child, practically starving."

"We'll put the rent on hold for now," Madame Demarais said. "You can pay us when you can. Sooner, of course, is better, but I know the *boches* have their own pay schedules."

"I don't have the job, not yet. And anyway, my aunt has just returned to her house in the *banlieus*. She left in 1940, in the *exode*, and just now got it back from the Germans. She said I could live with her."

"Ah, so your life is looking up," Monsieur Demarais said. He ran his fingers through his thinning hair. "That's good, that's good for you."

It was a lie. There was no aunt, no house in the suburbs. She was packing up to move in with Alfonse. She had no intention of ever returning to the little pit where she'd spent the last eighteen months. Still, she couldn't stand to see the old couple's desperation. She knew that Monsieur Demarais had searched for months for a job. Once, during a horrible bout of hunger, she had scoured their cupboards for something to steal. All she had found was a little salt and eleven cans of beet soup, German military issue. A year earlier she would have turned up her nose at the beet soup, but upon finding it her stomach rumbled. Except that the discovery of the pitiful state of the pantry had made her feel too guilty to follow through with her planned theft.

"As soon as I get paid, I'll see what I can do to help you. You've been very good to me. Even when the police thought I was a Jew, you vouched for me."

"That's right," Madame Demarais said, eagerly. "We never told anyone you were Spanish, not one. We helped you as best we could."

It had been a commercial arrangement, of course. They had to protect her. If she were denounced or deported or even arrested and held for a few weeks, they would have lost their tenant. It was shocking to see their desperation, but she'd never harbored any illusions that they could do without her pitiful rents.

Monsieur Demarais was still pacing, and his wife still pleading when Gabriela finally broke away. She made her way from the flat and down the stairwell where she came across a man passed out on the stairwell. Someone had stolen his shoes.

A few feet down, someone had written in charcoal on the concrete wall: "*Du beurre pour les francais, de la merde pour les boches.*"

Butter for the French, shit for the Germans.

CHAPTER EIGHT

HELMUT DROVE THROUGH THE RURAL heart of France, stopping only when he reached the town of Valence, roughly a hundred kilometers south of Lyon. He'd studied his maps and knew when to depart from the main auto routes and onto narrow-shouldered country lanes that took him through small stone villages populated largely by dogs and old women in wooden shoes.

By the time he reached Valence, he hadn't seen a German for hours and only two other cars. On the outskirts of town he had to pull over to let two lorries go past. The driver of the first truck was a German and gave him a nod of recognition. He fought his way through an increasing number of carts and bicycles as he entered the town. Most people hurried to the side of the road when they saw the German car, but other times he had to lay on his horn.

He pulled up to a warehouse where men were loading lumber. Huge piles of cut boards lay stacked around the perimeter, which was fortified with fences topped with barbed wire.

A man signaled for him to stop as he entered the yard. The man was dressed with a wool cap, a beaten jacket, old boots, but when Helmut rolled down the window and the man leaned against the car, the hands were not calloused.

"What you want?" he asked in broken French with a strong Italian accent.

"I am looking for Pierre."

"There is not stone here. This is lumber yard."

It was a deliberate mishearing. Helmut had asked for Pierre, not *de la pierre.* It was the sign that he had the right man.

"Philipe Brun?" he asked. At the nod, Helmut said, "Where should I bring the car?"

"Around back, behind the horse carts." The accent had vanished, replaced by proper French. Even his mannerisms had changed and suddenly he looked very French, of a Mediterranean, thick-set type that was common in the south. "We can work without being seen from the road."

Once he'd pulled around back, the two men opened the false compartment in the trunk and hefted out the box. Helmut had already pried off the lid to get to the ration coupons he'd given Marie-Élise, and Brun lifted the lid. He whistled.

"How much?"

"Five thousand roosters."

Another whistle. "Where did they come from?"

"Do you expect an answer to that?"

"No, I guess not. But you say there are more?"

"It's just the start. Question is, do you know what to do with them?"

"I do and so do my men," Brun said. "You know this will kill a lot of people."

"Killing is not my goal."

"No, but it's the end result. It'll be bloody. If we're lucky. If we're unlucky, pure carnage. Frenchmen will die. There will be reprisals. More will die. What I want to know is if it will be worth it."

"You're French," Helmut said. "You tell me. Is it worth it?"

"It would be worth it to buy France's freedom. But this isn't about saving France."

"It isn't just about France, no. But what does that matter to you? You'll work with the English, with the Americans, with the Russians. Belgians, Arabs, Spaniards, whatever it takes. Don't tell me you draw the line at Germans."

"I'd deal with the devil himself if necessary."

Brun looked sincere, he sounded sincere. But thieves, traitors, and spies infested France.

"Why? Love of France? Is that your only motivation?"

"No motivation is ever that simple or pure. I've got other reasons. Hatred, for one. For the German bastards who did this to us." Brun gave a half-smile. "With apologies to the present company, of course."

"Of course."

"And glory."

"Glory?"

"It's a fantasy I have. That someday there will be a statue of me on the Champs Elysees. A *mounted* statue, of course. A big war charger and me atop, holding out a sword to direct the attack." He smiled. "And underneath, a placard that reads, 'Philipe Brun, Hero of France.'"

"Personal glory, that doesn't sound very French," Helmut said. "I thought it was glory for France. Never for one man."

"I have to keep this little story running in my head, it's what keeps me going. Otherwise I start to think about St. Claire and then I'm paralyzed. I'm a coward."

Helmut thought about the lies he told himself, like practicing for the stage, and thought Brun's method wasn't so different in the end. "What happened to St. Claire, anyway?"

"Typical story. Caught by his landlady. Suspicious old bag. Aren't they all? The French secret police have an army of fifty thousand agents, all working for free. Fifty thousand toothless, thin-lipped, shawl-wearing agents, waiting and watching and reporting. Landlady reported him to the secret police, who turned him over to the Gestapo."

"And they tortured him?"

"No, thank god. They never got a chance. I thought he'd roll over and give up everything. But you never can tell what a man's going to do. St. Clair killed himself before they could get anything out of him."

Did he really? Or was Philipe Brun the very member of the secret police who had arrested Helmut's previous contact? Was he now stumbling into a trap? Or being scammed by St. Claire's less-scrupulous replacement? Again, no way to be sure.

Truth was, Helmut wasn't sorry to see St. Clair gone. When Helmut handed over the first box of coins last summer, not long after the meeting in Gemeiner's castle, St. Clair couldn't stop staring at the gold coins, licking his lips. Helmut had half-expected him to start rubbing his hands together with a greedy cackle. How many of those coins had simply vanished into St. Clair's pockets?

Still, the loss of their contact had been a blow. Gemeiner had further segmented their operation after that. Too many people knew too much. It increased their vulnerability. So when the operation made contact with another official high in the Vichy regime, Helmut got the contact information via another route. Gemeiner didn't want to know the man's name or personal details.

Helmut was relieved to find in Philipe Brun a serious sort. Instinctively, he trusted him more than he'd trusted St. Clair.

"Now, this is very important," Helmut told Brun. He replaced the lid and opened his briefcase. "You can't actually spend the gold, not you, not your men, nobody."

"I thought you said it was clean."

"Clean? What does that even mean? I didn't exactly use ration cards to get my hands on this stuff. And even if I'd pulled the gold from my private vault — and I didn't — it still wouldn't count as clean."

"But if that's the case —"

"I'll tell you what I told St. Clair. There are dozens of Gestapo agents who are solely concerned with finding gold. The instant this gold starts to circulate, someone's going to catch wind. More than a few coins and it'll be someone very important. Then they're going to look for the source. Do you understand?"

"Yes, I understand."

"You spend this gold before we work things out with the Americans, sooner or later someone is going to get caught. And that someone will either bite a cyanide capsule or face torture, you understand that."

Brun stood more stiffly. Good.

"Say it's one of your men. When he's tortured, he'll talk. They always do. And he'll finger the guy who gave him the gold. That's you."

"I understand."

"You can't give it to your men. Not yet. When we get closer, when it's too late to do anything stupid or greedy. For now, you've got to hold onto it. Anything else is terribly dangerous."

"I understand."

He could see Brun working it through, coming to the same understanding that he had in those months after the meeting with Gemeiner in Prussia.

Helmut snapped shut the briefcase and handed it over. "Now let's talk about legitimate business. Have you got my shipment?"

"I've got the picket rails and the round rails ready to go, and fourteen thousand of your 1.83 millimeters at a lumber yard near the rail station. All I need is the train and the labor."

"Arranged."

"Hmm, well the 3.6 millimeter boards will take another six

weeks to complete."

"I need them in four."

Brun shook his head. "Six to get them all, but I'll ship as they become available. You should have eighty percent in four weeks."

It would have to do. He held out his hand and they shook. "Thank you, you have been helpful."

A sardonic smile. "Anything for the Reich."

ᛋᛋ

Helmut drove all day and reached the border just before dusk. With his cargo deposited and not even the 25,000 reichsmarks in his briefcase to give suspicion, the only thing to worry about now was the discovery of the false compartment, now empty. But there were a million legitimate reasons why a man about the Reich's business might have such a compartment.

The wipers flicked away the cold rain, now mingled with sleet. The car was low on petrol, but it would be easier to refuel on the other side. Two French officers slowed him down a kilometer south of the border, but when he held up his German papers, they nodded and waved him on. They looked relieved not to have to step out of their enclosed guard posts.

He was not so lucky when he returned to the border crossing. Two men with submachine guns took one look at his papers and ordered him out of his car. They led him back into the stone cottage. A man stood up behind the desk.

"Helmut von Cratz." It was the young SS officer who had interrogated him on his initial crossing. "Glad to see you have returned so soon. Your absence might have caused me difficulties."

One look at the hard edge to the man's expression and a knot of cold fear formed in the depths of Helmut's gut.

I am an enemy of the Third Reich. I am undermining it from within.

He took on an irritated air. "I don't have time for this. What do you need?"

"I have orders to arrest you. You are wanted for questioning in Berlin."

ℋ

A pack of zazous assaulted Gabriela as she walked along the Boulevard Saint Michel, in the Latin Quarter. She didn't see them coming until they were upon her, pulling at her sleeve and taunting.

"Hey, *boche* lover. Hey, you eat any German sausage lately?"

She turned, startled. She was returning to Le Coq Rouge for the first time since she'd left with Alfonse. In her handbag was perfume, underwear, lipstick, all bought with Alfonse's money and for his pleasure. It made her feel dirty, and worse, when she passed hungry Parisians, standing sullenly in queues in front of the shops, she couldn't help but notice the warm, full feeling in her stomach and feel like she should be suffering with them.

And so she distracted herself by thinking about Monsieur Leblanc's note. "Please, find out what happened to my son." She'd pulled it out of her bag at least twenty times.

Leblanc appeared to be laboring under the delusion that Colonel Hoekman was somehow friends of either Alfonse or Helmut, not, as Alfonse seemed to fear, that he'd come to investigate the major personally.

She was so distracted by her thoughts that the zazous caught her by surprise. "Leave me alone. I'm just passing through."

"Oh, I bet you're just passing through," one of them said. "You're passing through the entire German army, aren't you?"

The zazous wore oversized jackets with multiple pockets, tied off with belts and half belts, long, greased hair. It was evening, but three of the four men wore dark glasses. Teenagers, really. The tallest of the four wore a colorful scarf around his neck and his hair turned up in a duck tail at the back. A pencil-line mustache, and he walked with a swaying jazz-step as he followed her.

They were passing one of the vegetarian restaurants of the Latin Quarter that were well-known zazou hang-outs. The sound of jazz music came from a pair of open doors that seemed to defy the winter chill.

He reached out and gave her left breast a tweak. She slapped his hand. "Go drink your carrot juice, swing boy."

"I've got a carrot right here. Nice and firm and fresh. You can juice it yourself."

The other boys laughed.

She'd been accosted by zazous before. Riff-raff. They weren't political — they wouldn't have survived so long if they had been — but they were still detested by the French police and the Germans alike. And ordinary Parisians, for that matter, had little use for them.

He reached out and grabbed her bottom. "Come on, *boche* lover. Ten minutes. That's all I need. No?" He let out an exaggerated sigh.

Gabriela felt a surge of relief at the sound of disappointed boredom in his voice. Hopefully, this meant they would leave her alone. She wouldn't come this way again.

A car squealed to a stop at the curb. Out jumped Major Ostermann and his driver. Alfonse grabbed the zazou accosting her, spun him around and punched him in the face. The boy fell back with what sounded like a startled laugh, completely at odds with the shocking violence of the major's blow. His hands flew to his nose, which spouted blood.

Alfonse and the driver laid into him with their boots. The other three teens scattered. Two of them ran toward the staircase descending into the basement of the building to their right, the same vegetarian restaurant with the jazz music. The other fled down the street.

Alfonse screamed in German as he kicked. The young man curled into a ball and tried to protect himself. Boots to the ribs and head. A moment longer and they would kill him.

She grabbed Alfonse's arm. "Leave him alone! It was harmless, I wasn't in danger. Alfonse! Please!"

He snarled something at the other German and the two men stopped kicking. The young man lay whimpering. Alfonse turned, saw the door swinging after the two who'd run for the building and took out his handgun. He aimed at the window and fired two bullets. The window shattered, screams from inside. The sound of overturning tables and chairs as people scrambled for whatever entrance lay to the rear. Such places always had a rear exit.

Alfonse turned calmly back to Gabriela as he holstered his gun. "Come on, the car is warm." He took her arm.

She was shaking as she got into the car. She stared back at the young man lying on the sidewalk, groaning, barely moving. He was only a few years younger than she was.

"How was your day?" Alfonse asked in a casual voice. He draped an arm over her shoulder. "Did you buy the hats you were talking about?"

"Alfonse, he was just a boy. I can handle myself."

"What?" He looked momentarily confused. "Oh, you mean the zazou. Forget about it. It was nothing."

"You can't do that, you can't just attack people like that. He didn't do anything, you should have just given them a hard word or something, not...what you did." Her heart was still pounding and she fought to keep her voice from rising into a shriek.

"Oh god, don't start in on that. The sooner the French deal with these zazous, the better. We had Swing-Heinis, too, you know. Listening to that degenerate negro music. Swing, jazz. It's a moral rot."

"But what about the music at Le Coq Rouge?"

"That's different. You don't see sexual dancing, moral degeneracy."

She stared at him, trying to figure out if he was being deliberately ironic.

"Come on, it's nothing. There won't even be a police report." He put a hand on her leg and slid it up under her dress. A raised eyebrow.

"Alfonse, stop it."

But he didn't stop. He leaned over and kissed her neck. His hand slipped higher, reached her panties. He slid his finger under the edge. She stifled a gasp and glanced at the driver. The young soldier kept his eyes focused on the road.

"Alfonse," she whispered. She wanted to push his hand away, but couldn't.

And then, abruptly, he did stop. He pulled his hand out and his entire body went rigid.

She opened her eyes to see that they'd pulled up in front of Le Coq Rouge. There was another car parked in the alleyway. A soldier wiped it down with a rag, buffing the glossy black surface with the same care one might devote to polishing a general's boots.

"Alfonse, what is it? Is something wrong?"

The car stopped, but he made no move to get out. "To be honest, I'm not hungry."

"But I am, I haven't eaten since breakfast."

"Fine, we'll pick up something in Montmarte. I know a little cafe in Pigalle, and then we can go to the cinema."

Montmarte was a grittier part of the city and full of the same jazz and swing clubs that he'd just been deriding. And Pigalle was the site of official brothels, for the girls *en carte,* as they said, inspected by the police to keep vice strictly regulated. She didn't want to go anywhere near the place.

"I don't know, that doesn't sound very nice."

"I'm sick of all these Germans," he said. "I just want get away from war talk for a few hours. Did you know the Americans bombed Hamburg again? And the Sixth Army is about to give up the ghost in Stalingrad. They're eating rats. The air drops have been completely cut off. They say by February it will be all over."

She was pretty sure that such talk could get him in trouble for defeatism. For his sake, she hoped the driver spoke no French. You never knew who might denounce you. Not that she felt any sorrow to hear about the German troubles in Russia.

The major said something to the driver and he started to back the car out of the alley. "It's all they'll want to talk about, the war. And it will be so much *scheiss,* you know? Everybody knows how the war is going."

He was trying to sound casual, she could tell, but there was an underlying strain that he didn't seem able to disguise.

"You were fine a minute ago," she said. "Did something happen?"

"That's Colonel Hoekman's car. I don't want to see him."

"Wait!" she said. It came out loud enough that the driver turned with a frown. He stopped at the head of the alley, asked Alfonse a question, but the major just gave him a dismissive wave and he pulled back onto Rue Saint Remy.

"We can't leave," she said. Colonel Hoekman was there; she had to talk to him. "I told Monsieur Leblanc I'd help at the restaurant tonight."

"What, you mean you've got to work? Why didn't you say anything before?"

"I do, I promised."

"You don't need that job." He lit a cigarette. A little distance from Hoekman's car seemed to put him at ease. "What does Leblanc pay you, anyway?"

Pay her? She was lucky he didn't charge for the privilege of working the room.

Gabriela wasn't stupid; within five minute of meeting Monsieur Leblanc three months earlier, she'd known exactly what he wanted from her. It wasn't, as it turned out, the ability to clean and buff a fine Sarreguemines serving platter.

But first, he'd showed her to the back, explained the staff rules, warned her that she'd have to work out with the other dishwashers how to split up the leftovers. And no stealing from the ice box or he'd show her the door.

Meanwhile, Leblanc studied her as he might study cuts of beef brought by the butcher. How much could he charge for this piece, so nice and juicy? She'd felt a twinge of misgiving, tempered only by Christine's earlier promise that Leblanc would treat her fairly. "He's not going to corner you in the closet I mean," she'd promised.

Christine listened to Leblanc explain Gabriela's new job, and occasionally jumped in with a cynical comment like, "Turn the light on before you enter the kitchen to give the vermin a chance to run for cover," or, "Keep the back door locked. There's a pack of small boys who will come in and raid the ice box while your back is turned and Leblanc is too soft to turn them into the police."

Leblanc permitted these intrusions with nothing more than a scowl. But after explaining how Gabriela should not expect money of any kind for her job, Leblanc now glanced at Christine. "Which sounds like it might be a problem. I understand you're short of money."

"I've been selling some of my ration cards," Gabriela admitted, "so that I can afford to use the others. And it's not like my rations were all that high to begin with."

"You've come to the right place, then," Leblanc said. "It's true that our food loses something in presentation by the time our clients send back plates to the kitchen, but we cook with the best ingredients we can get our hands on. It still tastes fine. You'll never go home at night feeling like a gorged lion, but it's enough, while you figure out what to do. Job wise, I mean."

"I don't understand. Whether I keep washing dishes or not?"

"It helps if you think of dish washing not so much as a job, but as a stepping stone."

Gabriela looked at Christine. There was a bruise on her cheek and love bites that crept above her high collar. She seemed more tired today, older. It must have been a rough night.

A stepping stone to what? Not onto dry land, that's for sure.

"I don't want to hostess," she said. "I know that's where the money is, but really, I can't do that, so if that's what you —"

"Nobody is going to pressure you," Leblanc said. "You work in the kitchen, you work in the kitchen. You're expected to wash dishes and wash them well and nothing else. If you ever change your mind—" He held up his hand. "I know, I know—but if you ever do, then I'll change my expectations. But that's your choice."

True to his word, Leblanc left her alone once she started working. She'd had no money to pay rent or to buy new stockings or any of the other little expenses that added up, and so she'd continued to sell her ration cards. But she'd at least eaten real food (only slightly used) five nights a week and the work wasn't strenuous.

More importantly, she'd discovered that Le Coq Rouge was a great place to watch for Germans. There were all types: businessmen, young officers on leave from the Eastern Front, pilots, Gestapo Agents. Practically everything except enlisted men.

She couldn't see from the kitchen, but she asked Christine or Elyse about the officers, if there were any young, handsome men. Who were they tonight, regular army or maybe SS agents? Whenever it was SS, she'd make her way to the alleyway when they were leaving, to watch for her man. And one day, he'd come. And she'd discovered that his name was Colonel Hans Hoekman. Better yet, he'd be back.

"But what exactly does Leblanc pay you?" Alfonse repeated, interrupting Gabriela's thoughts.

"It's not much, but it's still my job, and I promised."

"The point is, it can't be much, and it's not worth it. If we go back there you're going to run into Colonel Hoekman. He might still be angry from the other night. What if he wants to interrogate you?"

"I'm just a girl. Surely he won't care."

A snort. "He'll care. You can be damn sure he'll care. Hoekman never turns down an opportunity to interrogate someone." Another drag from the cigarette. He offered a cigarette to Gabriela, but she shook her head. "And I'm not just talking about you. Worried about myself, too, goddammit. I didn't want to sit at that table, but if that bastard says he's your friend, what choice do you have? You're French, you don't understand."

"I don't understand about the Gestapo?"

"If you understood, you wouldn't want to be anywhere near Hoekman. Just let him do his thing and then he'll move on to the next hunting ground."

"What's he doing here?"

"I don't know, but I guarantee he's after bigger game than petrol thieves and faggots. That makes him rather eager. And there's nothing more dangerous than an eager Gestapo agent."

"But why would you be worried, you haven't done anything, have you?" she asked.

"No, of course not." It came out a bit too quickly. "But suppose I get into a conversation with another officer and he says something imprudent about the war. And suppose Hoekman overhears? I'd be guilty of nothing, but it wouldn't matter. The Eastern Front always needs reinforcements. He's just that type of man."

"I know it."

Alfonse tried to put his hand on her leg, but this time she refused to be baited. Instead, she looked out the window at the Paris streets rushing past. She had to get rid of him and get back to Le Coq Rouge, but how?

As they crossed the Seine on the crowded Pont au Change, Alfonse rolled down his window and flicked the half-smoked cigarette into the street. Immediately, a small boy scrambled into the road, dodging bicycles, to retrieve the cigarette. There was a brisk market in half-smoked butts and the city had no shortage of hungry, enterprising children to gather them. But one of the bike riders had also spotted the smoldering butt and hopped down off his bike. Gabriela turned her head to watch through the rear window, hoping the boy would reach it first.

The boy reached the smoldering cigarette a fraction of a second earlier, but the bicycle rider pushed him out of the way and snatched it up. A moment later he was smoking it while the child sat on his backside and watched.

Alfonse's driver cursed in German. The end of the bridge was clogged with bicycles and carts and they weren't moving. He honked his horn. Alfonse leaned forward with an impatient frown.

Behind them, the boy wandered off, while the man continued to puff on the found cigarette. At last he picked his way through the crowd to where he'd abandoned his bicycle, only to stand with a helpless expression. His bicycle had disappeared while he'd scrambled for the cigarette. She hadn't seen it either, and it was impossible to spot the thief in the sea of bicycles.

Her first thought was the bastard deserved it. The boy had won fair and square; it was a petty cruelty to shove him out of the way and steal his prize. One theft begat another. But the man looked around him, then lifted his hands to his face with a look of such bewilderment and despair that she only felt sorry for him. He'd stolen the cigarette, not out of any real malice, but simply to grab a moment of pleasure in this hard city. And now the hard city had made him pay.

"Finally," Alfonse said as the crowd responded at last to the continuous honking. He did not appear to have noticed the drama playing out to their rear.

Her resolve stiffened. She had to get back to the restaurant and if Alfonse wouldn't take her, she'd have to find her way back herself. An idea came to her.

Gabriela put a whine in her voice. "I'm still hungry."

He patted her knee. "We'll be there in a few minutes."

"Do you know a place called the Egyptienne?"

"Sure, Boulevard de Clichy, short walk from the Moulin Rouge. It's a *maison close*, isn't it? I've heard Goering is a regular when he's in Paris. But why would you want to go there?"

"Of course we would never go there," she said in a shocked tone. Again, that illusion that she'd just been a hard-working girl at Le Coq Rouge, who just happened to find German majors attractive in their own right. "But there's a good restaurant in front. I thought we could eat there."

Truth was, the *en carte* girls and the nude dancers at the Egyptienne stepped into the restaurant during breaks in the action. During her long, fruitless search for employment, Gabriela had once entered to ask about jobs and been taken for one of the working girls. She'd huffed off, offended that anyone could think such a thing. Remembering the humiliating incident made her aware that she was wearing panties, nylons, dress, shoes, perfume, and lipstick gifted by her German patron.

In appearance and behavior, she would fit right in with the *en carte* girls. Life had a way of punishing you for your hubris in the most ironic fashion possible.

"Okay, if that's what you want." Alfonse gave instructions to the driver, then sat back and ran his hand beneath her dress again. A moment later he was nibbling her ear. "On second thought, this could be fun."

How hard would it be to deflect his attention to some other pretty thing? Not particularly difficult, she suspected.

CHAPTER NINE

T HE TRAIN CAME UNDER ATTACK several hours into its trip. Boredom and fatigue had replaced Helmut's initial rush of fear at being taken into custody. The prison car had no windows and he leaned against the wall, dozing as much as possible against the rattle of the train and the discomfort of his manacles. He sank into a lethargy, only occasionally punctuated by moments of full-blown panic as he remembered what awaited him upon his arrival in Germany.

The first indication of trouble was the sound of the roof-mounted anti-aircraft gun chattering from several cars up. All at once the guards were diving to the floor. Helmut and his fellow prisoners — a mixture of *maquis*, communists, intercepted spies, captured airmen, and even a Jewish banker expelled from Vichy and taken into custody by the Gestapo — did not have this option, hampered as they were by chains and manacles. Shouts for help in German, French, Italian, English.

The train shuddered and the roof peeled open. Something splattered across his face. Shards of sunlight thrust into the car. The gunfire receded, replaced by screams. No more words. Dying, all men sounded remarkably the same.

The guard stationed near Helmut lay on the ground, writhing like a man in the grip of a seizure, his face clenched into a grimace. The heavy caliber machine guns of the strafing fighter had turned one of his arms to pulp. Moments earlier, he'd been talking to a fellow guard about an Austrian girl they both knew named Helen. Apparently Helen had red hair, a shapely bottom, and freckles on her breasts. A lively discussion about the color of hair between her legs. Copper? Full-on red? A lovely auburn shade?

This young man would never find out unless someone stopped the gush of blood from his ruined arm.

As Helmut looked for someone to help, he noticed the Jewish banker at his side seemed to be in trouble. The man was a quiet little man with a pair of thin lips and a mustache that looked, ironically, rather like Hitler's. A couple of hours earlier, he'd asked, improbably, if Helmut knew the time difference between New York and Berlin—as if he were expecting a call from Wall Street upon their arrival—then, when Helmut said he guessed eight hours, had nodded and said cryptically, "It will have to do. And I suppose I don't have much of a choice in any event."

The gunfire had liberated the man from his chains. He slumped to the floor, until it looked like he was resting his head in the injured guard's lap. And then Helmut saw how he'd freed himself from his chains; the lower half of his body remained in its seat. Helmut turned and the biscuits and milk they'd given him for lunch came up.

A dark shadow passed overhead and an engine that screamed like some hideous bird of prey. It breathed fire onto the train and several rows ahead prisoners and guards jerked and jived, and suddenly the screaming of the engine sounded like a tuneless song, and the dying men looked like dancers. When the plane passed, the screams and shrieks and curses filled the empty space. The smell of blood and hot metal. Helmut ducked down and clenched his eyes shut, sure that the next pass would be the last for him.

But then he heard a blessed sound in the distance. The familiar whine of Messerschmitt interceptors, two from the sound of it. He'd spent three weeks running supply trains to Calais early in the war and heard that sound hundreds of times as Messerschmitts raced off to battle Spitfires over southern England and the Channel.

The anti-aircraft continued its angry chatter for a few more seconds and then the sound of both the Messerchmitts and the attacking plane disappeared in the distance. The train didn't stop.

The guards collected themselves, turned to injured comrades. A medic appeared. They shot a prisoner in the head; presumably, his injuries were too great to survive. Injured men moaned, then cried out as they were moved.

A very pale, very young soldier checked Helmut's restraints. Just a boy, really. His hand trembled. It was the second of the two men who'd spoken so lovingly about Helen's freckles, breasts, and bottom. They'd carried off his friend. He met Helmut's gaze with a haunted expression. "My god, I can't take this," he said in a low voice. "I've got to get out of here."

Helmut grabbed the soldier's hand and squeezed. "It's over. You pulled through."

"I'm a coward."

"No, you're not. Look around you, men are dead and dying. You're standing and doing your job. You're one of the brave ones."

The boy swallowed hard and something like gratitude passed over his face. He gave a brisk nod and then continued down the row, checking prisoners. The train continued to clatter its way into the heart of the Reich. Apparently the engine — no doubt the real target of the strafing run — had emerged from the attack unscathed.

Helmut closed his eyes and tried to remember the day

with Marie-Élise at Chenonceau. The sunlight, the smell of the garden, the bread and cheese and wine. Marie-Élise's face, so young and vulnerable and beautiful.

⚡⚡

"Gaby!" cried a familiar voice as Gabriela waited in front of the Egyptienne.

Loud laughter and music from inside. A Frenchman in a crisp blue uniform with gold epaulettes festooned with tassels stood at the door and let people enter or turned them away, depending on some mysterious criteria. Gabriela had been afraid to approach the gatekeeper until Alfonse returned from parking the car. Maybe the doorman would look at her and say she wasn't pretty enough or ask if she was a Spaniard or a Jew.

She turned at the sound of her name. It was Christine. She was dressed glamorously, with a shimmering skirt, a glossy blouse, white gloves, and a long cigarette holder in her hands, but no cigarette. Christine greeted her with a kiss to each cheek.

"I thought you were supposed to be at the restaurant," Christine said.

"Planning to go later, what about you?"

"Not until curfew," Christine said. "Until then, I'm trying to get in here."

"And you can't just walk in? You're plenty pretty enough."

"A few weeks ago there was an…incident. I can't get in without a man, so I've been waiting to see if there's anyone I know."

"Oh." She started to ask what kind of incident, but just then Alfonse came back from the car. No sign of the driver; she didn't suppose the Egyptienne was the sort of place that welcomed corporals.

Christine gave Gabriela a significant look before turning her charms to the major. "Alfonse, my love, how are you?"

He gave her a charming smile. "Leblanc must be frantic

with his two prettiest girls out. I'll bet the clients take one look inside and decide to go somewhere else."

Another German officer passed, accompanied by two elegantly dressed Frenchmen. They smiled at the girls, who returned the look coquettishly.

"You might be right," Gabriela said. "Look at all the men who are following us here. Handsome men, too."

Alfonse gave what sounded like a good-natured grunt of faux jealousy. "Hmm, maybe we're safer inside, where the two of you have some competition."

"Let's go then," Gabriela said. "It's cold out here. Oh, I asked Christine to dine with us. I hope that's okay."

"Bringing two pretty girls to the Egyptienne?" He grinned. "Isn't that like bringing sand to the beach?"

⚡⚡

Gabriela had claimed she wanted to go to the restaurant to eat, but she put on a pouty, capricious act once they got inside. It was empty, that was boring. And she wasn't hungry anymore anyway. "Let's go to the lounge instead."

"Are you sure? I thought you said — "

Gabriela tugged on his arm. "Oh, come on. It'll be fun."

She caught Christine watching with a thoughtful expression, but her friend said nothing.

They continued through the restaurant and into the lounge at the rear of the gentleman's club. There were twenty men or more smoking water pipes, drinking, eating on the floor, propped against pillows on luxurious carpets like they were in some Turkish harem. Others played billiards, cards, or darts at the back, or sang bawdy songs around the piano.

For every man in the club there were two or three women. Young, attractive and, to Gabriela's shock, each and every one of them was topless. They drank and sang and sat on laps, giggling. One girl went hand-in-hand with a German into a back room.

Alfonse's face lit up and he turned to look at each and every pair of jiggling breasts. "Did I ever tell you how much I love Paris?"

"Hmm, South Sea Islands night," Christine said. She shrugged and started to unbutton her blouse. "We don't want to stand out."

"I don't see anything that looks like the Pacific Islands," Gabriela said. "Shouldn't we wear coconuts or something?"

"Oh, come on, Gaby," Alfonse said as he watched Christine undress. "Don't be such a prude. You're among the natives, you need to act like one. Come on, I'll help."

She slapped away his outstretched hand and forced a light smile to her face. "So now you want to undress me in public? Oh, you naughty man."

Christine had by now removed her blouse and unhooked her brassiere, liberating her breasts. They were small and very firm and she fluffed them a bit. Tweaked her nipples to make them stand up. Alfonse watched with a delighted expression.

There seemed to be no choice and so Gabriela reluctantly unbuttoned her blouse and took off her own brassiere. A topless waitress came by with drinks and took their discarded clothing without prompting. Gabriela resisted the urge to cross her arms over her chest.

"Very nice," Christine said with an admiring glance. "You're such a beautiful girl, makes me jealous. Don't you think she's beautiful, Alfonse?"

He stared. "Oh, you're both ravishing."

When Gabriela couldn't stand the self-conscious feeling any longer, she said, "Let's get something to eat. I'm starving."

"And I'm dying of thirst," Alfonse said.

"I believe we can satisfy all appetites tonight," Christine said. Other girls passed them by, sizing them up. She saw one girl in particular eye Christine with a frown and Gabriela found herself wondering about the "incident."

They took a seat among the stuffed pillows and the food appeared within moments. Scallops in garlic and butter, olives, beef tips in wine sauce, sauteed champignons, shrimp, apricot pork loin; the food was so rich and in such quantities that Gabriela forgot for a moment the rations, the queues, the time she'd found the torn-out pages of a cookbook on a bench in the Luxembourg Gardens and spent the next two hours pouring over the recipes with the same naughty pleasure as if she'd just found a smutty novel.

Christine leaned over from her pillows at one point. "Don't eat too much," she whispered. "No blouse, we don't want to show the bulgy tummy look. It's not very erotic."

Alfonse nibbled now and then while the girls ate, but he took everything offered to drink. His bonhomie increased after two or three. He greeted and toasted every man who passed, got distracted by a cute girl at least a head shorter than Gabriela, then waved her off with a laugh when she whispered something in his ear. "No, no, I've got company already, see."

A trio of Germans stopped by who seemed to know Alfonse and they engaged in what sounded like good-natured banter. A topless girl hung onto one man's arm, ran her fingers through his hair while he talked. She nibbled at his ear. There were love-bites on his neck.

Alfonse laughed and waved his hand. "*Nein, nein. Ich bin beschäftigt.*"

"No, you're not busy," Christine told Alfonse. "Go on, enjoy yourself. We're not going anywhere."

"In that case, I'll be back in a few. Just have to show these boasters how to play a good hand of *Schafkopf.*"

"Where did you learn German, anyway?" Gabriela asked after Alfonse left with his friends.

"Two years of horizontal German lessons." Christine lifted her wine glass in a mock toast gesture. "Here's to another ten. By then, my boobs will be too saggy to do this anymore."

"Horizontal collaboration, more like." Gabriela looked around at the decadence of the Egyptienne. It seemed almost frantic in its defiance of the reality outside these doors. Hungry Frenchmen, Germans getting shipped off to the Eastern Front or bombed in their barracks by the Allies. "It's going to get ugly if the Americans show up."

"Nah, the *boches* aren't going anywhere. I mean, the Reich's not going to last a thousand years, nobody believes that bullshit. But they'll be here long after we're toothless old hags begging centimes in front of Notre Dame."

"Let's hope not."

"Oh, the Germans aren't so bad. Big and dumb and gauche, but do you remember what it was like when the English were in town? No, probably not. The Germans are better behaved. And if the Americans ever came, it would be like ten thousand zazous in uniform. And this place? The only mistake I made was getting thrown out." A wry laugh. "They heard about me at the One-Two-Two and the Sphinx, too. Nobody works harder than a whore looking for revenge. Five whores looking for revenge? I'll take a Gestapo interrogation before I face that again."

"What happened?"

"Oh, it was all my fault. A misunderstanding about a wealthy German officer, but I should have known better. He was spoken for."

A roar of laughter from the Germans near the piano interrupted Christine. One man, a brandy snifter in one hand and cigar in the other, stood on a chair and shouted something that brought cheers from the other Germans and tinkling laughter from the girls, most of whom seemed to be laughing along without understanding.

When the hubbub died down, Christine's mind had apparently turned elsewhere. "How is Alfonse? He can be generous, no?"

"Yes, generous." And brutal, in turns.

"You wanted me for something," Christine said. "Did he ask you to arrange a *menage a trois*? I can be convinced."

A week earlier, that suggestion might have shocked Gabriela, but now she merely shook her head. "I need your help getting rid of Alfonse when he comes back."

"Get rid of him? Whatever for?"

"I need to go back to Le Coq Rouge. We pulled up and he saw Colonel Hoekman's car. Soon as he knew the Gestapo was back he wanted nothing to do with the place."

"Don't blame him. What I can't figure out is why you don't feel the same way."

She considered how much to tell Christine, had been on the verge of confiding moments earlier, until the off-putting bit about the Germans. "I'm trying to help the *patron* find his son."

"You mean Leblanc's note. I'd love to find him, too, but it's been three days. Roger's probably in a camp by now, or 'volunteered' to work the coal mines. God help him if he really is a homosexual."

"Can you help me?"

"Come on, Gaby, I don't want to get mixed up in this. I'm here to go back with someone to the baths. It's been so damn slow at the restaurant, I need to pay my rent. Look at that man over there, he keeps watching us."

"The fat, drunk slob?"

"The rich, drunk slob," Christine said. "And if I get him into the baths, lather him up, I won't even need him inside me." She held out her hands with their long fingers and their carefully groomed nails. "I've got everything I need right here."

"He's old, bet he's old enough to be someone's grandfather."

"Old enough to be rich, you mean."

"How about this?" Gabriela said. "I have a little money in the car Alfonse gave me to buy a fur wrap."

"And what'll you tell him when he asks to see your new wrap?"

"If he bothers to remember, you mean. I'll tell him I lost money buying some silly thing or other. You know, like girls do."

Christine seemed to consider for a moment. "No, I can't take your money. That's what the *boches* are for."

"I need your help."

"Help getting yourself killed? I don't think so. God, you're obsessed with that Gestapo bastard. Can't for the life of me figure out why."

"I'm not obsessed."

"Just stay away from Hoekman. Why won't you trust me on that?"

"Everyone takes a risk," Gabriela countered. "They threw you out of the Egyptienne, but here you are, you came back."

"That's different. Worst thing happens, they throw me out a second time and my name gets dragged through the mud again. In case you haven't noticed, my name wasn't that clean to begin with. You mess up with Hoekman, how does that turn out? Not too damn well, does it." She waved to the waiter for another glass of champagne.

"Fine, I'll do it myself."

"Oh, god." A big sigh, then finally, a nod. "*D'accord.* You want Alfonse to go back with another girl? I know just the girl. And she owes me a favor, too." She stood up, scanned the room. "I saw her here just a minute ago. Ah, there she is."

"How long do you need?" Gabriela asked.

"Five minutes. Get your clothes, find the corporal and have him bring Alfonse's car around. I'll meet you out front." She disappeared and Gabriela went to retrieve her clothes.

Outside there was no sign of Alfonse's driver, but the doorman knew just where to find him. He sent a boy off running and a few minutes later, the driver came around with the car. His clothes looked rumpled and one of his shirt buttons was still unfastened. Looks like she'd interrupted his own little party, wherever the enlisted drivers went to relax when they weren't driving spoiled majors and their mistresses back and forth across Paris.

She climbed in, said, "Sorry. I didn't mean to spoil your evening. If you want, maybe — "

"*Je ne comprends pas*," he interrupted in heavily accented French.

True to her word, Christine swooped down the stairs to the car a few minutes later, once again fully dressed. She got in the car and gave instructions in German to the driver, who sped off.

"You'll have to make up a convincing story," Christine said, "but I think you're good until morning. The private party I arranged will keep him occupied. What's your plan?"

"I need to get the colonel to take me home."

"Oh, Gaby."

"Think I can do it?"

"A few nights ago I thought you were crazy for trying to seduce that *boche*, but you know, I think he was warming up. Too bad Roger had to steal the petrol and mess everything up."

"So you think I can do it?"

"You're so damn pretty and confident, too. Just keep doing what you were doing and *ouais*, I think so. But why the hell would you want to?"

Gabriela leaned back in the seat. "I have my reasons."

CHAPTER TEN

HELMUT'S TRAIN STOPPED AT THE vast Anhalter rail station. Papers changed hands; the prisoners shuffled off in different directions. Two hard-faced men in a difficult-to-identify uniform took custody of him.

The station was chaos. Troops coming and going, supplies, civilians, work crews repairing bomb damage. Half a dozen beams of trickling snowflakes penetrated the station through holes in the glass skin thirty meters up. The main atrium was too cold to melt the snow and they formed white patches on the tile.

Even as prisoners poured out of the train from France, soldiers herded a different group of men onto a Poland-bound train parked on the opposite platform. They shuffled along, putting up no resistance, and Helmut couldn't see if they were Jews, communists, homosexuals, or merely enemies of the Reich.

"May I ask where you are taking me?" he asked the two men as they led him from the station in handcuffs.

"Just move along." They loaded him into a car.

The scene in Berlin reminded Helmut of the heady days after the Anschluss, when joint German and Austrian parades clogged the streets of the city and hundreds of thousands of people joined in celebration.

Tens of thousands of troops paraded beneath the Brandenburg Gate and along Unter den Linden. Hulking, intimidating Tiger tanks rumbled through the streets, flanked by smaller Panzers and mechanized infantry in trucks. The air lay heavy with fumes.

But even from his vantage in the military car—twice blocked and rerouted by the parade—Helmut noted important differences from those earlier spectacles. The crowds were thinner, the cheers defiant or anxious instead of jubilant. Half the marching soldiers looked like either fathers or boys, barely able to shave. Not the stiff-marching, cocky troops of a few years earlier.

What would an observer of a similar scene in Moscow have seen? Were the Russians also pushed to the brink? Or were there endless supplies of fresh Mongolians, Turks, Cossacks, and other yellow-teethed, beady-eyed types from the vast hinterland of the Soviet Empire? Feasting on promises of rape and pillage in the German countryside?

These thoughts fed his despair.

The car took him to a nondescript concrete building on Bendlerstrasse, not far from Wehrmacht headquarters. They led him into a room with two chairs and a table and a single overhead light bulb. They handcuffed him to the table, then bolted the door behind him. It was cold in the room and he shivered in a cold sweat. A sharp chemical odor hung in the air, like the kind used to clean up after blood and shit and vomit. His fear grew with every passing minute until he thought he would faint. At last the door opened and he whipped his head around to see the face of his torturer.

But it was a familiar figure who stepped through the door. He felt a flood of relief.

"Gemeiner?" Helmut said. His relief turned to cold anger. "What the hell are you playing at?"

"Very sorry about that," Gemeiner said. "Here, let me get you out of those cuffs."

He was dressed in civilian clothes with no visible weapon. After uncuffing Helmut, he took a seat opposite and set a thick envelope on the table between them.

"Please forgive the theater."

"Theater?" Helmut demanded. "Is that what you call it? Do you have any idea what your little show cost?"

"Ah, yes, the attack on the train. You realize the train would have been attacked or not, regardless of whether you were on it. Of course, I was relieved to hear you were uninjured."

"I'm not talking about that. I've got a hundred and fifty men in France left unattended. No doubt word has spread of my arrest. If they think my business is defunct, the STO will round up some of them. The rest might be drafted into Todt work crews. The lucky ones. There are Jews, Poles, refugees. Do you have any idea how hard I worked to put together that team and hold it?"

"Noted," Gemeiner said. "I'll put in a call as soon as we're done."

"But why? Why not just send a courier? Or better yet, pick up the phone?"

"You came to the attention of an overzealous SS agent. He called for advice."

The young captain at the border crossing near the Molynaux farm.

Gemeiner continued, "It was only with the greatest of fortune that he called our man instead of going higher up to Berlin or calling someone who would have alerted Colonel Hoekman. But you see, we couldn't do nothing. Instead, we had to pretend to take you into custody and continue the fiction all the way to Berlin."

"Ah, I see." His anger began to fade. "So what now?"

"Now we create a false file and send you on your way. You were investigated, found clean, and we'll be sure to keep an eye on you just in case. In the meanwhile, take a few days, visit your wife, look after your affairs in the Reich."

"And Hoekman knows nothing?" Helmut asked.

"No, not yet. But he's getting close. How close, we don't know, but if he keeps sniffing around, it's only a matter of time. He's smart as Satan, we can't fool him forever." Gemeiner folded his hands in front of him. They showed liver spots and extruding veins, but the old soldier's hands still looked strong and firm. "It might be necessary to sacrifice your friend."

"Major Ostermann? No, I don't think so."

"He is engaged in a number of petty illegalities. It wouldn't be hard for you to forge a few invoices, make it look like he's requisitioning more than he reports. Let them think they've found their culprit and they'll move on to something else."

It was a repellant thought, especially in light of what Helmut had been facing just moments earlier. Things would go very badly for his friend if he fell into the hands of the Gestapo.

"Apart from the obvious treachery of turning over an innocent to our enemies," Helmut said, "there's a flaw in your plan. Alfonse is a talker. He talks too much after a glass of wine. What's he going to say when they rip out his fingernails?"

"Nothing much, there's a reason we didn't bring him into the conspiracy. He knows nothing, he can tell them nothing."

"But he'll say he does, if only to get them to leave him alone," Helmut said. "And then they'll have reason to dig into my organization and they'll still find us out."

Gemeiner looked thoughtful. "You might be right. Any suggestions?"

"We could have Hoekman killed. Make it look like the *maquis*."

"No, that's impossible," Gemeiner said.

"Not at all, it'd be quite easy. I can probably arrange it myself. There's a Jew who works for me, his brother's family was recently —"

"I'm not saying he couldn't physically be killed. But when you kill someone like Hoekman you double the resources searching for you until pretty soon you've got someone you can't kill. No, I can't risk it, not until we're sure Hoekman is looking into us and nobody else."

"Problem is, we need a man on the inside, someone to get close to Hoekman, and we haven't got one."

"Not yet," Gemeiner said with a smile that looked vaguely predatory. He unwrapped the cord on the envelope in front of him and removed some papers. "Tell me, what do you know about Gabriela Reyes?"

Helmut frowned. "The prostitute from Le Coq Rouge? Gaby? How do you know about her?"

"We have files on everyone who works in the restaurant and many of the clients as well. I've been trying to figure out who or what has drawn Hoekman's attention. It's not that young thief he collared last week. He was a nobody."

He wondered who fed Gemeiner his information. It could have been anyone from the dishwasher with the hook to one of the working girls, to one of the many Germans or French who dined every evening in Le Coq Rouge.

"I figured out she was Spanish, but other than that, I have no idea."

"Her father was a Republican in the civil war. Fled to France a couple of years before the present conflict. Educated man. A little too bookish for his own good. Raised his daughter as an atheist, didn't know how to keep his mouth shut about politics."

"Really?" He remembered how he'd dismissed Gaby as just another prostitute.

Gemeiner slid a file across the table. "The French, bless

their bureaucratic little hearts, made dossiers of half a million foreigners living in the country. They've been useful to a good number of parties, and not just the Gestapo. Go ahead, read."

The documents were in French, but not original; someone had retyped the file on a German typewriter and there were a number of spelling and diacritical errors. Gemeiner's monolingual secretary? Or was there a warehouse-sized room somewhere filled with a thousand young women with typewriters, copying anything and everything that might be of use? His French reading skills were weaker than his speaking ability and he could feel Gemeiner's impatience as he labored over the file.

For a moment he suffered a shock to discover that Gaby was only sixteen years old, but then he saw that the uppermost document was from early 1939. She would be twenty now, but still. It was a hard world that turned a girl from a good family to prostitution. The rest of the story was all too typical.

"I don't see anything surprising here," he said. "Her mother and older brother died in Barcelona. Killed by fascists. The girl and her father escaped to Paris, where the father supported himself by writing for a newspaper and giving Spanish and English lessons. The girl lived with her mother in France for several years as a child, that's why she blends in so easily." He thumbed through the last document, which included an arrest warrant. "And apparently the father was picked up as a communist sometime during the invasion and the girl is on her own."

"Read the signature of the arresting agent," Gemeiner said.

"Obersturmführer Hans Hoekman." He looked up. "Is that our Hoekman? I don't recognize the rank."

"Senior Storm Leader. Like a lieutenant, but usually Waffen-SS. I don't know, but it appears that Hoekman was in an early military unit before transitioning to the Gestapo."

"Unusual to have risen so fast," Helmut said. "He must have impressed someone with his cunning and cruelty."

"That you can say such a thing without a hint of irony is a certain indictment of what our nation has become, don't you think?"

"Quite." Helmut considered. "So Gaby's father was arrested by our own Hoekman. That's a hell of a coincidence."

"That's exactly what I was thinking."

Helmut looked at Hoekman's signature, smooth and sure, a man who was supremely confident of his own judgment. "What about the girl's father? He still alive?"

"I don't know, I haven't been able to find out. Probably not. Let's be realistic, he's a communist and it's been two and a half years. But I'm guessing the girl doesn't know he's dead, or probably dead."

"I'd noticed she'd showed up at Le Coq Rouge shortly after the colonel. I wondered for a minute if she were somehow working for him and the whole seduction attempt and then how she tried to help the young thief was an act to put Alfonse off his guard."

"It's still a possibility," Gemeiner said. "Stranger things have happened."

"I doubt it. No, she's found him, she's trying to get close enough to either figure out what happened to her father or get revenge, if she already knows"

The older man collected the papers and returned them to the envelope, tied off the string. He pulled out a cigarette, offered one to Helmut who declined. He lit, took a drag and said, "Tell me what happened when the girl tried to seduce the colonel."

"Not much at first. But Gabriela is excessively pretty and even more persistent. I think she might have gone home with Hoekman, if not for the incident with the petrol thief."

"And that. Tell me how it happened."

He explained exactly what he saw and his impressions of the event. "Could be that Roger was working for the *maquis*, but mostly, I think he chose an unfortunate target for petty theft. In any event," Helmut added. "Hoekman is still around. He left a message a couple of days ago asking if I wanted to join him at the restaurant."

"And? Did you go?"

"That would have been tonight. Arrest and transportation to Berlin has a way of interfering with one's social calendar."

"It occurs to me that Gabriela Reyes is not the only exceptionally attractive person you will find at Le Coq Rouge."

"They're all pretty," Helmut said. "Monsieur Leblanc has a good eye for talent. Although some of the girls have a hard look around the eyes, if you know what I mean."

"I'm talking about you, Helmut. You've got just the look that makes the *frauleins* swoon, or in this case, the *mademoiselles*."

Helmut couldn't help the snort. "Assuming that were true, what does that have anything to do with anything?"

"You're only what? Twenty-eight?"

"Twenty-nine. Thirty next month."

"But a young man, good-looking, and wealthy. From a prosperous family. Daddy left him the business, but he didn't stop there, he doubled it, tripled it even. A kid like that is going somewhere. And as an important businessman, unlikely to be shipped off to reinforce the Sixth Army outside Stalingrad. Don't underestimate the value of that in these hard times."

"I'm already married, if you'll remember."

"Come on, Helmut," Gemeiner said. "Have a little imagination. First of all, nobody in France cares about your family in Germany. Second, you take a girl like Gabriela, she doesn't want to be a prostitute, she wants to escape her situation. She practically begs to be seduced. I'd seduce her myself if I were about thirty years younger and twenty kilos lighter."

"And spoke either French or Spanish."

"And that," Gemeiner said with a shrug. He set down his cigarette in the ashtray, where it smoldered, then leaned forward across the table. "Point is, you can seduce her and then she'll spy on Hoekman for us. She's trying to get information from him anyway. She can help us at the same time."

"So I get the information and then what?"

"And then what?" the older man asked. "Then we know if Hoekman is investigating us or if he's solely focused on Major Ostermann."

"But what do I do with the girl once I've seduced her? Say she gives us everything we want, then what?"

"End the affair, of course," Gemeiner said. "I'd say you could keep her for awhile, but she'll be toxic at that point, so yes, figure out a way to get rid of her."

"As in letting the Gestapo discover her and haul her off to some camp, too?"

"You're a good man for the cause, Helmut, but you're too sentimental."

"Human, you mean."

"It's a cold, hard world. Our whole country is getting fucked over by these bastards. It's an ugly thing to use someone and throw them away, but for god's sake, she's a refugee turning tricks. The world has already used her up and thrown her out."

"And my wife?"

"I know about your marriage," Gemeiner said. "Is it really going to matter to Loise?"

"What's that supposed to mean?" he demanded, even though he knew exactly what it meant. It was silly to get prickly about something that was only the evident truth of the matter. But it was the building anger with this entire manipulating sequence, from the time he was arrested in France to the horrible scene on the train, to the casual dismissal of his marriage.

"Calm down, calm down. Look, sleep with the girl or don't, it's up to you. In fact, it's a useful seduction technique to stop just short of intercourse, at least at first." His voice turned harder and he leaned forward. "But this is not a request. Gabriela Reyes is pretty, smart and resourceful and she's a prostitute. She's both imminently useful and easily manipulated. Do it."

At last Helmut let out a drawn-out sigh. "Very well. And the next shipment?"

"We'll have it in a Paris warehouse by next Monday. You'll need to be creative in moving the goods. The operation is working at full tilt."

CHAPTER ELEVEN

Colonel Hoekman was more than receptive to Gabriela's advances. Seducing him was so easy, in fact, that it should have raised suspicions from the moment she and Christine stepped into the restaurant and the Gestapo officer gave her a toothy smile. He gestured at Gabriela with his hand. "*Mademoiselle*, come, come."

Christine headed for the kitchen, then gave her a significant look over Hoekman's shoulder. *Be careful!*

Gabriela calmed her nerves and took a seat at the table where Hoekman dined alone. Better to have Helmut von Cratz here. Rude as he was, he didn't scare her like this Gestapo man. She had two memories now of his casual violence, and Christine's warning was still fresh in her mind. But he looked genuinely delighted to see her. The work of the other night hadn't been wasted.

"You remember me," she gushed. "I was afraid you'd have met some other pretty young girl and I so wanted to meet you again and get a chance to know you better. You're such a handsome man, I'm sure every girl in Paris is thinking the same thing."

"Please to speak slower. You talk too fast for me."

"Oh, I'm sorry, I was just so excited to see you." She forced herself to slow down. It was the nerves. "Your French is fine, Colonel."

Hoekman's French was improved, but still halting.

"Please, Hans you will call me."

She laughed. "Hans I will call you." She put a hand on his knee.

"You are hungry, yes?"

"Oh, no, Hans, I already ate. I just came for the company."

She looked around the table. The wine was barely touched and a plate of *jambon aux haricots* daintily picked at. He'd ignored the cheese, the bread, and the large plate of escargots. Monsieur Leblanc had more trouble getting butter and garlic than the actual snails, which seemed oblivious to rationing. She supposed that edible garden pests weren't on the German requisition lists.

"You just started?" she asked with a gesture at the uneaten food.

"No, not true. I am here some time already, and I eat already, yes?"

"But you've barely eaten."

"Too much rich food is...how do you say? Unhealthy for body." He wagged his finger. "You French could learn a lesson."

Ah, so that was it. The Germans had imposed austerity on the French for their own health.

"Well then, let's just have a drink and we'll get to know each other better. I'm sure you have many, many interesting things to say. You seem like such a fascinating man."

"This is such boring place," he continued in his bad French. "We go to my house and get to know each other. You will like. I have chocolates."

"Oh, chocolates!"

"We go then, yes?"

She didn't want to, now that it came down to it. She'd expected, planned a further seduction, with the hard-edged

Gestapo man only gradually yielding to her charms. But then once she had him, he would need her, desperately. He would do anything, give her any information, if she would only sleep with him. And she would find Papá.

His acquiescence was so sudden and unexpected that she didn't have a chance to mentally prepare herself for what it would actually mean to get into a car with this man who had brutalized her father. To let him touch her. To take her, it would be worse than being raped. And she would have to pretend to like it.

"Gabriela?"

"Call me Gaby. All my friends and lovers have called me that."

"Gaby, then."

She'd waited too long to back out now. Two and a half years now, and she owed it not just to Papá, but to everything her family stood for and everything they had lost.

A sudden decision. "Yes, of course, let's go."

He gave that same toothy, shudder-inspiring grin and they stood up. Gabriela gave a glance back toward the kitchen. Monsieur Leblanc stood there with a tray in hand and she thought he would be happy to see her leave with the colonel. His pleading note that she do something; this would be her way of helping him find Roger. Or so he must be thinking.

But Leblanc shook his head, gave an urgent little gesture with his hand that she not go. But why?

No chance to think about it as Hoekman had her arm and now led her from the restaurant. He gathered their coats at the door, but declined to turn over hers. "We are not outdoors for long, the car is waiting."

Outside, the chill cut her bare skin. Hoekman's grip tightened painfully on her arm.

"Ow, what—? Hans, what are you doing?" she asked, now

growing alarmed.

"Come along. Make no noise." He took her purse. "You do not need bag."

There was such a dark menace in his voice that she almost screamed. But there were two more gray-uniformed men who fell in behind. Gabriela's knees buckled as she almost fainted with terror.

A truck pulled into the alley and then they were pushing her into the back and shutting the doors. Hoekman came in with her as the other two shut the door behind them and the truck pulled away. There was a dim light in the interior and some sort of radio equipment to one side with what looked like a big bowl with wires coming out of it attached above. She didn't know what it was, but the machines and the electric apparatus terrified her.

"*Ay, diós mio*," she said, the Spanish spilling from her mouth without thought.

"A Spanish girl." Hoekman smiled. "Yes, I knew it."

Gabriela recovered. "What is going on? I really didn't mean to come with you if — "

"You think to play me. You cannot play me, I am the player. You understand, I know what you are doing."

He dumped her purse on the floor. He picked up her knife. "And this?"

"Paris is dangerous at night for a girl."

"A weapon." He shook his head in what looked like mock disgust. "And reichsmarks. So many. Does your major friend give to you? This is illegal, surely you know."

She forced anger into her voice. "Are you just here to rob me, or are you arresting me? If so, do it and let's be done with it."

"I do not arrest you," Hoekman said. "I bring you to talk."

"What? Then I'm not interested in talking. Please, stop the truck and let me out. I have work to do at the restaurant."

He cut her off with a withering look. "You will now cooperate or your father will suffer."

She let out a gasp. "My father?"

"You think I do not remember? I remember you. I remember everything. And he talks. He tells me your name and when I meet you I remember."

"He talks? You mean he's still alive?" She was breathing very quickly now. "But where is he, what did you do with him? Please, for god's sake, I'm just a girl, I need to find my father and help him."

"Yes, you may help him." He paused, as if struggling to find the right words in French. "You may help him by helping me."

The truck stopped. It had only been a few minutes; they must still be close to the restaurant.

"I told you," she said. "I don't know anything, I'm just a girl trying to stay alive, how could I possibly help you?"

"Very easy, *mademoiselle*. You return to your lover, the major, and you...how you say?"

"What?"

"You learn certain things and you tell me."

"I spy on Alfonse you mean?"

"Yes, that is the word, you *spy*."

The thought was repellent. She had no great affection for Alfonse. She was only with him to feed herself and stay close to the restaurant where she'd hoped to meet Colonel Hoekman again. And yes, she'd responded physically to the man, but so what? He was just another *boche*, ravaging *La Belle France*, Marianne in chains, who had no choice but to spread her legs and smile.

Yet knowing that Alfonse was this man's prey made him more endearing than the money, food, warm bed and bath, the touches that her body had craved. Who cared what kind of man Alfonse was, Hoekman dragged people away and they were never seen again.

But Papá. He's alive!

"It is your choice," Hoekman said. "You help me and I help you. You do not help me and your father...suffers."

"Okay, I'll do it." The words tasted heavy and foul on her tongue. "I'll spy on him. Tell me what and how."

"Be careful, be very, very careful. I see when I am double-crossed."

"Double-crossed," she muttered. "Is that on the vocabulary list at the Gestapo language school?"

"What?"

"I won't double-cross you, but I need proof my father is alive. I need to know he is still alive and well," she repeated, more firmly this time.

"No, no. First you spy, then if no double-cross, I help with father."

Liar. She'd help him and then he'd forget all about the bargain, but it wouldn't matter because she'd be stuck. There had to be some way to stake out a small measure of autonomy. To keep from being swallowed whole and digested by this thing.

"No, first you prove he is alive, then I help. And after I help, you must promise to let my father go."

"Let him go? We don't let people go. I promise not to kill him, that is all."

There was one thing. The one weapon that every attractive woman still wielded. She put her hand on his leg. "Please, be reasonable. If you are reasonable, I can be reasonable too."

He looked down at her hand, then licked his lips with a disgusting motion that looked like a night crawler coming in and out of its hole. "Yes, yes. Reasonable. I like that."

"See how easy that is?"

He put his hand on her breast and gave a clumsy squeeze. "Come to my flat, you show me reasonable."

She slid her hand higher on his thigh. "No, first you prove to me my father is still alive, then I will be reasonable."

Hoekman stared. Again, the tongue. He was breathing heavily now. Slowly, gently, Gabriela removed her hand from his leg, then pulled his hand off her breast.

"You can be reasonable, too, Hans. I know you can."

He could force her. Gabriela had no illusions about that. Men could always force what they couldn't earn. But most men—even someone like Colonel Hoekman—wanted to *believe* it was earned. She could see it going through his mind right now.

At last he nodded. "Yes, okay. We shall both be reasonable. I find you proof your father is still alive. You find me one piece of information in return. Yes?"

"What kind of information?" she asked, suspicious.

"There is man I look for. I don't know his name, but they call him...how do you say? The lowest rank of enlisted man."

"*Simple soldat?*"

"Yes, that. A common soldier."

"You are looking for a private? Is he a deserter?"

"Of course he is not a true private," Hoekman said with some irritation. "That is what they call him. I search for his true identity. You find if Major Ostermann knows this man, I help with your father. It is small thing. A reasonable thing."

She nodded. "Yes, okay."

Hoekman smiled. He leaned forward and rapped twice on the metal that divided them from the cab. The truck shifted into gear and pulled away.

"Where are we going?" she asked.

"To Ostermann's flat. You must not go again to restaurant, not tonight because we leave together. I take you to his flat."

Gabriela let out her breath. "Can I have my money back?"

"No, the money stays with me. The knife, too. These

are illegal."

Illegal and also leverage. It was a fair amount of money Alfonse had given her; she couldn't ask for more anytime soon.

But Gabriela was alive and soon to be released, that was all that mattered.

𝔰𝔰

Alfonse staggered in shortly after dawn. He was still drunk, but wore the bleary look of a man with a fading buzz and a budding headache. Gabriela lifted herself on one elbow to look at him.

He sat heavily on the edge of the bed, peeled off his shoes and chucked them in the general direction of the closet, then tossed his jacket at the chair. It missed. He sank back onto the bed with a groan.

"God, that was a night. And I've got to meet with General Shoenkopf at ten. That's what, three hours from now? He's going to scream at me about that ball-bearing shipment. Goddamn factory was bombed to hell by the Americans last week so of course the shipment is *kaput*. He's going to take one look at me and wonder why I was out drinking all night instead of finding his precious ball bearings. The Luftwaffe will fall from the sky for lack of ball bearings and it's all going to be my fault. What was I thinking? You should have stopped me. Or Christine. Or common sense. Someone or something."

"There was no stopping you."

He chuckled. "No, there wasn't, was there?" And then, when she didn't answer, he rolled over to look at her. "You're not angry, are you?"

"Why would I be angry?" Truth was, she'd been caught up in memories of the ugly meeting with Colonel Hoekman and barely listening.

"Oh, you know. I left you at the lounge and when I came back you were gone. I knew you didn't leave with someone else, you'd never do that, so I figured you'd sulked home on your own. Is that what happened?"

"No, really I'm okay. Did you have a good time, what happened?"

He raised an eyebrow. "You want to know?"

"Sure."

"You say you want to know, but I don't think you really do. You'll get jealous and then there will be a scene and my head is starting to hurt already."

"How about if I express just enough jealousy to let you know I care."

"And how much is that?" he asked.

"I'll aim for an appropriate spot somewhere between dozing off to sleep and chasing you out of the flat with a hail of broken plates."

He laughed. "Okay, so there was this little Spanish girl, some friend of Christine's, and she was doing this dance where she took slices of an apple and put them in her—wait, are you sure?"

"Oh come on, I'm not easily shocked. Go on."

"So anyway she took these apple slices out of her...you know...and then she picked out the men and forced them to eat the pieces. If they resisted, she took her legs and—well, it was funny."

"And how did the apples taste after they'd been moistened up a little?"

He actually blushed at this. "You know, it's not usually my style, but I'd had a little too much to drink."

"So is this the girl you took into the back room?"

"Oh, come on, I wouldn't...well, sure. I didn't mean to, but she was insistent. You know how these peasant girls are. Horny as hell, every one of them. I think a girl grows up in a small town in Spain there's no cinema, no art, no culture of any kind. She gets really good at screwing."

"What do you mean, no culture of any kind? You make it sound like Spain is the Belgian Congo or something."

"It's the Congo of Europe," Alfonse said.

She found herself bristling. "No, it's not. There's all kinds of history, architecture, music. It's a great country. They had a huge empire. Spaniards discovered the Americas."

"No they didn't. Columbus was Italian."

"Funded by the Spanish queen."

"Oh, what do you know about it?" he said. "Look, I've been to Spain, you haven't. Donkeys and bicycles. Dogs pooping in the street. Really bad food."

"Bad food? What about paella?"

"Paella? What's that?"

"What's paella? Are you serious? And you're lecturing me about Spain? Oh, never mind."

"Fifty years from now, when Germans and Americans are living on the moon—probably killing each other up there—you'll see, the Spaniards will still be riding donkeys and bicycles. I can't believe it, you're getting mad. It's the girl, right? You *are* jealous that I went back with another girl."

"I'm not jealous."

"Women are all the same, I should have known. Oh, my head."

"You should sleep a little," she said, "so you'll be ready for the unpleasant discussion about ball bearings."

"No way, falling asleep will make it worse. I'll wake up, I'll be groggy with bags under my eyes. No, I'm just going to lie down for a few minutes, then get cleaned up and get some coffee. Lots and lots of black coffee."

Gabriela reached for the water carafe and poured a glass. "You'll feel better if you drink some water."

"What? No, not right now." He yawned. "Say something so

I don't fall asleep."

"So, you buy ball bearings and ship them to Germany? Is that your job in the army?"

"Why would you want to know about that?"

"You told me to say something, so I said the first thing I thought of."

"It's really complicated. I'm not sure you'd understand."

"Probably not," she said, deciding that there were upsides to having him continue to underestimate her intelligence. "But you need to talk, remember, so you don't fall asleep."

"Okay, yes, it's something like that. Everything is wrapped in with the war effort. You've got guys like Helmut working as private businesses, but military orders take top priority at any and all times. You know, it's kind of like how there's not always flour and cooking oil on the shelves because our soldiers need the food so they can keep the Russians from penetrating the Reich."

Sure, because "our" soldiers needed French flour and cooking oil more than hungry French children. It reminded her of the Demarais, hungry in their freezing apartment in the 14th Arrondissement.

"But I thought it was the Germans who invaded Russia, not the other way around," she asked in an innocent voice.

"Purely a preventative war. I mean, you can argue about details of this thing or that. Maybe we shouldn't have gone into Poland in the first place, and I always thought we should have come to an understanding with the British early on. They're a reasonable race, they didn't want a wide-scale war anymore than we did. And you know, as soon as the Brits started fighting, it was only a matter of time until Roosevelt forced the Americans into the war."

"I thought that had something to do with Japan."

"Well, the Japanese are another problem. But my point is,

there's nothing you could do about the Russians. They want to turn every country in Europe into little Soviet republics. Overrun the world with Slavs. Sooner or later the civilized races had to confront them."

"So it's purely a defensive war, then?"

"If you take a wide enough view, yes."

"If there's one thing you Germans are good at, it's taking a wide view. In your narrow sort of way, that is."

"Let's not talk politics," he said. "It's an exceptionally boring subject, especially if I have to explain the background of everything for you to even understand what I'm talking about. Isn't there something else you want to talk about?"

"Well, I'm still wondering about your job," Gabriela said. "Sounds like you and Helmut do pretty much the same thing, just that you're military and he's a businessman. Is there a lot of money in it?"

"More money than you can imagine. Not that a major like me would see any of it. It's just my job, I don't make a profit."

"You look like you're doing pretty well."

"I have access to a few nice things. That's different." He must have misunderstood her question, because he added quickly. "I'm not poor or anything, you understand."

"Of course not."

Ball bearings, money, big trainloads of goods. The major's lavish lifestyle. Possible motives for Gestapo interest in Alfonse's affairs came into focus.

And Helmut von Cratz, who seemed positioned between Alfonse and Colonel Hoekman. Which side was he working for?

She decided to push for that last bit of critical information. "One more thing, I was wondering about. I never see any of these other men you work with. You're a major? Is that important?"

"Of course. There are higher ranks, sure, but I have my hands in everything. Many men answer to me."

"Officers *and* enlisted men?"

"Yes, of course."

"Do you ever have much contact with any of the simple soldiers?" Gabriela said it casually, *simples soldats,* in a way that might mean any lower rank. She watched his reaction.

"As little as possible," he answered with a smile. "The privates, corporals and the like are good for a strong back and a weak mind. They respond best to shouts and threats." If she'd aroused any suspicion, he didn't show it. Alfonse's face betrayed nothing except his usual boastful attitude, mingled with exhaustion from the previous evening's debauchery.

She'd asked. Now what was she supposed to do?

CHAPTER TWELVE

HELMUT WASN'T USED TO THE naked vulnerability in his wife's face. He'd phoned Loise as soon as Gemeiner let him go, then stayed in a hotel last night so as to allow her a chance to adjust to the idea. It hadn't been enough.

"Please, come in," she said stiffly as he stepped into the big foyer, as if inviting in a guest instead of the owner of the house. "I'd take your jacket, but you'll want to keep it on, I'm afraid."

He stepped inside and understood what she meant. His breath came out in puffs. Loise wore a sweater and heavy wool trousers.

"How are you, my dear?" he asked.

"As good as can be expected."

Helmut looked around the front hallway, noted a pair of children's boots, a brightly colored umbrella, and a box with some building blocks. "You have guests?"

She followed his gaze. "Ah, that would be Della and Jarvis. Their parents work in Leipzig and they've been evacuated."

"Are the British and the Americans bombing that far inland?" he asked, surprised.

"I don't know, I don't think so. Not yet."

"It's only a matter of time."

"Yes."

"And the children are difficult, or no?"

"No more difficult than any other child. But I don't always miss them when they go off to school."

If the moment hadn't already been awkward enough, the mention of children made it doubly so. They stood and looked at each other for a long moment before she cleared her throat. "Well, they're at school now, we have the house to ourselves. Come in, please."

She led him further into the house. Her gait shuffled and he caught a grimace of pain. It was dark in the house; most of the windows had blankets nailed over the frame to cut down on drafts. Loise led him into the salon and shut the door behind them. She made to shovel coal into the fireplace. "Let's warm things up and then I'll make some coffee."

"Let me do that, you get the coffee." He took the shovel and their hands met. Hers felt like ice. "You've had trouble getting coal?"

"No, you've sent plenty. But it doesn't look good to have smoke pouring out of the chimney when we've seen coal rations cut three times since October. I gave some of it away. Discretely, of course, don't worry."

"And the oranges?" He smiled. "Please tell me you didn't give those to the neighbors."

"Oh, god, were they good. I shared them with the children, and Della actually started crying. I ate more than my share, I confess. I took a little sugar and used the peel to make cookies. Here, I still have two left, let me get them. We can have them with the coffee."

The cookies were good, the coffee weak, and the conversation stilted. Loise was a beautiful woman, blonde and with blue eyes; Helmut had been prodded many times about all the beautiful little Aryans they were sure to produce. Alas, this particular bloodline of the Master Race had apparently run its course.

When the conversation sputtered and died, Helmut picked up the newspaper Loise had left on the coffee table. It was full of the usual propaganda, wishful thinking, and outright lies. So many British bombers shot down, this many American ships torpedoed. The usual stories of Soviet atrocities, which may have been true enough, except for the part about the valiant efforts of Germans to spread peace and prosperity throughout Eastern Europe.

"I can't read this rubbish," he said at last and tossed down the paper.

"Have you been following the news from the Eastern Front?" Loise asked.

"This doesn't exactly qualify as news."

"Some of it is true."

"Not enough," he said.

"Maybe not, but you can learn a lot even from what they don't say." She picked up the paper and flipped to the third page. "The Fuhrer is talking about the great sacrifice of the Sixth Army and how they'll be known as heroes."

"Sacrifice?"

"Exactly. Nothing about victory or pushing the Soviets into the Volga River like what they were going on about last fall."

Helmut nodded. It was an exceptionally grim sign.

"You know what I think?" Loise said. "I think they've given up the Sixth Army for lost. The Bolsheviks have them surrounded, that much is clear. There's some nonsense about holding out until spring and a massive new push. An air bridge, reinforcements, a counter-attack, all that sort of nonsense. But then you see that some of the generals have been airlifted out of the army. Why would you do that?"

"Because you think the cause is lost."

"And what then? Is the war turning against us, Helmut? You see these things, you have to know."

"We've lost the momentum," he admitted. "And there are so many of them. But it all depends on whether or not the Soviets can sustain an offensive."

"Do you know Frau Schneider?" she asked.

"The lady with all the dogs?"

"Not so many dogs anymore, but yes," Loise said. "She has a Ukrainian servant girl. The girl's brothers are volunteers with the Wehrmacht and she volunteered to come work in Germany."

"The Reich is full of foreign volunteers these days."

"So this girl said that when the Bolsheviks recaptured her village, they committed outrages against every woman and girl in town. The soldiers were Mongolians and Cossacks. And Russians, too, of course."

"Our troops have not always behaved in an upright manner, either," Helmut pointed out.

"You wouldn't catch Germans behaving like animals," she protested, to which he said nothing. "And this was a Ukrainian village! The Bolsheviks were liberating it and they still committed outrages. There was a baby. Six months old. They took her and—no, I can't even say it. The stories were horrible, awful."

"You can't think about that. It's far away and you can't help by worrying about it."

"We simply must win this war."

"You can't worry about that."

"And if we don't? If we lose?"

"If we lose, it won't be to the Soviets. Don't forget about the Americans."

Loise got up to check the fire, returned to her seat. "I don't know, I just don't know what to believe anymore. They don't tell us anything, they're trying to protect us, I know, but I just want to know the truth. How can I prepare myself if I don't?"

Helmut made a sudden decision. "I have business in Switzerland in two weeks. Would you like to come?"

"A vacation, now? What would we do in Switzerland?"

"No, not a vacation. A vacation has limited duration."

Her eyes widened. "Oh. And you would come with me?"

"Of course. At least at first, to help you get settled."

"I see. Then what's the point?"

"You'll be safe, that's the point."

"Helmut, Switzerland isn't safe either. Nowhere is safe."

"There are safer places than here."

"No, I can't do it, not now. Maybe..." Her voice trailed out. "Maybe if the Bolsheviks come here, then—no, that is impossible. I just can't believe it will come to that. This is all temporary. We just need to work out a truce with the Americans and British and then we can win this war. We can still win, don't you think? Don't you think so? Helmut?"

He looked down at his empty cup. After a long, awkward silence, he said, "May I please have some more coffee?"

She got up wordlessly and took the cup. It was a relief when she left the room.

♯

They made love that night. Rather, tried to.

Loise had warmed the bed with the pan and then heaped the bed with extra blankets before going down to the WC. The electricity was out, so she took the lamp. Helmut wore socks, woolen underwear, and a hat. He resisted the urge to stoke the stove and throw off some of the blankets. Instead, he climbed in and waited in the dark.

The children had seemed intimidated by his presence at the dinner table. They shyly waited until he gave them permission to eat, then only spoke in whispers when they wanted something. Normally, he might have brought a tin of cookies to break down their defenses, but given the circumstances of his arrival, he didn't have so much as a piece of chocolate to share between the two. It took almost until bedtime to break them out of their shells, when Helmut sat at the piano and played old Bavarian folk songs, while Loise joined him in singing. By "Mir Ham's Vom Sauerkraut," they were laughing and clapping.

Loise returned from the bathroom wearing a nightie. She stood by the door, shivering, with the lamp held unsteadily in one hand.

"Is something wrong?"

"You look beautiful," he said, truthfully.

"Why are you looking at me like that?"

He tried to erase whatever expression he'd been wearing. "I was surprised is all. I thought it would be too difficult."

"To make love to my husband? I'm not so sick as that, just a little uncomfortable."

And yet Loise gave a distinct grimace of pain as she sat on the edge of the bed and extinguished the lamp. She moved like an old woman as she stretched herself beneath the covers. "I'll feel better once I'm warmed up a little. Want to help?"

It was stupid to get his hopes up, but in spite of the pain, of everything, at the first touch he wanted her. It had been so long. He needed her so badly he was shuddering. She kissed him and touched him and helped him out of his clothes and everything seemed to be just perfect. But when the time came to enter her, one, two, three movements and she was stiffening in pain. He tried to stop, but she begged him to continue and he did so until at last he knew she couldn't stand it anymore and he couldn't stand knowing she couldn't, so he pulled away and rolled onto his side. The ache was almost too much to bear.

"I'm so sorry," she said.

"No, no it's okay." He just needed to regain control. It would only take a minute.

"Let me touch you, let me do it that way. I can still do it for you, you understand."

"Loise."

She put her hand between his legs. "Shh, just let me, please. Let me try."

He didn't think it would be possible, but he was a man, after all, and it had been months. Within a few minutes it was over. She had a handkerchief by the lamp, which she used to clean him up. And then she leaned her head on his chest.

"Thank you," she said.

"Thank me? I didn't do anything. But maybe I could — "

She put a hand on his lips. "Shhh. No, maybe later. I just need to relax and it will feel better."

"I didn't mean to hurt you."

"I know."

They lay in silence for several minutes, but just when he thought she was asleep, she said, "France is a long way from home. It's almost another world."

"France is a lot like here. Just people, struggling. Things are getting the same way everywhere."

"Is it hard for them?" Loise asked.

"They're enduring the war. Hungry. My employees are so thin, are always talking about food and recipes. Their children are even thinner and hungrier. It's heartbreaking."

"You should help them."

"Oh, I do, believe me, whenever I can. Last week alone I gave out two hundred loaves, three hundred kilos of flour, plus cooking oil, potatoes, beans, coffee, and even some dried apples. Some weeks I can get more, some less, but it's always something, whatever I can get. But they're still hungry. I don't know how someone would survive on official rations, it's just not possible."

"I'm glad you can help. You're a good man." She put her hand on his face and stroked it. "You've got a whole separate life there, don't you? But I'm grateful you come to visit when you can."

There was something else she was saying, but he couldn't pin it down. "You need to stop worrying about the war. We'll be okay. You'll see."

"No. I mean, yes, I worry. But you've made a different life, you have to. An apartment, contacts. You probably live your life thinking in French half the time."

"Well, sure, that's just natural. I'm speaking it so much."

"And there are women, too, in France."

"What? Loise—"

"Wait, don't say anything, let me finish."

"You don't need to finish. There's nothing like that. Nobody shares my apartment and there are no women."

"Helmut, I know that men at war have special...challenges."

"War is hell for everybody. Everybody has to sacrifice. Why should I be any different?"

"You're gone so long," Loise continued. "And when you're back, it's so very difficult, I know. Maybe if I could see that doctor in Vienna, but he left for the Crimea, they say, with the army. But after the war, maybe the surgery."

"Of course. We'll do whatever it takes, pay whatever. Until then, there's nothing we can do but try to endure the situation as best we can."

"Yes, endure," she said.

"Then put this other stuff out of your head. I'm not going to replace you, that's just worried talk, it has nothing to do with reality."

"I know you'd never do that," Loise said. "You're too good-hearted to ever walk away from your commitments, maybe even when you should. I just want you to know I'm understanding, too. Some women aren't, but I am. If there were ever an indiscretion or a moment of weakness, well, it wouldn't really matter, would it? It wouldn't change anything."

"That will never happen," Helmut said firmly.

"But if it did, that would be okay. You wouldn't even need to tell me about it."

And with that, they lapsed into silence. A few minutes later and her breath turned heavy and regular, but he couldn't sleep.

He kept thinking about that day with Marie-Élise in the chateau gardens. Her hair smelled like lavender, her skin was soft. There was a light, warm breeze, and the flowers were a bright smear of colors. The scene colored his memories like a Monet. He ached with regret.

And wasn't that its own kind of infidelity?

CHAPTER THIRTEEN

T HE MAIN FLAW WITH EMPLOYING Gabriela as a spy — apart from her hatred for the man for whom she worked — was her lack of German.

Over the next few days, she caught several glimpses of papers and overheard conversations on Alfonse's private telephones. Once, a young man in uniform came late at night and told Alfonse something that made him angry. He berated the young man for a good twenty minutes while Gabriela and the maid stayed out of the way.

It was all in German. She caught nothing. Alfonse could have been either plotting the assassination of Marshall Petain or arranging the world's largest shipment of feather dusters, for all she could decipher.

"What was that all about?" she asked after the maid retreated to her quarters and Alfonse told her to get ready for bed.

"That? Oh, that was nothing."

"Didn't sound like nothing."

"He was supposed to get me some bacon. I'm so sick of eating chicken. Apparently, there is none to be had in Paris at the moment. I don't believe it. There's plenty of bacon, you just have to keep looking."

"Oh, is that all?" She didn't know whether to believe him or not.

And for all his carelessness with his words, Alfonse was careful with his documents. He kept them in envelopes for the most part, and tucked some of them into a safe. Some days Alfonse arrived with a bulging briefcase with paperwork to pour over, which he scattered in a haphazard fashion over his desk, but he always shoveled them back into his briefcase when he finished and locked it. One morning he had a young soldier in the house and spent the day dictating while the other man typed. Soldier, paperwork, and typewriter disappeared that afternoon.

As for money, Alfonse spent liberally, but kept a close eye on his billfold. She managed to pilfer a bit of loose change, but she was afraid that he'd catch her if she went to too much effort to take some money to replace what Colonel Hoekman had stolen. She'd meant to give some of it to the Demarais, but she'd have to find some other way to help the elderly couple.

And nothing more about the *simple soldat.* He gossiped about this officer or that bureaucrat often enough to ask prying questions, but rarely gave much time to the young men who drove him, typed for him, or delivered telegrams and packages, except to complain when they were late. It was a small piece of information she needed, but she couldn't seem to pry it out of him. She dreaded going back to Hoekman with nothing.

Six days after her encounter with the colonel, Alfonse announced over breakfast, "Helmut von Cratz is back in Paris."

"I didn't know he'd left."

"Neither did I, until I got word that he was in Berlin. Something urgent, apparently."

"That doesn't sound good."

"Oh, it's always urgent with the government. Probably nothing. Helmut mentioned you."

"What did he say?" she asked warily, prepared to fend off any denunciation.

"He wants your help with something, didn't say what."
Alfonse winked. "I hope it's not a problem with a certain
shipment of German sausage."

"Well, with no bacon in the house, maybe I'll order some."

"Hah. Well, if I thought there were any risk of his seducing
you, I wouldn't let you out of the house. But there's no risk.
Poor man is devoted to his crippled up wife back in Germany.
I've told him a million times to get a mistress, so long as he
doesn't try to take mine."

"What happened to his wife?"

"He's vague on the details, but apparently some sort of
growth in the nether regions." Alfonse let out a visible shudder.

"A growth? Like cancer?"

"How would I know? Apparently it's not life-threatening,
just debilitating. Imagine catching something like that. You
know, every day I thank god I'm a man. Disgusting."

He slathered butter on his toast and took an enormous bite.
"You know what would taste good with this toast?"

"You want me to get the marmalade?"

"Bacon. A big, fatty, salty piece, right here. When you're
out with Helmut, keep an eye out, will you? I'll pay whatever."

She spotted her opportunity. "How much should I pay?
And do you want to give me a little money so I'll be prepared?"

"Don't worry about that, they probably wouldn't sell it
to you anyway. Just tell me where you saw it and I'll send a
German. Dammit, you know I drove past a farm yesterday and
the farmer had at least half a dozen pigs. He wouldn't sell me
any bacon, said it was impossible. Said the requisitioning officer
had already inventoried the meat for slaughter. 'Goddammit,'
I said. 'I *am* the requisitioning officer.'" Alfonse snorted. "You
know what I'm going to do? I'm going to tell Colonel Hoekman
to arrest the bastard."

"You can't do that. He was just afraid."

"He wasn't afraid, he was a greedy old peasant. Fatter than Goering's hound dogs. I'm serious, his belly was hanging over his belt like this. And some people claim the French don't have enough to eat." He patted her hand. "Come on, Gaby, don't get alarmed, I'm not serious. I wouldn't tell Hoekman if his pants were on fire. I'm sure as hell not going to send him after some farmer with too many pigs."

"You   promise?"

"I promise." Alfonse stood up. "Helmut will be here in an hour. You'd better go get prettied up. Not too prettied up, though."

⚡⚡

Alfonse was gone by the time Helmut arrived. The man was smartly dressed in a freshly pressed suit and polished black shoes. He removed his hat and his blonde hair was gelled, combed into perfection. With his sharp features and blue eyes, he looked the epitome of Aryan supremacy. His Nazi masters would be proud.

"You look very nice today *mademoiselle*. Thank you for agreeing to assist me."

"You're welcome, I suppose."

"Your particular talents will be indispensable."

She looked at him with irritation. "Are you setting me up for another cruel insult?"

"Not at all. I'm genuinely grateful, as you will see."

"After the other day, formality sounds like condescension to my ears."

"I was out of line. Please accept my apology."

That deflated her. "Oh, well thank you. I let my temper get the better of me."

"No, you were right to be angry. Come on, the car is ready."

It was a bright day, with the sunlight melting the frost that glistened on the metal grating outside the building. Smartly dressed women clicked by and men in uniform or suits hustled to and from private automobiles. Few animals or bicycles. Just a few blocks away, the scene would be entirely different.

Helmut drove his own car, which he'd left running. With gendarmes patrolling on foot, he apparently felt no risk leaving it temptingly at the curb. Gabriela remembered the scramble for Alfonse's discarded cigarette. It had taken the scavenger just seconds to lose his bicycle. This was a different neighborhood entirely.

"Where are we going, anyway?" she asked as Helmut pulled away from the curb.

"To my office. I have some papers I need you to look at."

"Me? Whatever for?"

"It's a translation problem."

"You don't need a translator, your French is perfect."

"Who said anything about French?" They turned off Rue Dupont. The gendarmes, in full collaboration mode, touched their hats as they drove past.

A tickle of doubt. "I don't understand. How could I possibly translate into German, I don't speak any of it."

"You've forgotten your native tongue? I find that hard to believe."

"What are you talking about?"

"We didn't get a very good start the other night, but I want to start over," Helmut said. "To do that, we need to be honest with each other."

"Paris is not the sort of place for honesty. You start being honest, the Nazis line you against the wall and shoot you."

"I'm not a Nazi."

"You look like a Nazi, you act like a Nazi. You steal for the Nazis."

"I told you before, I don't steal anything. I buy and I sell."

"You forced us to ruin our currency at the exchange rate you set," she said, "and you force us to sell at the price you agreed would give you maximum profits. That's just a clever way of stealing."

They'd crossed over the Seine to the Left Bank and instantly there was a line halfway around the block of people waiting for one thing or another. "Look, a food queue. Do you think those people would agree with my definition of theft or yours?"

He was silent at this for several long seconds. "Who told you all that?"

"I'm not blind, I can see what's in front of my eyes. Look, there's another queue, and another one right there."

"I mean, who told you about the exchange rates and the system of commerce?"

"Because I'm not bright enough to figure it out on my own? I'm just a whore, you mean?"

"You're not a whore, I know that now."

"Helmut, what do you want? A quick lay in your apartment? I work on contract, not by the hour."

"I'm not interested in that."

"Sure you're not."

"Soon as I figure out how, I'm going to prove it to you," he said.

If it wasn't sex, then what? If he was working for Colonel Hoekman, it would explain how he seemed to know she wasn't French. His French was good, but not so good he would have picked up on minor quirks in her pronunciation. Even when the rare Frenchman caught her accent, he usually guessed that she was from Langue d'Oc, where she'd spent some of her childhood, not from a foreign country.

But if Hoekman had sent him, why not just say it?

They were edging their way through the bicycle and cart traffic of the Quartier Latin now and she got a sudden idea. "Okay, if you're sincere, turn back toward the Sorbonne, then take a left on Rue St. Jaques."

"Whatever for?"

"You asked, but if you're not sincere, go ahead and forget it. Let's get your so-called work out of the way and then you can take me home."

Helmut nodded. "Fine. Tell me where to go."

He balked again when she directed him down the actual street in question. "This isn't safe. Maybe for you, but I'm German."

"Pull over right here."

"Gaby..."

There were people in the streets, ragged, lean-faced people, and many of them stopped whatever they were doing and stared at the car. But it was daylight. In any event, she was enjoying his discomfort. Let him see what it was like.

"You've got a pistol, don't you? Take it out if you don't feel safe. I'll only be a few minutes."

"Okay, but hurry."

"One other thing. I need some money."

"Money? Whatever for? You're not doing anything illegal, are you?"

"I just need some money. I've got to help some poor people, that's all."

"I don't have any money."

"You have some money," she said. "Let's have it."

"Some pocket change, that's all. A couple of coins."

"I can't believe it. Well, hand it over."

"Why?" he asked, his tone belligerent.

"There's an old couple up there living on dry crusts and rotten potatoes. Even a few coins would help."

"Who are these people? How do you know them?"

"It's where I used to live. Yes, here, in this rat hole. You don't think I'm screwing your friend because I'm bored with my daddy's mansion in the 7th, do you?"

He looked up to the decrepit, soot-stained building with a frown.

"They're my former landlords," she continued, "and it was a blow when I moved out. My pitiful rent was all they had."

Helmut fished a few coins from his pocket. "This is really all I have, but hold on one second." He got out of the car, lifted the trunk a few inches, then slipped something out and underneath his coat. He gave her a bag. There were two baguettes and a big wedge of cheese, quite hard from the cold. "Give them this. Tell them to let the Beaufort soften at room temperature before eating. Never mind, they're French, they'll know that already."

"Thank you," she said with genuine warmth. "But they'll have to sell this cheese. It's too valuable to eat."

"Then tell them to get a good price. I paid...well, never mind. Just get a good price."

She tucked the prizes under her coat, left Helmut in the car. The same hungry eyes followed her. She kept her distance. The smell of freshly baked baguettes might be enough to start a riot.

⚡⚡

Madame Demarais fumbled with the latch for several moments before she finally got it open. She eyed Gabriela with a look of desperate hope. "You've come back? Henri! Gaby has come back, we have a renter. Henri!"

Gabriela stepped into the flat. It was colder inside than it had been in the street, if that were possible. Or maybe it was just being out of the sun that did it, into the gloom of the flat.

It looked dirtier than she remembered: the paint more faded and peeling, the floors more worn, the few pieces of furniture more shabby. It was quiet, too, and it took a moment to realize why; there was a dusty spot in the corner where the radio had sat for the last two years.

"You sold the radio?"

"We can't eat the BBC," Madame Demarais said. "You

wouldn't believe what that nasty man at the *marché aux puces* offered. Theft, I tell you." She leaned against the wall and her hand trembled. "Sorry, I feel a little faint."

"Sit down." Gabriela took the woman's arm to help her to the chair. Her skin hung off her bones and there was a sharp, bony look to her face that hadn't been there a few weeks earlier.

"We kept your room in the back. I knew you'd come back."

"I'm sorry, but this is just a visit. I'm living with my aunt, remember?"

"But, we...oh."

The old woman sagged into the chair with such a defeated expression that Gabriela couldn't stand it. She fished out one of the loaves. "But I brought you something."

"Bread? White bread? And cheese? *Mon dieu*." She blinked. "But how did you get that?"

"My uncle, he works for the ministry."

"What ministry?"

"You know, the ministry of ah, food and rations."

"The Ministry of Food and Rations? I've never heard of such a thing. Never mind, it doesn't matter. Would you terribly mind breaking me off a piece of bread? Henri!" she called again.

There was an answering cough, deep and wet, from their bedroom.

"That damned fool," she said. "Spent three hours in a food line, outside, in the rain. There was some kind of riot, he fell in the water, came back chilled to the bone. You know what he got? Two tins of potted meat product. Potted meat product, is that even food? Henri, I'm warning you, I'm going to eat this all myself."

Madame Demarais took the piece of bread, closed her eyes with a rapturous look as she put it in her mouth. "Oh, this is... oh, you couldn't understand. You don't know. Henri! For god's sake, come out here."

The man said something in a feeble voice. Another wet cough. Gabriela was growing alarmed. "Is he all right?"

"Oh, he's fine. Just a little cough. Bring him a piece of that bread — not too much, mind you — and he'll be *en pleine forme,* you'll see."

But when she went back, he could barely lift himself to a sitting position in the bed. He was covered with blankets, but still shivering. He took a small piece, thanked her wordlessly with watery eyes and chewed unenthusiastically at the bread. She tried to get him to eat some more, but he just shook his head.

"How about a piece of Beaufort, then? Just a tiny piece." She unwrapped the cheese and held it under his nose.

"*Mon dieu,*" he said with a hoarse, damp voice. "That smells good enough to wake the dead." He broke into another fit of coughing. Whatever gurgled in his chest, he couldn't cough it up.

They should sell the cheese, not eat it, but she felt a desperate need to get him to eat. "Still cold, but smell that. Isn't that good?"

"Okay, just a tiny piece." He put it in his mouth, chewed, swallowed, but shook his head when she tried to give him some more. "No, I can't."

"We've got to get you to a doctor."

"I have no money for a doctor," he said. "Not a centime."

"I brought a few coins. Maybe the madame could buy you some medicine."

"It's too late, you know that. Even that old hen knows, if she would admit it."

"Don't give up hope, you'll see. You'll bounce back. All you need is some medicine."

"I have no money."

"I'll find help."

✠

"Did they appreciate my precious Beaufort?" Helmut asked as she climbed into the car. He pulled away at once.

"I gave it to them."

She didn't want to face Helmut's disdain. He'd just shrug and say it wasn't his problem, it was a tough war, there were lots of hungry people, the Germans had it tough too, or some similar *merde*.

But what else could she do? She had no money; even Madame Demarais hadn't thought much of the few coins she'd left. A meal, maybe two if they stretched it. Who, then? Alfonse would just laugh, she couldn't borrow from Christine again. Maybe if Gabriela had kept working, Monsieur Leblanc would have loaned her a few francs. Or if she'd made any progress in locating his son. Could she lie to him, or lead him to believe she had something from Colonel Hoekman?

"How were they?" Helmut asked after a few minutes of silence.

"Hungry and sick."

"How hungry?"

"Starving. And the *monsieur* has a horrible cough, down here in the chest."

"Dry cough or wet?"

"Wet, like he breathed in some milk and it's stuck down in his lungs."

"Was he shivering?"

"Constantly," she said, "but the apartment has no heat, so of course he's cold."

"And when he coughed up the phlegm, what did it look like?"

"I don't know, I wasn't looking at his snot."

"I think he has pneumonia," Helmut said.

"You don't have to be a doctor to guess that, but so what? They can't do anything about it. They can't see a doctor, they have no money for medicine. I couldn't even give them a few francs for food and coal."

"Actually, a doctor would be time-consuming. I know a man in Dijon who could probably see him right away, but, well..."

"There's no way to get to Burgundy." She tried to stay calm, but his words gave her hope. "I think they're going to die, first the *monsieur*, then his wife. Unless someone does something about it."

"They don't have to die. Let's forget the doctor. What he needs is a chemist. Sulfite drugs are the surest treatment. They're hard to get, but not impossible, if you want them badly enough. You'll have to help them."

"Helmut, I can't help. I have no money and no contacts."

"Yes, but I can and I do." He took the next right, then a left. "We'll make a quick detour."

"Really? Thank you so much." Her gratitude was deep and genuine.

"There are all sorts of things money and contacts can buy. Not just drugs and doctors." He turned and fixed her with a significant look.

"Yes, so your friend is always telling me."

"Alfonse is a braggart. You can't believe everything he tells you."

"You want me to move in with you instead, is that it? You have more money and contacts than he does, so you'd make a better lover. I should have known."

"Gaby, give me a little credit. I'm trying to help you."

"How."

"I have friends and those friends talk to other people and sometimes this information can be quite useful. Tracking down missing people, for example. People taken by the Gestapo."

"What? Do you know something about Roger Leblanc? Is he okay?"

"I have no idea. But I have heard about another of the Gestapo's victims. He's a Spaniard by the name of Ricardo Reyes."

"Papá!"

CHAPTER FOURTEEN

"I HAVE TO CONFIDE IN SOMEONE," Gabriela said. "I have no friends, you understand."

"I'm your friend."

"Yes, except you. And I have no family, except my father, and I don't know where he is or even if he's still alive."

"Then go ahead and tell me," Christine urged. "I'm your friend and always interested in hearing your problems, at least where a good piece of gossip is concerned."

Gabriela sighed. "This isn't gossip and you can't act like it is."

"Okay, I won't. So what happened after you left your old landlords?"

"We got the sulfides, just like Helmut promised."

"Wait, hold that for a second." Christine turned to study a pair of bicyclists who passed on the left. They were two older men and whatever she'd been looking for on the path through the forest, this apparently wasn't it. She turned back to Gabriela. "Go on."

"Are you looking for someone?" Gabriela asked. "Is that why you dragged me out here?"

Two hours down the Champs Elysees and through the 16th Arrondissement on foot to reach the park of Bois de Boulogne. Her feet were tired; she wanted to sit on a bench and talk, but

Christine insisted on walking up and down the paths through the forest. Mostly old people and kids who should have been in school.

"*Ouai*," Christine said.

"Well, who?"

"You'll understand when you see. Go on, tell me what happened."

"So after I brought the drugs to the Demarais, Helmut took me to his office to translate something from Spanish. I kept thinking he was going to find some weak premise to stop at his flat. Try to seduce me."

"If he did, it would be a first. He's famously and faithfully married."

"Alfonse reminds me that every time his name comes up."

"If your friend looked like Helmut, you'd try to remind the girls of that, too," Christine said.

"Hmm, well, he's not my type. Too proud and Nordic looking."

"Isn't that like saying he's too rich or too good looking?"

Christine's grip tightened on Gabriela's arm. Two young men came around the bend. They were smoking, laughing. Gabriela caught a fragment of conversation as they approached on foot. "...and the old man actually quoted Petain. Work is the duty of every Frenchman. 'No,' I said, 'Bending over and taking one up the arse from the *boches* is the duty of every Frenchman.'"

The other young man guffawed. "And?"

"Bastard chased me out of the house with his cane. I barely had a chance to grab my sunglasses."

The two men had slicked-back hair, carried rolled-up umbrellas over their arms even though the sky was clear, and slouched along in that idle gait so beloved of the zazous. Gabriela stiffened in memory of her last encounter.

But they merely smiled, gave an ironic tip of their nonexistent hats. The one who'd been sharing the anecdote said, "Good day, ladies. It's a lovely day to be idle and beautiful and French, *n'est-ce pas?*"

Christine turned to watch them go, then shook her head. "Maybe I was wrong." She sounded disappointed.

"You came here to study zazous?"

"Not exactly, no. So Helmut didn't seduce you."

"No, he didn't even try," Gabriela said.

"*Tant pis pour toi.* Well, Alfonse is good enough for a Spanish girl. And a hell of a lot safer than that Gestapo agent."

"Helmut offered me a job. Offered you a job, too."

Christine frowned. "A job? What kind of job does he think we could do?"

"He didn't say. He made it sound like there were a number of things. A little of everything, I guess. It was very strange, I can't explain it."

"There's an explanation. I know the type. He's trying to save us from a degenerate life."

"Like how you rescued me that day in the flea market?"

"That was different. You were starving. We're not starving. Helmut wants to save us from a degenerate life. No thanks for me. I prefer to earn my living lying in bed. It's an easy living. You going to take the job?"

"Maybe. It will give me something to do while Alfonse is out. There's something else."

"*Ouai?*"

Gabriela took a deep breath. Here was the danger, when you opened your mouth and you confided in someone. And that someone confided in someone else and that someone else denounced you for an extra ration coupon or to get her POW husband assigned to an easier work detail.

Christine must have read her thoughts. "Don't worry, I can be discrete."

"Are you sure?"

"You've never heard me admit that Monsieur Leblanc is a captain in de Gaulle's Free French, have you?"

"Christine!"

"I'm just joking."

"That's the kind of joke that gets people deported."

"Why, are you going to report this conversation to someone?"

"Of course not," Gabriela said.

"And neither am I." Her voice held an uncharacteristically serious edge. "You can trust me one hundred percent."

"I've got a problem. I got close to Colonel Hoekman and it turned out all wrong."

"Of course it did. I warned you."

"You did, but I had no choice. I had to do it, I had to get close to him."

"For god's sake, why?" Christine asked.

She took a deep breath. "I'm looking for my father. Hoekman is the man who arrested him."

"Oh." And then, a moment later. "Oh, I see."

"I've been looking for my father for two and a half years. Two and a half years of nothing, of worrying and wondering, and dead ends. And now I finally had a chance to do something. But what am I going to do? He's Gestapo and I don't have anything to trade for my father's freedom."

"Except for a pair of tits and a nice wet spot between the legs."

"Exactly."

Christine looked thoughtful, and Gabriela could see her working everything out. Why Gabriela took the job at the restaurant, why she'd questioned the hostesses about the officers who'd come to the restaurant, why she'd eventually decided to take a job as a hostess herself. Reevaluating everything that had ever happened between them, just as Gabriela had reevaluated their initial meeting in the *marché aux puces*.

"Why didn't you tell me before?" Christine asked.

"You can't just open your mouth and blurt these things out, not these days."

"Yes, but I'm your friend."

"I didn't know that, I just knew that...well, that day in the flea markets."

"You mean because I got you the job at Le Coq Rouge," Christine said. "You thought I was just another hustler, trying to pimp you out for some favor with Leblanc."

"Well, yes," Gabriela admitted.

"Let me tell you something. I know what I'm doing, I'm not an idiot. Just because I'm trying to make the most of my situation doesn't mean I never think about how things might be different. If this war hadn't come, if I hadn't gone into the One-Two-Two Club the first time. The thing is, you can either starve with dignity or you can forget about what's good and proper and whether a girl should feel certain things or not. You can either die or you can find a way to stay alive."

Gabriela thought about how her body had responded to Alfonse's touch and how she knew it shouldn't. There was some truth in what Christine said.

"I saw you that day," Christine said. "And you looked so fresh and beautiful. So innocent."

"Innocent. After everything I've seen?"

"You can be hit hard by the world and still be innocent."

"So what, you thought you'd save me?"

"Well, help you," Christine said. "Yes."

Gabriela let out a laugh that felt more than a little bitter. "Isn't that like Helmut's plan, in reverse? You're going to rescue me, but not by saving me from prostitution, but by pushing me into it."

"We're not prostitutes, and you know it. A prostitute changes sex for money. Do you really think that's all we're doing?"

"I don't know," Gabriela said.

They were silent for a moment as they continued along the path, then Christine said, "So Hoekman wants to trade sex for information about your father?"

"I'd make that trade, but the Gestapo doesn't play nice. They don't make a trade one for one. They take what you offer and they take something else, too."

"You knew that already, but okay. What does Hoekman want?"

"What does he *demand*, you mean? There's no wanting. He *demands* me to betray Alfonse."

Christine stopped with a frown. "Really, how?"

Gabriela described how Hoekman had hauled her into the truck and made his demands, but left off the details about searching for someone called "the private."

"It's easy to see how Alfonse would attract Gestapo attention," Christine said at last. "He spends too much, he talks too loud. No way the army pays him enough for that kind of lifestyle. He's skimming the cream off the top and anyone can see it."

"You've just described anyone and everyone in Paris who is living the good life. What makes Alfonse special?"

"Maybe nothing. He's boastful and lives in a big, flashy way. Like a general. Only maybe a general can get away with that, but not a major. In fact, he might have just irritated one of those generals, who thought he was living a little too...*loud*, I guess you could say. Maybe the general set the Gestapo hounds on his trail." Christine nodded, clearly liking her theory. "And about this sex. Did you give in to Hoekman already?"

"No, not yet. I made him promise to bring me something about my father, first."

"That's good. It's your only tool, so don't give it up easily."

"I won't."

"But when the time comes, spread 'em and spread 'em eagerly, know what I mean? Moans, kisses, whatever the bastard wants. In the mouth or up the arse, it doesn't matter. Give him the whole wheel of cheese and let him eat it. It's just sex and you can pretend he's anyone and you're anything. Just get through it and live to fight another day. It's just sex."

"You said that already."

"Tell yourself it's just sex enough times and you start to believe it."

"That was my plan all along," Gabriela said. "Colonel Hoekman has been talking to Helmut, by the way. He told Helmut my father is still alive. Why would he do that?"

"They are friends of a sort, aren't they?" Christine said. "They've come to the restaurant together more than once. So Hoekman talked, that's good. It corroborates the story."

"I don't know what to think. I don't like Helmut, and I don't think he likes me, but he doesn't scare me like the Gestapo. I asked him if he knew anything more about my father, but of course he said he doesn't. I need to convince him to dig deeper."

"So you *are* thinking of seducing Helmut. Well, good for you, if you can pull it off." Christine's voice abruptly changed. "Oh, my god, look at that. I knew it."

They'd emerged from the woods to find themselves in a clearing in an isolated part of the park. There was a dry fountain, surrounded by benches. Dead, wet leaves lay unswept and blown into piles. The isolated corner was a perfect place for a meeting away from hostile attention. That's just what they found.

There were at least twenty young people idling about the clearing. The teens slouched on benches, smoking and playing cards. Umbrellas, thick-soled shoes, boys with long, narrow ties, girls with bright red lipstick and sunglasses. Two more arrived on bicycles from the path on the far side. A girl sat on one boy's lap and the two were kissing. The next bench over, the scene played out with two kissing boys.

Gabriela and Christine stopped at the edge of the clearing. A few faces glanced in their direction, then, apparently deciding they were neither friend nor enemy, turned back to what they were doing.

"I thought I was going blind," Christine said in a low voice, "but I was right."

"Yeah, so what?" Gabriela said. "The secret meeting of the International Order of Zazous? Lazy, shiftless youth of the world unite? Come on, let's go."

"Look at those boys, kissing."

"So what?" Gabriela asked. "They should just be glad we're not informers."

"Look!"

Irritated, she paid the kissing boys more attention. And stopped, shocked. "Oh, my god."

"You see," Christine said, triumphant. "You see. He's not dead, he got out. My god, somehow he got out."

And how was that? Could that even be possible? One of the kissing boys was Roger Leblanc, recently arrested by the Gestapo.

CHAPTER FIFTEEN

COLONEL HOEKMAN'S OFFICE IN THE 16th Arrondissement had an expansive view across the Seine toward the Eiffel Tower and the big Nazi flag at its top. There was a breeze today and the flag snapped arrogantly over the city. The first thing Hoekman did when his lieutenant led Gabriela into the room was draw the curtains.

There was a shelf by the window, but instead of books or photos, it held three glass cages. In each cage was a snake and a bowl of water.

The lieutenant gave Hoekman a Heil Hitler and left her alone with the colonel.

"Sit please," he said. He locked the door behind him, then removed a bottle from the liquor cabinet. "You want a drink?"

"No thank you, Hans." Gabriela took a seat on the couch.

"Drink, I insist."

She fought the tremble in her hand as she took the offered drink, took the tiniest sip possible, then set the drink on the table. Hoekman sat down and put a warm, sweaty hand on her leg.

"So, my dear. The thing you need to understand about these things is they take time."

"You've been practicing your French," Gabriela said.

"Two months ago, I speak none of it," he said. There was a

hint of pride in his voice that Gabriela took note of. "Only two months, not bad, right?"

"Very impressive." It was true. His accent was better, his vocabulary less searching. Who could learn a language in two months?

"Every day I practice, I learn new words. I have a tutor, he is best in France. The thing is, I cannot know this country unless I speak its tongue."

"What brought you to France?"

His mouth tightened. "To serve the Reich."

The question was too direct. She could feel him closing off. "You must be a very smart man, Hans, to learn so quickly. Another month, maybe two and you'll speak better than I do."

He rubbed at her leg. The hand left a streak of sweat. "We shall see. Perhaps I will leave this country first." His hand went higher.

She stood up. "Do you have water? I'm just a girl and this drink is too strong."

"Yes, of course. In the bottle on the...*zut!* I know this word."

"On the counter?"

"Yes, on the counter."

She picked a larger glass, poured about half the whiskey into it and then filled this larger glass with water. She took another sip, remained standing.

The cages drew her attention. One of the snakes—a big, dark, ugly thing—was crawling up the side of the glass and nosing at the lid.

"You like my snakes, I see."

"Are they poisonous?"

"No, but they are deadly all the same." He walked over to the cage. "This one, he is rat snake, from Bulgaria. When he is not hungry he can be quite tame. When he is hungry, which is most of the time, he is very aggressive."

"Is he hungry?"

"Yes, I suppose. Let us find out."

Hoekman slid open the cupboard below the cages and removed a wooden box. Something was scratching around inside. He pulled out a white mouse by the tail and held it upside down while he worked with a latch on the snake cage. The mouse didn't seem to be in any discomfort, but twisted around, tried to lift itself to see what held it captive.

Hoekman opened the lid opposite where the rat snake was climbing the glass and with a practiced motion, flicked the mouse into the cage. It landed on its feet and immediately began nosing around in the sawdust. All at once it came to the back end of the snake, draped across the bottom of the cage, and froze.

The snake continued nosing at the lid but suddenly grew still. Its tongue flicked out again and again and it turned its head first to one side and then the other. It lowered itself to the ground.

"It is a strange thing, do you not think?" Hoekman asked. "The mouse is smart, it knows it is in danger. The snake is very dumb. It smells something, but can not...how do you say? Cannot *organize* itself for the hunt. But the mouse is trapped. It searches for an escape that does not exist, while the snake wanders. Eventually the head of the one meets the head of the other."

"Oh, please, take the mouse out. You can feed the snake later."

"It is not smart to insert a hand between a snake and a mouse. Let us watch and learn. It is very interesting."

She didn't want to watch, but neither could she look away. The mouse edged around the corner of the cage, while the snake nosed in seemingly random directions. The mouse was coming inevitably around the front of the cage while the snake doubled back on itself to head in the same direction.

"Watch! Now we see."

The snake caught sight of the mouse. It drew into a partial coil, its head perfectly still, except for its tongue, always flicking. The mouse twitched its way forward, closer and closer to the snake's head.

The strike, when it came, was a blur. Nothing could move that fast. And yet, the mouse moved even quicker. It took a flying leap backwards, just as the snake's open mouth brushed its fur. The snake missed.

Gabriela's hand flew to her mouth to stifle a scream. Her heart was pounding. It was just a mouse, it didn't matter.

"Yes!" Hoekman shouted. "Now we start again. Now we see. Now it is game."

The mouse had lost its caution in favor of panic. It scrambled around the edges, tried to burrow in the sawdust, only to find the glass floor, and then scampered across the cage toward the other side. The snake had recoiled and waited. And a moment later they came face-to-face for a second time.

The mouse tried to jump out of the way again, but the snake moved too quickly. It grabbed the mouse and in an instant, embraced it in its coils. The mouse's head bulged out the top; its back legs twitched and kicked.

"Oh," Gabriela said. "That poor mouse."

"This is strange," Hoekman said, "but I always feel guilty at this point. I ask myself, is it natural for snake, which is low form of life, to eat mouse, which is higher form? And yet, this is nature. One is strong, the other is weak."

The struggle was over. The snake loosened its coils. It nosed the mouse until it found the head, the eyes staring glassily skyward. The snake opened its jaws wide. She looked away.

"The snake is natural part of world, yes?" he asked. "It is just following its nature."

"I suppose so."

"Without snakes and other animals to eat them, mice would infest the earth. The earth would not be in a natural state, it would be ill." He looked at her, as if waiting for her to come to some conclusion. She wasn't getting it. "Isn't that what happens now in Europe? It is not in a natural state."

Natural state? There's a swastika flying atop the Eiffel Tower, for god's sake.

"Only when we return Europe to a natural state is there peace." Hoekman strolled back to the couch. "Tell me, how is your work?"

"My work?"

"With Major Ostermann. What progress do you make?"

"I'm not so quick at languages as you. I don't speak German. It makes it difficult to figure out what he's doing."

"Yes, but you talk to him. The major talks, talks, talks. It should be easy to get him to talk about the private."

"I couldn't get him to admit anything about the *simple soldat*."

"No?" He looked disappointed. "And what else have you noted of his behavior? Tell me now. Tell me everything."

She told him everything without telling him anything. She shared what Alfonse ate for breakfast, when he left for the day, when he returned, but when it came time to recollect phone calls, documents, visits, her memory grew confused, uncertain. Hoekman pressed for details, she furrowed her brow and said, "I can't recall."

"This is useless," Hoekman said. He stood and paced over to the window, then whirled around. "Are you such stupid girl, who cannot notice important details?"

"I'm just so worried about my father. It makes it hard to concentrate. Perhaps if I could see him, just for a few minutes, see that he's okay."

His look hardened and she grew afraid that he'd seen

through her scatter-brained act.

"Please," she said.

"No, impossible."

"Why is it impossible? If he's really in good health, like you said, it should be easy enough."

"He is in Germany. I cannot release him, not yet. And I cannot permit you to leave Paris."

"Then bring him here. Surely the Reich has a house where he could be kept under arrest, given food and care, and his daughter could see him."

"You do not want to help me? Is that it? You prefer the alternative?"

Gabriela went to his side, put her hand on his shoulder. "I am helping, I promise. But you have to give me something. We each promised to be reasonable. I'm trying to help you, but you have to do something."

"You play dangerous game. I grow tired of this game and then you learn I can be not so nice to get what I need."

She ran her fingernails along the nape of his neck. "I'm not political, Hans," she said in a quiet voice. "It doesn't matter to me what happens between the Germans and the French. I'll help you in any way I can, I don't care, but I love my father, I need to be sure he's okay."

"No. It is too soon, you do nothing."

Her mind turned to the side, tried to find a way out of the stalemate. If she backed down now, she'd never get anything. "If you won't help me with my father yet, could you tell me something else?"

"What?"

Gabriela glanced back at the snake's cage. The tip of the tail was just now disappearing down the snake's throat. A lump eased its way through the snake's body. "How about Roger Leblanc? Is he okay, too?"

"Roger Leblanc? Are you serious?"

"Yes, I'm serious. I'm worried, we're all worried."

"What do you care? I know he is not your boyfriend."

"But he's the son of my *patron*, who is in a terrible state. Maybe I could bring something back to Monsieur Leblanc, a bit of hope. If you could let me see him, it would be a way to show me that you really are important enough to help a prisoner."

"Impossible."

"So you can't. You can't help a prisoner."

"It is impossible because he is a homosexual. We ship him to a camp in Germany for reeducation through hard labor. If he cannot be cured, we send him to an asylum. If he can be cured, we return him to France, but not until then. We do this for the good of France, you understand. These homosexuals, they are like a disease. They weaken your country."

Except that she'd just seen Roger this morning, sitting on a boy's lap, engaging in deviant, decadent behavior. He'd been arrested, then released? Why? And why would Hoekman lie about it?

⚡⚡

The first thing Colonel Hoekman did when arriving at the office was order Alfonse's secretary to shovel more coal into the pot-bellied stove in the corner. It was soon shimmering with heat. The room smelled like coal gas.

Two more Wehrmacht corporals brought in boxes of papers: requisition orders, manifests, packing lists, invoices, and the like. It was haphazardly arranged, but the Gestapo colonel's own men—three sharp-eyed, green-eye-shade types—devoured the piles, furiously scribbling notes.

Meanwhile, Helmut and Alfonse sat in their chairs, sweating. Hoekman hadn't so much as unbuttoned his jacket. Every few minutes, one of the men would hand the colonel a paper. He would scan it, take a few notes and then tuck the paper into a folder.

Helmut feigned disinterest in the process. Alfonse, on the other hand, craned forward with obvious intent to see whatever had drawn the attention of the green-eye-shade men.

After almost an hour, Alfonse burst out, "Are you almost done?"

"Of course not, we are just starting."

"Well how long is it going to take?"

"It will take as long as it takes," Hoekman said.

"You know, we're awfully busy, isn't that right, Helmut?"

"I've got time," Helmut said. Alfonse gave him a hard look in response.

"Is there a problem, Major Ostermann?" Colonel Hoekman asked. "Something you would like to tell me? Perhaps you can save us all some time by telling me what to look for."

"There's a war going on, in case you haven't noticed. Who's going to explain to General Dorf what happened to his shipment of grain?"

"The general is well aware of my investigation."

Helmut put a hand on Alfonse's arm and shook his head. He wore the most serious expression he could muster. "The colonel is only doing his job, Major Ostermann. Let him work, it will save us all time."

Alfonse fixed him with a frown. "Thank you, *Herr* von Cratz." He turned back to the colonel. "You don't understand. General Dorf may have sounded understanding, but he's got a ruthless schedule, I tell you. And if he doesn't get that grain..."

"I report to Heinrich Himmler," Hoekman responded. "I say this not to boast, but so that there can be no misunderstanding. If General Dorf has problems with my methods, he may take it up with the Reichsführer-SS himself. Himmler might prove less than understanding of interference with my investigation." Hoekman turned to Alfonse's secretary. "Corporal, there's a chill. I think the fire is dying down."

"Yes, *Polizeiführer*."

"Stoke it high."

"Yes, *Polizeiführer*."

It continued this way for another hour. Part of Alfonse's problem, Helmut suspected, was that he ran his military affairs the same way he managed his personal life. There was style, there was a flair for the dramatic. He could organize spectacular operations one week, then drown under a sea of minutiae the next week. Behind the scenes, a platoon of bookkeepers scrambled after him, trying to clean up the mess. It couldn't be easy.

Helmut, on the other hand, had much more to hide and therefore his paperwork appeared, superficially at least, more ordered. Colonel Hoekman's green eye shades had spent fifteen minutes and proclaimed Helmut's records impeccable.

One of Hoekman's men loaded paper into a typewriter and began writing a memo. Periodically, he would glance at his notes or those of the other two. Some half hour later he hand-delivered the memo to the colonel.

Hoekman read the memo for several minutes, then took off his glasses and tucked them into the breast pocket of his uniform. "There would appear to be some gross irregularities."

"What do you mean?" Alfonse said. "There are no irregularities."

"Let me show you something." He pulled out a piece of paper and showed it to the two men. "This is Helmut von Cratz's document reporting a shipment of sixty thousand tons of coal through Méricourt in Pas-de-Calais on October 14th, 1942. Von Cratz reports that he sold forty-six thousand tons of coal to Todt Organization and fourteen thousand tons to the military. The requisitioning officer for the Wehrmacht is listed as Major Alfonse Ostermann.

"Now this is your record of the same transaction." Hoekman smoothed out some folded and double-folded papers. "Quite a mess. Look at all these hand-scrawled figures. Barely legible, and look at these basic math errors, corrected later. It's like a child did this. That would be your handwriting, wouldn't it? You seem to have taken fourteen thousand tons, but then General Dorf only signs for twelve thousand. There are two thousand missing tons of coal."

"I don't recall the shipment in question," Alfonse said, his voice sullen.

"Is that so? You purchased fourteen thousand tons of coal with state money. That is a non-trivial quantity. And this is your signature. Here, and here. And here, too."

"I'm sorry, I don't remember."

Helmut remembered the shipment. He remembered the missing two thousand tons, too. Because he had stolen them. It was not the first time that he had taken advantage of Alfonse's carelessness.

"I'll look into it. I'm sure there's a reasonable explanation," Alfonse said.

"There had better be a lot of reasonable explanations."

"It's a war," Alfonse said. "We're getting bombed out there. The *maquis* target the tracks, raid our yards. Turn your back for five seconds and the workers will slip half a rail car into their pockets. Then we've got to cross into Belgium and those rats are even bigger thieves than the French. Every shipment we get to Germany is practically a miracle. Talk to General Dorf. He'll vouch for my work. Helmut, tell him. I'm the best man in the whole damn army at what I do."

"I'm afraid we are getting nowhere." The colonel turned to the corporals and his own men. "Leave us, now." The others obeyed at once.

As soon as Hoekman was alone with the two men, he stood,

pulled on a pair of black leather gloves. He wore a predatory expression. Alfonse paled. Helmut thought about his gun in the car, wished he had it with him.

"There would appear to be something wrong in France."

"There are a lot of wrong somethings," Helmut said. "I'm not sure that Major Ostermann's missteps necessitate a Gestapo investigation."

"Do you really accept that this man is merely guilty of minor negligence?"

"I don't think he's corrupt, if that's what you're implying. But whatever his crimes, you replace him and the war effort will suffer. Even if you found someone better, it'd be months before the man knew what he was doing."

"Thank you," Alfonse said. "About time you defended me here."

Colonel Hoekman looked surprised. "You are a serious businessman, Herr von Cratz. If one of your men produced these papers, would you let it pass without question?"

"Well, no. There are some irregularities here, I'll concede that. But..."

"But what?"

"Ostermann has friends. General Dorf, General Vogel in Berlin. If this is all you have, you'll have a hard time getting them to sign off on the major's arrest, or even demotion. I know what you said about Himmler, but I've dealt with the Wehrmacht enough to know they can be prickly bastards when someone steps onto their turf. In the end, wouldn't it be better to avoid conflict between the regular army and the SS?"

"Exactly," Alfonse said. "You see —"

"But if it makes you feel better," Helmut continued, "I can send over some of my accountants, help them sort out this mess." He gestured at the table, strewn with documents. "See if I can track down Major Ostermann's errors. I'll prepare a report."

"Hmm. Perhaps."

"You've done a good job here," Helmut said. "The Wehrmacht requisitioning effort has grown sloppy in France. Cleaning up their books is the best thing that could be done. In fact, I can positively state that you've personally helped the war effort with your investigation."

"That is not my job," Hoekman said. "My job is to find the corrupt and the incompetent. Not to help, but to find people who would harm. To uncover defeatists, spies, communists, profiteering Jews, and other enemies of the Reich. And then, when I have found them, to utterly destroy them."

CHAPTER SIXTEEN

HELMUT JERKED HARD ON THE wheel to pull the car to the side of the road. "Get out, now."

Gabriela hesitated, confused. But Helmut had already thrown his door open and was racing around the other side. She was just opening the door on her side of the car when he grabbed her and dragged her from the car.

"What are you doing? Ow, let go."

An airplane came whining in, fast. Helmut shoved her into the ditch and threw himself on top of her. The plane screamed overhead, no more than thirty feet off the ground. She caught a glimpse as it passed. A fighter plane with red, blue, and white circles painted on the undersides of its wings. British RAF. It disappeared.

Helmut got off and she was surprised to see he was shaking. It had all happened so fast, she hadn't had time to be scared. She rose to her feet and brushed mud from her dress the best she could. It was a mess.

"False alarm," she said.

He scanned the sky, as if looking for other aircraft, but the countryside was calm. The sound of a cow lowing in the distance. "Not necessarily. It's a German car, probably obvious from that height. It would have been easy enough for that pilot to squeeze off a few rounds."

"But he didn't."

"No, he didn't."

"Why?"

"Life is random sometimes," he said.

They returned to the car, but Helmut walked around and shut the doors instead of getting in. He shrugged out of his greatcoat, loosened his tie. The weather continued unseasonably warm and there was a hint of spring in the air. Too early, she knew. It was just a late January thaw.

It had been a quiet morning driving through the French countryside. She'd been nervous at first, not knowing what he wanted. He stopped in one town to arrange some sort of grain purchase, then, at noon, pulled into a sleepy, medieval village for lunch.

She couldn't remember the name of the town. Saint Something-or-Other. Helmut used his ration cards, his reichsmarks, and a bit of charm to acquire wine, cheese, and a fresh baguette and they made a picnic in the meadow-like park just outside the crumbling village walls.

Like every town in France, it had a monument to the last big war, an obelisk at the edge of the park with the names of the young men and boys *morts pour la France.* Couldn't have been more than two thousand people in the village but the names of the dead scrawled down the entire front of the obelisk. She counted eleven boys with the surname of Traineur. Brothers and cousins? An entire generation of Traineur men pruned from the family tree?

Helmut studied the monument for several minutes before he said, "You see enough of these and you understand why the French were so quick to capitulate."

He'd kept his thoughts to himself after that and Gabriela found herself studying him as they continued on the road, wondering just what he was thinking, how much she could trust him. Now, with the shock of the near miss by the RAF fighter still exposed on his face, he looked young and vulnerable.

Helmut leaned against the car. He pressed his hands to his temples. "I'm so tired of this war. Why didn't we learn our lesson last time around? It's not like there aren't a few of those monuments in Germany."

"Maybe you should have thought about that before you invaded Poland."

"Me?"

"Yes, you."

"And you're responsible for the Spanish Inquisition, I suppose."

"Okay, fine. Why are you tired of the war? You're doing quite well, personally. All this killing must be profitable."

"I was making money before the war and I'll be making money after the war. My father gave me his business and his talent and I can make it work under any circumstances."

She snorted. "At least when Alfonse brags, it's about his car or his way with women. He doesn't try to sound better than other people."

"I don't mean it as a boast, it was just something that happened. Some people are born smart, others are born beautiful. Like you, for example."

"Is that a compliment to my looks, or an insult to my intelligence?"

"It's just a statement of fact. I have a way of getting things organized, that's what I was born with. Alfonse, he's rich by circumstance, but I'd be rich anywhere."

"So if it doesn't matter, then why do you care if there's a war? Just the inconvenience of diving for the ditch when the enemy flies over your car?"

"Because in war, you've got to do ugly things. The government orders me to supply ten thousand tons of coal, where does it come from?"

"Presumably you dig it out of the ground."

"Right, and who does the digging? Are they there by choice? How much are they paid?"

"So Helmut von Cratz has a conscience, is that what you're trying to tell me? I'm not sure I believe it."

"Why do you hate me so much? You don't hate Alfonse and he's nothing but a womanizer and an opportunist."

"Maybe he doesn't aspire to more, that's why. Maybe you do, but it's obvious how you fall short."

"Am I such a bad person? I helped your friends. The old man is getting better."

"He is," she admitted. She'd returned two days ago to discover that Helmut had sent them flour, oil, turnips, carrots, and leeks. Even more amazing, he'd somehow found a doctor to visit Monsieur Demerais in their flat. "A German doctor," Madame Demerais had whispered. "The neighbors didn't like it, but I don't care. He knew what he was doing."

"And I told you your father was alive."

"The Gestapo already told me that." She was struggling to maintain her anger.

"The Gestapo could be lying," he said.

"So could you. You haven't brought any proof, agreed to take him a message, found even where he's at. Anything."

"I will when I can."

"Here's the thing," Gabriela said. "You want something. Every man wants something from me, so you're not so different. Monsieur Leblanc wants a girl to seduce the marks from German pockets. Alfonse wants a steamy romance in Paris, someone he can impress."

"And Colonel Hoekman?" he asked.

She fixed him with a stare, wondering what he knew. His face gave away nothing. "Hoekman wants spies. He needs a steady stream of victims so he can take the credit for exposing people. This will help him rise in power. That's my guess."

"It's a good one."

"But these men are open about what they want. You, I don't know. You're not driving me to rail yards and country villages to impress me. You haven't tried to seduce me yet. You haven't asked me to spy on anyone. But I know you want something and that makes me suspicious."

"Maybe we have a mutual enemy."

"You mean Hoekman."

"Yes, that's what I mean." He smiled. "There, you see, you're not just pretty. You're intelligent, too."

She fixed him with a hard look. "Helmut, I don't trust you. I don't think I ever will."

They both looked up as an army truck approached. Helmut bent and made as if checking the tire pressure. He gave a wave to the soldiers in the back, then dropped the pretense as soon as it disappeared around the bend.

He said, "If that truck had been passing ten minutes ago, it would have been an ugly scene. That Hurricane would have gobbled it up."

"Lucky for the Germans. Maybe now you'll win the war."

He didn't take the bait. "I went looking for Roger Leblanc."

This caught her attention. "Did you find him?"

"No, apparently he was sent to a reeducation camp in Germany. Problem is, once they shipped him off, it became almost impossible to do anything about it."

"Hoekman said they were trying to cure him. Is that possible?"

"Sure, if you stretch the meaning of the word cure. They'll force him to admit he's a homosexual—which he'll do, whether or not he really is—then the fun starts. They'll hook him up with wires, show him photos of nude males, then administer electric shocks to the genitals."

"That sounds horrible."

"If he convinces them he's cured, they'll send him to a labor camp. Short rations, sixteen-hour days making munitions."

"And if he's not cured?"

"I don't know, but there are terrible rumors. Come on, let's go. We're supposed to meet Alfonse in twenty minutes."

"But what if you're wrong?" she persisted as they pulled back onto the road. "What if they just took Roger in for questioning and decided he wasn't a threat? Let him go?"

"It's not about containing threats, Gaby. It's about control and suppression of deviant elements of society."

"But say, just for argument, that they let him go. Is there any possible way he's been freed? That he could be back in Paris?"

"Gaby, if I went to the restaurant tonight and saw Roger Leblanc carrying on as if nothing had happened, I'd suspect treachery."

CHAPTER SEVENTEEN

G ABRIELA AND HELMUT ARRIVED AT the rail depot to find Alfonse in uniform, snapping instructions at soldiers, who, together with a small army of civilian workers, scrambled everywhere with crates, boxes, and laden wheel barrows.

Two trains sat huffing on the tracks, facing opposite directions. Half the cargo movements were between the west-bound and the east-bound trains and the rest came from a huge barbed-wire enclosure on the north side. Boxes and barrels stacked almost to the height of the enclosure.

Helmut jumped out of the car and pushed into the fray. He seemed to have forgotten about Gabriela. She followed.

"What is the train still doing here?" Helmut demanded. "It was supposed to leave the yard two hours ago. You know we got buzzed by a Hurricane."

"Dammit, I know that," Alfonse said. "It flew over, strafed us a couple of times, and flew off."

"Then what are you playing at? Why aren't these trains gone?"

"If you'll shut up, I'll tell you." Alfonse stopped as a junior officer came over with a question. Alfonse snapped his answer and the other man saluted and raced off in the opposite direction. "The goddamned *maquis* sabotaged the bridge and we had to reroute one of the trains. It only just got here."

"But the other train isn't even unloaded yet. Why?"
"Ask your man," Alfonse jerked his thumb over his shoulder.

He was gesturing at a young man in civilian dress with a notebook who argued with two other civilian workers. Helmut strode up to the young man and spun him around. "Jesus Christ, Mayer. How many times do I need to tell you?" He dragged him away from the others and snatched the notebook. He looked ready to explode with anger. "What in god's name are you thinking?"

"Sorry, boss," the young man said, "but Raymond is sick and these other morons screwed up the paperwork. We were going to be here all day getting it sorted out. I had to come out, should have done it sooner, in fact."

"Well I'm here now, so get the hell away from these soldiers. Next time I see you, you'd better be so goddamned pale from lack of sunlight that I mistake you for a corpse."

"Yes, sir." He turned and ran for the depot offices.

"Not all Jews look so obviously Jewish," Helmut explained when the young man had run off. "Unfortunately, David's face looks like something from a Gestapo how-to manual. You know, 'recognize a Jew with these three easy-to-identify facial features.'"

"Unlucky for him," Alfonse said without so much as a glance up from his papers.

"Right, and I can't have him running around all these soldiers looking like a fucking rabbi."

"You can't protect him?" Gabriela asked.

"Yeah, I can protect him. I can protect him by keeping him inside." He turned to Alfonse. "Didn't I tell you? Wasn't I clear enough?"

"I've got my own problems without keeping an eye on your Jews."

A soldier came running up to Alfonse. "Thirty minutes!"

"*Scheiss.*"

"Thirty minutes till what?" Helmut demanded.

"That Hurricane was part of an advance fighter screen," Alfonse said. "I got a radio an hour ago saying a huge wave of bombers penetrated France near Calais. They've apparently veered in this direction."

"Probably targeting the truck factory," Helmut said.

"Probably, but they won't pass the depot without bombing the hell out of us. And if the trains are still in the station..."

"What should we do?" Gabriela asked, alarmed.

Helmut turned, blinked, as if just remembering she was there. "What you should do is get into the bomb shelter. Now."

"No," Gabriela said. "I can help. Alfonse, what can I do?"

"Tell her to get inside," Helmut said.

"He's right," Alfonse said. "I've got no use for girls. Get inside."

The two men broke into German without waiting to see if she'd obey. Moments later, they split up. There was a good deal of shouting in French and German. The soldiers and workers picked up speed. Men were cursing, sweating, knocking into each other. Not one of them paid her any attention.

It was obvious the mountain of goods wasn't going to get loaded in thirty minutes. There was too much and the pile was dropping too slowly. And that wasn't even counting unloading the incoming train.

She grabbed for a box from the dump in the enclosure, found it was too heavy, picked a smaller crate instead, just managed. She joined the group of jostling, swearing workers and soldiers. There were men on the train, taking boxes. One of them took her box easily, eyed her dress and hat with a scoffing look.

"Don't just stand there, girl, keep working."

She went back for another box. The work exhausted her within minutes. An air raid siren started its miserable whine. Low, then a high shriek, then low again. And still the men worked.

Alfonse screamed at the men in German and French. "Goddammit, get those boxes in there. Move! Move!" One soldier stumbled and Alfonse cuffed him on the ear, grabbed the box and carried it away.

The men heaved like blowing horses, groaning. Sweat stained their armpits and backs.

Helmut ordered the trains to leave before the work was done. They whistled in turn, competing over the wailing air raid sirens. They crept out of the stations in opposite directions. Even as they picked up speed, men ran to and from the trains, heaving crates in and out. One fell, broke open, and spilled nails across the ground. They joined a mess of bolts, tools, gears, mashed-up food, and broken boards and equipment.

And then men were jumping out of the moving trains, some of the soldiers swung themselves up, and everyone else raced for one of the warehouses on the edge of the depot.

"I hear them!" someone shouted and then there were shouts in German and French and what sounded like Dutch. Within seconds, the movement had become a panicky stampede.

Alfonse spotted her, grabbed her and dragged her into the building. They stumbled, staggered down the stairs. Men poured down the stairwell into a dimly lit basement room well below ground. Soon, they were packed in, crushed one against the other and still more men forced themselves into the shelter. Gabriela grabbed Alfonse's arm to keep from getting separated.

Men were snapping at each other, some close to blows.

"You bastard, move over."

"Move yourself, you French faggot," the soldier snapped.

"Shut up, both of you!"

And then there came a point where the basement held as much as it could fit but there were still men on the stairs, trying to get down. Cursing, screaming back and forth, and a fistfight near the stairs from people trying to get down and men trying not to get crushed. Someone knocked out the light and they were plunged into darkness. More shouts and curses.

Gabriela felt like a mouse in the coils of Colonel Hoekman's snake. Every time she breathed in, the bodies crushed her tighter until she was gasping for air. Alfonse shoved and snarled to try to clear men off her, but his efforts were useless. And then at last came a horrible thump and the ground shook. A deathly silence fell over the men.

"I'd hoped to meet you in a dark, sweaty place," Alfonse whispered in her ear. "But I was counting on more privacy."

The light came back on. It illuminated dozens of terrified faces.

Another thump and shake. And another, harder. The floor seemed to lift up. It would have thrown them from their feet, but they were packed too tightly. Men screamed.

Thump, thump, thump, thump.

The bombs came in rapid succession. She expected every explosion to be the last.

It was quiet again. She braced herself for the next attack. Only gradually did it dawn on the group that the bombers had passed and they were still alive.

Men shouted their relief. A fresh crush as some fought to free themselves from their claustrophobic tomb and others were too afraid to leave the shelter so soon. It took a few minutes to sort itself out.

Above ground, Gabriela, Helmut, and Alfonse found each other near Helmut's car.

Surprisingly, the rail yard was largely intact. A bomb had detonated on the tracks, leaving a tangle of tracks and signals, and one of the outbuildings burned crisply. But most of the bombs had fallen errant on the cow field to the north. Smoking craters pockmarked the field and the hedgerow was burning. There was a cow on the tracks that looked like it had just lain down on its side to take a nap, but it must have flown a good fifty meters through the air. The cow appeared to be the only casualty of the attack.

There was a tremor to Alfonse's hand as he lit a Gauloise. "That was an exciting day of work."

"Heil Hitler," Helmut said in a flat voice.

"*Vive la France,*" Gabriela offered.

"Shall we retire to my hotel?" Alfonse asked. "I have a bottle of *crème de cassis* and I get the feeling we could all go for a drink."

Meanwhile, the common soldiers and workers didn't have that same luxury. They were already working at the wrecked tracks. Already cleaning debris, securing the perimeter against *maquis* attacks. There would be hours of back-breaking labor before they could rest.

"You two go on ahead," Helmut said. "I'll meet you later."

⚡⚡

Alfonse mellowed after a couple of drinks. "The only thing killed was a cow, can you believe that? All of us squealing like girls and those stupid Brits were bombing a cow pasture."

It was warm enough to enjoy the terrace and the glow of the black current-flavored *crème de cassis* as it went down. Gabriela was well into her second glass before she stopped hearing the *thump, thump, thump* of bombs repeating in her head.

The waiter of the hotel restaurant arrived in a black jacket with a white shirt and a cravate tied in a bow. He explained a few of the available dishes and their prices, then added in an apologetic tone, "And you will need one meal coupon for the young lady if she orders separately. There have been...*inquiries* about our adherence to the current rationing program."

"Fine, no problem," Alfonse said. "Last time I was here you

had this excellent plate with shrimp in garlic butter sauce. Is that still available?"

"We do have shrimp, but...*desoleé, monsieur*, the butter is a problem. We only have margarine tonight."

"Margarine?" Alfonse grunted. "May as well cook it in melted candle wax. Well, forget the shrimp, then. How about cheese, you still have that?"

"Yes, of course. We have an excellent selection."

"Fine, fine, bring me that. Just a plate of whatever."

The man returned a few minutes later with a plate of cheeses. Alfonse said nothing, but eyed the cheese tray with a scowl as the waiter left. "This is a goaty selection. You like goat cheese?"

"Some, if it's not too strong."

"Helmut loves the stuff, we can save it for him. The stinkier the better. So, how is it working for my friend?"

She shrugged. "All right, I guess."

"He just needs to relax more. I mean, you saw me, I know how to get it done when it's time. But when the crisis passes, you've got to let it go. Relax, enjoy life. He shouldn't be down there breaking his back on the heavy lifting. That's why the army drafts privates."

"Maybe that's his own way of relaxing," she said. "If he keeps busy, he'll forget faster."

"He relaxes by working? Hah." Alfonse shook his head. "No, that's not it. Not it at all."

"Then maybe he wants to make sure it gets done right."

"Again, you're wrong. I'll tell you what it is. It's his messed up marriage, that's the problem. That wife of his...oh, there he is."

Helmut came through the terrace doors. He'd mostly cleaned up his face, but there was a smudge of soot over his right eyebrow. Gabriela picked up a napkin. "Here, you've got something above your...yes, right there." She stood, rubbed at the spot, mostly got it out.

Helmut took a seat. "That Dutch engineer is a genius. He'll have those tracks repaired by morning." He took the glass Alfonse offered, drank.

"We were just talking about you," Alfonse said.

Helmet fingered a hole in his suit, which had taken a beating. It was torn, muddy, and splotched with oil. "Discussing my impeccable sense of style?"

"I was telling Gaby about your wife. God, she's a beauty. Do you have a picture?"

Helmut reached into his jacket pocket and removed a billfold, handed her a small photo. The woman was very beautiful, severe looking, with light hair pulled into a bun at the back.

"About what you'd expect from this handsome wolf," Alfonse said. "Pick the most beautiful girl and seduce her."

"She's very pretty," Gabriela said. "What's her name?"

"Thank you, her name is Loise."

"Did you know Helmut almost married some French peasant? It's true. Black hair, hazel eyes, beautiful breasts." Alfonse held his hands in front of his chest and pantomimed a generous bounce. He grinned and held up a hand as if to stop Helmut's anger. "Not that I ever saw them, but you could imagine."

"What happened?" she asked.

Helmut shrugged. "The war happened."

"Excuse me for saying," Alfonse said, "but you know, I've already had a couple. I talk too much when I drink. Which is often. I think you should have taken the Frenchy with the big *busen*. Not the ice princess."

"Alfonse," Gabriela said.

"It's true. That French girl — what was her name? Come on,

what was it?"

"Marie-Élise."

Alfonse snapped his fingers. "Yes, that was it. Marie-Élise. She was alive, she loved everything about life. Okay, Loise is a smart woman. She's got a clever tongue, she can match wits. The peasant girl, I don't know. Maybe she's a *dummkopf*, but I know I'll take the simple, but passionate girl." Alfonse tweaked Gabriela's cheek. "If she's beautiful naked, like Gaby, and always horny, so much the better."

Helmut got up as if to leave. There was something in his eyes that looked like pain.

Alfonse grabbed his arm. "Oh, come on, Helmut, don't go. I'm a little drunk already, you know how I get."

Helmut sat back down, finished his drink, and held it up for Alfonse to refill. The pained look faded, or perhaps was masked.

Gabriela looked back and forth between the two men, wondering. "How did you two become friends?"

"Flatmates at Oxford," Alfonse said.

"You studied in England?"

"That's right, we're college mates," Alfonse said. "And the rowing team. We formed a coxless pair. We were good, right Helmut?"

"We were good."

"Remember that race against the so-called Cambridge Invincibles? They had style, you've got to give them that. They sent an ornate letter with Gothic letters in the post claiming they were going to give us the old Viking blood eagle, then eat our still-beating hearts. God, that fired us up, I'll tell you. We had those cocky bastards by a full length going into the last fifty meters. Then came the premature celebration."

"What do you mean, premature?" she asked Alfonse.

A half-smile crossed Helmut's face. "He means he stood up and gave some sort of Viking cheer as we approached the line."

"I didn't need to row," Alfonse said. "All we had to do was coast across the line."

"Soon as he stood up, he unbalanced the boat and over we went. So there we were, in our whites, clinging to our boat, hats floating down the river. Three meters from the finish. I'll never forget the smirk on the Invincibles' faces as they slid past us. Or Alfonse's hangdog expression, for that matter."

"Oh, god, you'll never let me live that one down."

"Me?" Helmut said. "You've told that story ten times for every time I mention it."

"Good times, I tell you, good times."

"Immature times."

"Ah, we had fun," Alfonse said. "You know, Gaby, we both speak perfect English. They came to me a few years ago, asked me if I wanted to infiltrate the UK as a spy. I told them espionage was not really my thing. It's true, I would've made a piss-poor spy. I don't like danger."

"And you talk too much," Helmut said.

"And I talk too much. Cheers to that." Alfonse tipped back his glass. "You'd never know it from that grim look plastered to his face, but Helmut was quite the ladies man at the university."

"Oh, I believe it. He's a handsome man."

"Those English girls swooned over him."

"Come on, don't exaggerate," Helmut said.

"There were dozens," Alfonse said. "Couldn't take a walk without making every girl in the park blush and giggle and stare."

Gabriela gave Helmut a teasing smile. "Is this true?"

Helmut snorted. "Hardly. In four years, I remember all of two girls. A girl who wanted me to take her home with me to Bavaria so she could escape her father's farm in Sussex. Then there was that earl's daughter, from Scotland. She was, uhm, big-boned."

"Goddamned Amazon, you mean," Alfonse said. "Remember that time you played tennis? And she caught you one in the beak with a forehand smash? Blood everywhere. Like a slaughtered turkey."

"I swear, her whole family was like that," Helmut said. "I visited her estate in Scotland and the friendly croquet games turned into the Second Battle of Bannockburn. Broken mallets, shouting and cursing, fist fights. And that was just the ladies match."

"Shame we're enemies with the Brits, now," Alfonse said. "We had some good times, made a lot of friends. It's unnatural for the Germanic peoples to be at each others' throats. Why should Britain and America be allied with Slavs? And who are our allies? The bloody Japs and the Italians. Tell me, does that make sense?"

"Your voice is awfully loud," Helmut said. "Maybe we should talk about something else."

Alfonse leaned forward and spoke in a conspiratorial tone, still too loud. "I'll tell you something else. When's that bastard Hoekman going back to Germany?"

"We're stuck with him for awhile," Helmut said.

"That other night, that was horrible. When he pulled on his gloves?" Alfonse let out a nervous-sounding chuckle. "I half expected him to say, 'We have ways of making you talk, Herr Ostermann.'"

"So watch yourself," Helmut said. "Keep your paperwork in order. The Wehrmacht can only protect you so far when the Gestapo is involved."

"Hmm, well we'll see about that. General Dorf has pull in Berlin, too. He'll cover for me."

"Maybe, but Hoekman has two things General Dorf doesn't. One, he's impressed the hell out of Heinrich Himmler. Two, he's on the side of justice."

"Justice," Alfonse sneered. "Fascist bastards will piss on your face and tell you it's raining. Cut off your hand and send you a bill for the surgery."

"But it is justice, isn't it," Helmut said.

"You're not actually taking Colonel Hoekman's side," Gabriela said. "Are you?"

"God, no. Men like that have turned Germany into a perverted nightmare. But if you take Hoekman's general assumption about what is good and right for the Fatherland — and I'll be damned if most Germans don't seem to agree — then everything the colonel is doing is right and proper."

"I was at his house once, in Prussia," Alfonse said. "You listen to his accent, you can tell he was born to working parents, but you'd never know it by his house."

"Is it big?" Gabriela asked.

"Used to belong to a Baron von Something or Other. Hoekman isn't married. Can you imagine a girl marrying him? And his parties are dreadfully dull, tedious. With what he's got, you'd expect him to fill the place with paintings and statues. Half those places look like a bloody museum."

"Like a *French* museum," she said. "Which is not a coincidence."

"Well yeah, whatever. Not that Hoekman doesn't have taste, he doesn't bother to try. He has a more unusual collection."

"Snakes?" Gabriela said.

"Exactly. How did you know? Yes, he's got two rooms filled with the disgusting things. It's like a zoo in there, he breeds vermin to feed to his animals. Smells like mice. Piss and shit."

"I've heard about the snakes," Helmut said. "First thing he does when he visits a new country, is go collecting."

Helmut seemed to have warmed to the *crème de cassis,* and poured himself another glass. He took a nibble from one of the more pungent goat cheeses.

"Wonder who takes care of the snakes when he's not home," Alfonse said. "Can't imagine the maid or the cook would be too keen to clean up snake turds."

"He brought some with him," Gabriela said. "One is this big, black rat snake from Bulgaria."

"How do you know that?" Alfonse asked.

"Uhm, the girls like to gossip." She thought of a convincing lie. "He took home a girl from the Egyptienne and made her watch while he fed mice to his snakes."

"There's got to be a better way to seduce a girl. *Mademoiselle*, do you want to see my snake? It is big and strong." Alfonse chuckled. "It lacks a certain subtlety."

"Interesting," Helmut said. A thoughtful look came over his face. "How many snakes has he got in France? Did this girl tell you?"

"I don't know. Three in his office, anyway."

"Wait," Alfonse said. "Let me get this straight. He took a girl to his office and made her look at his snakes? Is that supposed to make her horny or scare the hell out of her?"

"Does it have to be either, or?" Helmut asked. "Hoekman probably doesn't know the difference."

Some time later, after they'd finished the *crème de cassis* and moved on to a bottle of wine, Helmut asked to be excused to visit the WC.

"Probably won't be gone long enough for us to slip upstairs," Alfonse said when Helmut was gone. He was slurring some of his words now.

"The longer you wait, the hornier you'll be."

"And that's a good thing?"

She leaned across the table until their lips were almost touching. "That will be a very good thing, I promise."

"Come on, let's go now. Helmut's a big boy, he can take care of himself."

But Helmut came back moments later. Alfonse looked disappointed.

Helmut poured more wine for everyone. "Let's have a toast."

"A toast? Whatever for?" Alfonse asked.

"To the piss-poor British pilots who bombed a cow pasture instead of our railway depot."

Alfonse laughed. "I'll drink to that."

"We're alive," Gabriela said, "and that's a good thing."

They drank their wine and Alfonse started a story about a midget sex show he claimed to have seen in Pigalle. It sounded suspiciously like a setup for a joke, with a punchline that would make the others groan. But then one of Helmut's sarcastic asides distracted him and soon he was talking about Oxford again.

Helmut stood up some time later. "I'm going to my room. All this wine has gone to my head."

"That's what it's supposed to do, you know," Alfonse said.

"Nevertheless, I think I've had enough."

"Finally," Alfonse said after he'd left. "Come on, let's go to bed, I'm horny as hell."

Gabriela had no enthusiasm for it. The drinks had calmed her nerves after the bombing at the rail yard, but she wasn't particularly aroused by Alfonse's loud, drunk voice and red face.

"Come on," he said in a pleading tone. He tugged at her sleeve.

"Okay, okay, I'm coming."

⚡⚡

Later, when Alfonse was snoring in bed with all the noise and enthusiasm of a Ruhr Valley steel mill, she slipped into her clothes and stepped onto the balcony. The air was brisk, and a welcome change from the booze and sweat that radiated from the bed. The village slept below her, dark but for a few lamps in windows and the moonlight overhead. Swallows flitted above the tile roofs.

Helmut stood on the adjacent balcony. "Good evening."

"Can't sleep?"

"Too much running through my mind. You?"

"With Alfonse snoring like that? It'll be a miracle if I get any sleep at all."

"I can hear it from here. He keeps up that racket and the Brits will think they discovered a secret munitions factory and come drop a few bombs on our heads."

"They'll never bomb here. There aren't any cow pastures next to the hotel."

He smiled. "I'm glad you came out. I've been called away. We might not see each other for a few days."

She was surprised to feel a twinge of disappointment. "Oh? Where are you going?"

"Called away. You know, the war effort."

"Always the war effort. Well, be careful. I don't want to see you killed or worse."

"I need to ask you something before I go."

"You can ask."

"What does Colonel Hoekman want?"

"I told you before."

"Right, you said he wants spies. Gaby, please be open with me. He didn't bring you in for a herpetological exhibition."

She didn't say anything.

"Gaby, I'm trying to help you, you've got to understand that."

"I don't believe it."

"What does Hoekman want? Are you spying on Alfonse, or is it someone else?"

There was no reason to deny it, was there? If he suspected already, he could say something to Alfonse whether she lied or not.

He must have read her worries. "Alfonse is a big talker," he said, "but I'm not. He's careless, he lives above his pay grade, and that attracts attention. We sat through a hell of an inspection of Alfonse's paperwork the other day and it could have gone even worse."

"I'm worried about him," Gabriela said, truthfully. "He's always going to be that guy who stands up in the boat before it crosses the finish line."

"That's why his friends have to look out for him."

She didn't answer.

"Look, if you can tell me, we can help—quietly, without making Alfonse panic and do something stupid."

"You really think so?" she asked.

"I do think so, and you know what?" He leaned over the railing that separated the two balconies. "I might be able to help *you* with Hoekman, too."

"How? What could you possibly do against the Gestapo?"

"Nothing, directly. But I'm a rich man. Hoekman himself is untouchable, but I can work on other people."

"Sounds a lot like Alfonse's General Dorf solution to me."

"I'm not Alfonse. Surely you've noticed by now."

"Fine, you say you can help. Could you help me find my father?"

"Your father." He hesitated. "I want to lie and say yes, of course, but I don't know. Gaby, surely it has occurred to you he might be dead."

"He's not."

"It's been how long? Two and a half years? A lot of people have died in camps."

"He's not dead and I'm going to find him. Can you help me or not?"

He sighed. "I can try, but I want to be honest. They're tough odds. But if I'm going to look, you've got to give me something."

"Give you something. That's exactly what Colonel

Hoekman told me."

"I'm not Colonel Hoekman, either. Surely, you've noticed *that* as well."

"You're more sophisticated in your technique, I'll grant you that."

"Give me some credit, please."

She'd been vacillating, but now she made her decision. She had few allies, and the friends she had—Christine, the Demarais, perhaps Monsieur Leblanc—were weak. Alfonse? He'd never help, she couldn't trust him. So what about Helmut? Did she have any choice?

"Hoekman's looking for a private in the army," she said. "He thinks the man works for Alfonse."

Helmut frowned. "A private, you say?"

"That's what he said. A *simple soldat.* I don't know if he's French or German."

"A private." The frown deepened. "None of Alfonse's aides are privates. Even his driver is a corporal. He give you a name?"

"No name." Gabriela remembered how Hoekman had put it. "Actually, *simple soldat* was my word choice, since he couldn't remember how to say it. His French is getting better, but it still has gaps."

"How exactly did he say it, then? How did you know that's what he meant?"

"He said, 'the lowest rank of enlisted man.' I filled in words in French."

"The lowest rank of enlisted man. *Simple soldat,* that would be *Schütze* in German." Helmut looked blank for a long moment and then a worried expression crossed his face. "*Mein Gott!* Oh, I see. Yes, that must be it." Helmut turned from the balcony.

"Wait, what is it?"

"Tell Alfonse to drink lots of water, it will help with the hangover." He opened the door to his room.

"But what about my father?"

"Later," he said. "Later."

CHAPTER EIGHTEEN

"SIMPLE SOLDAT?" GEMEINER REPEATED. THERE was static on the line; perhaps he was unsure he'd heard right.

"It's something like *Schütze* in German," Helmut said. "Literally, a simple soldier. Listen, are you sure your line isn't tapped? There's a lot of crackling and popping."

"Positive," Gemeiner said. "Both phone lines were chosen at random. The call is going through a switchboard in Flanders."

It was pouring rain outside the phone booth in the village of Villejust. Helmut had called from another booth near the depot, said a certain thing to Gemeiner's secretary, received a number in return: 965391. The first two numbers — 96 — corresponded to a phone booth location on a map Helmut kept in his possession. The second number, taken backwards, worked out to 19:35, or the time he should wait at the booth for Gemeiner's call. The call had come precisely on time.

"So who is this private?" Gemeiner asked.

"It's not actually a private," Helmut said. "It translates as 'simple soldier' in French, but what Hoekman said literally was, 'the lowest rank of enlisted soldier.' What are the other ways you could say that?"

"*Kanonier*? *Pionier, Kraftfahrer*? Let's see...*Flieger* for the Luftwaffe."

"The old way."

A pause, then, "Oh. Oh, I see."

The old word had been replaced by newer words and had since become merely slang for a country fool. But it used to mean a man drafted up from the village with a pike or musket thrust into his hands and ordered to the front lines. It had been the word for private before the reformation of the army in the last big war. Common man: *Gemeiner.*

"That's right," Helmut said. "He's looking for you."

"So he's on to our operation."

"It would appear so, except he thinks Major Ostermann is your liaison, not me."

"We can't count on that confusion forever."

"No," Helmut said.

He looked out the glass doors, but it was dark outside the phone booth and the rain pounded so hard that it ran in rivulets down the glass doors.

"They arrested our man in Provence yesterday," Gemeiner said. "He bit a cyanide capsule before they could interrogate him, thank god."

More disquieting news. "Who is taking his place?"

"It might be you," Gemeiner said. "I'm rather short of English speakers."

"Needless to say, I'm not in a position to meet with American agents in Provence."

"Last resort only. First, we need to deal with our Gestapo friend before he penetrates the organization."

"You know my answer," Helmut said. "We need to kill him." He thought about Roger Leblanc, dragged out of Le Coq Rouge, still protesting his innocence. "We'll be doing the Reich a favor, believe me."

"I'm sure we would, but that bastard keeps notes. It'll be obvious he was onto us and if he dies, that would probably double the attention turned our way."

"Unless we make it look like an accident. A car accident, a robbery gone bad, something like that."

"Damned   tricky."

"Did you know Colonel Hoekman fancies himself an amateur herpetologist?" Helmut asked. "He keeps snakes in his office and probably his flat, too. Raises mice to feed them. It occurs to me we could do something with that."

"Go on."

"Do you remember the Arab who put us in contact with the Americans in Algeria?"

"Mahmoud Something-or-Other, right? Smuggles goods between Algiers and Marseille."

"Something like that, yes," Helmut said. "He has cohorts in North Africa. There are some deadly snakes in the Sahara."

"What are you thinking?"

"We get an asp or a viper or whatever is most deadly and release it in his office. It bites him, he dies, and everybody shakes their heads and says, 'That crazy Colonel Hoekman, keeping all those snakes. He was bound to get bit sooner or later.'"

There was a long moment of static and Helmut began to wonder if they'd lost the connection, but then Gemeiner said, "It's just weird enough to throw people off, if you could manage the details."

"Should I contact the Arab?"

Another long pause from the other end. "No. I don't think it would work. I was in Africa in the last war, a base outside of Windhoek. We lost a man to a cobra bite once. It's a horrible way to go, but not as fast as you might think. The snake was longer than a man and as big around as a child's arm, but it still took all night and half the next day for the guy to die. Same thing happens here and that will leave plenty of time for Hoekman to linger, to tell people he never had a poisonous snake. Oh, and to say, 'I'm on the trail of a major smuggling operation, maybe something more. Maybe even traitors. It was probably them who planted the snake.'"

Helmut felt deflated. It had seemed like a clever idea. "Maybe in the night, then? He gets bit, he lies down to sleep and never wakes up."

"And how do we slip the snake into his bed? How do we keep it from slithering off to the warmest part of the flat? Snakes aren't guard dogs. You can't make them attack on sight. But I like the way you think. If we could somehow make it look like a hazard of his job or his lifestyle that has nothing to do with us. That reminds me," Gemeiner added, "how are you getting on with the girl?"

"Gaby? She doesn't hate me anymore, I guess that's a start."

"She doesn't hate you? That doesn't sound like she's ready to take her pants off."

"She's suspicious by nature. You would be too after what she's been through, and with the Gestapo putting her thumbs in the screws. Besides, she gave up the information willingly, and I didn't even have to sleep with her."

"Here's what I'm thinking," Gemeiner said. "We get your prostitute to do the killing."

Helmut recoiled from the suggestion. "What? How?"

"The girl hates Colonel Hoekman, she just needs a nudge. You feed her hate, and you sleep with her. Once she's fully in your confidence, you recruit her to our side. You'll give her the means to get to Hoekman."

"Let's say it's possible," Helmut said. He switched the phone to the other ear. "If she kills Hoekman, they'll catch her. And when they catch her, they'll kill her."

"Yeah, probably." There wasn't quite a shrug of indifference in Gemeiner's tone, but close. "That's an ugly truth. It's a necessary truth. In fact, we can't wait for it to happen. She gets caught, she'll give you up under torture and you'll give me up and so on. We won't all bite our cyanide capsules in time. So we'll have to stage her suicide. She was so distraught over her father she murdered his persecutor and then took her own life. She'll leave a helpful note. Everything will wrap up nicely."

"That's repugnant." Just hearing the plan spoken out loud made him feel ill. "Besides, people aren't guard dogs either. You can't make them attack on sight."

"No, but unlike snakes, they're warm-blooded creatures. They have passions. Control those passions and you can get them to do what you want."

"No," Helmut said. "It's too much. Gemeiner, she gave me the information willingly. It's the whole reason we know Hoekman is looking for us. It's wrong to push her into this."

"How many Germans are dying every day?"

"Don't you think I know that?"

"And now we have Stalingrad," Gemeiner said.

"I know the situation is dire, but if they break through the encirclement—"

"My god," Gemeiner said. "You haven't heard, have you?"

"Heard what?"

"It's all people are talking about in Germany."

Helmut felt himself growing alarmed. "I've been away from the radio for a few days. It's all propaganda anyway, I can't stand listening to it."

But surely if there were big news someone would have known about it. He couldn't imagine that Alfonse's men wouldn't have started discussing it as soon as the bombing at the station had ended, but somehow Helmut hadn't caught so much as a word.

"This isn't propaganda. For once, that bastard Goebbels came right out and told the truth, bleak as it was."

"Dammit, what happened?"

"The battle is lost. The Sixth Army is no more."

The news shook Helmut. In spite of the false hope (which he'd also been deluding himself with just moments earlier), the outcome at Stalingrad had been obvious for weeks, and yet to hear it spoken was almost too much. "The entire army?"

"Surrendered. Quarter of a million men lost. Shipped to Siberia, most likely, to be worked to death in Stalin's factories. They'll never be heard from again."

"My god."

"A year ago, only a few of us could see where this was going. In fact, there were times when I wondered if I was wrong, the Wehrmacht seemed to be having such an easy time of it. On the outskirts of Leningrad, Moscow, Stalingrad. And now, it has to be obvious to everyone from the Reichstag down that we're in trouble. With the Sixth Army gone, the whole center of the Eastern Front is on the verge of collapse. I heard — and I hope to god this is just rumor — that General Zhukhov is amassing six million Soviet troops for a spring counteroffensive."

"Six million? How is that possible? And I know for a fact we're preparing our own spring offensive in the east. I've got the requisitioning forms to prove it."

"And how many men do you suppose we still have on the Eastern Front? Two million? Two and a half? Another half million by spring. Come on, Helmut, you know that we'll never mount a credible offensive again. That is a privilege possessed only by our enemies now."

Helmut fell quiet.

"So you see our situation becomes urgent," Gemeiner said.

"There's still time."

"There's no time. The war is turning and turning fast. How long until the Red Army pours into the Fatherland? You know what happens then? I'll tell you what happens. Your wife is a beautiful woman. They'll have Loise on the floor. They'll have her clothes off. They'll have their way with her. Loise will beg them to kill her, but they'll just keep at it. Again and again and again. Wonder how that will feel with her medical condition and all. If you're lucky, they'll put a bullet in your head first so you won't have to watch."

Helmut could hardly breathe. "You bastard."

"Why? Because I'm telling the truth? Wake up, man. Wake up and do what must be done."

"I don't care, it won't work. Gaby is searching for her father. Hoekman's the only man who could help her. She's not going to kill him."

"And what if I told you I found her father and he's alive?"

"He's alive?" Helmut asked. "Is that even true?"

"Oh, it's true. And when Gabriela Reyes sees what I've seen, when you show her, she won't just agree to kill Colonel Hoekman, she'll beg you to give her a chance."

CHAPTER NINETEEN

GABRIELA AND CHRISTINE RETURNED TO the Bois de Boulogne in the 16th Arrondissement and made their way toward the secret rendezvous spot of the zazous. This time, however, they looked the part: short skirts, colorful socks, sunglasses.

"I still think we should tell Monsieur Leblanc," Christine said. "He's sick with worry."

"If that's what you think, why didn't you tell him first thing?" Gabriela asked. "Or last night, at the restaurant, you could have told him then."

"I don't know, maybe I just want to be sure first."

"Be sure of what? We both saw Roger. There's no way we made a mistake."

"Okay, then," Christine said. "So why didn't I tell him? He'd want to know, he's frantic. He'd be so grateful."

"You had a bad feeling, that's why."

"A bad feeling? That doesn't make sense. It's good news they let Roger go, right? Well, isn't it?"

"Something's wrong, that's what," Gabriela said. "It doesn't make sense that he'd be free and back with his friends. Come on, we'll find out for sure."

It was chillier today, though still dry, and the girls pulled their sweaters tighter when a gust of wind picked up.

"You think those zazou girls have wool underpants?" Christine asked. "Because these silk panties aren't doing the job."

"Maybe our socks aren't long enough."

"They make them that long?"

They came upon the clearing. There were even more zazous around the dry fountain than before. They were sipping drinks, laughing, smoking, playing cards, or simply doing nothing but leaning back with hands behind their heads.

A boy in a long coat spotted them and approached. He wore a yellow star on his breast, like a Jew, but instead of *Juif*, it had the word *zazou* sewn into the center.

The boy tucked his hands into the pockets of his sheepskin coat. "Are you swing?"

Gabriela had no idea what he was talking about, but she arched an eyebrow. "Are you?"

"*Mais, ouis.* Did you bring anything to drink?"

"We were hoping you'd have something," Christine said.

He looked disappointed. "Someone brought fruit juice, but we could use some grenadine syrup. JPF keeps cruising by the Pam Pam, so we're stuck here."

Christine pulled her cigarette case from her purse and took out a couple of Gauloise stubs. She handed the longer one to the young man and he brightened. "Thanks. You girls alone?"

"We're looking for a friend," Gabriela said. She scanned the crowd, but couldn't see Roger anywhere. "You know Roger Leblanc?"

"Whitey? He's drawing again. Know that bird statue by the cascade?"

Gabriela shook her head. "Which way?"

He gestured with his cigarette. "Follow that path, take the left. Just around the bend."

Roger was close enough they could still hear the zazous

talking through the trees when they found him. He had his pastels out and a partially-completed sketch on an easel.

But Roger wasn't actually drawing. Instead, he sucked at a cigarette, paced back and forth, and muttered to himself. "It's not right, it just doesn't look the same." He glanced back to the easel, shook his head. "What's wrong with me? God."

Gabriela stepped closer to see what it was about the drawing that so disgusted him.

She expected to see a picture of the park scene facing Roger. A stone crane stood at the edge of the pond, and water spilled over the edge of the stone cascade, into the pond, where it churned up sticks and dead leaves. A tree stood on the hill next to the cascade, still leafless in late winter, leaning over the cascade pool. But the drawing had nothing to do with the park. Rather, he'd drawn a flat, gray landscape of dead, broken trees, with what looked like a factory and its smokestacks rising in the upper-right corner. The building was tall with severe lines, and no windows. Curiously, a red rooster perched on top of the building.

"What are you drawing?" she asked.

Roger turned, his expression startled.

"Gaby? What are you—? Christine? Jesus, don't sneak up on me like that. I thought you were—never mind. What are you doing here?"

"We're looking for you, what do you think?" Christine asked.

"But you're dressed like zazous."

"And so are you," Gabriela said. "Roger, what is going on? What are you doing here? Did you escape? Are you hiding out, is that it?"

He started to say something, stopped, took a drag from his cigarette. "No, no, you really have to go." He looked over their shoulders. "Just go."

"Your father is dying from worry," Christine said. "And

here you are wasting time with the zazous. We saw you kissing a boy the other day."

He blushed. "Oh, surely not. You must have made a mistake, that wasn't me."

"It was you," Christine said. "Don't lie. Listen, it doesn't matter. What matters is that your father...look at me when I'm talking to you. Don't you even care? How could you do this to him?"

"At the very least you could have passed him a message," Gabriela said. "Did that even occur to you?"

"Oh, god, is he really worried?"

"What do you think?" Gabriela said. "He's frantic. The Gestapo carried you off, what's he going to think? You could be dead, you could be tortured, you could be anything."

"You don't understand, you couldn't." A burst of laughter from the zazous gathered on the other side of the trees. Roger jumped, then turned back with a nervous look. "I just—listen, you have to go. Get out of here. Now, hurry, before it's too late."

"What do you mean, too late?" Gabriela said. "We're not going anywhere until you tell us what's going on. Does Hoekman have something on you? We can help, but you've got to talk to us."

"How could you possibly help? You don't know anything about anything."

"We're trying to understand. Why don't you talk to us?"

"About what? Nobody listens to us, nobody cares. Fascists, the *maquis*, they all hate us. Can't everybody just leave us alone? We don't care about you or your stupid war."

"Roger, I saw Hoekman, he interrogated me," Gabriela said. "And you know what happened? He—"

She was ready to tell him everything. Whatever had him spooked, it couldn't be worse than what Hoekman had over her. Maybe there was something he knew about the colonel that

MICHAEL WALLACE

could help her find her father. Or maybe Hoekman played the
same game with both of them and they could help each other.

But at that moment there was the sound of screaming and
shouts from the other side of the trees. A harsh, jeering laugh.

"Oh, no," Roger said. "Oh, god. No, it's all wrong."

A girl ran through the clearing, screaming. Her clothes
were dirty, her blouse ripped open.

"Listen to me!" Roger said. He snatched up his portfolio.
"You've got to hide. Do it now!"

Roger's warning snapped Gabriela from her stupor.
Christine looked frozen with fear. Gabriela grabbed her arm
and pulled her from the footpath. Just off the path she spotted
a bare patch of dirt curving up the side of the hill toward the
top of the cascade, perhaps leading to a secret rendezvous spot
for lovers. Gabriela dragged Christine up the hillside. They
scrambled up on hands and knees.

The women reached the bushes at the top of the hill. "Gaby,
I'm scared!"

Gabriela pulled Christine to the ground. "Keep down!"

A young man burst into the clearing, spotted Roger.
"Whitey!" he screamed. "It's the JPF. Run!"

Two other young men caught him and threw him to the
ground. They wore the blue uniforms and black berets of
the JPF—Jeunesse Populaire Française—the youth fascist
organization. "Scalp the zazous!" one of the men yelled.
Another man yanked back the long hair of the zazou. The other
had a pair of shears and hacked away. The two men laughed
while the boy tried to free himself.

Roger clutched his portfolio to his chest and shrank back
with a pale expression until his back pressed into the statue of
the crane.

"Whitey!" the young man on the ground yelled. "Roger,
help me!"

206

Roger didn't move.

As soon as they finished with the hair, the JPF tore at the zazou's clothes, then started kicking him in the ribs. Other zazous fled past, pursued by JPF. One girl was completely stripped to her panties. A red-faced man pursued her with a leer. He caught her and pushed her to the ground just out of view. The girl screamed. More zazous and their attackers. Nowhere did Gabriela see any of the zazous fighting back.

Christine was crying. "Oh my god, oh my god, oh my god."

Gabriela slapped a hand over her mouth. "Shut up, now."

And then there were others joining the fray. Men in gray uniforms and hats with silver skulls and eagles clutching swastikas. Gestapo. The JPF thugs shrank out of their way. Time to let their masters do the real work. The Gestapo beat the zazous with clubs, pistol-whipped one boy who resisted. They slapped them in cuffs, threw them on the grass. Minutes later, they were dragging them away, kicking them, hitting them about the head. The boys and girls were weeping, begging for mercy, half-naked and filthy. Soon, a quiet descended on the clearing, disturbed only by the water that spilled over the edge of the cascade into the pool.

Nobody had touched Roger Leblanc. He sat frozen with his drawings clutched to his chest until they were gone. And then he moved with a terror of his own, grabbing his easel and turning to flee. The drawing on the easel fluttered to the ground. He didn't seem to notice.

Gabriela stood up. "Roger, wait! Roger!"

"Go away, just leave me alone." He fled.

Gabriela rose to her feet and made her way down the hill. Christine followed.

"Did you see that?" Christine asked. "Did you see how they went right past him? How did they miss him? He was right there, they didn't even see him."

"They saw him."

"What are you talking about? They left Roger alone. If they saw him, why wouldn't they take him, too?"

"Yeah, why?"

The ground was marred with heavy boot prints, the signs of a struggle here and there on the grass. Gabriela picked up Roger's drawing. The bleak factory, twin smokestacks that stretched toward a leaden sky.

"Gaby, for god's sake, can we go now? Please?"

She'd missed a detail in her initial glance, something about the red rooster perched on the edge of the factory, out of proportion to the rest of the scene. It was detailed for something so small, drawn with pastels. The rooster wore a gold star on its breast, with the word *zazou* written across the center. The rooster had a beak, feathers on its head, but wore a human face.

The face of Roger Leblanc.

CHAPTER TWENTY

HELMUT'S FACE WAS WARM AND sympathetic as he leaned across the private train compartment. He rested his hand on Gabriela's. "How did they catch your father?"

"It was my fault. If I hadn't been there, Hoekman never would've arrested him."

"Why don't you tell me about it."

She would have recoiled from his touch just a few days earlier. She'd distrusted him, hated everything he represented. But then, as was usually the case, the truth was more complex than she'd initially guessed. Helmut was more complex.

Now she found his touch comforting. Of course some of it was this train ride, the culmination of all her hopes and fears, that did it. But the truth was, she'd been fighting to maintain her dislike for some time now. Since the day he gave Monsieur Demerain the sulfide drugs for his pneumonia, probably saved his life. It was a relief to just give it up.

Any residual defenses had melted yesterday when he'd arrived at Alfonse's flat and handed her an envelope. "Train tickets for Strasbourg."

"The occupied zone? Whatever for?"

"We're going to take a little trip."

"Why? Seriously, I can't figure out why you keep dragging me around the country."

She thought about what Christine said about men who tried to rescue prostitutes. Was he acting through some sort of misguided charity or was it all about Colonel Hoekman? The last two times she'd seen him he hadn't mentioned the Gestapo.

"Do you have something better to do?" he had asked as she retrieved her coat and a bag with a few personal effects. "Surely you don't want to sit around Alfonse's flat all day, moping about until he comes home."

"Well, no. But you're always busy and working. What am I doing, just keeping you company?"

"I like your company, I admit it."

"Oh? And why is that?"

"Because when I'm with you I can think about something other than the war for a few minutes, I can pretend the world is a simpler place."

"So you're bored, that's all."

"Not today I'm not." A mysterious smile flickered across his face. "Today is a big day for you. I've got a surprise."

"I'm living in Paris under occupation. I'm not sure I like surprises. They usually turn out badly."

"You'll like this one."

"Oh?"

"I found your father."

She caught her breath, felt light-headed. "Papá? Is he...? Is he...?"

"He's alive. Would you like to see him?"

The next few hours had been the slowest of her life. But finally, the Alsatian countryside clattered outside her window. It was hilly, with German-looking villages, which was presumably why Germany kept insisting on ownership. It had been two years since she'd been more than fifty kilometers from Paris; she found the escape exhilarating. Now that they were approaching Strasbourg, her heart was thumping.

Gabriela wanted to share with Helmut; she'd never told anyone before what had happened. She was very aware of his hand resting on hers.

"You must love your father very much to keep searching after so much time," he said. "Most people would have given up, but you keep hoping."

"I have to. He's the most wonderful man in the world and he would have done anything for me. You know, I loved my mother, of course, and my brother, too, but it wasn't the same."

"Tell me about him."

"I can't even think of where to start."

"How about what he did for a living. That usually defines us more than anything."

"He owned a bookstore in Madrid before we came to France. New books, used books. Carried everything you could imagine. He'd point me to the best novels, sometimes something subversive. He loved to read, himself. I guess that's why people usually go into books, isn't it? Not for the money."

"No, I wouldn't think so," Helmut said.

"He could read for hours at a stretch. Anything, like his bookstore. When he wasn't curled up with an adventure novel he'd bury himself in philosophy. Too much for his own good. He loved to talk politics or anything philosophical."

"He raised you on philosophy? That sounds dry. And I'm a German, I'm supposed to love that stuff."

"I know, it makes Papá sound like a bore, but he wasn't, not at all. He was a writer too, always making up stories. And he had a wicked sense of humor. He liked to play practical jokes. Nothing mean, he just loved seeing people laugh.

"He was an idealist at heart," she continued. "Not a compromiser. When the civil war started in Spain, he published a tract and smuggled it into Nationalist territory. They tried to arrest him when Madrid fell. They got my mother, and he turned himself in to serve time in her place, since he was the one they really wanted."

"How did you end up in France?"

"Franco won the war, half the country fled to France. My mother turned Nationalist—at least she claimed as much—but my father couldn't, and wouldn't make pretenses. She came with us to France, but then went back with my brother. Didn't matter if she'd turned Nationalist, the fascists still came for her in the end. She died 'resisting arrest,' whatever that means. My brother in prison, a year later. Typhus, they said."

"I'm sorry."

She nodded. Painful memories, not helped by the estrangement between her parents those last couple of years. Papá had sent numerous letters from Paris, but mother always refused his pleas.

"Paris looked like a safe bet at the time. We spoke French and knew the country well. There was trouble with Germany, but nobody took it seriously. I mean, if there was a war, it would probably turn out like the last one, right? Years of trench warfare with life carrying on behind the lines. We didn't count on the *boches* overrunning the country so fast."

"The Germans, as a people, are frequently underestimated."

"Nobody underestimated the Germans. They were terrified of them. It's why France fell apart like it did."

"Sorry, go ahead. Why did the Gestapo arrest your father?"

"My father got a job for the British embassy, translating intercepted documents between Madrid and Berlin. They were worried Franco would join the Axis. The other Spaniards at the embassy were all former Republicans and anti-fascists. We fled the city, reached the coast just as the British and French armies were evacuating Dunkirk. My father bought passage on a fishing boat—he said it was for both of us—but he lied. He couldn't get us both out, so he was going to send me on alone."

She hesitated at the horrible memories of her struggle through Dunkirk. The bombings, the dead bodies. The screaming women and children. A man's leg, lying in the road.

Helmut said nothing, and at last she regained control and was able to continue.

"I couldn't leave him, so I went back."

"You should have gone. He made a great sacrifice."

"That's where you're wrong, Helmut. And so was my father. Either together or not at all."

"And what happened?"

"I begged, threatened, lied my way back to the hotel where he was waiting out the siege with the rest of the low-level embassy staff. I got there too late. Or not late enough, depending on your point of view."

Was that right? Would it have been better if she'd arrived ten minutes later, when the Germans had taken everyone away? If she hadn't seen Colonel Hoekman, hadn't known any of it?

"The Germans had figured out who they were by then, and were lining them up against the wall. It looked like they were going to gun them down. I came running, I had to stop it."

"Maybe they weren't going to kill them. Maybe they were just searching."

"Well, yes, I know that now. They took some of them away, but most of them they let go. How could I know?"

"You couldn't. Don't blame yourself."

"As soon as they figured out who I was, the Germans singled my father out for a more rigorous search." She pressed her fingertips to her temples, wishing she could erase the horrible memories. "It was all my fault."

"How was it your fault? It was nothing more than bad luck. You were trying to help."

"No, it was my fault. Even after that, we still almost got away. They took out my father's trunk and searched it. He had his questionable books and papers but it was all in Spanish. They didn't see what he'd written about the Germans in Spain. They confiscated everything, but you could see it in the officer's eyes. He was disappointed, but he was going to let us go. There were too many other suspicious people, and not enough Germans to hold them all and they could only fit the most important embassy staff in the truck."

"You're lucky you were in France," Helmut said. "In the Ukraine they would've taken you off the road, shot you just to be sure."

"Yeah, lucky us."

"I'm sorry, I didn't mean it that way."

"I know it could be worse. I could be a Jew or a Pole or a communist. I could be my brother. He's dead. It's just hard to feel fortunate given everything I've been through."

"I understand, it came out wrong. So what happened?"

"The officer decided to give us one last humiliation before sending us on our way. He barked something at his men and they stripped me naked in front of everyone. As soon as they started groping me, my father lost control."

She took a deep breath. Helmut squeezed her hand.

"The officer threw him to the ground. I begged Papá to be still, but by the time he stopped it was too late. They beat him. And the officer wanted more. He said his men would rape me unless Papá confessed everything."

"Confess what?"

"Exactly. He had nothing to confess. He was just a translator, he wasn't a spy."

"The officer?" Helmut asked. "Was it—?"

"Yes, it was. Hans Hoekman. I don't think he was a colonel then."

"The bastard."

"Of course Papá confessed. He said he was a communist.

It was sort of true, I guess. He helpfully explained his books and papers, everything they hadn't understood before. 'Don't worry, *hija*,' he said, 'I haven't done anything, they'll let me go.' I knew he was lying. It's not like the fascists in Spain hadn't already taught me better."

"And they arrested him?" Helmut asked.

"Dragged him away and let me go. Hoekman kept his word. His men left me alone after that. I wish they hadn't. I wish they'd raped me and my father had kept his mouth shut. I could have taken it."

"That's a horrible thing to say." A terrible look came over Helmut's face and he looked out the window. When he returned his gaze, the look was gone. "It was a great thing your father did. He must love you very much."

"I know it, I never stop thinking about it. I looked for him, I wrote letters to the police and to Vichy. I bribed a French official. I queued for days at the German embassy. Nobody told me anything."

"So what did you do, how did you survive?"

"I sold my father's possessions and I looked for work. There wasn't much, but I did what I could. Laundry once, sweeping. Even some trash picking. But there were still things I told myself I wouldn't do. I despised girls like Christine, I never would have sold myself. I didn't understand they were just girls trying to survive, like anyone else."

"Then how did you end up at Le Coq Rouge?"

"I was desperate, and I met Christine, who got me a job washing dishes. Leblanc fed me leftovers, but there was no salary. I still wouldn't have turned to prostitution, but then Hoekman came into the restaurant and I could tell he was going to return. Luck, I guess."

"Not so lucky. You were smart to get a job where the Germans come."

"I didn't think about that at the time," she admitted. "I was just hungry. But then I discovered it was a great place to watch for Germans and eventually Hoekman came in. The night they arrested Roger was my first night as a hostess."

"With the idea of seducing Hoekman?"

"Yes, exactly. I'd seduce him and convince him to release my father."

"It's a horrible thing to become the lover of the man who arrested your father."

"But you know what," she said. "I never slept with him. I was going to, but you saved me."

"I didn't save you, you saved yourself. Not many people can do that. This war crushes people, but you managed to fight through it and come out on top. And you found your father."

"I can't believe it. After all this time. It's almost too wonderful to believe."

Gabriela took a deep breath. Helmut was still holding her hand. She felt an unfamiliar flood of emotions. A warmth that spread through her body with such a rush that she felt light headed.

Helmut must have seen it on her face, or maybe he was feeling the same thing, because suddenly he was leaning forward. Their lips met. There was nothing tentative in his kiss. He held her in a fierce embrace.

She could feel his hunger. It was almost desperate. And she wanted him with such a need that it overwhelmed her. Her heart hammered. Was the door of the private compartment locked? How quickly could they be out of their clothes? How long until the train pulled into the station? She didn't care. She wanted him.

But then Helmut pulled back. "What?" she asked. "Is something wrong? We have time."

He flushed. "I'm sorry, I shouldn't have done that."

"You mean Alfonse?" She was having a hard time catching her breath. "He's just...that is, I don't want to say he's just a ration book, but you know I don't love him. I was doing what I needed to survive and if we — "

"No, I know what that's about. I'm sure Alfonse doesn't feel any special attachment for you, either. Not that he'd be happy about what I just did, but frankly, I don't give a damn about that. The thing is, I'm married."

"Oh, of course. I'm so sorry, I can't believe I forgot."

"There's so much distance between Loise and me, and there's the war, and, well, it's easy to pretend that I'm not married, or that it doesn't matter. Circumstances, you know. I could do whatever, and she'd probably forgive me. She already has, and I haven't even done anything. But it still matters, I still need to remember that. I'm married," he repeated, as if trying to convince himself.

"I'm sorry," she said again. "I forgot."

"Don't be sorry, it's not your job to remember. That's my job." He stood up, made for the door. "I've got to get some air. I'll be back in a few minutes."

She watched him leave, confused.

⚡⚡

Helmut wasn't much of a smoker, didn't even carry a cigarette case, although he enjoyed a cigar when offered one, but he understood the appeal. He needed something to calm his nerves. And he was torn by guilt and desire.

"I can't do it," he muttered.

A man pushed by in the corridor. The train rattled and Helmut caught his balance against the wall.

Gaby was there, he had her. A few seconds longer and she'd have torn off her clothes. She wanted him, she was dying with desire.

It was probably good for his plans that he'd walked away.

Her desire would build even in absence. God knows his own was about to explode. He could take her to her father, let her emotions climb until they left her wrecked, and then take her to a hotel room. Too late to return to Paris today. A glance, a touch, a sympathetic word, and the seduction would be complete.

They would make love, then make love again. By the time they left the hotel she would love him. And that love would be mirrored by the deepest possible hate for Colonel Hoekman. He would whisper his plan, she would agree, and then he would send her on a one-way mission. Gemeiner would be pleased.

What would his wife say? Nothing. She wouldn't even imagine him contemplating such a betrayal. How about Marie-Élise?

Of course you would do it, Marie-Élise would tell him. *Your precious war is more important than love or promises, or trust.*

"I can't do it," he said aloud. "I can't."

But he had to.

⚡⚡

Gabriela shuddered in recognition when she glanced out the window as the train pulled in the station in Strasbourg. It was raining and the droplets running down the window turned the industrial outskirts of the city into an impressionist painting in gray cement and steel.

A single factory stood out from the rest in its angular lines and twin smokestacks. She reached into her purse and unfolded Roger's drawing. It was the same factory, no question, right down to the dark streaks on the windowless walls. The only difference was that Roger had wiped away the surrounding industrial zone and put the factory on a flat plain of dead trees. Here and there were stumps, or maybe the footings of other buildings, long since obliterated.

Helmut peered over her shoulder. "That's creepy."

"Look out the window."

He did. The train inched past the factory. "Even creepier. What's with the rooster with the human face?"

"You don't recognize him?"

"Should I?"

"Roger Leblanc. This is his drawing. He put his own face on the rooster."

"Whatever for?"

"I have no idea."

Helmut looked out the window at the factory, then back to Gabriela with a frown. "How did you get this drawing?"

"Roger dropped it in the park and I picked it up. I've been trying to figure out what it means, especially that rooster on the wall."

"Le Coq Rouge." *The Red Rooster.*

"And why does the rooster have Roger's face on it?" she asked.

"I don't know. You say you found this in the park?" A frown came over his face. "But when? Hoekman arrested him weeks ago. If he'd seen this place already, then why —"

"Your timing is off," she said. "I saw him two days ago, in the Bois de Boulogne. He was with his friends, a bunch of zazous. The JPF beat them and then there was a mass arrest."

"Two days ago? You saw him in the Bois de Boulogne two days ago? How is that even possible?"

She told him how Christine had spotted Roger in the Bois de Boulogne and how they'd tracked him to an isolated corner of the park. How she and Christine had returned dressed as zazous and found Roger drawing by himself. And about the attack.

The train came to a complete stop and an official knocked on the door, checked their transit papers. He glanced at Helmut, studied Gabriela, then said something in German. Helmut nodded. The official left them alone.

"He says ten minutes, then we can get off," Helmut said. He was silent for a long moment, looking out the window at the factory and occasionally glancing back to Roger's drawing. "I'd heard the Gestapo arrested several dozen zazous. They're being shipped off to work details. That must be the raid you saw. But this part about Roger, how is he free?"

"That's what I've been asking myself."

"There's only one answer. You remember what I told you?"

"You said if I saw Roger Leblanc free, I should be suspicious."

"I thought it was a rhetorical question. But you'd actually seen him, hadn't you."

"It's Roger's doing, isn't it? Hoekman let him go and he promised to spy for the Gestapo in return. He told them about the secret zazous parties in the Bois de Boulogne and that's how they arrested them. He was a collaborator. He's denounced his friends."

"I'm afraid so."

It was one thing to guess, another to hear it laid out, naked and ugly. "How could he do such a horrible thing?"

"Who knows? We don't know what they did to him or what they threatened. These are desperate times, Gaby. People resort to desperate measures."

"You're never so desperate as to betray people you love."

Helmut fell silent with a troubled expression. She wondered what horrors he'd seen to make him doubt what she thought a self-evident declaration.

"Roger must have come through this train station," she said, "but why would he draw that particular building?"

"They brought him here, that's what must have happened." He looked out the window. "It's the same place they keep your father."

She caught her breath. "My father's working in a factory? And that's what Roger was doing? What is it, work duty for dissidents?" She felt a rising hope. Her father, alive and on a labor crew. He'd be fed, at least. Probably healthy enough to keep working.

Helmut shook his head. His expression was grim. "It's not a factory, Gaby."

"It's not? Then what is it?"

"It's an insane asylum."

CHAPTER TWENTY-ONE

THE STRASBOURG CENTER FOR THE *Criminally Insane.*
The wording over the gate was in French, Alsatian, and German. Both the Alsatian and the German were decipherable only through their proximity to the French, but the German, with its Gothic letters, appeared especially menacing. One word stood out: *geisteskrank.*

Below: *Deadly Force Zone - Unauthorized Access Forbidden.*

A pall of coal smoke and a chemical smell hung over the town. It had stained the factories, and the windowless, cement thrust of the asylum was uglier than most. Dark streaks down the side of the building. An oily smoke seeped from the stacks.

Gabriela and Helmut approached the gates. The feeling of dread had been swelling since they stepped off the train.

"Papá isn't insane."

"It does look like a factory," Helmut muttered. "We've even industrialized insanity."

"I'm telling you, there's nothing wrong with him. He's not insane, never has been."

"That's the wonder of the thing. We're in a war and that's what industry does in war, when faced with shortages. It finds substitute materials. You don't have enough petrol so you make it from coal. Not enough grain, you invade Poland. There weren't enough insane people in the Reich, so we had to make more."

A pair of chain fences surrounded the building at roughly fifty meters. Curled bundles of razor wire filled the space between the fences and looped cruelly along the top. A guard post squatted outside the gates, with a second inside the second fence. A guard at the first post inspected their papers while a second kept his submachine gun trained on them. Helmut showed his papers and answered the questions curtly in German. The guards let them pass.

To enter the compound was to enter another world. A world of concentration camps, islands of suffering that dotted the landscape. She heard the whispered names in her head: Fort de Romainville, Le Vernet, Buchenwald. They devoured people.

The double barrier of chain link and razor wire blocked most of the view of the outside world, except for a handful of buildings that rose on the right side just high enough to see. From behind came the hiss of train brakes. In front, a desolate expanse between the gates and the asylum stairs. Bare dirt, without a tree or blade of grass. Two more guards stood by the door, alert as they approached.

Helmut showed his papers, but the guards waved them in without further inspection.

The smell of formaldehyde and harsh chemical cleaners assaulted her as she entered. The floors in the foyer were bare linoleum, alternating green and white squares, visibly worn from years of foot traffic.

A man in a white lab coat and rubber gloves to the elbow emerged from a door to the left. A nurse pushing a man in a wheelchair came from the hallway to the left and turned onto the main corridor. The eyes of the man in the wheelchair were bloodshot, vacant. He wore a dingy gray straightjacket and a leather mask that covered his mouth and strapped at the back of the head.

Gabriela stared, transfixed with dread. As they passed, the man's eyes swung in her direction and she drew back in horror. The nurse snapped something in German and jerked his wheelchair around so he could no longer make eye contact.

Helmut took her arm. "You can do this."

"Yes, I can. I can do this and I will."

Helmut spoke with a doctor in a white lab coat, who pointed down the hall and gave instructions in German.

They passed through another locked and guarded door. Beyond lay a long hallway with doors on either side. Each door had a barred opening high up and a window lower down with a slider. The smell of industrial cleaners grew stronger the deeper they penetrated the building, mixed with the occasional sharp tang of something else from the rooms they passed.

Their footsteps on the bare cement were the only sound for most of the hallway and then someone stirred in a room to their right. A man hurled himself against the door and screamed in French, so high-pitched and babbling she could only pick out a few words. And then, as they continued, he lapsed into loud, shuddering sobs.

"*Maman! Où est ma maman?*"

Gabriela couldn't help herself. "Who are you?" she asked in French. "What is your name?"

But he only screamed incoherently.

Her French woke the other inmates. The hallway filled with a clamor of shouting, moans, pleas. A woman cried in Italian. Begging, pleading.

"What?" she said. "I can't understand. Do you speak French?"

Helmut pulled her along. "Gaby, listen to me. You can't, you'll just cause trouble. Only your father, that's all we can see. These other people...there's nothing you can do."

"My god." Gabriela resisted the urge to clamp her hands

over her ears. "How long has my papá been here?"

"I don't know," Helmut said. "At least two years."

Two years! Who could survive two years in such a place? Another doctor passed, pushing a cart. There were straps and electrical devices, forceps and long syringes. Something dark and greasy stained his white apron.

"Are they really doctors?" she asked. "Please tell me they're not."

"Real doctors, real nurses."

"But doctors and nurses help people, they don't...do they?"

"Sometimes they do." His voice was grim.

"But so many, all in one place?"

"These people always exist. They're everywhere in small numbers. What happens when cruelty is no longer proscribed? When sadistic behavior is not just tolerated, but sanctioned? Even enforced?" He shook his head. "It's not hard to staff insane asylums. Doctors, nurses, guards, there are always volunteers."

He started to say something else, but they pushed through another door and an orderly demanded something. Helmut pulled out his papers.

The orderly gestured for them to follow. "*Kommen Sie mit mir.*"

The man stopped in front of one of the doors and took out a ring of keys, counted through them one after another. This hall was quieter. In fact, Gabriela would have thought the cells empty, except for a solitary cough toward the end.

The orderly swung the door open and gave an expansive, almost ironic gesture for them to enter. Gabriela stepped through, heart pounding.

Dear god, let him be okay. Let him be healthy.

A man sat in a chair, his back to the door, facing the corner. He wore no restraints and rested his hands on his lap. There was a cot attached to the wall with a single, thin blanket. A metal chamber pot in the corner. One wall was scratched and gouged, as if by the claws of some animal, trying desperately to escape from its cell.

No books, no papers, nothing to occupy his hands or his mind. A bare stone wall, bare concrete floor. A single dim light bulb overhead. Two years in this place? Her father had once claimed it was impossible to be bored, there were too many things to read and learn. But he'd never imagined a room three meters by three meters, with nothing but a single light bulb to stare at day after hellish day.

"Go to him," Helmut murmured.

His words jolted her from her stupor. *"Papá? Soy yo, tu hijita. Ya vengo por ti."*

Her father didn't answer, didn't turn, even as she crossed to his side. She bent and took his hands. For a second she thought it was the wrong room; this couldn't be her father. He looked so old. His face drawn, his hair gone gray, face unshaven for several days. There was no spark in his eyes, no upturned mouth like she remembered. But the nose, the jaw, the cheekbones; it was him.

His once strong hands and arms were weak and trembling as she picked them up. She kissed his face. He smelled old and sick. He didn't look at her or respond to her touch or words.

"Papá, I came, I told you I would. I'm so sorry it took so long. Papá, it's me, Gabriela. Papá?"

No response.

"Papá!" Gabriela let go of his hands, which flopped to his side, and took his face in her hands. "What's wrong? Can't you see me? It's your daughter, me, Gabriela, Papá, for god's sake, can you hear me?" She turned to Helmut in a panic. "What's wrong with him? Why isn't he answering?"

"Oh," Helmut said. His face was pale. "I didn't know."

He stepped forward and touched her father's forehead and

she saw for the first time the scar traced in a curve above the eyebrows. Raised and pink, where someone had carved into him. A long, angry gash across the skull.

"What is it? What did they do?" She heard her voice as if from a distance, a high-pitched sound, like a scream from one of the asylum cells.

"He's been cut." Helmut spoke with an audible shudder. "They cut through his skull across here and inserted something into the brain. I've heard of this, it's called a lobotomy."

"A what? For god's sake, what is that?"

"They stick something in and they stir it around to break up part of the brain."

"No! No, they couldn't. Why would they do such a thing?"

"It's to pacify the criminally insane. But he's so non-responsive, they must have given him an especially violent surgery."

"He wasn't insane!" That distant screaming again. "He wasn't insane!"

She couldn't tell if she were screaming or if that sound came from her head. A tiny, distant part of her brain observed that this must be what it felt like to be actually, genuinely insane. Right before they cut open your skull and stirred your brains as casually as if they were a pair of egg yolks.

She felt violently ill. She turned, coughed twice as her stomach heaved and she tried to force it down. And then she threw up, not on the floor, but all down the front of her dress. Helmut caught her as she fell. She fought to regain her balance. He was wearing some of her vomit.

The door opened to their rear. The orderly stood there with a frown. "*Fraulein?*"

His face was a mask of perfect sanctimony, self-righteous priggery. She wanted to tear that look off his face, to gouge out his eyes. To smash his head against the stone wall again and again until *he* was the one with the senseless look.

Gabriela lunged at him with a cry of rage. He staggered back, seemingly caught unaware, and lifted his hands. She was about to catch him, her only thought to go for his eyes, when Helmut grabbed her arms.

"Gaby, no! Gaby, listen to me. Not like this."

She tried to pull free, to hit him until he let her go. But he was too strong, he had her hands pinned and she couldn't move, could only wail. "My father, look what this bastard did to him. Look!"

"No, Gaby. He didn't, he's not the one. He's a functionary, a nobody. You can't do anything by hurting him. You'll just get yourself arrested."

"I have to do something. They've destroyed my father, don't you see? Can't you understand?"

"Who took your father, Gaby? Who sent him here? Gaby, who is responsible? It's not this man."

The answer came to her and suddenly everything about this horrible concrete building made sense. It was a giant snake cage, with a man dropping mice down to be destroyed inside.

"Colonel Hoekman," she said. "He's the one. He did this."

ᛋᛋ

Gabriela spent a few more minutes with her father before the orderly returned. Helmut argued with him and managed to send him away. "We only have ten more minutes."

She stroked her father's hair, then rubbed his neck. Scars ran like ribbons down his back; she could feel them through his gown. A lump on one shoulder, like a broken bone that had improperly healed. None of it seemed to cause him any pain.

And yet he wasn't completely unresponsive. He turned at one point and stared at her with liquid eyes and she swore she saw a glint of recognition.

"Oh, Papá, I'm so sorry. I love you so much."

He gave a deep sigh, then turned back to the corner.

It wasn't ten minutes, more like five, before the orderly returned. Helmut argued, but the man was insistent. A soldier with a submachine gun appeared in the hallway and at last Helmut said they had to go.

"No, I won't."

"You have to," he said in a gentle voice. He pried her fingers from the chair.

"Papá, I'll be back for you."

She was in a daze as Helmut led her back through the building. The same man was screaming for his mother and they wheeled a man past on a cart who stared at the ceiling with eyes so glazed she thought he was dead. At last they were out of the damnable place and outside. Even the smoggy air of Strasbourg was a relief after the formaldehyde and ammonia and blood that suffocated her lungs.

She glanced back at the building as they reached the chain link gates, up to the roof where Roger had drawn the rooster with his face. "I know what made him do it."

"Hmm?" Helmut looked up from staring at his hands.

"I know why Roger turned on his friends. They took him here and showed me my father. Or someone like him."

"Perhaps."

"It was an ugly thing Roger did," Gabriela said. "His friends are going to suffer for it. But imagine they strap you into a chair and draw a line across your skull. You see a saw and a chisel on a tray and other horrible tools. The doctor comes and there's blood on his apron and he's wearing rubber gloves and a mask, so you can only see his eyes. You're screaming, but nobody seems to be paying attention."

"Gaby, please, stop. Don't do this to yourself."

"Then they wheel my father past. There's a scar on his forehead that matches what they've drawn on your own skull.

He's alive, but there's nothing behind his eyes but an empty hole. Colonel Hoekman comes into the room then and you stop screaming, but only because the terror has sucked it out of you. He tells you what you have to do for the Gestapo and you beg him to let you do more. You'll betray anyone, denounce anyone. You'll prove how useful you can be, because there's no torture or death that's worse than the empty hole."

Helmut stared at her with a horrified expression. "Where did that come from?"

She couldn't say anything, just turned away from Helmut to face the train station. She could feel the asylum squatting behind her, gray and menacing. Her father remained inside.

CHAPTER TWENTY-TWO

I T WAS TOO LATE TO return to Paris, but Helmut didn't want to stay in Strasbourg. "I've found that constant air raid sirens and bombings tend to ruin a good night's sleep."

Gabriela didn't care. She walked in a choking smog. It was all she could do to take her next breath.

The line was bombed out near Nancy, so they took the train south instead and stopped in a village near Mulhouse, at a hotel a few blocks from the train station. The owner spoke German to Helmut, Alsatian to his wife, but then, when she passed later on her way to the water closet, she overheard them speaking French behind closed doors.

There was hot water and she took a bath. She scrubbed herself until she couldn't smell any formaldehyde, vomit, or ammonia. Just the scent of lavender soap. When she came out, wrapped in towels, she discovered Helmut had gone into the village and found her a change of clothes.

The hotel room was small but clean, with a hot, noisy radiator. Helmut retrieved a kettle from the kitchen downstairs and made her tea, mixed with brandy. By the second cup she felt herself relaxing. Or maybe it was impossible to sustain the anger, horror, and despair she'd felt since seeing her father.

It wasn't fair. After everything her father had suffered and years of searching for him. They deserved a happy ending, like in one of the books from the store.

Helmut stood by the window, parted the curtains to look down to the street.

"The problem is," she said, "I want two things and I can't have them both."

"What two things?"

"First, I've got to get my father out of there. Get him out and find a safe place where I can take care of him."

"It won't be easy. It was hard enough getting in to see him. And expensive. Not to mention dangerous. I took some risks."

"You have no idea how grateful I am."

He sat on the edge of the bed. "It's nothing. I wish I could do more."

"So you don't think it can be done. Get my father out, I mean."

"I didn't say that," Helmut said. "I said it won't be easy. Let me think about it. What's the other thing?"

"I want Hoekman to pay for what he did."

"If there were any justice, he'd hang for his crimes. The man is a monster. But what could you possibly do?"

"You're right, it's probably even more hopeless than helping my father. Like you said, people like Hoekman profit from their cruelty these days. But there's got to be a way."

He was quiet for a long moment, then said in a quiet voice, "There are other ways to get justice. Quicker, more sure ways."

"Tell me."

"Did they search you the last time Colonel Hoekman summoned you?"

"No. The first time, yes. I used to carry a knife for protection, and he took it. Second time, he didn't bother. He must have known I wouldn't dare."

"So you could easily conceal something on your person next time you saw him."

"I suppose I could. Another knife, maybe, if I could get one."

"A knife isn't good enough. He'd overpower you and take it. You need a gun."

"Could you get me one?"

"I could. In fact, I've already got one. There's a Mauser semi-automatic pistol hidden in my luggage."

The idea was tempting. She imagined the look on Hoekman's face as she pulled the trigger. When he realized that he was about to suffer for his crimes. When he looked into her eyes and saw, *knew*, why she was killing him.

"I'd never survive. They'd hear the gun, come in and arrest me, unless I could kill myself first."

"That's the risk," he said.

"That doesn't matter. Papá deserves whatever sacrifice I make, except that one thing."

"Your father is still alive."

"Exactly. He's still alive and if I kill Hoekman, they'll arrest me and my father will spend the rest of his life in that horrible place. I can't do that, I need to get him out first, then take care of Hoekman."

"Except that as soon as you got your father out, that would be impossible. They'd be looking for you; you'd have to stay in hiding." He shook his head. "No, if you get your father first, you'll have to forget about Hoekman, he'll be untouchable."

"And if I get Hoekman, I can't save my father."

Helmut looked thoughtful. "What if...? No, you should drop the whole idea. It's too dangerous."

"What were you going to say? Tell me," she urged.

"Let's say you get close to Hoekman and take care of him with the gun. If I helped you, if I got you out of there then I could hide you. Smuggle you out of Paris."

"And my father?"

"Supposing that at the same time you were shooting

Hoekman there was a fire in the records room at the insane asylum. With the arresting agent dead, his records destroyed, your father would be just another patient. At least until they sort through Hoekman's files and figure out his cases. In the meanwhile, I'll pay someone to look the other way while we wheel your father out of the asylum."

She put down her drink and sat next to him on the bed. "You could do that?"

"I think so."

She took a deep breath. "Do you think I could pull it off? Could I kill Hoekman or would that be throwing my own life away?"

"If you are prepared. If you want it badly enough. Yes. You might get caught in spite of everything, but at least you'd have tried."

"I can't get caught. I can't stop imagining what it would be like to be strapped down on an operating table while they draw a line across my forehead. I couldn't do it, I'm not that strong."

He took her hands. "I swear to you that whatever happens, I won't let that happen."

"If they catch me you'd have to kill me. I can't do it, I can't go through what my father did. Please, could you do that for me? Could you find a way to kill me first?"

"Gaby, if I have to, I'll pull the trigger myself. It would be the hardest, worst thing I'd ever done, but I'd do that for you, I swear it."

She felt such a swelling of emotion that she had to speak. "Helmut, I think I'm falling in love with you."

He stroked her face, stared into her eyes. His were shockingly blue. He was beautiful, almost too pretty to be a man. "I want to make love, Gaby."

Gabriela nodded. "Me, too."

After their crush of passion on the train, she was afraid.

That feeling was unexpected and she didn't know exactly what to do with it. She was more tentative when she reached out this time. He leaned forward and kissed her, not on the mouth, but on the cheek, then the eyelids. He stroked a hand along her face.

Gabriela let out a sigh. She could feel him trembling. A light kiss on her lips.

She undid the top two buttons on his shirt and slid her hand inside. His skin was warm, she could feel his heart beating.

"Oh, Gaby."

"Take off your clothes," she whispered.

But without warning, he pulled away. He groaned and put the heels of his hands to his eyes, shook his head. "I can't do it. It's wrong."

"I'm sorry," she said. "I shouldn't have, I know you're married, I wasn't thinking."

"No, it's not that. It's not you. It's nothing to do with you at all and it's not even about Loise." He rose, paced the short distance between the bed and the window.

"Helmut, what is it, what's wrong?"

"You can't do it. You can't kill Colonel Hoekman. You need to get away from him, go into hiding." He turned around. "I'll help you do it."

"I'm not going into hiding. And you're wrong. I'm strong enough to do this."

"No, you can't. And you won't. I won't let you use my gun, I won't help you in any way. I'll help you hide, that's what I'll do."

"Helmut, for god's sake, you practically talked me into it yourself."

"Well, I changed my mind, is that so hard to understand?"

"I know the risks, I know it's dangerous, and I still think I can do it."

"You think? You think? There's no *thinking* you can do it, there's only doing on one hand and dying on the other. A horrible, nasty death. No, you can't. You'll die, I promise you. And they'll make you suffer."

"I won't die! I've got too many reasons to stay alive."

"Reasons? You think that matters? The world is full of people with good reasons to stay alive. Some of them are dying right now."

She thrust out her chin. "I'm going to do it. There's nothing you can do or say to talk me out of it. Either you're going to help me or I'm going to do it on my own."

Helmut started to say something, but then his mouth snapped shut. It was hard to say what he was thinking. Of course, all the same arguments that she'd used herself minutes ago still held. If she killed Hoekman on her own, who would help her father? She'd never get him out. Helmut had to know that, had to wonder if she was serious.

He stood up, buttoned his shirt and headed for the door without saying a word.

"Helmut?"

"I'm sorry, I need some air. I'll be downstairs."

And with that he was gone.

ꜱꜱ

Helmut retreated to the hotel bar. He intended to drink himself senseless. He'd maintain just enough consciousness to crawl into bed and pass out. In the morning he'd think more clearly.

He ordered a straight whiskey and sat by himself near the fireplace. It crackled with a small, but cheery fire. The only other clients in the bar were two men speaking in Alsatian. He couldn't understand a word. Good. He downed the liquor, waved his hand for another, then a third.

"Too much strong drink can have deleterious effects on the

mind," a man said from behind his shoulder.

He turned, startled, to see Gemeiner standing with a sardonic smile at his lips. Gemeiner wore a business suit and not his uniform. He took a seat next to Helmut.

Helmut returned to his drink. "I thought you never left Germany."

"Alsace is Germany now, haven't you heard?"

"What are you doing here?"

Gemeiner pulled up a chair. "Have you bedded the girl yet?"

"Not yet, no. She's ready though. I'll do it when I go back."

"Not if you don't stop drinking. At that rate, you'll be sleeping on the floor in a puddle of your own vomit."

"I know my limits. She's already offered herself to me."

"So why didn't you do it?"

"Waiting for the right moment. You can't rush these things."

"Well, enjoy yourself," Gemeiner said. "It's a hell of a job, you have to enjoy the extras when they come."

"Goddammit."

"Oh, come on. I know what you're going through, and I appreciate it, I do. But compared to what that girl gave up, is going to give up, what are your problems?"

"Exactly right," Helmut said. "She's agreed to kill Hoekman. She's insisting on it, in fact."

Insisting on it even when he tried to talk her out of it. He couldn't go through with it, he just couldn't.

"And I think she can pull it off," he continued. "She'll go in there, gun down the bastard, and there will be a car waiting out front to carry her to safety."

"Only it won't be you in the car," Gemeiner said, "it will be two hired men. And they'll kill her."

The levity was gone from Gemeiner's voice, replaced by a grim certainty. Good thing, too. Helmut was ready to throw himself at the man, beat him senseless. One more joke would have pushed him over the edge.

"No, I can't do that," Helmut said. "I've got to do it myself."

"Don't be a fool."

"I'm not being a fool, I'm doing what's right. If I'm going to sign off on her death, I've got to be a man and do it myself. Otherwise, I'm no better than the people we're fighting, no better than Hans Hoekman."

"Oh, Hoekman would happily do it himself. He loves that sort of thing."

"You know what I mean."

"You know your problem?" Gemeiner asked. "You let yourself get emotionally attached."

"Is there some other way? Because please, tell me if there is."

"The thing is, I can't trust you any more. Your intentions are right, but once she steps into the car, you won't be able to follow through. You'll remember her soft kisses, her caresses and then you'll think, 'It wouldn't be so bad, would it, to let her live? We could make it look like she died without actually killing her.' And then you'll disobey orders. That's why it's got to be someone else."

Helmut had nothing to say to this. The man was almost right, in fact, but not quite. Truth was, he'd already decided as much, he didn't intend to kill her at all. He was going to claim he had, that was all. Sure, Gemeiner insisted that without a body and a note, the Gestapo wouldn't believe it was a crime of passion. They'd keep digging, but with more men, more resources, until they uncovered the conspiracy. But Helmut was sure he could work out something almost as good. He just needed to think of something.

"You never answered the question," Helmut said. "What *are* you doing here?"

If Gemeiner's voice had been serious before, it now sounded positively grim. "We lost another man to the Gestapo."

"Really, who?"

"Who is unimportant, except that he knew too much, was too critical to our plans."

Helmut felt a tight band of worry in his gut. "Did they take him alive?"

"I don't know. He was our man on the inside, so he was the one who would have fed us the very information we are now lacking. Did he bite his capsule in time? We have no way of knowing."

"And if he didn't?"

"Then we are all dead. The safest thing, in fact, would be to fall back on our contingency plans. You have one, I presume?"

"Yes, of course."

His contingency plan was a hundred thousand Swiss francs in Geneva and ninety thousand American dollars in a safe-deposit box in Buenos Aires. Enough to flee Europe and rebuild somewhere else. Nobody knew about this contingency, not even Loise.

"That's the safest course," Gemeiner said. "But the coward's way out." He shook his head. "I don't intend to back out. There's too much at stake, we're too close. If I die, so be it. I assume you feel the same way."

"Let's say your man killed himself," Helmut said. He had finished his drink, but when the bartender on the other side of the room caught his eye with an implied question about refills, he shook his head. "What do we lose besides intelligence?"

"We lose our liaison with Vichy and the American General."

Helmut drew in his breath. "That's a hell of a lot of responsibility for one man."

"We didn't have much choice in the matter. But that's not all. Our man had arranged to transport the gold to Marseille, but how? With whom? I have no idea. I know where the gold is, but that's all."

"*Scheiss.*"

"What we need is someone who can move freely throughout France, who can speak English and French. Someone who already knows our contact in Vichy."

Suddenly, he understood everything. "So this is what brings you out of Germany. It's not to keep an eye on me, it's to give me this."

"You are a smart man."

"I don't know Brun, I've met him exactly one time."

"That's one time more than anyone else."

"And I certainly don't understand the military situation. As soon as I open my mouth to Brun and the American agent, they'll know I'm hopelessly ignorant."

"All you need to know is that the French need to stall the German Seventh and hope the Italians are too weak to push in from the east. The operational details are for the Americans and the French to work out.

"But all of this hinges on evading the Gestapo," Gemeiner added. "Hoekman has taken down two of our men. He knows there is someone in requisitions and suspects this person is Major Ostermann."

"It's a stroke of luck that he's focused on Alfonse," Helmut said.

"Yes, but it can't last. Ostermann was protected by his position, a few well-placed friends in the Wehrmacht, and the fact that Hoekman had nothing but suspicions. He has more than suspicions now. An hour after he has Ostermann under questioning he'll learn his mistake. Another hour of questioning will turn his attention to you."

"Hoekman must be killed."

"I have an Opel outside with a full tank of petrol. I want to drive you to the Egyptienne."

"Tonight? You can't possibly be serious. It's seven

o'clock already."

Gemeiner looked at his wristwatch. "Quarter of."

"There are two military checkpoints before we reach the border of Alsace. At least two more between there and Paris. Six hours drive, add three, maybe four, five hours at checkpoints, depending on luck...it's impossible."

"And don't forget, you have to go upstairs and sleep with the girl, first."

"And how long are you allotting for that?" he scoffed.

"An hour, two tops. Meanwhile, I'm going to make a few phone calls, drive out to the first checkpoint just outside the city — that will be the toughest one — and prepare the groundwork. By the time you finish seducing the girl — "

"Gabriela. She has a name."

"By the time you finish seducing the girl," he repeated, "I'll have the journey trimmed to seven hours, tops."

"You're serious, aren't you?"

"Absolutely."

"Okay, so I go upstairs, sleep with Gabriela. Let's say it takes me an hour. Seven hours on the road, just to be safe. We arrive in Paris at three in the morning."

"And there's a small problem entering the city. I know the colonel in charge of the checkpoints that run in a ring from Saint-Denis, around the east side, and down to the south of Paris. A real by-the-books officer. I can't drive into the city through any of those checkpoints. Too risky that I'll be spotted. The regime thinks I'm in Kiev."

"At least we still hold Kiev."

"For now. There's not much of a city left. You think Paris is hungry."

"You don't have to tell me," Helmut said. "I've got requisitioning contacts in the Ukraine. The Kievans have been deemed 'superfluous eaters.'"

"If the Gestapo discovers me in Paris, I'll find myself a superfluous breather." Gemeiner shook his head. "I can't be seen on the east side and we don't have time to circle around and approach from the west. We'll stop and I'll climb in the trunk before we reach the city."

"Okay, so we make our way to the Egyptienne. It's now three o'clock in the morning."

"Where the party will still be in full-swing, from what I understand."

"True, but Hoekman won't be there," Helmut said. "He'll be in bed, resting up for a full day of arrests and torture."

"Unless he has just received an urgent message from Gabriela that she has information about the *simple soldat.* She'll insist on meeting him at the Egyptienne for her own safety. A back room, the kind reserved for private debauchery. He'll have no reason to suspect a trap, not in such a public place. Soon as they're alone, she pulls out a gun, and murders him."

"Hmm."

"The girl thinks we're waiting to drive her to safety." Gemeiner said. "Instead, I kill her, dump her in the Seine with a soggy, but readable suicide note."

There was a sick feeling in his stomach.

Gemeiner leaned over and rested a hand on his shoulder. "It's a war, my friend. Horrible things happen. We can't go soft."

"I'm not getting soft."

He pulled his hand away. "Good, there's no room for it."

"And me? Where am I while you're stabbing her in the back?"

"In a bakery truck, speeding toward the French Riviera with a cargo full of gold."

"Just like that?" Helmut asked.

"Just like that. Or rather, as the French would say: *voila tout.*"

CHAPTER TWENTY-THREE

Helmut found Gabriela sitting in the chair by the window when he returned.

"Helmut, I don't know what's wrong, but I think we should talk. First of all—"

"Shhh, please. I have to think."

He couldn't figure out how to wiggle free from the situation.

Technically, there was little fault with Gemeiner's plan. Helmut believed the man could handle the checkpoints. He thought Hoekman would fall for the trap. Gabriela had the nerve to pull the trigger. There might be some difficulty getting her out of the Egyptienne after she fired the pistol, but he guessed Gemeiner had a plan for that.

The plan was risky, of course, with a million things that could go wrong. But that described everything these days. Still, it stood an excellent chance of succeeding. Other than that, it was all wrong.

"Helmut?"

"Just a minute."

"You're scaring me. Talk to me, please."

"I've got to think. Please, give me a moment."

"This isn't about what just happened between us, is it?"

"No, it's not," he admitted.

"Something's wrong. No, something *new* is wrong."

A hint of a plan started to form in his head. He turned to Gabriela. "Two things happened you might find interesting. First, I ran into a friend downstairs at the bar. He offered to drive us to Paris tonight."

"Tonight? Well, if that's what you want," she said after a moment of hesitation. "We can go back instead of spending the night here."

"Second, I learned Colonel Hoekman is going to be at the Egyptienne tonight. We'll get there before he leaves, you can lure him to the back room and we can be done with the matter once and for all."

"Oh."

"Unless you're not ready, if you don't think you can do it. If you need more time..."

"I can do it."

"Are you sure?"

She drew in her breath. Again, a long moment of silence. "Helmut, is there something you're not telling me?"

"There are a lot of somethings."

"You left here insisting you wouldn't let me kill Hoekman." A slight tension in her voice. "Downstairs, you happen to run into a friend who somehow knows where a Gestapo agent will be several hours from now."

"I know, it's funny how that happened, but—"

"Funny? Don't insult me by claiming this is a coincidence."

"Listen to me for a second. You already know Hoekman is my enemy. I'd like nothing better than to see him dead. You might be the tool to do that."

"The tool? I'm a tool?"

"No, not a tool. That was a poor choice of words. Listen, we both need the same thing, is that so bad?"

"There's something wrong here. Why do I feel like you've been lying to me?"

"I haven't told you the whole truth, no."

"Oh, Helmut." There was disappointment in her voice. "I should have known. You're just a man, you just wanted what a man wants."

"What a man wants? If that's all I wanted, I would have slept with you just now. I would have sent you in there to your death but I tried to talk you out of it. Don't pin crimes on me I never did."

She walked to the curtain, lifted the corner, and peered down at the street. When she turned back, the anger was gone from her face, replaced by something flat and cynical. "I see. It's a practical relationship. Well, let's not pretend it's something it's not or pretend we had something we didn't."

"I know I should have told you more, told you earlier," he said. "You're angry, I understand. You have a right to be."

"Don't be an idiot. I saw my father with part of his brain cut out. I tried to seduce the man who arrested him. I spread my legs for your friend so I could get something to eat. And I just told a *boche* war profiteer that I was falling in love with him."

Her words felt like a punch to the gut.

"Well, are you going to say anything?" she demanded. "What's this all about? Who are you and what do you want?"

"I'll be honest with you," he said.

"I doubt it."

"Yes, I will. I won't tell you everything, but everything I say will be the truth."

"Let's hear it."

"I'm an enemy of the Reich."

"Come on, you don't expect me to believe that. I saw you at the rail yard, ordering those men. They were stealing the wealth of France and shipping it east."

"I didn't say I was an enemy of Germany," Helmut said. "But I'm an enemy of the Nazi regime. There are a lot of us.

People try to kill Hitler all the time. They fail, and generally their goal is to overthrow the government and prosecute the war in a more intelligent fashion. We're not like that. We accept that the war is lost, our enemies are too strong and we're surrounded."

"Surrounded all the way from Brittany to the steppes of Russia. Of course."

"That's an illusion. The German war machine is like a runner who sprints to a big early lead, but has nothing left to finish the race. I'm not sure we could beat just the Russians, and with the Americans massing in England and North Africa, it's hopeless."

"Anyone who is not German has figured that out a long time ago. So how do you plan to save Germany if you have no hope?"

"We have no hope of winning the war, but we can choose who we lose to."

"What do you mean?"

"If we lose to the Soviets, Germany dies forever. What takes its place is a crippled client state, populated by the offspring of Soviet troops and their German sex slaves. The German men will finish their short, miserable lives in Siberian work camps."

"And if the Americans win?"

"I don't know what will happen if the Americans and British defeat us, but it will be better. It certainly couldn't be worse."

"This all sounds fine," she said, "but how can you possibly determine which of your enemies defeats you?"

"I can't tell you that part."

"Hmm, but you want me to kill Colonel Hoekman for you. Why?"

"He's a threat to our plan. He's been distracted by Alfonse, but that won't last. We were fortunate. Alfonse isn't and never has been part of our conspiracy."

"Of course not. Alfonse doesn't care about anything but

Alfonse. And he talks too much. Only a fool would include him in a conspiracy."

"Colonel Hoekman is looking for us, that's what brought him back to France, not Alfonse's petty embezzlement."

"Never mind, you don't need to tell me any more. Say I kill Hoekman for you, then what?"

Helmut said, "My friend downstairs doesn't care what happens to his tools after they're used. He's planning to throw you away when he's done with you."

"In other words, I do your dirty work and then you let the Gestapo kill me?"

"Not quite, but close enough. Don't worry, I've got a plan to get you out of there. I'm not going to let anything bad happen."

"How very noble of you."

⚡⚡

Downstairs, at the phone cabin, Helmut placed a call. He looked first to see if Gemeiner was lurking about, but the older man seemed to have made good on his word to prepare the way at the first checkpoint. There was no sign of him or of his Opel.

The call took most of his phone tokens and two switchboard transfers. And then the phone rang and rang and rang at the house in Traunstein.

At last Loise picked up. "Hello? Who is it?"

Her voice was small, practically overwhelmed with static. The phone lines were shockingly degraded since last time he'd called.

"Hello, it's me. Are you alone?"

"What? I can barely hear you. Helmut, is that you?"

"Are you alone? Can we talk?"

"What? Helmut? Are you okay?"

"I'm okay. Listen, remember what we talked about last time, about Switzerland? I need you to get out. It's time, you have to go. Tonight, if possible, but if not, first thing in the morning.

You have to get out of the country, do you understand?"

"Helmut? What? Can you repeat that?"

He repeated his instructions, reminded her about the box in the basement with the Swiss francs and the papers and the bank information. Without saying box, basement, or Swiss francs, of course. Couldn't take a chance that a switchboard operator was listening. Again Loise interrupted, unable to hear him, and again he repeated it.

"Did you get all of that? Loise? Loise?"

The line was dead. How much had she heard? Any of it?

He looked down at the tokens in his hand. He didn't have enough to try Germany again and still make the call to Paris. And without the call to Paris, he had nothing.

He called his man in Paris. David Mayer picked up on the second ring.

"David?"

"Who is this?" The voice was cautious.

"It's von Cratz. I'm in Strasbourg and I need your help."

"Hey, boss. Sorry, I didn't recognize your voice. Did you get the Belgian order shipped?"

That was code. *This call is unexpected. Is everything okay?*

"Day after tomorrow," Helmut said, which meant that he was not under any duress. "But let's hope we don't have an overly inquisitive switchboard operator. I'm full of risky calls tonight. My luck is bound to run out."

"You don't have to tell me about risky calls."

"Been chatting with your banker friends again?"

"How did you guess? And ordering gefilte fish for the gathering of the Elders of Zion in Berlin next month. I hear Dr. Goebbels is going to be the keynote speaker. No, I had a conversation with a cousin. Still alive, thank god, far underground."

The tenor of the conversation started to worry Helmut.

If they were being listened to—and every minute they kept chatting increased that likelihood—they'd now put David's cousin at risk and anyone that man might be helping or hiding.

"Listen, David," he said. "Do you have the Dupuis papers?"

"Yes, they're here. Safe."

"Tonight is when you will use them."

"Tonight as in tonight?" David's voice tightened. "What is it?"

"There's no immediate risk. Wake your wife and daughters, pack everything of value. But nothing...religious, you understand. Nothing that would give you away. You have several hours to get them to the train station. You will pick them up in the car in Dijon."

"You're sure? You're positive they're not in danger?"

"I'm in danger, David, not you, and not your family. But I need your help."

"You know I'll do anything for you. Except I can't risk my girls, you understand."

"I'm not lying. You're perfectly safe for the moment. By the time you're no longer safe, your family will be out of the city and you'll be on your way to Geneva. I have an account there under the Dupuis name with more than enough for your needs."

"So this is it, then. I'm done."

"You're done," Helmut confirmed. "Thank you for your years of service, enjoy your retirement, etc. After tonight, it will no longer be safe for you in France, if it ever was. I'll be sorry to lose you, but there's a good chance the Gestapo will roll up the whole organization."

"You're kidding, everything? After all we've worked for?"

"You'll call Henri and Stephan, warn them? They've got their own contingency plans. Oh, and Damien, call him too. He'll take care of the others. Nobody is going hungry."

"Yeah, but boss..."

"There's no other choice. It's over. Do you understand?"

"Yes, sir."

"Now, here's a question. Do you own a gun?"

"Yes, I do."

"What kind of gun?" Helmut asked.

"I keep a Luger in my flat. I also own an Italian Beretta, although I only have a few rounds."

"The German gun will be better. Yes, that will be perfect. Now, can you impersonate an agent of the secret police?"

David laughed. "Remember the rabbi comment? I don't think so."

"Not Gestapo, your German isn't good enough and we have to fool a German. A French agent."

"Well, I still look pretty ethnic. Not too many of our kind in the Franc-garde. Although it helps you haven't let me see the sun in two years."

"Cut your hair to the scalp, that will help."

"And the nose? Got a good surgeon? My brother could pull it off, he looks more Aryan than I do."

"And your brother, where's he?"

"Deported."

"Right. I'll work with what I've got. Wear a hat, keep your head low."

A moment of hesitation. "Yes, okay, I can manage."

"Good, now here's what you'll do."

CHAPTER TWENTY-FOUR

G ABRIELA SPOKE NO GERMAN AND the older man driving the car spoke no French. They fumbled through mutually unintelligible greetings, then never spoke again. The man sat up front and Helmut in back with Gabriela. She didn't want him there.

"Please," Helmut murmured as they pulled away from the hotel, "act as if we're on friendly terms."

She kept her tone sweet. "Why, am I disturbing your aura?"

"It's important that Gemeiner think we're lovers."

"In that case, *mon cherie*, come closer so that we may nuzzle each other's necks and act like foolish children in love."

He slid closer and put his arm around her shoulders. "There, that's much better."

She leaned over and kissed his ear, then whispered, "Go to hell."

He laughed as if she'd said something funny, then spoke in German to Gemeiner for a few minutes. She couldn't read the older man, except that he was deadly serious about whatever they were about.

There was a checkpoint at the edge of Strasbourg, but the soldiers simply waved them through.

"That's a good sign," Helmut said. She didn't respond.

The headlights sliced a narrow beam of light through

the Alsatian countryside. Here and there they saw a light in a farmhouse, but mostly the villages, towns, and countryside remained dark except for the occasional car traveling in the opposite direction. Once, Gemeiner pulled over to let a convoy of military trucks pass. It went on for several minutes before it was done. And then it was the dark road again.

Gabriela had plenty of time to consider Helmut's betrayal. No, not betrayal. His loyalty to his German cause. No doubt he thought his cause very noble and important. No doubt it was just as important to Helmut as her own goal of helping her father was to her.

That didn't soothe the bitterness that consumed her now. The humiliation, the anger, the despair. She'd been vulnerable, needy, even desperate for affection. That night after she'd met Alfonse at Le Coq Rouge she'd responded to him sexually; what hope did she have when touched by actual feelings of tenderness and love? None, really.

Of course it was all fake. Helmut lied his way into her trust.

They reached the second checkpoint. Gemeiner and Helmut went out to argue with the soldiers. She sensed some difficulty explaining their presence on the road at this time of the night. For her part, when a soldier flashed his electric torch into the back seat, she smiled coquettishly. The soldier returned a cheerful grin.

"That was the hardest part," Helmut said when he returned to the car.

"I think the hardest part is when I shoot Colonel Hoekman."

"Well, yes, there is that."

"And when I see if you care enough to save me."

"Gaby."

Again, silence. They crossed into France. The car grew warm and she dozed off, then woke at the next checkpoint. They passed without difficulty, then Helmut and Gemeiner returned to arguing in German for the next ten or twenty minutes.

When they finished, Helmut removed his gun from where he'd concealed it beneath the seat and handed it to Gabriela.

It was heavy and solid and had a smell of metal and oil. She'd never held a gun before. There was a thrill, a feeling of sudden power, holding the thing. He held out his hand and she returned the gun with some reluctance.

He loaded bullets into the box magazine in front of the trigger. "Watch what I'm doing. I want you to repeat this a few times."

"Will I need to reload?"

"No, but I want you comfortable with the gun. There's no chance to practice shooting. We can't even risk stopping and letting you fire a few rounds. Loading and unloading the gun will give you some comfort with the weapon. Go ahead, do it."

It was surprisingly tricky to slip the bullets in and out of the magazine. The near dark inside the car didn't help. She loaded and unloaded six or seven times until he said that was enough. Helmut emptied the bullets and peered into the chamber, then returned the unloaded gun. "Point it at my chest."

"Are you sure?"

"It's unloaded. Go ahead, I want you to know what it feels like."

She did it.

"Good, now pull the trigger. I know that might be hard, but I want you to get the feel so that—"

Click.

"Or maybe not so hard," Helmut said. He took the gun, reloaded, then returned it. She held the loaded weapon in her hand. "Okay, point the gun at my chest again, but don't pull the trigger. Uhm, obviously."

"And you trust me?"

"Of course."

Yet even in the darkness she could see a twitch at the corner of his mouth as she pointed the gun at his head.

"I said aim at my chest."

She lowered the gun until it pointed at his chest. Gemeiner's eyes watched through the rear view mirror before shifting back to the road. The trigger felt light under her finger, almost as if it wanted to be squeezed. Her hand didn't tremble. At last she lowered it. Helmut let out a sigh.

"Worried?"

"No, I wasn't worried. Well, maybe a little bit."

"Then why did you give me a loaded gun and tell me to point it at your chest?"

"Because this is not a game. I needed to see how you'd react. And I want you to know I trust you. Maybe it would help you trust me back."

"I'll do what I need to do, but you'll never see my trust again."

"I'm sorry, Gaby, I really am. Can you at least trust me enough to do what I say when you get to the Egyptienne?"

She studied his face. It looked sincere enough, but she'd learned better. Still, what choice was there? "Yes, I can do that."

"You'll want to point the gun at his head, that's the natural tendency. Don't. Too great a chance you'll miss. Aim at his chest. Squeeze the trigger and keep squeezing until there are no bullets left in the magazine. Keep shooting even when he goes down. Aim every shot at his chest. Even if you miss some of the shots — and you won't after the first shot or two — these bullets are 7.63 millimeter. He'll go down and won't get up. You just need to make sure you finish the job."

"I've been thinking about those pleasure rooms," Gabriela said. "Christine was telling me about the One-Two-Two and I'll bet the Egyptienne is the same. They're padded for privacy. And there will be music out front, and people talking in loud voices. It could be nobody hears the gunfire."

"Even then, the Mauser is awfully loud. They make suppressors you can attach to the end of the barrel. It doesn't eliminate the sound, but it muffles it. Too bad we don't have time to look for one. No, I think we have to assume people will hear the gunfire."

"So what then?" Gabriela asked.

"We can account for that. After you take care of Colonel Hoekman, drop the gun and come screaming out of the room, yelling something about an assassin in the back room. The man driving our car—whose name I don't want to say out loud, because I don't want him to know we're talking about him— will whisk you away. Nobody will be quite sure if you're being arrested or hustled off to safety. I'm counting on the fact you're a beautiful young woman to confuse matters, but you'll need to do some acting, too. Like that night at Le Coq Rouge, when you pretended to be Roger Leblanc's girlfriend. That should be good enough."

"I can do that. But what happens then?"

"This is where you're supposed to believe that the man currently sitting in the driver's seat in front of us is going to take you to safety. Unfortunately, he has other plans, so I've arranged a contingency."

"He has other plans? What kind of plans?"

"Let's just say this. If anything goes wrong, they'll find your body floating face-down in the Seine."

⚡⚡

They'd been on the road so many hours it was almost a surprise when they approached Paris. They pulled onto a dark farmhouse lane several kilometers outside of the city. Gemeiner climbed into the trunk and Helmut and Gabriela moved to the front seats. Helmut ground the gears of the Opel the first time he shifted, then it was smooth driving.

"Too bad your friend didn't spend the whole trip in the trunk," she said. "It suits him. And now I can stop pretending we're in love."

"That was pretending? Our troops in Russia are getting a warmer reception."

"I was pretending to be a girl whose lover is sending her to get killed by the Gestapo. A girl in that situation is not likely to be sitting on his lap, nibbling his ear."

"Well here's the checkpoint," he said stiffly. They approached the barricades and the floodlights, a soldier in the road holding out a hand for them to stop. "You'd better act now."

She snuggled up to his arm and leaned her head against his shoulder. Soldiers walked around the car, but when the officer at the window saw Helmut's papers, he waved them off and sent the car through. As soon as the checkpoint retreated to their rear, Gabriela pulled away and looked out the window.

They slipped through one of the *banlieus* to avoid another checkpoint, came into Paris from the south along Avenue de Choisy. As soon as the streets became lit, she took out a brush, her lipstick, and a mirror from her bag and went to work salvaging her appearance. Her new dress had suffered during the long drive.

"Next stop, the Egyptienne," Helmut said. "Get the gun, put it in your bag."

A car pulled behind them as they turned onto the Boulevard de Clichy and repeatedly honked its horn. "Open your bag, set it there." He slipped his hand inside her bag where she'd put the gun. He stopped the car.

The car drew beside theirs on the driver's side. It was Alfonse's Horch Cabriolet. The window rolled down; Christine sat in the passenger side and Alfonse leaned over her lap. Christine waved and smiled.

Alfonse flashed a grin. "Aha, I just knew some filthy *boche* had stolen my girlfriend."

"That didn't slow you down, I see," Helmut said, with a nod toward Christine.

"What was I supposed to do? Spend the evening in a bar, crying over my drink?"

"They should post a general service announcement whenever you go out. 'Horch spotted, all virtuous Parisiennes please run for the nearest shelter.'"

"Virtuous Parisiennes? Do such things exist? And if they did, what would I need them for? When I see a girl with virtue, I make a point to divest her of it as soon as possible." He winked at Gabriela. A car pulled behind the Horch and honked, but Alfonse paid it no attention. "So, when did you get back from Belgium?"

"Just now," Helmut said. "It's been a long day, we thought we'd go out for a drink."

"Hey, us too. We're on our way to the Egyptienne. Care to join us?"

There wasn't a moment of hesitation in Helmut's voice. "Sure. I've got to stop at the flat with these papers, but I'll drop Gaby off first. Give me fifteen minutes and I'll catch up."

"Great, see you then." He roared away.

"This is an unneeded complication," Helmut said.

"Let me out behind the Egyptienne and I'll tell Alfonse you couldn't make it."

"And when Hoekman shows up? What'll you tell Alfonse?"

"If it's a problem, your friend in the trunk can distract him. You're not losing your nerve, are you?"

"No, not at all," he said. "I just, well, as soon as I drop you at the Egyptienne, I'm going to pick up a shipment at the warehouse and then I'm leaving Paris at dawn. We might not see each other again and I don't want to end it like this."

"How *do* you want to end it, Helmut?"

"I don't know. I just wish that for once it wouldn't end with regret."

CHAPTER TWENTY-FIVE

COLONEL HOEKMAN SAT BY HIMSELF at a table in one corner of the lounge. Virtually alone among the men in the lounge, he wore his uniform. His hat rested on the table in front of him. A girl came and put a hand playfully on his arm, but he waved her off. He glanced up and met Gabriela's gaze.

She turned away. Her stomach lurched.

The Egyptienne was set up tonight like a 1920s Chicago speakeasy. The girls wore pearls and flapper dresses. Garish lamps, bartenders in gangster suits and hats. A jazz quartet played in one corner, but they were white men with painted black faces and painted pink lips.

Gemeiner had come in a few minutes before she did. He also sat by himself. Unlike Hoekman, however, he'd allowed himself to be surrounded by pretty girls and signaled the bartender for drinks for his new companions. He slid her a glance, then looked back to the girls at his side.

"Gaby! Over here!" It was Alfonse, standing by the pool table with cue stick in hand. Christine stood behind his shoulder.

"Watch this shot," he said after she'd made her way over.

He lined up, gave a confident hit to the cue ball, then watched with a smug expression as it struck the three ball, which in turn ricocheted at an angle and knocked the nine into the corner pocket. The other German player snorted as Alfonse lined up for another shot. Two more shots and he dropped the eight ball. The two racked up for a return game.

"I've been thinking about Roger Leblanc," Christine said to Gabriela.

Gabriela gave a sideways glance to Colonel Hoekman, still staring in her direction. She had to go over there, and soon, but first, how could she get Christine away from danger? Alfonse, too. She owed him that much.

"*Ouai?*"

"How did he convince the zazous that he was one of them?"

"What do you mean?" Gabriela asked.

"He infiltrated their group," Christine said. "They just trusted him, why?"

"Because he was a zazou, of course."

"No, he wasn't," she said, her tone defensive. "You saw what happened. They let Roger go. He was with the fascists, he had to be. He must have been all along. He was nothing but a JPF and he grew his hair out so the zazous would think he was one of them. You saw how they accepted us when we dressed up. It can be done. That's what Roger was doing."

"And took on an effeminate air so people would think he was homosexual? Learned how to draw? Cultivated an attitude of not giving a damn for months so people would believe it?"

Christine nodded. "He was good, wasn't he?"

"He wasn't good, Christine. He was a zazou all along. He turned on them."

"I can't believe it."

"Believe it. He was a collaborator."

She tossed her hair. "We're all collaborators, Gaby. Doesn't mean we denounce our friends. No, I don't believe it. It can't be true."

Gabriela looked at Alfonse. He was in the middle of another series of excellent shots and laughing and joking in German.

She glanced over to Colonel Hoekman. When she turned back, Christine was watching her.

"You're not going to that Gestapo bastard again, are you?" Christine asked.

"Yes, I am. "

"I don't understand you, Gaby. I try, but I can't. Do you need help, are you in trouble? If it's money —"

"There is something you can do. How quickly can you seduce a man?"

The concern vanished, replaced with a sly smile. "Faster than you."

"You're sure about that?"

"You've got the face and the tits, but I've got the cunning and the experience." Her expression changed again. "Wait, you're not talking about Hoekman, that's not what you want me to do, is it?"

"No, of course not. What I'm asking is how quickly you can get Alfonse out of here and back home with his pants off."

"He's into his pool game now. I figured another hour and then —"

"There's no hour, Christine. You've got about two minutes to seduce him."

"Two minutes? What kind of a girl do you think I am?"

"I'm serious, Christine, listen to me. If you can't do it, you've got to get yourself out at least. Say you're going out for fresh air, whatever." She turned to go.

Christine grabbed her arm. "What? Why?"

"Just do it. It's a question of life and death."

Gabriela left Christine staring after her and made her way toward the colonel. She felt the extra weight in the handbag over her shoulder. Inside, Helmut's Mauser. She imagined her hand closing around it, pointing it at Hoekman's chest, pulling the trigger. It would be loud. She needed to be prepared. She couldn't let it startle her.

Colonel Hoekman stood as she approached. A wary look.

She licked her lips, tried to look nervous. It wasn't hard. "I-I've got that information. Can we go talk?"

He came around the table and put his hand on her arm. "Let us go to my car."

"No, we need to stay here, inside."

"Come, be reasonable."

"I won't go to your car. I'll only tell you here, where I'm safe."

"Really, I must insist. This place is too public." He tightened his grip.

"I'm warning you. I'll scream."

"Do you think that matters? I'm in charge here, not you. Don't forget it."

Again, his French was greatly improved from the last time she had seen him. Both accent and grammar. It was a sharp mind against hers. Could he suspect her? She felt a trickle of fear.

"I don't trust you. If you take me in your car, you'll force me. Maybe my friends will never see me again. So I'm going to scream. Maybe it won't matter, but I'll do it anyway. I'll scream and there will be a big scene."

"You are making me angry."

She changed her tone. "Please, I beg you. Be reasonable. I'm going to tell you everything I know, there's no need to force me. Now please, people are going to notice. That doesn't help you, either. Alfonse is here, you don't want to alarm him when he's with all his army friends."

To her relief, Colonel Hoekman released her arm. "Where, then?"

"How about one of the pleasure rooms in back?"

"Any one in particular, *mademoiselle*?" An edge of suspicion in his voice.

"Oh, it doesn't matter, so long as it's private and we can talk. You'll be interested in what I've learned."

He was hesitating, she could see, weighing his options, his risks. She had to give him more.

Gabriela leaned forward and whispered with her lips touching his ear. "I've found your *simple soldat*. He's been right under your nose. In fact, he'll be here tonight."

"What? I knew it. Who is it?"

"It's not Alfonse, he's apparently completely innocent. But someone close to him."

"Yes! It's Herr von Cratz, isn't it?"

"I can't tell you here, not in the open."

She'd stopped just short of denouncing Helmut, but it didn't matter. A few seconds alone and Hoekman would be dead. He'd never tell anyone.

"When is he coming? What do you know?"

"Not here. We have to go somewhere where we can talk freely. And you have to give me proof my father is alive. You promised."

He pulled back a pace, seemed to study her, then nodded. "Let's go back."

Colonel Hoekman went first and it gave her a chance to glance around the room. She saw Gemeiner studiously not watching, but she also saw two other men who were. They played a game of darts to one side and both gave a quick glance as Gabriela and Hoekman passed. She pretended not to notice.

Who were they?

Gemeiner's fellow conspirators? Undercover Gestapo agents?

She followed Hoekman through a doorway that led to a hallway lined with doors. Men with dark suits and cigars, Chicago gangster style, stood in front of each room. Signs hung from some of the doors, reading "*ne pas déranger*" and "*bitte nicht stören.*"

Hoekman made to step through one of the doors without a "do not disturb" sign and one of the faux-gangsters waggled a cigar. "What's the password to the speakeasy?"

"What do you mean, speakeasy?" Hoekman demanded.

The man didn't break from character. "The password, Mister."

Gabriela said, "You have to pay a small fee."

"Ah, I see." He handed over a few bills and they stepped into the room.

It looked like a small hotel room with a bed and pillows. Everything red. Prints of topless dancers and nude women reclining on couches lined the walls. There was a window at the back, drawn with a heavy red velvet curtain.

Hoekman examined the décor. "Disgusting."

As soon as the door shut, Gabriela reached into the bag. Hoekman's back was partially turned.

Her fingers brushed the box magazine, found the handle. Her finger slipped into the trigger. His back was still turned. He wouldn't know what was happening as the pain sliced through him. She would be deprived of the satisfaction of seeing the look on his face. But there would be a brief moment, after the pain started, when he would know everything. He'd know she'd discovered what he'd done to her father. He'd know he was going to die for it.

Gabriela pulled out the Mauser.

The gun made a little snicking sound as it brushed the metal clasp of her handbag. Instantly, Hoekman whirled around. She had the gun free. It rose toward his chest. A bright look of alarm on Hoekman's face.

He had her wrist, he was twisting to the side. She pulled the trigger. A sharp retort. The gun bucked. She could feel the power of it. Hoekman twisted the gun out of her grasp. He was too strong. She didn't get off a second shot.

Hoekman swung the Mauser and it connected with the side of her head. Pain exploded in her temple. She crumpled to the ground.

Hoekman stood with a stunned look on his face. He clutched his side. Blood soaked through his uniform and oozed through his fingers. He looked down at his bloody hand. His face turned pale.

"No."

"You bastard," she said through clenched teeth from where she lay at his feet. "I saw what you did to him. And now you're going to die."

He unbuttoned his coat with the shaking fingers of one hand and peeled back his jacket. Pulled out his shirt. And then gave her a look of triumph. "I don't think so, not today."

It was true, oh, god, it was true. A nasty gash on his side, but no penetrating hole into his gut. He'd twisted the gun away just in time. He was only grazed. He'd been too strong, just too strong. She felt a crush of despair.

Hoekman grabbed her by the hair. He dragged her to her feet.

"I tried to be reasonable."

Where were they? Someone had to have heard the gun. It was so loud. There were men standing outside. Why didn't they come see what was wrong?

"Help! Somebody, help!"

"It seems these rooms are quite private, as no doubt you considered when you brought me here to murder me. If anyone hears a faint whisper of screaming, it will no doubt be taken for amorous behavior. So go ahead, scream in passion. It is expected."

"Let me go!"

He held her at arm's length, so high that she had to stand

on her toes to avoid being lifted entirely from the ground. She clawed at his arm, but couldn't get through his gloves or shirt. He tossed the gun onto the bed.

"I have exhausted reasonable possibilities," he said. "All you leave me are the unreasonable options." He used his free hand to reach into his pocket. He pulled out a pair of long-nosed metal pliers.

"What are you going to do with that?"

"I am going to extract information, of course."

"Please, no."

"Yes, *mademoiselle*. Yes, we must."

CHAPTER TWENTY-SIX

HOEKMAN THREW GABRIELA BACK TO the floor. He fell on her, pinned her with his knees. He grabbed her jaw with his left hand, and lowered the pliers toward her mouth with the other.

"No, please." She felt weak with terror.

"Who is it? Is it von Cratz?"

"I don't know, I barely know the man."

"Why is he going to Marseille? What is he doing there? Who does he keep meeting in Germany? Is he working for Major Ostermann, or the other way around?"

"I don't know anything, I was bluffing. Please."

"You will tell me now, or I will pull your teeth."

"I don't know anything, I swear, I don't."

"You will change your mind."

Hoekman squeezed her mouth, forced it open enough to jam the nose of the pliers in, and grabbed one of her teeth. She screamed.

"*Hör damit auf!*" shouted a man at the doorway. More shouting in German.

Hoekman dropped the pliers and climbed slowly to his feet, raised his hands. Gabriela scrambled away, reached the edge of the bed, pulled herself up. She was shaking, she could barely hold herself steady.

It was Gemeiner. He stood at the doorway with a gun in his hands, which he pointed with steady hands at Hoekman. He'd shut the door behind him.

Hoekman snarled something in return, but Gemeiner shouted back. Neither man moved. Gabriela spotted Helmut's Mauser, lying on the floor where Hoekman had dropped it. She snatched it up.

"Tell your friend to lower the gun," Hoekman said. "He is making a big mistake."

"He doesn't speak much French. Tell him yourself."

Gemeiner looked to Gabriela. "You have gun. You shoot now? Yes? We go."

"You're making a big mistake," Hoekman said. He directed another angry tirade at Gemeiner, but now there was an edge to his voice. Desperation, she thought.

She pointed the gun. The gun had felt so solid in her hands before, but now she was shaking. She felt lightheaded. She had to get control before she fired.

And then the door flew open again. Two men entered. The first one slammed into Gemeiner. The two men went to the ground. The attacker was younger and quickly disarmed the older man. The second seemed to size up the situation, then pointed a handgun at Gabriela.

"Put the gun down *mademoiselle*, or you die."

He was French. She recognized the men now. They were the two who had watched her go back with Colonel Hoekman. She dropped the gun.

"You, by the bed," the man said in French. "Put your hands on your head."

"I am a Gestapo agent," Hoekman said. "Who the hell are you?"

"Franc-garde. Nobody move."

"Listen to me," Hoekman said. "These two intended to

assassinate me. I am Gestapo. I have papers."

"It's a lie," Gabriela said. "He's a saboteur. This older man is a German officer. He saw the saboteur and came to arrest him."

"Look at my uniform," Hoekman said. "Gestapo, you see it. And I'm bleeding. This whore shot me. My papers are in my pocket. Come look at them, quickly. There may be others."

"He's a liar!"

But she could see the French secret service men coming to a decision even as they dragged Gemeiner to his feet. She was a girl, after all, and Gemeiner spoke no French; he couldn't corroborate her story.

"Are you badly injured, *monsieur*?" the lead man asked Hoekman. "Shall I call for a doctor?"

"Not seriously. Give me the girl. I must take her away at once for questioning." He jabbed his finger at Gemeiner. "Keep this one. I will send someone for him shortly. He is highly dangerous. Do you understand me?"

"*Oui, monsieur.*"

Gemeiner broke free momentarily. He fumbled with something. It wasn't a weapon, it was something he was trying to get to his mouth. He almost got it there but one of the Franc-gardes seized his wrist and twisted. A small capsule dropped to the floor. One of the men picked it up, handed it to Hoekman.

The colonel let out a nasty laugh, said something in German. The older man looked stricken.

"Make sure he has no more cyanide pills. Strip him naked, search him thoroughly. I want him alive and unharmed. Then you will empty and secure the building. I will be back shortly."

Hoekman grabbed Gabriela's arm, shoved her toward the door, then spent a moment buttoning his jacket. He fished out his own sidearm, which he showed to her before pocketing it again.

"Don't let him take me, for god's sake," Gabriela said to the lead Franc-garde. "You know what they'll do to me. Don't let them, I beg you."

"I am sorry, there is nothing I can do."

"Do not scream," Hoekman said as he pushed her from the room. "In the first place, the lounge is filled with German officers. I doubt your fellow whores will come to your aid. Second, if you scream, I will order Monsieur Leblanc killed, your friend Christine, the old man and woman who rented you an apartment. And your father."

"I saw what you did to him, you bastard."

"Yes, he is quiet now. Not so much trouble. It is a much-needed improvement in his personality. But he can still suffer and die. Is that what you wish?"

She made a direct path toward the exit. The party continued its raucous ways. There was no sign of Christine or Alfonse, thank god. If only she'd told her to run, flee for Marseille.

The doorman asked about Gabriela's coat, but Hoekman shoved him out of the way. They pushed through the doors and into the cold night air. Hoekman spotted his man, shouted orders, and the young soldier left at a sprint, presumably for the car. Hoekman glanced from side to side, looked behind him and even up at the roof. He had one hand on Gabriela's arm and the other in his pocket.

A car squealed up to the curb. She thought at first that it was Hoekman's, but it didn't have swastika flags and the colonel yanked her back and pulled out his gun. A man jumped out and ducked behind the hood with only his head and a submachine gun visible, which he propped on the hood.

"Hand over the girl," the man said.

She recognized him. It was the man from the rail yard, what had Helmut called him? David Mayer, that was it. He had a cap pulled over his head and a greatcoat. No insignia, but he had a vaguely official air about him. A serious set to his jaw.

MICHAEL WALLACE

It occurred to her that things had played out almost as Helmut had thought they would. She had come out with a man who was going to drive her away. Helmut had arranged for Mayer to come and pretend to abduct her.

"I am a Gestapo agent. Who are you?"

"French police. Give her over at once or you die."

"No you are not, you are a Jew." Hoekman turned to Gabriela. "Your friends sent a Jew?"

The man with the gun let out a hiss. He might have fooled Gemeiner, but not a man like Hoekman, who no doubt saw Zionist conspiracies in his scrambled eggs every morning.

"I'm going to count to three and you'd better let the girl go. I'll kill you both, I don't care, but you're not taking her."

"And if I let her go, you'll still kill me?"

"I don't care about you. I won't shoot you. My orders are to take the girl."

"What for? Who are you?"

"One. Two."

"Very well," Hoekman said. "Don't shoot, I'll hand her over. Although what you all find so interesting about this whore, I can't tell. She's not even that pretty and she wears too much perfume, it's sickening." He snarled in her ear, "I'll find you anyway, you know that. All of you. You, your major friend, von Cratz, the other girls at the restaurant, and now this Jew." He shoved her toward the car and took a step back.

"Shoot him," she cried to Mayer. She ran toward the car.

"Get in. Hurry."

"Take him down, do it. Kill him, for god's sake!"

"Those aren't my orders."

"It's not him, it's not who you thought it was. You have to shoot him. Please, listen to me."

"Get in, *now!*"

She had no choice, so she opened the door and scrambled

into the car. Mayer sped away from the curb. She glanced back at Colonel Hoekman. He was not waiting for his car, but sprinting back into the Egyptienne. Where the Franc-garde held Gemeiner.

Helmut's friend was shortly to have a very rough time of it.

⚡⚡

"You should have killed him," Gabriela said. "Why didn't you listen to me?"

"The boss told me to get you in the car but leave the old man alone. I wasn't, under any circumstances, to harm him."

"Old man? Are you blind?"

"Yes, that was strange." David Mayer pulled onto the Champs-Élysées. It was almost empty of traffic at this hour. She could see him fighting the urge to punch the accelerator.

"So why didn't you shoot him?"

"I didn't get where I am by disobeying von Cratz."

"Except that time at the rail depot, when he'd told you to stay inside and you were out among all those Germans, what about that?"

"I had no choice, the shipment was sitting there, it needed to be loaded. The Brits were about to bomb us to hell. But this was a direct order. I thought it best to err on the side of caution."

"Yeah, well caution left that monster alive. You know how many people Hoekman's killed? I bet half of them were Jews."

He turned briefly with a flat expression. "And how long would I last if I got worked up about every Jew-killer I saw?"

"You're not listening to me. Colonel Hoekman is alive. He's not coming after some random Jew, he's coming after you."

"Monsieur von Cratz has arranged for that contingency."

Mayer turned off the avenue onto a smaller side street. He cut through a residential neighborhood, then back onto one of the boulevards. She lost her bearings.

"Where are we going?"

"Gare de Lyon. I've got fake transit documents and two train tickets for Geneva."

"Geneva? Whatever for?"

"The war is over, for both of us. Von Cratz has taken care of everything. We've got papers, we have money, and we have foreign contacts. We can wait out the war in Switzerland, or, if they get dragged into the war, fly to South America." He shrugged. "So you see why we can't worry about one Gestapo agent. That son of a bitch will get his punishment in the end, you can be sure of it. Either the Americans, the Russians, or God himself."

"You're taking me out of the country?"

"Tonight."

It was a tempting offer and she might have taken it if not for her father. But there was also Helmut to consider. He had to be warned.

"We can't run away."

"Yes, we can. And we will. I have my orders."

"Listen to me for a second. Remember the old man who was supposed to bring me out of the Egyptienne? Hoekman took him prisoner. They're torturing him right now. We have to warn Helmut."

"Von Cratz said —"

"The old man tried to kill himself with a cyanide capsule. And now he's going to get tortured and tell them everything and you know what happens next? He tells them about Helmut. Listen to me, this is no different than the rail depot. We've got to think for ourselves."

David Mayer pulled to the side of the road. "He didn't tell me what he was doing or where he was going, just told me how to get you and how to safely get out of the country. He wasn't planning to see me again, so he didn't even tell me how to get him a message."

"I don't know either." Her mind was racing. She could figure this out. "He had to pick up a shipment, but he's not leaving the city until dawn. He's probably gone there and is waiting for daybreak. Where would he get a shipment?"

"What kind of shipment? Arriving by rail?"

"I don't know. Couldn't be too big, because he was going to drive it out of the city himself. Something that could fit in a small truck or the trunk of a car. And I think it was already in Paris."

"That doesn't help. Could be anywhere."

"A warehouse? An office?"

"There's one warehouse I know about that's not attached to a rail depot, but there have to be fifty, sixty men working there at all times. It's not the place to pick up secret shipments." He was quiet for a moment. "Problem is, I don't come very often to Paris. I work mostly between Le Mans and Orléans. Too many Gestapo in the city. Too many *milice*, too many Franc-gardes."

She had an idea. "Turn the car around."

"I told you, it's no good. I don't know where he is."

"But I know someone who might."

⚡⚡

Gabriela pounded on the door to Alfonse's flat. There was no answer. She pounded harder. "Alfonse!"

The stress and pressure of the last several hours was catching up to her. Had Alfonse and Christine been in the lounge when Hoekman led her out? She couldn't remember. Had the Gestapo already come to arrest them?

At last the door cracked. Alfonse peered past the chain. "Oh, Gaby. It's you. I wasn't expecting you to spend the night."

"Can you let me in? We've got to talk."

"The thing is, I'm, uhm, kind of busy at the moment. You were gone with Helmut and then I heard you'd left the lounge and...well, I didn't know."

There was enough light spilling through the crack that she could see he wore the silk robe he preferred when he played the sophisticated seducer. No doubt Christine was in the bedroom in some state of undress.

"I don't have time for this, Alfonse. Let me in. Hurry up."

"Who's that man with you?"

"He works for Helmut."

"I can't right now. Why don't you come back in the morning. We can talk over coffee. By then I'll be feeling better. I've got this terrible headache."

"Dammit, Alfonse, I know Christine's in there. There's no need to pretend. Just open the door."

"Please, don't be jealous. You've been gone a couple of days and she—well, I couldn't resist. You know how I get."

"Jealous? Don't be an ass."

"You're not angry?"

"Of course I'm not angry, just open the goddamn door. I need your help. It's an emergency."

He shut the door and she thought he'd given up arguing and locked her out, but then she heard him fumbling with the chain and he opened up. He sighed and gave an exaggerated wave of the arm to indicate that they enter.

"Thank you," she said with a note of sarcasm. "I'd hate to be any bother."

"I let you in, didn't I?" He looked at David with a frown. "Wait, it's the Jew? You brought Helmut's Jew here?"

"So what?"

"I don't hate Jews, I don't care, really. But if the Gestapo sees..."

"The Gestapo is on its way already."

"What?"

Christine came into the hallway from further back in the flat. She wore one of Alfonse's heavy cotton bathrobes. It hung open at the neck, showing most of her breasts. She glanced from Gabriela to David Mayer, and the corners of her mouth quirked.

"Glad to see you're still alive, Gaby. You keep playing with Colonel Hoekman, I'm surprised every time you surface."

"Never mind that," Alfonse said. "What's this business about the Gestapo?"

"There was trouble at the Egyptienne. They arrested Helmut's friend. He's under interrogation now. They'll be hunting down Helmut as soon as they get some information."

"Oh, god."

"And then they're coming here."

"But I don't have anything to do with that." Alfonse sounded almost frantic.

"I knew it," Christine said. "I knew Helmut was involved in something. He was too pure to be believed. So what is it? What's his crime?"

"He's an enemy of the Reich. Undermining the war effort."

"*Zut*," Christine said.

"My god, he is?" Alfonse asked. "I should have known. Always going on about helping people, it was all a front. Why would they come for me? Someone's got to tell Hoekman I had nothing to do with this. My god, someone's got to tell him."

"Don't worry, dear," Christine said. She put a hand on his shoulder. "Paris is full of people who can vouch that you're not involved in anything but yourself."

Alfonse shrugged her hand away. "But where the hell is Helmut? He's got to tell them, they've got to hear it from him. Now, before they arrest him, while he'll still be believed."

"That's what you need to tell us," Gabriela said. "You have to help us find him."

Alfonse shook his head. "I don't know, I have no way of finding out. Please, all of you just go, I don't want to get involved. I've got to make a phone call."

"It's too late for that. It's not just Helmut, all of us in this room are in danger."

"No, I don't believe it. All of you go. Please, for god's sake."

"What happened to the man who defended me on the Boulevard Saint Michel?" Gabriela asked.

"That was different."

"Right, it was just a zazou. Easy enough to beat up some kid. But if there's real danger, Alfonse is nowhere to be found."

"It's the Gestapo. There's nothing I can do."

"I was this close to killing him, Alfonse. If not for goddamn French collaborators, Hoekman would be dead. Now why are you scared?"

"Why am I scared? It's the Gestapo. The *Gestapo.*"

"Alfonse, listen to yourself." Christine said. There was an element of disgust in her voice. "Be a man and do something. We're two whores and a Jew. If we can stand up to Colonel Hoekman, so can you."

"You're wasting your time," Mayer said. "Come on, both of you. Let's get out of here and leave this coward to the Gestapo. Maybe his friends in Berlin can save him."

"Oh, come on, that's not fair." Alfonse licked his lips. "What can I do anyway?"

"You can tell us how to find Helmut," Gabriela said.

"I already told you, I don't know."

"You have an idea, you have to."

He looked back and forth between Gabriela, Christine, and Mayer. "He's not at his flat?"

"No, but he's somewhere in the city," Gabriela said. "Waiting for a shipment."

She explained what she knew, how the shipment had to be small enough to fit in a small truck or the trunk of a car.

"There's a place Helmut goes to pick up packages," Alfonse said. "A little warehouse in the Fifteenth Arrondissement. I once saw a truck pull up and a man go in with a large satchel and come out empty-handed. I later saw the same satchel in the back seat of Helmut's car, but empty. I'm guessing it was fake papers for his workers, that sort of business. The thing about this place is that it has a private garage, big enough for three, four cars. It's an excellent place to take a small shipment because nobody can see what you're loading or unloading."

"That sounds exactly right," Gabriela said. "Can you show us how to get there?"

"If I do, will you promise I'll never see any of you again?"

"With pleasure."

CHAPTER TWENTY-SEVEN

HELMUT WAS NOT PLEASED TO see Gabriela, Mayer, Christine, and Alfonse arrive at the warehouse. Alfonse, especially, was a bad sign. And the look of terror on his face made it instantly clear that something had gone horribly wrong.

He listened with growing alarm as Gabriela gave a summary of what had happened at the Egyptienne. Hoekman alive, barely wounded. Gemeiner taken captive. Thank God Gabriela was alive and free; other than that, the operation had been an unmitigated disaster.

"So why did you come here?" he asked when she finished.

"To warn you," Gabriela said. "And you need our help. You'll never get out of the city alone."

"Out of the question. You're going with David to Geneva and that's final."

"No, I'm not. I'm going to help."

"I don't need help. I've loaded the truck and I'm ready to go."

The driver of the first truck had helped him move the boxes without comment, then driven off. All he had left to do was clean up a few incriminating papers here in the office and then he'd have been gone. Five more minutes. And then captured at the first checkpoint he reached, based on what he'd just heard from Gabriela.

"There were police in the streets, already," she said. "I'll bet every Gestapo agent in the city is awake and looking for you. How many in Paris?"

"Dozens," Helmut said. "Add to that probably hundreds of informers. Plus the police, the *milice*, the Franc-gardes. Even those laughable junior fascists. They'll be out looking for us."

"You won't be laughing when JPF kicks in your face," Alfonse said. He sat at a desk in the corner, smoking and muttering to himself, none of his traditional bravado. It occurred to Helmut that he was the sort of officer who, when caught in a surprise attack, would cringe in the foxhole while his men begged for leadership, until finally the position was overrun and everyone killed.

David Mayer kept guard in the front room of the safe house, peering through the windows. The cars and the panel truck sat in the garage, out of sight. There was a back alley where they could slip out without emerging onto the main street. Unless the Gestapo surrounded the entire block, of course. If Gemeiner were alive, and under torture, it would only be a matter of time until they found him.

"It's going to be a hell of a chance getting out of Paris," Helmut said.

"I know the streets," Christine said. "I've lived in Paris long enough, I could practically drive a taxi. I can get us out of here."

"No, forget it." He paced the room. "And you're sure? Gemeiner is alive?"

"He was an hour ago," Gabriela said.

"I can't believe it. After all of that, you'd think he'd have that cyanide capsule pinched between his teeth where it could do some good. Not in his pocket."

"It's not his fault," Gabriela said. "Just bad luck having Franc-gardes on a mission to impress the *boches*. Gemeiner wasn't expecting trouble."

"Of course not." He forced himself to remain calm. "Nobody is. That's why you carry the goddamned capsules, it's a contingency."

"There's nothing we can do about it now."

"No."

"What does he know?" Gabriela asked. "Everything?"

"Thank god, no. I got a sealed envelope from the man who helped me load the shipment in the truck. From our Vichy contact. Gemeiner doesn't know his name."

It had seemed a needless complication earlier, but now Helmut was glad for the precaution.

"But that's the only good news," he added. "He can find this place, or close enough for the Gestapo to finish the job."

"Any chance he can stand up to torture?" she asked.

Helmut considered. "For a little while, maybe. He's no coward and he lived through the trenches in the last war. POW camp for eleven months. Who knows what the Russians put him through? But Hoekman can be persuasive. Sooner, rather than later, he'll talk."

"Do you have extra cyanide capsules? One for each of us?"

"Forget about it," Alfonse said. " I'm not taking a goddamned capsule."

"Nobody expects you to," Helmut said. "We expect you to babble everything you know in the first five seconds of interrogation."

"Interrogation? Hell, no. I'm going back to Germany. I've got friends who can protect me."

"Sure they can, Alf."

"You'll see, I'll come out of this just fine."

"But I need one," Gabriela said. She closed her eyes as if remembering something terrible. Her father, no doubt, and that angry scar across his forehead. When she opened her eyes, she looked resolute. "He's not getting me. I won't be taken."

"Me, either," Christine said. She looked pale. There was a tremble at her lip that somehow made her look more brave, rather than less.

"Come on, think this through," Helmut told them. "I can get a third ticket for Geneva. You'll be safe from the Gestapo there."

David Mayer popped in from the front room. "Time's almost up, boss. A suspicious car swung by here twice. How long until they start beating down doors?"

Alfonse ground his cigarette in the ashtray and rose to his feet. "That's enough for me. Open that back door so I can get my car out, I'm going."

"Sit down," Helmut said. He turned to Mayer. "Keep watching. We'll be done in five minutes."

"I'm not sitting down," Alfonse said. "I'm done."

"Please listen," Gabriela said to Helmut. "We can help you, you need us."

"Yeah, how?"

"Let Alfonse go, first," Gabriela said. "I don't trust him. The less he knows, the better."

Alfonse turned with a flash of temper on his face. "You don't trust me? Who showed you how to get here?"

"No offense," Gabriela said, "but you don't care and if they catch you, you'll tell them everything. The sooner you get out of here, the better. For all of us."

"You were nothing when I found you." His voice rose in pitch. "You're still nothing. Listen to you, couple of working girls who think they're going to be heroes. Go ahead, Helmut, give them the cyanide, let's see just how brave they are."

"Calm down," Helmut said. "There's a residential flat upstairs. Someone will hear you."

Gabriela was right about Alfonse. Helmut hadn't wanted to send him away until he figured out what to do with him. But if they caught him, he would talk. Helmut wasn't bringing him along—even if Alfonse were to agree to go—which meant it was either kill him or let him go. Gemeiner would say to shoot him, but that was something he couldn't do.

"Mayer will let you out. You're done. Get back to your friends in Germany, if you can."

"Sure, send me off with the Jew. Great, wonderful." He turned to go, but stopped as he reached the threshold to the front room. "I never asked for any of this, it really isn't fair."

"Alf," Helmut said.

"Fine, yes, I'm going."

He could hear Alfonse still grumbling to David Mayer as the two went out the back door.

Helmut sighed, then turned back to Gabriela and Christine. "I'm listening. Give me a reason."

"For starters, it's a long drive to Marseille," Gabriela said.

He started. "What? What makes you say Marseille?"

"Colonel Hoekman asked me. You keep going down there, he said, so why?"

The entire plan balanced on the edge of a razor. Hoekman knew too much already. Gemeiner had only to fill in the gaps. It made Helmut want to give up, sprint for his car, and flee in some random direction.

"Lots of checkpoints between here and Marseille," Gabriela said. "Your French is almost perfect, but you have an accent. They'll be looking for you. I can drive us through the checkpoints."

"I can help, too," Christine said. "My family lives in Toulon, not far from Marseille, and I've paid the smugglers five, six times to smuggle me in and out of the Occupied Zone. I know how to get in contact with them so we can bypass the checkpoints."

"Maybe," Helmut said. "You'd certainly be safer there than in Paris with Hoekman looking for you." He turned to Gabriela. "But why do *you* want to go? It'll be dangerous."

"I know."

"And what I'm doing is for the German people, not France. You were furious with me before, so why help me now?"

"I'm not finished, that's why."

"You could be."

"No. You send me to Geneva and then what? I wait out the war. That could be years, or maybe it never ends. And meanwhile, Colonel Hoekman keeps hurting people."

"With any luck, you'll never see him again."

"With any luck, I will. And this time I won't fail."

"Be reasonable."

"I'm not a reasonable girl, Helmut. I never have been. I don't forget, and I don't forgive."

"What about your father?"

"Yes, what about him? I can't help him from Switzerland."

"You can't help if you're dead."

"I'm not going to die."

"You might not. It could be worse than that."

"Hoekman had his pliers in my mouth. He was going to rip out my teeth. Nothing you can say will scare me more than that."

Helmut glanced between the two women, came to a decision. "If you're going to help, there's something you should know."

"Yes?"

He reached into his pocket and pulled out a 20 franc gold coin. On the front was Marianne with a laurel wreath, on the back, the proud Gallic Rooster, the *Coq Gaulois*. "Do you know what this is?"

"Looks like contraband," Gabriela said.

"French Rooster, 6.45 grams of gold. Enough to bribe a French police officer to stay in bed instead of making his rounds. Enough to pay an *ancien soldat* to get his gun from where it's hidden in the barn, because he can feed his family for a month with this coin."

"And what are you going to do with it?"

"A man will do a lot for a single French rooster." Helmut returned the coin to his pocket. "I've got 70,000 in the truck."

CHAPTER TWENTY-EIGHT

C OLONEL HOEKMAN DROPPED A MOUSE into each cage in turn. Within thirty seconds, three mice lay twitching, eyes dulling, in the coils of three snakes. Below the snakes, in the cabinets, he could hear rodents in their cages. He'd have reason to bring out more in a few minutes.

The old man—Hoekman still didn't know his true identity—lay strapped to the table, staring up at the ceiling. He could have watched, but he did not turn his head or show any interest. He wore a sullen expression, not fear. You couldn't break a man until he was afraid. That was Hoekman's first task.

Hoekman had made multiple mistakes at the Egyptienne. Underestimating Gabriela Reyes, of course, that was one. Secondly, where had this old man come from, and why hadn't he noticed him in the lounge? Next, he should have taken his chances with the Franc-gardes. Instead, his first instinct had been to run here with the girl, come back for the old man later. First the girl had tried to kill him, then this old man. Who else was there? Was Major Ostermann about to burst through the doors, maybe von Cratz? He should have secured the building, then left with both prisoners. Instead, he'd stumbled into the night air and been surprised by a Jew.

The other mistake was not realizing the old man was more important than the girl. What had he been thinking in those few seconds of chaos? That the old man was Gabriela's lover, he supposed. She was a prostitute, after all, and prostitutes couldn't be picky. Any man with money would do, and if he were old and ugly, he'd be that much easier to play. And of course old men like this one usually convinced themselves the girls loved them.

So he'd left the old man in care of the Franc-gardes. Only upon his return, when he was carting the man off for interrogation, did something about his demeanor make him reconsider. Hoekman called him Gemeiner and the old man hadn't answered to the name, nor shown any surprise or confusion. The lack of response was telling.

And so Hoekman's mistake with the old man proved fortuitous. If he'd known then what he knew now, he'd have been outside the lounge with Gemeiner when the Jew pulled up. He'd be left with the prostitute to interrogate. This was much better.

Hoekman didn't turn away from the cages until all three mice were reduced to lumps inching down the length of the snakes. "A rodent is a warm creature, curious, passionate. A reptile is cold, analytical. You'll never see it afraid or angry."

Gemeiner sounded bored. "I'm not scared of snakes, if that's what you're trying to do. And I'm not afraid of torture. I'm not fond of it, but I can endure it just fine."

"Is that where you got the scars on your back?" Hoekman asked. "They are old, you are old. Were you perhaps captured by the Russians in the last war? Did they burn you? Were they looking for information, or torturing you for their own amusement?"

"My, what a skilled investigator you are." Gemeiner turned his head to where Hoekman stood by the cages. "Did you go to a special school to develop that penetrating insight? And such searching questions. They have rendered me quite helpless."

"Your arrogance is tedious, but not particularly surprising. You are in the reptile phase right now. You still think you control the situation. You will eventually pass to the rodent phase. We will see what you say then."

"Reptile phase? Rodent phase? Is that supposed to be profound?"

"Merely an observation of human nature," Hoekman said. "My point is simply this. You will talk eventually. They all do."

"Maybe, but it will be too late to help you. Two hours, three, it will be too late."

"Too late for what?"

"Too late to stop our cavalry of magic unicorns from flying over Berlin and dumping ten thousand kilograms of gummi bears onto the city."

He was tired of being mocked. Time to take control of the situation. "Do you know the difference between a hungry snake and a hungry rodent, Herr Gemeiner?"

"I'm sure you're going to tell me."

"A hungry snake will curl into a ball and wait. It can wait for months, with nothing but hunger to occupy its time. A snake can wait until it is almost dead and there's nothing left but a lean, starving hunger. It never panics, it just waits. Sooner or later something will crawl into its den and then, just like that," he said with a snap of the fingers, "the snake is fed."

"Fascinating."

"A rodent, however, is quite frantic with hunger after twenty-four hours. A mother mouse, unfed, will devour her blind, hairless young. Put two starving mice in a cage and one will attack and kill the other. Eat its brains first. It's true, that's where the most energy is and somehow the rodents know it."

"I'm sure they do."

"Now, rats, they're even nastier. You know in Stalingrad, when our troops were trapped in the *Kessel*, it was widely reported that hunger reduced our men to eating rats."

"They taste okay if you clean them properly and use plenty of salt. Not much meat."

"What is not widely known is that hunger also reduced the rats to eating our men." Hoekman opened the cabinet, removed one cage, then another. Inside, the frantic sound of scratching, squealing. They were desperate to be fed.

"One sniper fell asleep at his post," Hoekman continued. "When he woke, there were rats on his face, tearing at the soft tissue on his lips and ears, biting at his eyeballs. Hundreds of them. But rat teeth are small. Their bites, individually, are far from fatal. It took some time for the soldier to die while they ate him alive."

"And how do they know this is what happened?" Gemeiner asked. Hoekman detected a note of uncertainty in his voice. "Was he writing it down while they ate him, or was there someone watching and taking notes?"

"You're right. Perhaps he was killed by a Soviet sniper and then eaten. It does sound like conjecture. A story told to scare other soldiers. Keep them from falling asleep at their posts."

He brought the two cages over and set them on the table next to Gemeiner. "Look at these cages. You can open them from the top, or you can slide open this panel on the bottom."

"I'm not afraid of a few lab mice."

"Not even hungry lab mice? After everything I've told you?"

"No, sorry, you'll have to do better."

Hoekman pulled up Gemeiner's shirt. There were rope-like scars on his abdomen that matched the ones on his back. Too bad he couldn't know what had caused those scars. It would be interesting to know what techniques the Russians used and whether or not they'd been effective. He checked the straps on Gemeiner's hands and feet, then turned to the bin of tools next to the table. He fished out a razor blade, held it up to the light

MICHAEL WALLACE

and check its edge. Sharp.

"This is my favorite part of the job," Hoekman said.

"I'll bet it is."

It was warm in the office—both snakes and rodents preferred temperatures that could make a man loosen his collar—but that didn't fully explain the sweat beading at the old man's forehead.

"Don't get me wrong, I do not enjoy torturing people. Causing them pain. I am...*indifferent,* I suppose you could say. I am not like some men for whom the pain is everything. What I enjoy is the learning. You learn a good deal about people doing this. Human nature, the capacity to resist, the need to please. Who talks, who stays silent. And why. I believe that every man has his breaking point.

"One man starts babbling at the first glimpse of a pair of forceps. Another man can handle pain, but if you keep him awake, standing on his feet, he'll beg, cry for mercy after three or four days. Most cooperate fully if you threaten their wives and children, but not everyone."

Hoekman bent to the man's stomach. This would be more interesting if he didn't get carried away at first. He drew the blade across the flesh. One, two, three, four, five times. Gemeiner drew in a sharp breath, but didn't cry out. Blood welled to the surface and ran in rivulets down his side.

"Very good, Herr Gemeiner. Some pain, some fear, but your reptile side still holds sway."

He lifted the two cages and put them side by side across the man's stomach. It was slick with blood now and Hoekman had to hold the cages in place to keep them from simply sliding off. The animals inside scratched, squeaked.

"So what, you're going to let some hungry mice bite me?"

"They'll lick at the blood at first. Your bucking and thrashing will confuse them, but they are too hungry and there

288

is nowhere for them to go in any event."

Gemeiner was panting and his eyes watered. "Go ahead. The sooner you start, the sooner you'll see I can't be broken."

"That sounds like quite a challenge."

"You'll see. I'm not afraid of lab mice."

This *would* be interesting.

"When did I say anything about lab mice? They're not from a lab. They were brought to me from the Eastern Front. And they are not mice. The rats of Stalingrad are nothing more than a few bones at the bottom of a cook pot by now, but there are still plenty of rats in Kiev."

Colonel Hoekman slid open the bottoms of the cages. The rats were starving and needed no encouragement to start their work.

𝅘𝅥

It was just before dawn and Gabriela was dismayed to discover the streets of Paris already flooded with enemies. Gendarmes on foot, waving over cars, German checkpoints, bunches of *milice* in black shirts, pulling on black berets. Hoekman, it seems, had roused the entire city to look for the fugitives.

Helmut wore a cap and a fake mustache that wouldn't hold up to serious scrutiny, but was close enough to the real thing if Gabriela didn't look too hard. The truck had *"Farine du Quartier"* painted on the side, together with a helpful picture of a sack of flour and three baguettes for those who might not speak French.

Problem was, if they were stopped, subjected to even a rudimentary inspection, it would all be over. Those weren't bags of flour in the back.

Gabriela tried to shake off the fear. "A million people living in Paris, and half the city is awake already. They can't stop everyone."

"Until we try to leave," Helmut said. "The city is strangled with checkpoints. They'll double- and triple-check every transit document and open every car trunk and every truck."

Christine leaned forward to look over Helmut's shoulder. "That's what I'm here for." She sat behind the seats, near the boxes of gold coins. "Take the second left. Yes, here." A moment later she said, "The edge of the 15th is like a sieve. You want to get out of the city, I can find at least four routes into the southern *banlieus*."

Make that three. The first road they tried had two policemen, questioning a man with a cart filled with cabbages. The man was shouting, pointing at his cart, then giving exaggerated, disgusted shrugs. The police were so focused on the arguing man that Helmut had time to turn around without getting stopped.

"Try here instead," Christine said a moment later. "Left, then bear right."

It seemed they were doubling back on their tracks, but then they hit a cobbled street and they were slicing due south. Minutes later, the city fragmented into villages and then unbroken farmland.

"I told you she knew the city," Gabriela said.

"Nicely done," Helmut said.

"Stay on this road until you cross a green iron bridge," Christine said, "then take the immediate right. Follow it... oh, about half an hour. Then you'll see what looks almost like a cow trail on the right. That'll carry us all the way to the Lyon highway."

"How long?"

"Another hour, hour and a half maybe."

Gabriela looked down at her clothes, glanced back at Christine and her coat and dress. "We can't go all the way to Marseille like this. Sooner or later we'll hit a checkpoint and it's going to be sticky explaining why a flour truck is carrying two girls who look like they stepped out of a city lounge and spent the night in a warehouse."

"I don't have to be there until tomorrow morning," Helmut said. "We have all day and night to get to Marseille."

"Perfect," Christine said. "We can bypass those old Vichy check-points at night. Meanwhile, I'm dead tired back here. Can you find the bridge and the dirt road on your own?"

"Sure, get some rest. My jacket is tucked behind my seat. You can use it as a pillow. Feel free to pull off those tarps and do something with them, if you can."

"Can I open the boxes?" Christine asked in a teasing voice. "70,000 gold coins might not make the most comfortable bed, but I'm willing to give it a try."

"They're booby trapped, so maybe not."

"Booby trapped? Are they really?"

"Maybe, maybe not. If they're not, the guy who packed the box should really be deported."

"Gaby, hand me Roger's drawing," she said. "You know, the rooster on the building, you still have it?"

"Yes, it's here."

"I want one more look. There's something that's bugging me."

⚡⚡

After Christine had fallen asleep in the back, Gabriela looked out the window. A gray, rain-splattered dawn greeted them. The truck heater thawed her feet, but it wasn't enough to warm the front, so she was cold in spite of her coat.

"So here we are," Helmut said. "Together again."

"Yes."

"Thank you for coming back to warn me," he said.

"I need your help getting my father out of that pit. You can't help if Hoekman arrests you."

"Is that all it is?"

"No, it's not," she admitted. "I wouldn't have left you behind anyway, I hope you know that."

"I wouldn't have left you, either."

"I know." Gabriela thought about what Alfonse had said about Helmut. He was wrong. It wasn't an act; Helmut was a good man who cared about people. Flawed, like anyone else.

"It wasn't my idea," he said. "I never wanted to hurt you. I don't know if you'll believe that, but it's true."

"You were playing the good soldier, I understand."

"No, not really. If I'd played my part, I would have seduced you, sent you to kill Hoekman, and then never thought about it again."

"It's a strange time and place for a German to grow a conscience."

"I always had one. I never managed to lose it, that's the problem."

"I'm sitting here, thinking and thinking, and I can't figure out who you're going to bribe with those 70,000 French roosters. And how it can help the Germans."

"It's safer if you don't know."

"It doesn't matter anymore, what could go wrong? David Mayer left for Switzerland. Hopefully, he's on the train by now. Hoekman has Gemeiner. I don't even want to think about that. You've got employees, but by now Nazis are dragging them out of bed."

Helmut's grip tightened on the wheel. "My men have contingencies. I hope to God they followed them. If they did, they'll be long gone by the time the Gestapo arrives."

"And your wife?" she asked, gently. "What about her?"

"I called, or tried to, at Strasbourg. David is going to try again from Switzerland. She knows what to do. She's smart and resourceful."

"But not so smart and resourceful that she can help all the way from Germany. You're down to two friends and they're both in this car."

"I don't plan to put you in danger."

"Too late for that, now." She put a hand on his arm. "Why don't you tell me what you have planned. Maybe I can help."

"I don't suppose it could hurt," Helmut said. "If you're captured, I'm likely either dead or also in custody."

"That's right."

"Did you know there was almost a second war with the French army last fall?"

"What French army?"

"Vichy kept its army. Small, weak, pathetic, true, but it existed. It had to police Algeria, for one, protect the coast against Allied attack. When Algeria fell to the Americans, the Wehrmacht launched a second invasion to occupy the south."

"I heard that. I couldn't figure out why they had to invade."

"Hitler couldn't leave the south of France exposed, especially not the coasts. He didn't trust what remained of the French in any event. But what wasn't reported was that the French almost fought back."

"You can destroy the French army, but you can't do anything about French pride," she said.

"Fifty thousand troops took defensive positions around Toulon. The Germans surrounded them and there was almost shooting. The French cause was hopeless and they disbanded at the last minute. The thing is, they still have their weapons."

"What's changed? I don't know much, but I know fifty thousand troops is nothing. They couldn't hope to defeat the *boches*."

"Exactly. That's why they disbanded and that's why the Germans simply let them. But Gaby, they don't have to defeat the Germans. All they have to do is seize the port of Marseille and hold off the Wehrmacht for five days. They'll have the element of surprise. It will take the Germans time to mount a counterattack. Meanwhile, the British and the Americans control the western Mediterranean. If the port of Marseille stays open..."

"You're saying you want the Americans to invade."

"They're going to invade anyway. They might come through southern France, maybe across the Channel, or via Belgium. Denmark, Italy, Greece, it doesn't matter. The Americans are too strong, they are winning and the Western Front is too thinly protected. It's just a question of timing. Because meanwhile the Russians have turned the tide in the east. If the Americans wait another year it will be too late. The Soviet Union, not the United States and Britain, will win the war. Tell me, would you rather be liberated by Stalin or Roosevelt?"

"I see. And the gold coins?"

"Bribing Vichy officials. Paying mobsters, saboteurs. Payment for French soldiers."

"Why gold?"

"Because gold has no value unless they win. A man spends his gold and the Gestapo will be kicking down his door. If a man takes the gold, it is worthless unless the Americans win."

"French roosters?" she asked.

"Robbed from French vaults when France fell. I merely bought it back to return to the French people."

"But where did you get so much money?"

"I'm a good businessman. Or was. I've saved my profits, liquidated half my capital. All for this. Saved some currency to tie up loose ends."

"Loose ends like David Mayer."

"All my employees. And my wife, you, Christine. Hopefully, myself, if I survive the next few days. But yes, it's over. I'm almost broke. Maybe in a few years I'll rebuild."

"I'm sure you will, you have a talent."

"I've got it," Christine said from the seat behind them.

"I thought you were asleep," Gabriela said. "Got what?"

"I was asleep, and that's why I've got it. I figured it out. The red rooster, I understand. It's France. Roger Leblanc thinks he's France. That's why he made a rooster and put it on top of that building. It's looking down, it has his face on it."

"That doesn't make any sense," she said. "You're still dreaming."

"Listen! The German prison. The rooster is a *Coq Gallois*, like on the gold coins. It's just sitting up there, doing nothing, while the *boches* run their horrid little factory."

No, she wasn't asleep. In fact, she sounded more awake than Gabriela had ever heard.

"And Roger put his face on it," Gabriela said. "When the Gestapo came and arrested the zazous, Roger sat and watched."

"That's me, too," Christine said. Her voice was softer now, rippled with a current of anguish. "Do you think that's how my face looks? When the *boches* come to me, when I lie on my back and do nothing. Is that what I look like?" Her voice rose in pitch. "That dead look, is that me? Please, tell me."

"Christine, no. Don't do this to yourself."

"I can't help it. My god, I'm a collaborator."

"Christine," Helmut said. "Listen to me. In war, everybody is a collaborator."

CHAPTER TWENTY-NINE

THE HUMAN SMUGGLER LED THEM along a hedgerow just after dusk, then into a thick copse of trees and up to the edge of another farm. He stopped Helmut and Gabriela and waited. They could see a ramshackle stone cottage with a single lit window. Ten minutes passed.

The smuggler was a nervous young man, wiry with a thin mustache. Maybe eighteen, twenty years old. Gabriela couldn't understand what alarmed him about the farmhouse. At last, he whispered, "All right, it is safe. Go."

Helmut had paid him five hundred reichsmarks, agreed to pay five hundred more for every crossing, of which there would be several. Five hundred more when he brought the truck across the border, loaded with bags of flour. It was an exorbitant fee, but it was a complicated undertaking.

Gabriela carried a heavy bag as did Helmut and the smuggler. Her arms ached.

They stopped again some distance on, this time in a wide ditch. Trees on either side, but clear pasture in front. The stars glittered overhead. A chill breeze blew down from the Massif Central just to their south. In the distance, a dog barked. Then it was silent again. Still they waited.

Gabriela could sense Helmut's impatience as he stirred by her side. "What is this about?"

"They come through this wood," the smuggler whispered. "They're dangerous to both sides."

"You mean the Resistance?" Gabriela asked. "The *maquis?* Why would they care what we're doing?"

"They're always on the lookout for collaborators." Again, that whispered urgency. "Some are no more than common criminals. They don't care, they'll rob anyone."

But then later, when they set off again, the man said, "Stay back from the road. They come down this way in their trucks, even in the middle of the night. Always looking for contraband."

"You mean the *boches?*" Gabriela asked. "German military, is that who we're looking out for?"

He didn't answer. A few minutes later, however, he warned, "These farms are dangerous. If they see you passing, know you have a little money, they won't hesitate to rob you."

"Who will rob you?" Helmut asked. "You mean the farmers?"

But again, he refused to clarify. It was never more specific than "they" or "them." It occurred to Gabriela that the smuggler classified everyone as either *us* or *they.* And *they* were always a risk to *us*, no matter who *they* were.

At last, they reached the safe house, a small inn at the edge of the village of Gaudet. And just in time; Gabriela's aching arms couldn't take any more.

"Be careful, they can't entirely be trusted," the smuggler warned. "Sometimes they'll take advantage of travelers."

But when they arrived, the innkeeper took their money and gave them a key. He was an *ancien combattant* from the last war, with a crooked nose and a thick neck marked with mustard gas scars. One eye was cloudy gray and blind. He fixed Helmut with a hard look with his remaining eye, but said nothing, just pointed them toward the room. He disappeared into a back room and didn't reappear. Helmut carried the bags upstairs

MICHAEL WALLACE

one at a time while she stayed with the smuggler.

The whole setup, dividing trusted people to stay with the bags of gold coins, reminded her of the old logic puzzle from the *colégio* in Barcelona.

You have a wolf, a goat, and a cabbage and you have to get them across the river.

Helmut looked tired when he came back downstairs. He leaned forward to speak in her ear. "You've got the Mauser? Good. Lock the door. If someone tries to enter, shoot them. I don't care who they are or what they say."

"And have you figured out yet who *they* are?"

He laughed. "I have no idea."

"Helmut, be careful. I don't trust that guy, either."

"I'll be careful." He lowered his voice further. "Only four hundred more kilos to go."

She retreated to the room and locked the door. She lit the lamp, then lay down on the bed with the gun in her hand. It wasn't her intention to fall asleep, but she was exhausted and long past the ability to maintain the constant tension she'd felt since the previous night at the Egyptienne. She woke to Helmut pounding on the door. She let him in and helped him with the bags of gold.

He woke her about once an hour with two more bags. Sometime after midnight, he brought Christine and they paid off the smuggler. The man slipped the wad of bills into his pocket. "The truck will be parked around back first thing in the morning."

"And the guns?" Helmut asked.

He reached into his coat and pulled out a pair of handguns and then a box of shells. Helmut turned them over in his hands. "Lugers. German sidearms. Where did you get these? Wait, never mind, I don't want to know."

"Probably not," the smuggler said.

"Well, thanks." The two men shook hands.

"If you come back, need to get north again, ask for Yves in the village. *Bonne chance et bon courage,* I hope they don't catch you."

Helmut turned to Christine once they were alone. "Your man came through, I'll give you that. I half expected to be robbed by armed men. Or worse."

"I've used him before. He's expensive, but he's good and he can be trusted."

"You girls can have the big room. I'll take this one. Lock your doors, keep the guns at hand."

"Nah, I'll take the smaller room," Christine said. "And I'll be fine by myself. I think you two have some unfinished business."

"It's okay," Gabriela said. "I mean, we're not, we haven't..."

"No need to explain it to me," Christine said. "Go ahead, I'll be fine. I'm only too happy to have a few hours alone, by myself, in a comfortable bed."

She took the key to the second room and left them alone, staring awkwardly at each other. The sound of the door in the adjacent room closing, the lock turning.

"I'll sleep on the floor if you'd like," Helmut said.

"No, don't do that. Go ahead, sit down. You look exhausted." She helped him out of his shoes, took off his jacket, then sat down beside him on the bed.

"Thank you." He rubbed at his temples, then gave her a direct look. His eyes were piercing and startlingly blue. "I'm so sorry for everything."

She put her hand on his. "Shh, I know. I think I understand."

"You do?"

"It's the war, it makes everything wrong and it justifies everything."

"Not everything, there has to be a line."

"But you didn't cross it," she said. "You could have and I'd have never known. But you didn't, you stopped, you told me."

He reached a hand and rested it against her cheek. She leaned forward until their noses touched and they looked into each other's eyes. His gaze was so intense it was hard not to look away.

Slowly he leaned forward. His lips brushed hers. She responded. It was a gentle kiss. The second kiss was more passionate. They put their arms around each other and kissed longer, harder. She was burning with desire and she could tell if she pushed, they would be undressing each other within moments.

There was nothing said aloud. Gabriela didn't pull away, and she sensed no reservation from Helmut. Nevertheless, there came a point where an unspoken agreement passed between them. They disengaged, first pulling back just a few inches, crossed again by a brief kiss, then further. At last they separated.

"Oh," he said. "That was nice."

"Yes."

And then Gabriela was helping him under the covers. She crawled in next to him, still clothed in what she'd worn the previous night—they had picked up fresh clothes earlier in the day, but were saving them for the next day—and put her arm around him. She lay her head against his chest. He pressed his face into her hair, kissed her head. Then leaned back against the pillow.

She could feel his heart beating furiously. But gradually, minute by minute, it calmed. Helmut sighed. His breathing turned regular. He was asleep, she could feel exhaustion pulling at her as well.

Gabriela put her hand to his face and stroked his cheek.

It didn't seem fair, none of this seemed fair. A different time, a different place. Things would have been different.

⚡⚡

They unloaded the bags of gold coins into the safe house in Marseille. It was already spring in the south and Christine went upstairs and threw open the shutters.

A light breeze blew in off the Mediterranean. It smelled of salt water with an occasional whiff of fish from the docks.

They'd come down from the hills on winding roads choked with cars, bicycles, motorcycles, and trucks. Goats sometimes crossed the road *en masse*, blocking traffic. Germans built concrete casements along the hillsides, mounted with machine guns. More Germans were bulldozing a pasture for an airstrip, others dug tank traps. One entire stone village, clinging to the side of a cliff, had been emptied and turned into a fortified camp. They were never stopped or challenged.

The Marseille safe house itself sat back on a narrow lane, with a hillside view down toward the aquamarine blue of the bay. Scrubby trees stretched up the hill behind them. The hill sloped sharply down from the house to a small alley cut through the scrub and along the edge of the hill. It twisted down to some houses fifty or sixty meters below them. But no immediate neighbors. A rooster crowed in the distance.

"I'm not turning over the gold until I meet with the Americans," Helmut explained as he double-checked the Mauser, then handed it back to Gabriela.

She didn't like it. "And you want us to stay here, while you go off alone? How can you be sure it's not a trap?"

"If Philipe Brun were setting me up, he could have turned me over to the Gestapo a long time ago."

"Unless he's just a bandit, then he'd want you to come down and bring the gold before finishing you off."

"Maybe. I'll take that risk."

"Then why not take the gold with you?" she asked.

"I don't know the man, so I'd be a fool to blindly trust him.

Just in case they really are trying to rob me, I don't want to make it too easy. Besides, a thousand things could go wrong. It could be nothing more than running into a gendarme who wants to inspect the truck. A thousand kilometers across France and we could lose the gold in the last kilometer."

He pulled out his own pistol, unloaded it, reloaded, then aimed at a spot on the wall. He put the gun away, then pulled it out again and aimed a second time.

"Tell me where you'll be, at least."

Helmut tucked the gun in his jacket pocket. "I'm going to the *vieux-port*, near the fish market in Quai des Belges. One of the shops has a wooden sign painted with a blue dolphin. That's where I'll be. But don't come, it's not safe."

"And when you're done, then what?"

"Then I'll take you to Switzerland."

Christine came down the stairs. "What about me? Just go home?"

"You've done so much," Helmut said. "We'd never have got out of Paris without you. There are seventy thousand roosters in those bags, more or less. Nobody would notice if there were a few missing, do you know what I mean? A girl wouldn't have to go back to working nights if she had ten or twenty gold roosters."

Christine blinked, nodded. Ten or twenty gold coins would be more than she'd ever seen in her life, but she had to have been thinking about those heavy bags already. You didn't stand next to bags of gold coins without being aware of it at all times.

"But you'll be caught as quickly as anyone else if you try to spend them, you understand. You have to wait until the Americans are here, or..." He hesitated. "Or bury them until the war ends, whenever that is."

"I understand."

"Just one more thing and you're done," he said. "Stay

with Gaby until I get back. You'll be safer together. Then go home, get your family away from the coast. Inland, at least—I don't know—forty kilometers, maybe. This will be the most dangerous real estate in France if everything goes according to plan."

"And if it doesn't go according to plan?" Gabriela asked.

"If I'm not back by nightfall, you'll know I failed. Christine, take Gaby if that happens. Your family can protect her. Don't either of you go back to Paris, for god's sake."

"But what about my father?"

Helmut chewed on his lip. "I don't know. Find David Mayer. Maybe he can help. Just...I don't know." He looked at his wristwatch. "I have to go."

The next few minutes proved to be a bitter parting. She wanted to tell him that she'd forgiven him and to thank him for finding her father. She wanted to tell him she loved him. But there was no time, and the moment was too awkward, so instead they exchanged chaste kisses to each cheek and best wishes and then he was gone. She heard the crunch of his tires as he backed the truck out of the lane.

After he was gone Christine sat in a chair in the salon, tapping her foot. "The problem is," she said at last, "I don't know anything else. My parents think I'm working as a seamstress in Paris. I send them money and ration coupons. Imagine a seamstress doing that. But they don't want to think about it."

Gabriela wondered about that. Probably they helped Christine maintain her fiction, but they'd have to be blind as well as stupid not to guess what she was doing in Paris.

"You're not seriously considering going back to the city," Gabriela said. "Not after all that about being a collaborator."

"Do you think I'm a collaborator?" Christine asked.

"No, but you do, that's what matters. And why would

you go back anyway? Especially after what Helmut said about the gold."

"It's not about the money. I told you, I don't know anything else, what would I do? Move home to Toulon and marry the son of the *boulanger*, like my father says?"

"Those are your only two choices? Surely not."

Gabriela felt like she was going insane waiting. She cracked the front window, then opened the front shutters a fraction, looked down at the street at the bottom of the hill. An old man on a bicycle, a dog trotting by with something nasty in its mouth.

"What are you looking for?"

"This is crazy," Gabriela said. "Sitting here, doing nothing."

"We're guarding the gold."

"We're not guarding the gold. If someone wants to steal 70,000 gold coins, will a couple of girls deter them? I don't think so. We'd be an added bonus. The only thing keeping this gold safe is nobody knows it's here. That's it."

"We've got guns."

"Yeah, and we're sitting on them, doing nothing. We could be out there helping Helmut."

"Helping him do what?" Christine asked.

"I don't know, but you saw what he looked like when he left. He's expecting trouble. What if Colonel Hoekman gets there first, he'll be dead."

"Helmut told us not to go."

"And he also told us how to find the fish market with the blue dolphin sign," Gabriela said. "He wants us to come or he wouldn't have told us."

"You're just rationalizing. You don't want to wait is all."

"No, I don't want to wait. Do you?"

"I think we should stay here. We've done all we can."

"No, we haven't. Listen, Helmut's in trouble, so what I

want to know is are you coming, or staying? I won't make you. I understand either way."

Christine sighed. "Oh, come on, are you sure?" Finally, when Gabriela didn't answer, she gave a firm nod. "Fine, then, I'm coming."

"You know how to find the Quai des Belges?"

"Of course. We can walk, it's not far."

"And the market with the blue dolphin sign, would that be hard to find?"

"I wouldn't think so."

Gabriela nodded. She looked down at the bags of gold. "How much did Helmut say? Four hundred kilos?"

"*Oaui,* something like that."

"We can't just leave it in the open."

"What then?"

"If we're going to hide this stuff before we leave, we'd better get busy."

⚡⚡

Helmut walked along the Marseille waterfront.

Fishermen tossed their catch from boats and into baskets. Other men waddled away with the heavy baskets balanced on shoulders. A babble of language; French, Italian, Catalan, Spanish, Arabic. Gulls wheeled overhead, screamed and squabbled. The sun was bright, the air cool and saturated with the smell of fish and seaweed.

He removed the cyanide capsule from his pocket and tucked it into his cheek. The glass felt smooth and cool. How easy to crush it between his teeth. He imagined the sharp glass, the bitter taste.

And it was surreal, because apart from the glass capsule, Helmut felt like he'd stepped out of the real world and into the pages of a book. A book where there was no war, where a German tourist with a battered copy of the Michelin Guide might stroll the docks of Marseille, taking in the crisp spring air, the sights and smells of the old port. Where he might stop for lunch and eat oysters with mignotte sauce and a bottle of chenin blanc.

That had been his life at one time. School in England, business in Germany, holidays in France. He'd met a pretty French girl, held her hand, whispered sweet French things in her ear. Marie-Élise was like a dream now, like a story he told himself.

Offshore, hundreds of fishing boats with sails skimmed the azure surface. A few steamers with varied flags. He could see the Château d'If, fortress and prison, a kilometer or so offshore on its island. German guns commanded the coast and a pair of Messerschmitts buzzed the harbor, but military presence was lighter than he'd expected. He knew the Luftwafte was currently constructing a major airfield nearby and that several thousand men of the First Army defended the city from American attack across the Mediterranean, but Marseille looked nothing like the ports along the French and Belgian coasts, subsumed as they were in war.

As for the docks themselves, it was clear why Philipe Brun had chosen this place to meet the American. There were no Germans or French police patrolling the dilapidated piers. Just fisherman dragging their catch from the sea, as had happened on this very spot for thousands of years, since the Romans. Since before the Romans, most likely. A few hang-abouts looking for food or day labor.

He rolled the glass capsule to his other cheek. It wouldn't take much of a bite to break the glass.

It was gas that killed. A bit of cyanide powder vaporized, you breathed it and it entered the bloodstream immediately and then the brain. Death took two or three minutes, Gemeiner said; unconsciousness was almost immediate. But there would be something in those few seconds. Dizziness? Nausea?

But only if you bit the capsule, that was the step Gemeiner neglected.

You coward. After all the warnings, you didn't take your own advice.

The docks grew seedier the further he walked. Rotting piers, the overwhelming smell of fish guts and sewage. Scavengers and rubbish-sorters picked through piles of refuse. Men sat repairing nets with calloused, saltwater-blasted hands. Pickpockets, Arabs, a man slumped drunk against a building. Women queued in front of a fish stall, waving their ration coupons. An even bigger crowd gathered around a man with a cart, illicitly selling shellfish. A withered beggar held out a hand to Helmut and muttered something incomprehensible. He handed over a few francs.

Helmut stopped on the docks between two piles of ceramic pots. A man with a cigarette dangling between his lips stacked pots, while his friend unloaded buckets from his boat. Screens capped the buckets and here and there an octopus arm reached through, probing for an escape route. The empty pots stood in shoulder-high piles, pyramid-style. From here he could see the sign with the blue dolphin opposite the pier.

The doors of the shop were closed. A man sat on a crate in front, his face buried in a newspaper. Black hair poked over the top. He had thick legs and hands with short fingers. Didn't look in any way like Gestapo or police, but the man didn't appear to be reading the newspaper either.

Helmut slipped his hand into his pocket. His fingers wrapped around the grip of the Luger. He'd rather have the familiar feel of the Mauser, but Gabriela had grown accustomed to the weapon and it would be harder for her to adapt. In any event, the pistol was probably worthless. He was alone; if it came to gun play, he'd better crush the capsule in his teeth and be done with it.

Once he'd studied the street and become reasonably sure that none of the men were anything but fisherman and dock workers, he made his way toward the closed door. The man folded his newspaper and studied him.

The man nodded. "Von Cratz."

Helmut felt a surge of relief as he recognized the man. "Brun."

"You're late. I was beginning to wonder if something had gone wrong."

"Something is always going wrong, but I'm here now. Is the American inside?"

"Yes."

"And your men?"

"You have the payment?"

Helmut smiled. "Perhaps not on me. Didn't fit in my pockets."

"But in the city? It's somewhere we can get to?"

"Yes. Your men?" he asked again.

"They're ready. You work a deal with the Americans, we can promise four days."

Helmut stopped while two men walked by carrying a length of heavy rope. "You said a week."

Brun had promised a week and Helmut had hoped for four days. If Brun promised four days, did that mean he'd get two? The Americans, no doubt, would demand a month.

"Germans have reinforced," Brun said. "A fresh division within twenty kilometers of the city. Four days is all we can promise. I told the American. He said they only needed seventy-two hours."

"Really?"

Brun gave a typically Gallic shrug.

The Americans were massing in England, but hadn't yet made a serious attempt to cross the Channel. That was only fifty kilometers or so wide, depending on where you crossed. It was several hundred from Algeria to Marseille.

The problem was not so much the crossing, but getting ashore and holding a beachhead, then winning control of the skies while you simultaneously tried to ferry millions of tons of men and materiel across those hundreds of kilometers. He could almost picture the logistics in his mind. For every man wading ashore with a rifle in hand, there would be ten behind the scenes. Men like Helmut and Alfonse and David Mayer.

But if the French rebellion managed to seize the city for a few days, the Americans wouldn't have to fight to establish a beachhead. It would come down to an air war, and seeing what the Americans and British could already do over northern France, the Luftwafte couldn't control the skies. Once the Americans were in France, the Germans would rush troops south, but that would empty the coast across from England. And there would be no dislodging the Americans, not with half of southern France in rebellion.

"When do I get the gold?" Brun asked.

"So mercenary," Helmut said with a smile. "I thought your greatest wish was to be known as the savior of France. Is it just about money after all?"

"Motives are a complex thing, my friend."

"You'll get the gold as soon as I speak to the American."

"Well, you'd better get going, then." He held out his hand. "Your gun?"

"My gun?"

"I'm sure you've got a weapon. Hand it over, the American said no weapons."

Helmut felt a touch of doubt. "I've never met the man, I'd rather have my pistol, just in case. The Gestapo, you know."

Brun shook his head. "No guns, I can't unlock the door until you hand it over."

Helmut remembered his earlier thoughts. If this were a setup, there would be no point in fighting it out. Cyanide would be the only recourse. He felt the capsule in his cheek.

He turned his back to the docks and slipped the Luger from his pocket. Brun tucked it into his own jacket, then pulled out a set of keys and unlocked the door. "Go upstairs, it's the room overlooking the bay."

He stepped inside. "Thanks."

But Brun was already locking the door behind him. It was dark inside, with only a little light through a shutter high on the door. The overwhelming smell of fish guts permeated the room. Helmut made his way up the stairs. There was a small office on top, but it was empty except for a single chair, facing the window.

A man sat in the chair. He didn't turn around when Helmut entered. Too dim to see much of the man except his outline.

Helmut cleared his throat. "I believe you are expecting me."

The answer sounded muffled.

"Are you the American?"

Again, a muffled response.

And then, gradually, as Helmut's eyes adjusted, he saw that the man's hands hung down by his side. They were tied behind his back. There was something around his head.

Helmut crossed the room in three steps. The thing around his head was a gag. The man's head lolled to one side and his face was so bruised and swollen that Helmut didn't recognize him at first. Blood soaked his white shirt. The man lifted his head and met Helmut's gaze with anguished eyes.

It was Gemeiner.

CHAPTER THIRTY

GABRIELA AND CHRISTINE WALKED THE docks. They'd scavenged men's shirts and trousers from a closet in the house. They were too big, and the belt holding up Gabriela's pants made her feel more ridiculous still. Only the Mauser in her pocket gave her confidence.

People watched. One fisherman said to another in Spanish, "You can have the blonde, I'll take the one with the big boobs."

Gabriela turned to him and snapped, "*Tu puta madre.*" The man drew back with a surprised look, then grinned. His friend slapped him on the shoulder and laughed. It was stupid. She couldn't get rattled. Thankfully, the men didn't follow.

A minute later, a group of dock workers stopped unloading crates from a tramp steamer and whistled after them. "Hey, girls. Come over, come talk to us." After Gabriela and Christine passed, one said something in an unknown language that made the others laugh.

The whistles and the calls seemed to unnerve Christine as well. "What are we doing? We're just girls, we can't do this."

"We can and we will. Ignore them, it means nothing."

"A few days ago I was shaking my tits in the face of some old general with hair growing out of his ears. I told him I wasn't wearing any panties. And now I'm supposed to do this?"

"You said you wanted to come. Well, do you?"

"I just need you to talk me into this. I'm scared."

"Fine, here's what you have to ask yourself, Christine. Are you just a collaborator? Is that all you want to be?"

"No, but..."

"You can either collaborate or you can resist, it's up to you."

"I don't know, Gaby, I don't know if I'm strong enough."

"You're not Roger Leblanc. You can do this, I know you can."

"Helmut knows what he's doing, right?"

"That's right, we're just here to help. But we need to be strong, we can't be surprised by whatever happens. Can you do that?"

Christine nodded. "I think so."

"Good, just do what I tell you."

But Christine drew up short. A worried look passed over her face. "Oh, no."

"What is it?"

"Look. There it is, the place with the dolphin sign."

Gabriela looked down the street and what she saw destroyed her hopes.

⚡⚡

"They all talk in the end," a man said in German while Helmut stared in horror at the broken old man in front of him.

Helmut whirled around. His hand went to his pocket, but of course the Luger was gone. He'd surrendered it to Philipe Brun before entering the building.

Colonel Hoekman stood at the door to his rear. He held a gun in his gloved hand. The silver skull gleamed on his hat.

Helmut slid the cyanide capsule between his teeth, stuck it halfway out. "Not another step forward. I'll bite. You'll get nothing."

"I need nothing. I have everything already." Nevertheless, he didn't move from the doorway.

Bite, you idiot. It's over, don't let them take you.

Helmut's eyes darted to the window. Too small to crash through. And too high. The building was solid brick and there was too much noise on the docks and in the harbor. Nobody would even hear him scream for help. If they did, they wouldn't come. Not here.

Could he charge Hoekman, overpower the man? The colonel was a good ten centimeters taller and there was nothing soft about the way he carried himself. Oh, and the small matter of the gun. No, he didn't think so.

"I should have known it was you," Colonel Hoekman said. "All that business with Major Ostermann's files. You were hiding in the shadow of his incompetence. It was good, I'll give you that. You played the perfect snake, slithering around where no one could see you. I'm a snake too, and so I should have found you. But with all these people blundering about, waving guns and making feints, I was distracted. The major, your prostitute, the Jew. It almost worked. Too bad your friend blurted everything. Go ahead, ask him."

Helmut pulled off the gag. Gemeiner looked up. His eyes were shot with streaks of blood. He looked ten years older. "I'm sorry, I tried."

"For god's sake, why didn't you bite the capsule?"

"I know, I know."

"What the hell were you thinking?"

"I know, I'm sorry."

"What did you tell them?"

"Too much, my friend."

"Where's the American?"

Gemeiner let out a bitter laugh. "Ah, that's the irony. This bastard intercepted a message from the Americans. They're abandoning any plan to invade Provence, at least for now." He coughed. It was weak, gurgly. "Maybe they prefer Italy or

Calais. Maybe they want to wait."

"Your plan was pure fantasy," Colonel Hoekman said. "The Americans will never defeat us. They are cowards, happy to fly ten thousand meters overhead and bomb vineyards and churches, or play cat-and-mouse games in the desert, but charge fixed positions? No. They do not like to die. The Americans are quite the opposite of the Russians, in fact. And if they are afraid of dying, how will they ever penetrate Europe?"

"But what about Brun?"

"Not much help," Gemeiner said.

Hoekman gave a dismissive wave with his free hand. "That is the most amusing part of this whole plot. You put your faith in a Frenchman? Hah. One look at Herr Gemeiner and your Vichy traitor abandoned the whole plan. For a little incentive more, he happily led you in here."

"Kill me," Gemeiner muttered in a voice so low that Helmut wasn't sure he heard correctly.

"What? How?"

"Untie me, make him shoot us both. Please, let me die."

"You can charge me if you'd like," Hoekman said. "I am hoping to disarm you, subject you to questioning. I would like to discover where you've hid the gold, after all. I wish to count every last coin and submit a full report to Berlin."

"No doubt that will advance your evil little career," Helmut said.

"One would suppose." Hoekman looked thoughtful, as if, incredibly, this were only just occurring to him. "But isn't it curious that you would use the word *evil*. Any objective bystander would agree that I'm not the evil one in this room. That would be the two men working against their Fatherland, their Führer, even their own race. To turn against one's family is the worst kind of evil imaginable."

Helmut felt his body tense. Everything had collapsed, he

had nothing left.

"Come on," Hoekman said. "I'm ready. Are you going to bite the capsule, or charge me? The room is empty. You have no help. Your man here couldn't stand on his broken ankles even if you untied him."

"And what happens to Gemeiner?"

"What happens to him is inconsequential."

"What is it? A quick execution or some sort of medical butchery like what you did to Ricardo Reyes?"

"Not a quick execution, certainly not. But believe me, Herr von Cratz, you will have other worries. Your world will be reduced to figuring out how to please me, how to give me what I want. You will not give this old man another thought."

"He's suffered already, he's broken, nearly dead. Why not just shoot him in the head and be done with it. Do that and I'll tell you how to find the gold."

"You will tell me how to find the gold anyway."

Helmut made a quick decision. He spit the cyanide capsule into his hand, then shoved it toward Gemeiner's face. The old man grabbed the capsule with his lips.

"No," Hoekman snarled. He strode across the room.

Too late. If he had hesitated once, Gemeiner had long since learned the error of that path. The crunch of broken glass. There was something white around his lips and he took a deep, shuddering breath.

Hoekman reached Gemeiner, tried to dig the capsule out of his mouth with his gloved hands. But already the old man was convulsing, his head lolling back.

Helmut turned for the door and ran. He had a split second. He heard Hoekman turning, waited for the gunshots to the back. They didn't come. He reached the door, pulled it open.

And collided with two young Gestapo agents in uniform.

He was already tensed, ready to fight and so he had the

upper hand. He swung his elbow, caught the first man in the jaw. The man had a submachine gun and Helmut grabbed it by the barrel, tried to wrest it free. He had it, it was coming loose.

The other man bashed him in the head with his gun butt. Sharp pain. His vision turned black. He stumbled.

They were on him. Kicking, hitting with gun butts. He tried to regain his feet, but they knocked him down.

"Enough," Colonel Hoekman said. "I want him uninjured." He bent and grabbed Helmut by the hair, dragged him back into the room, threw him down. "Did you think I came alone? What a fool you are."

Helmut looked up. Gemeiner slumped over in his chair. His pain, at least, was over.

"It doesn't matter," Hoekman said. "You killed the old man, but so what? I already found his breaking point. It was impressive, but in the end he turned into a frightened mouse, cringing in terror. They all do. What I don't know is your breaking point. Can you hold up as well as the old man? Or will you be begging and whining within a minute, like that faggot from the restaurant?"

Helmut said nothing. His head throbbed, there was a fire in his side, like maybe they'd broken a rib. And he was terrified. But he wasn't going to show it. He could suffer some more, he had to. He couldn't tell Hoekman where the gold was, not yet. Not until Gaby and Christine had waited so long they knew he wasn't coming back.

"Very good, that is an excellent start, Herr von Cratz." He turned to the other two. "You, secure the door, make sure that Frenchman is not still lurking about. And you, get this man in the chair."

The second man untied Gemeiner and pushed him to the floor. The old man's body slumped at an unnatural angle. His eyes, glassy, dead, stared over his shoulder. White powder flecked his lips.

They bound Helmut's hands behind his back with the same ropes they'd used on Gemeiner, then shoved him into the chair. He sucked in his breath against the pain in his side.

"So you're going to do it here?" Helmut asked.

"There is no reason to leave, not yet."

"You're afraid of an ambush. All your boasting and insulting the French and Americans, you can't just drive through the streets of Marseille with your Nazi flags flapping in the breeze."

"You continue to underestimate me, Herr von Cratz. We have more than enough men to secure our absolute safety. That's right, there are twenty men in this building alone. I have thirty more searching Marseille, breaking apart the last of Philipe Brun's pathetic band of traitors. When they are quite finished, we will all leave together. I might even request a military escort." He leaned forward and smiled. "So if you are hoping for some sort of grand rescue, you might be disappointed."

The second lieutenant returned to the room, gave a Heil Hitler and told Colonel Hoekman that the building was secure. Helmut was facing the wall, but he heard the sound of a briefcase snapping open.

"I think we shall start with this. And how about this. We'll see how our prisoner reacts to that. Like a reptile or like a rodent." The briefcase snapped shut. "Get him on his feet."

The two lieutenants jerked Helmut out of the chair. He closed his eyes.

"So, Herr von Cratz. You will never see your wife again. And your French mistress seems to have abandoned you."

"What is your point?"

"Since you have been *de facto* unmanned by these events, it would not seem to be a hardship to see you unmanned *de jure*." He held a pair of forceps in front of Helmut's face and clicked them open and closed. "Lieutenant, drop Herr von Cratz's pants. I am going to remove his testicles."

CHAPTER THIRTY-ONE

G ABRIELA STARED AT THE BRICK building in despair. Six Germans in uniform stood beneath the sign with the blue dolphin. A truck pulled up and another German leaned out the window with a cigarette dangling from his mouth. He said something and the men outside the door laughed. They carried guns hung on slings around their necks.

The Germans attracted attention from the dock workers, but most apparently considered it prudent to keep working. A small army of stevedores unloaded a tramp steamer. They trudged past, carrying crates, forearms bulging. Gabriela and Christine stood in the shadow of a stack of narrow-necked octopus pots.

"What are we going to do?" Christine whispered. "We can't possibly — "

"Shh. Just a minute, I'm thinking."

Even among the fish and the men carrying baskets of shellfish, she caught glimpses of the ever-present French hunger. Thin boys watched with rat-like intensity from the alleys between buildings for the chance to steal or scavenge. An old woman took a bucket of fish guts and bones from a man while several gulls wheeled overhead, screaming their frustration. Gabriela didn't want to imagine what the woman intended to do with the fish offal.

The German soldiers, on the other hand, standing with content, well-fed expressions, smoking. One of them munched a croissant, and another sipped a cup of coffee and snacked on some sort of pastry. Two more Germans came around the side of the building. More laughter, some slaps on the back. Relaxing after a job well-done, apparently.

"So that's it, then," Christine said. There was a deadness in her voice. "It's over, the goddamn *boches* won."

"No, we can't...we have to..."

"Have to what? Gaby, we have no choice. Let's just get the hell out of here before one of them sees us."

She turned it over in her mind. They could run at the Germans, shooting. No doubt kill a few, before the *boches* cut them down. For nothing.

"You know I'm right," Christine said. "Come on, we can talk back at the house."

"Looking for octopus?" a man asked them in French. He carried two clay pots on his shoulders.

"Leave us alone."

"Pretty girls, dressed so ugly. Almost looks like you don't belong here. And why are you staring at the *boches*?"

Gabriela turned with a frown. The man was short, dark-haired, like a thousand others working the docks. "We're taking a walk, that's all." She took Christine and made to leave.

He swung one of the pots off his shoulder and blocked her path. "Listen to me, your friend might still be alive."

"What?"

"Come around here, where they can't see you."

They stepped to the back of the stack of octopus pots. "Who are you?" Gabriela asked.

A bitter smile. "I'm the man who would have been a French hero. They'd have built a statue of me overlooking the harbor and attached my name to parks and boulevards for generations to come. Now, I'm just trying not to be another French coward and collaborator."

"It's you, you're the Vichy official, the one who was going to seize the port for the Americans. What is the name? Brun?"

"*Oui*, Philipe Brun, at your service."

"But what happened? If it wasn't you, who tipped off the *boches*?"

He sighed. "It was a good plan. Or would've been, until the Americans balked and the Gestapo showed up. I led him right in there, right into a trap. A sniper had me pinned down, but that's just an excuse."

"Oh, god, no."

"But I couldn't leave, even when I had the chance. I saw you watching and knew, or at least guessed. You work with Helmut von Cratz, don't you?"

"Yes, and we're friends, too."

"I am so sorry, I thought it would work and I thought...I don't know, that I would be different. That when they took me, I would be a hero. I was not."

"You talked."

"I knew what to expect and that's exactly what happened. The usual Gestapo methods. And like a typical cowardly, craven Frenchman, I gave up at once." He gave a dismissive shrug, but there was a bitter edge to his tone.

Gabriela thought about Roger Leblanc, how he'd betrayed his zazou friends. Except this was a little different, wasn't it? "But if that's all you are, what are you doing? Why aren't you hiding somewhere?"

"I'm sitting here thinking about how many Germans I can kill before the bastards get me. I came up with a good plan, might even free von Cratz, but the problem is, I need two other men. I've got plenty of men I trust, dozens of them, but how long would it take me to get them? An hour, two?"

"And by then the *boches* are gone."

"Or else reinforced. The only hope is to act quickly, which means I'm two men short." He gave them a hard look. "Do you know any patriots in the area?"

"We know two."

"Can they be trusted?"

"They can. They're women, I assume that's not a problem for you."

"Man, woman, child, I'll take anyone who can do the job."

"Then we'll do it. What do you have in mind?"

"First thing, I need to get you guns."

"We're already armed."

"Good, very good. That buys us time. Now, can you shoot? And kill?"

"We can. Yes." Gabriela looked at Christine. "Isn't that right?"

"I-I don't know."

"Remember what you told me about sleeping with Colonel Hoekman? Just pretend you're someone else. Just survive and live to fight another day. Remember that?"

"Yes, okay." A grim expression crossed Christine's face. "I can do it."

"We only have one chance," Brun said. "Maybe ten seconds where they're distracted. Everything we do, we have to do in those ten seconds."

"And how do we get that distraction?" Gabriela asked.

"I've got a truck parked five hundred meters from here," Brun said. "I'm going to drive it around the corner and ram the Germans. With any luck, I'll kill a few. Then I'll start shooting. As soon as you hear the truck, you run for the door.

Gabriela couldn't see the soldiers from behind the octopus pots, but she could hear loud German voices, laughter. How confident they sounded. But were they *over*confident?"

"It won't work," she said.

"It has to work."

"Gaby, I think it's a good plan," Christine said.

"It's almost a good plan," Gabriela said. "But these men have seen a lot, they're trained soldiers. Wouldn't be their first ambush. They'll be ready. We might get a couple. The rest will turn those guns and we'll have to run across the open to get at them. There's no chance." She turned to Brun. "Meanwhile, it's suicide to drive at so many armed men with the truck. All it takes is one or two who aren't idiots."

"I'm not afraid to die."

"I'll die too, if it comes to that, but are we going to die and fail at the same time? That's the part I don't like."

"You have a better idea?" he asked.

Gabriela thought about crossing the Pont au Change in Alfonse's car. Alfonse had flicked a cigarette out the window and for a single half-smoked cigarette a boy had scrambled desperately through traffic. A man had abandoned his bicycle for the same prize. She thought about the bread queues and the children with pinched faces.

She looked up and down the docks. Fishermen, stevedores, laborers, beggars, scavengers, women queuing for fish, and many others with lean looks. Hundreds of people.

"I have a better distraction in mind," Gabriela said.

"I'm listening, go ahead."

"It starts with a spilled box of gold coins."

𝕾𝕾

It was the anticipation that was crushing, more so than the pain itself. Colonel Hoekman didn't go about the business at once, but in an exploratory fashion that gave Helmut plenty of time to think.

"That did not seem to be much pressure," Hoekman said, "yet you were quite out of your mind with agony."

He squeezed again with the forceps. Pain exploded in Helmut's groin, so deep and horrible that he turned lightheaded. The two lieutenants held him up. The pressure released and he gasped in relief.

Hoekman prodded at his testicle with a gloved finger. "Not even damaged yet, but look at the sweat pouring down your face. Every muscle in your body is quivering. You have not screamed yet, but I can tell you want to. You need to scream so badly and yet you don't. You refuse to give in and yet surely you know that this is only the beginning."

Helmut had never stared into the face of a sadist at work. He'd have expected joy, or sneering rage. But Hoekman was clinical, curious even.

"Do it, just do what you need to."

"And you can take it like a man, is that what you are saying?" A smile. "Patience, Herr von Cratz, we shall get there. First, let us continue to squeeze, a little more each time, until the left testicle bursts. Then I shall tear it out. Then, if you are strong enough to take it, the right testicle."

He reached the forceps forward, took Helmut's left testicle. A squeeze, harder, harder, harder, the pain building to terrific heights. Every moment Helmut thought it was impossible to stay conscious under such pain.

"Don't let him fall. Hold him up!"

The voice came from a distance, even though it was Colonel Hoekman's and he was right there. And then Helmut slumped to the ground, the pain releasing yet again. He curled. He needed to clutch his groin, but couldn't; they'd bound his hands behind his back.

Gradually, he saw that Hoekman and the two lieutenants crowded at the narrow window, looking down at the street. "Stay back you fools," Hoekman muttered. He grabbed one of the lieutenants. "You, go downstairs, tell them to stay out of it."

One of the men ran from the room. Hoekman and the other

man stayed at the window.

"What is it, *Polizeiführer?*" the lieutenant asked. "Why are they rioting?"

"I don't know, food, money, something. The crowd has gone quite mad for it."

"Look, more people. Half of Marseille will be pressing the building."

"That, we must not allow," Colonel Hoekman said. "It is not enough to push them away. Go down, tell them to shoot to kill. Do it now."

"*Ja, Polizeiführer.*"

The other lieutenant ran after the first. Helmut was alone in the room with Colonel Hoekman, and the Gestapo officer was at the window with his back turned. He should get up, attack the man, hands bound or no. But the pain rendered him helpless. He couldn't move.

"What is it?" Hoekman said. "*Ach du Scheiss.* Is that...is it gold coins? Shoot them you fools, shoot them all."

Gunfire.

⚡⚡

Gabriela and Christine forced their way through the mob. Old women on hands and knees, boys fighting, fishermen and dock workers. Dozens of people, and more joining every moment. Snatching up gold coins, stuffing their pockets.

Philipe Brun had driven past the building in his truck and then, as he approached the building, he tilted a bag of roosters out the window. Hundreds of coins clanked together, scattered, rolled in every direction. A moment of stunned silence, then pandemonium. As he drove past, he dumped the rest right in front of the startled German soldiers. The soldiers stood, stunned, as if unable to decide whether to scramble after the coins themselves or shoot at the truck.

He had stopped the truck and ducked out the opposite side, then gestured at Gabriela and Christine. The women hurried toward the building.

The SS officers pushed against the crowd with their guns. Another soldier came from inside and shouted at the others. Confusion on their faces, shouts. Two of the officers dropped to their hands and knees and grabbed for gold. Less than a minute had passed but already the mob bulged to well over a hundred people.

A gun barked three times in succession. One of the soldiers went down. Brun came around the truck, walking slowly, aiming, firing. Another soldier went down. The crowd screamed, pulsed. The soldiers started shooting indiscriminately. They hadn't yet spotted Brun.

Gabriela felt her hand close on the Mauser. Twenty feet from the soldier now. Gunfire rattled around her. She pulled it out, squeezed the trigger. A German turned, saw her, then spasmed, fell. Beside her, Christine's gun: pop, pop, pop. Another man fell. Two more soldiers disappeared within the mob. The gunfire hadn't stopped the scramble for coins.

Christine and Gabriela reached the door, flung it open, ducked inside.

She felt detached, like she was watching herself on a movie screen in a darkened cinema. Her hand reached into her pocket, scooped out more bullets. Christine was saying something.

She turned. "What?"

"We're still alive."

"Yes." She loaded bullets.

"My god, you were right, it's just like screwing the *boches*. I didn't think I could do it, but I did. I killed that man, I shot him."

There was a set of stairs. Upstairs, a man shouting in German. It sounded like Colonel Hoekman.

"Stay here," Gabriela said. "If anyone comes through the door, shoot him."

She climbed the stairs two at a time. When she reached the top, she burst in, gun outstretched.

Colonel Hoekman was waiting for her.

CHAPTER THIRTY-TWO

"You?" Hoekman asked, his voice heavy with disbelief. "Your *whore* came to rescue you?"

For one horrible moment she thought she'd caught him in the act of sodomizing Helmut. Helmut was naked, head slumped forward. Hoekman stood behind him, with his arm around the man's neck. But he was propping Helmut up and holding a gun to the back of his head.

"Move out of the way," she said.

He laughed. "If I'd known it was just you, I wouldn't have bothered. I thought there might be a band of *maquis* or some wharf rats, bribed with a few gold coins. I had no idea it would be a whore in love."

Nevertheless, he didn't remove his gun from the back of Helmut's head.

"I'll kill you both if I have to. I killed those soldiers outside. I liked it."

"You would kill your lover?"

"He's not my lover. Just another *boche*." She thought she saw a flicker of doubt in his eyes. "You don't get it, do you? I don't care about any of you. Germans, I want them all to die, every last one. You, von Cratz, Major Ostermann, all of them. I don't even care what happens to the French. Not really. The only person I care about is my father and you cut out part of his brain."

"Ah."

"And the only thing I want you for is to kill you, that's the only reason I did any of this."

"So shoot us."

"I'd prefer you put down your human shield first." She smiled. "I can shoot, but I'm not so confident as that."

"I don't believe you."

"What don't you believe, *boche*? That you are like that mouse in the cage and I'm the snake and there's no way out?"

"I think this man is your lover and you want to save his life." The uncertainty grew in Hoekman's voice. "I will make you this promise. If you put down your gun and walk downstairs, I will leave him and you alone."

In response to this pathetic offer, she lifted the gun, sighted it at his head. He ducked lower, trying to get as much of himself behind Helmut's head as possible.

As she squeezed the trigger, she let the gun buck in her hand. The shot went high. "*Merde.*"

Hoekman fell for the trap. He moved the gun from Helmut's head, leaned around and aimed. Helmut gave a jerk, pulled free. He threw himself to the ground. She fired a second time. She kept her hand steady.

Hoekman screamed. Fired a shot. It went wild. He collapsed to the ground. His gun dropped from his hand.

Gabriela didn't lower the gun as she made her way to his side. He was still alive. Blood soaked through his uniform on his chest. Red foam flecked his lips. His gun lay just beyond his outstretched hand.

Gabriela leaned down, met his gaze. She put the gun to his forehead. "Who is the snake now? And who is the mouse?"

She pulled the trigger.

"Oh, god," Helmut said. "That hurts."

Gabriela tucked the gun into her belt. "Are you okay?"

"I don't know."

"You're talking, that's good." She worked at the knots behind his back. "You looked terrible, and you didn't say anything. I was worried I was too late."

"Decided to keep my mouth shut and hope you weren't planning to kill me."

"It looked like he was raping you."

"He was, in a way. I didn't care for it much." He groaned as the knots came loose. He brought his hands around and felt at his groin. "Both still there. I wasn't sure." He looked up. "Did you mean that, about wanting all Germans to die?"

"I'd never hurt you. But some Germans could die horribly, and I wouldn't feel overly sorry. What do I know, I'm just a whore."

"He's a liar, you're not a whore. You never have been."

"I don't care about that, it doesn't matter anymore. But Hoekman was right about one thing, I do love you. Now, can you get up?" She looked for his clothes.

He closed his eyes and grimaced. "Give me a minute."

"We don't have a minute."

⚡⚡

Word had spread along the old port and lower Marseille. Thousands of people clogged the docks. The gold coins were long gone, but still they kept coming.

Nine Germans lay dead. Their bodies slumped where they'd fallen, except for one, who bobbed face-down in the water, pushed against the filth collected at the end of the harbor.

Soon the Germans would arrive and take their revenge. Probably be a massacre. The Vichy officials would be helpless to stop it. That's how these things went.

But how to decipher what had happened? Something about gold coins and a riot and gunmen. An old German dead from cyanide poisoning. A Gestapo colonel killed with a bullet to the head.

Gabriela, Christine, Brun, and Helmut left the port on foot. No way to get the truck out with the crowds. Helmut moved slowly, grasping his groin and wincing.

"Maybe they're all dead," Gabriela said.

"Who's all dead?" Helmut asked.

"Colonel Hoekman and his men, anyone who would know you were a part of this. He wanted to hog the glory, or at least solve the crime before anyone else got involved."

"Maybe. But they'll want to know what happened. The story of the gold coins might confuse them, but they won't let it drop. Not with gold. And there were eyewitnesses. Some might even be reliable. We need to cover our tracks or we're all dead just the same."

"What about the gold?" Brun asked. "You still have most of the coins."

"It's French. And I don't just mean the coins were made in France. Most of it was bought with French wealth. You take it." There was a worrying flatness in his expression. She didn't think it was the pain talking, she thought he'd given up.

"You want me to take it all?" Brun asked. "But I don't...that is, the plan, it failed."

"The war isn't over. You'll need it for something else."

"So why don't you keep it," Gabriela urged. "You don't know what will happen in six months. The Americans might change their minds or there might be something else you could do. There's so much money. Think of the possibilities. You worked too hard to give up now."

"If there's a use for them, someone else will find it."

"I'll keep them," Brun said, "but only until you figure out what you want. Then they're yours."

Helmut said nothing, just leaned his weight on Gabriela and Christine as they cut down an alley. The clamor from the docks receded in the distance.

CHAPTER THIRTY-THREE

THE OLD MAN STEPPED OUT of the building and blinked at the strong light. He looked up at the sky, a puzzled, but not unhappy expression on his face. It was October and a gust of wind blew a cascade of leaves over the fence and into the yard. He stared at a reddish gold leaf, spotted with brown, as it landed on an outstretched hand.

The nurse tugged his arm to get him moving. A pair of German soldiers watched with sideways glances from their post by the asylum door. He shuffled toward the gates.

Gabriela watched the nurse lead her father across the yard. Her heart pounded, she felt dizzy.

Helmut put a hand on her arm. It was steadying.

She turned over his pipe in her hands. Her fingers rubbed the soft meerschaum stone.

Guards unlocked the gates and the nurse led him through. She wore a sour, pinched expression, as if turning over her charge only under duress. Helmut had brought a wheelchair and he helped Gabriela ease her father into the chair.

Her father looked up with watery eyes. "*Hija.*"

Hearing his voice, seeing the recognition, she felt like she would explode with emotion. "Oh, Papá. *Que tanto te quiero.*"

"I love you too."

He recognized her, thank god, he recognized her. But there

was a childish expression on his face, unsophisticated, barely comprehending. There would be no more witty comments, wry observations about the world, deep conversations over a cloud of pipe smoke. She wanted to fall into his arms and weep.

Gabriela handed him the pipe. He turned it over in his hands. No recognition on his face, no spark.

"What is this?"

"It's your pipe."

"Oh, do I smoke?"

"Sometimes."

When you are reading philosophy. When you are writing. When you are railing against the injustices in the world. When you are yourself.

"I did not know that."

"Come on," Helmut murmured. "We have a train to catch."

"A train?" her father asked. "May I come?"

"Of course."

He glanced over his shoulder at the asylum. A confused look clouded his face, then passed. "What is your name again, *hija*? I'm sorry, I forgot."

"Gabriela, *Papá*."

"That is a beautiful name."

"You gave it to me, that's why it's so beautiful."

This brought a smile to his face.

$$\textbf{\textit{ss}}$$

Her father was worn out by the trip to Helmut's car, and then again to the train station where he had to get out of the chair to climb stairs to the platform. As soon as they were in the private compartment, he slumped back and fell asleep.

Gabriela sat next to Helmut. They held hands.

"I was so worried about you," she said. "I didn't hear from you all summer."

"I'm working on the Eastern Front. The war is going badly."

"But nothing happened, no interrogation?"

"Briefly questioned, that's all. Alfonse covered for me, can you believe it? General Dorf protected him. All that time, I thought he was just bragging, you know how he is. But apparently they really are good friends. Took care of me, too. It helped that Hoekman was dead and all their evidence was innuendo, but still, I owe Alfonse for what he did."

"Good for him." She hesitated. "How is your wife?"

"Sick, getting worse. But Loise is a Valkyrie, she'll keep fighting it. Maybe one day we'll get to this surgeon in Vienna who can help."

"I hope so."

The train whistled and pulled out of the station. Out the window, she could see another train arriving. More German soldiers with heavy packs, coming, going. Smart men in suits — the kind of men who profited from the war. Women with bundles and children in tow. Twenty, thirty men in manacles being loaded onto a prison car by a pair of soldiers. Did it never end?

They were shortly leaving the bustle and grime of industrial Strasbourg behind.

"How is Christine?" Helmut asked. "Did she stay in Provence?"

"No, she's in Paris again. Returned to the Egyptienne, but got in another argument, so she's back with Monsieur Leblanc at Le Coq Rouge, back sleeping with German officers. She got pregnant over the summer, ended it."

"Ah, that's too bad. I was hoping..."

"Yeah, me too. We divided the money you gave us and she spent her half the first six weeks. Gave most of it away, in fact. So that's some of it, but I don't think it's everything. She stops by my flat every Sunday afternoon and drags me out to the *Bois de Boulogne*, so we can look for Roger Leblanc. No sign of him, or his friends either. The zazous have either been deported or gone so far underground nobody will ever find them."

"Their day will come."

"As for the Germans in the city, they're older, less numerous, but more and more frantic to celebrate the good life of Paris."

"Like a last meal before an execution," Helmut said.

"Christine says the restaurant is packed. I couldn't say, I haven't been back."

"That's good." He turned and looked out the window.

"Your business is going well?" she asked, when the silence became too much to bear.

"Terrible." He turned back. "Lost most of my workers, of course. I couldn't pay half of them. Others got sent off as so-called volunteers to Germany before I could put them back to work. Still, there's always need for my skills, and I set some aside for emergencies, so I'm not hungry."

"But what about the gold?"

"That's Philipe Brun's now."

She tried to press him on that, but he started giving one-word answers or shrugs and they lapsed into silence again. Her father woke and looked out the window. He looked sad.

⚡⚡

The Swiss crossing was as heavily armed as anywhere she'd seen. The border on the Swiss side was a porcupine of casements, bunkers, and gun emplacements. Armed Swiss guards searched the train, inspected papers. They were interrogated in both French and German before being allowed to enter the country.

David Mayer met them at the train station in Geneva. He embraced Helmut. "Hey, boss. Good to see you again."

"How do you like Geneva?"

"*Comme ci, comme ça.* What do you know, the Swiss don't like Jews, either."

"I keep telling you," Helmut said. "You need your own country. This Palestine thing the British keep talking about."

"And live with a bunch of Arabs? No thanks."

"Hey, the Arabs get along with anyone. Bet they'd be happy to take the Jews, especially if it means swapping them for the British."

"What are you, a Zionist? No, soon as my papers come through I'm off to Brooklyn. I'll take my chances with the Americans." David looked at Gabriela. "You're looking good, Gaby. Finally put a little flesh on those bones, it suits you."

"I'm getting fat, you mean."

"Hardly. But I no longer feel the urge to stuff you with croissants. And you, you must be Señor Reyes." He held out his hand and then picked up the older man's hand and shook it for both of them. "Your daughter is quite a woman, it does you credit."

"*Merci, jeune homme. Muchas gracias.*"

"Come with me, sir, I have a car waiting."

Her father looked at Gabriela.

"It's okay, Papá, David is a friend. And I'll be there in a minute."

"Okay, *hija.*"

David carried her heaviest bag and wheeled her father out of the station.

Helmut gave her a sad smile after the other two had gone. "I guess this is it."

"Does it have to be?"

"Another year, two maybe, then this goddamned war will finally be over."

"That's not what I mean," she said.

"I know."

"But you'll be okay, right?"

"Maybe, who knows. The Allies are in Italy, what

about that?"

She knew some of it. The Americans had mounted a full-scale invasion of Italy since summer. The Italian government fell, the Germans occupied the north of the country. Seemed like the Americans were making slow but sure progress driving the *boches* north.

"But that could be good," she said. "The Yanks are in Europe, at least."

"Say the Americans conquer Italy, how will they cross the Alps? But it's got them committed, that's the problem. They should have come through Marseille. Now it could be another six months before they come at France. Meanwhile, the Soviets are pushing west, hard. You know, I heard a whisper the other day about a new plot to kill the Fuhrer, then arrest Goebbels, Himmler, and the lot."

"Could it work?"

"A coup? Sure, but you know what they're after? They want to put a general in charge, maybe Rommel, with the idea of better fighting the war. They still think we can win. No hope, it will only prolong the misery." He sighed. "I suppose I'm nothing more than a defeatist."

She took his hand. "So stay with us in Geneva. There's nothing left for you there."

His face clouded with pain. "I can't, Gaby, you know that."

"Because of your wife?"

"Yes, in part. Loise won't leave, she needs me. I have to stay behind."

"So you're going back to Germany to die?"

"To see what happens. Maybe rebuild after. Or yes, maybe to die."

"Oh, Helmut, no."

"We had a good run for awhile. Germany could have ruled the world if we'd gone about it the right way. We didn't, we did everything wrong. Now it's only fair to be punished for our crimes."

"But what does that have to do with you? You didn't do any of that. You're a good person, you helped people."

"Gaby, I cast my lot with Germany a long time ago. It made me rich. Now I need to pay the price for that loyalty."

"It isn't fair. You're just one man, you don't deserve to suffer. Please. Don't come with me, then, if you don't think it's right, but you have to get out."

"Gaby."

There was so much more she wanted to say, but then David returned from the car. He waited a few meters away.

Helmut put a hand to her face. "Thank you."

"For what?"

"For making me feel alive." He took out a piece of paper folded up in his pocket. "Christine left this in Marseille. I don't know if you want to keep it or if it's too ugly to remember. You can throw it away if you want, but I wanted you to decide."

She unfolded the paper. It had got wet at one point and the colors smeared along the side of one wall, but there was still a dark, chilling power in the gray building with its smokestacks. And the little bit of color, the red rooster with the human face standing on the roof of the asylum.

When she looked up, Helmut was walking away. He disappeared into a mass of men and women, all jostling on the platforms, arguing with station guards, haggling with porters, struggling with children, wrestling too much baggage evacuated in too little time, hurrying to catch a train, trying to communicate in some obscure language, and waging the millions of other individual battles being fought from London to Paris, to Berlin, to Moscow and every other station, street, and corner across the continent.

The individual battles of people, surviving.

ABOUT THE AUTHOR:

Michael Wallace has trekked across the Sahara on a camel, ridden an elephant through a tiger preserve in Southeast Asia, eaten fried guinea pig, and been licked on the head by a skunk. In a previous stage of life he programmed nuclear war simulations, smuggled refugees out of a war zone, and milked cobras for their venom. He speaks Spanish and French and grew up in a religious community in the desert. His suspense/ thrillers include The Devil's Deep, State of Siege, Implant, and The Righteous, and he is also the author of collections of travel stories and fantasy books for children. His work has appeared in print more than a hundred times, including publication in markets such as The Atlantic and The Magazine of Fantasy and Science Fiction.

Made in the USA
Middletown, DE
03 August 2015